Innocence

By Dean Koontz

77 Shadow Street · What the Night Knows · Breathless · Relentless
Your Heart Belongs to Me · The Darkest Evening of the Year
The Good Guy · The Husband · Velocity · Life Expectancy
The Taking · The Face · By the Light of the Moon
One Door Away From Heaven · From the Corner of His Eye
False Memory · Seize the Night · Fear Nothing · Mr. Murder
Dragon Tears · Hideaway · Cold Fire · The Bad Place
Midnight · Lightning · Watchers · Strangers · Twilight Eyes
Darkfall · Phantoms · Whispers · The Mask · The Vision
The Face of Fear · Night Chills · Shattered
The Voice of the Night · The Servants of Twilight
The House of Thunder · The Key to Midnight
The Eyes of Darkness · Shadowfires · Winter Moon
The Door to December · Dark Rivers of the Heart · Icebound
Strange Highways · Intensity · Sole Survivor · Ticktock
The Funhouse · Demon Seed

ODD THOMAS
Odd Thomas · Forever Odd · Brother Odd · Odd Hours ·
Odd Interlude · Odd Apocalypse · Deeply Odd

FRANKENSTEIN
Prodigal Son · City of Night · Dead and Alive
Lost Souls · The Dead Town

A Big Little Life: A Memoir of a Joyful Dog Named Trixie

DEAN KOONTZ

Innocence

A Novel

Bantam Books | New York

Published in the United States by Bantam Books,
an imprint of The Random House Publishing Group,
a division of Random House LLC,
a Penguin Random House Company, New York.

A signed, limited edition has been privately printed by Charnel House.
Charnelhouse.com

Title page art from an original photograph
by Agne Kveselyte

BANTAM BOOKS and the HOUSE colophon are registered trademarks
of Random House LLC.

LIBRARY OF CONGRESS CATALOGING-IN-PUBLICATION DATA

Koontz, Dean R. (Dean Ray)
Innocence : a novel / Dean Koontz.
pages cm
ISBN 978-0-553-80803-2 (acid-free paper)—
ISBN 978-0-345-53965-6 (eBook)
1. Social isolation—Fiction. I. Title.
PS3561.O55155 2013
813'.54—dc23   2013014516

Printed in the United States of America on acid-free paper

www.bantamdell.com

2 4 6 8 9 7 5 3 1

First Edition

Book design by Virginia Norey

This book is dedicated to Harry Recard for being a friend, for teaching me pinochle in college and thereby nearly ruining my academic career. And to Diane Recard for taking such good care of Harry all these years, an exhausting task.

*   *   *

Nothing pleases a writer more than mail from readers who claim that one of his books was life-changing or inspired perseverance in difficult times. But as I finished Innocence, a letter that I received from Elizabeth Waters in the state of Washington, regarding my novel From the Corner of His Eye, moved me more profoundly than most. Beth, your courage humbles me. The hope that you found in my book is matched by the hope that you have given me with your kind correspondence. You shine.

Rarely do great beauty
and great virtue dwell together.

—PETRARCH, *DE REMEDIIS*

Innocence

PART ONE

The Girl I Met in Lamplight
Near Charles Dickens

1

HAVING ESCAPED ONE FIRE, I EXPECTED ANOTHER. I didn't view with fright the flames to come. Fire was but light and heat. Throughout our lives, each of us needs warmth and seeks light. I couldn't dread what I needed and sought. For me, being set afire was merely the expectation of an inevitable conclusion. This fair world, compounded of uncountable beauties and enchantments and graces, inspired in me only one abiding fear, which was that I might live in it too long.

2

I WAS CAPABLE OF LOVE, BUT I LIVED IN SOLITUDE after Father died. Therefore I loved only the precious dead, and books, and the moments of great beauty with which the city surprised me from time to time, as I passed through it in utmost secrecy.

For instance, sometimes on clear nights, in the solemn hour when most of the population sleeps, when the cleaning crews are finished and the high-rises darkle until dawn, the stars come out. They are not as bright over this metropolis as they must be over a Kansas plain or a Colorado mountain, but they still shine as if there is a city in the sky, an enchanting place where I could walk the streets with no fear of fire, where I could find someone to love, who would love me.

Here, when I was seen, my capacity for love earned me no mercy. Quite the opposite. When they saw me, men and women alike recoiled, but their fear quickly gave way to fury. I would not harm them to defend myself, and I remained therefore defenseless.

3

ON CERTAIN NIGHTS, BEAUTIFUL BUT SAD MUSIC found its way into my deep windowless rooms. I didn't know from where it came, and I couldn't identify the tune. No lyrics accompanied the melody, but I remained convinced that I had once heard a smoky-voiced chanteuse sing this song. Each time the song came, my mouth moved as if forming the words, but they eluded me.

The piece was not a blues number, yet it weighed on the heart as did the blues. I might call it a nocturne, although I believe that a nocturne is always an instrumental. Words existed to this melody. I was certain they did.

I should have been able to follow those mellifluous strains to a vent grille or a drain, or to some other route of transmission, but every attempt to seek the source ended in failure. The music seemed to issue from the air, as if passing through a membrane from another, unseen world parallel to ours.

Perhaps those who lived in the open would have found the idea of an invisible world too fanciful and would have dismissed the notion.

Those of us who remain hidden from everyone else, however, know that this world is wondrous and filled with mysteries. We possess no magical perception, no psychic insight. I believe our recognition of reality's complex dimensions is a consequence of our solitude.

To live in the city of crowds and traffic and constant noise, to be always striving, to be in the ceaseless competition for money and status and power, perhaps distracted the mind until it could no longer see— and forgot—the all that is. Or maybe, because of the pace and pressure of that life, sanity depended on blinding oneself to the manifold miracles, astonishments, wonders, and enigmas that comprised the true world.

When I said "those of us who remain hidden," I should instead have said "I who am hidden." As far as I was aware, no other like me existed in that metropolis. I had lived alone for a long time.

For twelve years, I shared this deep redoubt with Father. He died six years earlier. I loved him. I missed him every day. I was now twenty-six, with perhaps a long, lonely life ahead of me.

Before I arrived, my father lived here with his father, whom I never had the honor of meeting. Most of the furnishings and books were handed down to me from them.

One day perhaps I would pass my belongings to someone who might call *me* Father. We were an enduring dynasty of the dispossessed, living in the secret city that the city's people never saw.

My name is Addison. But back then we needed no names because we spoke to no one but each other.

Sometimes, with a smile, Father called himself It. But that wasn't a real name. He called me Its It, or Son of It, which was our little joke.

By the standards of humanity, we were exceedingly ugly in a way that excited in them abhorrence and the most terrible rage. Although we were as much human as those who lived in the open, we did not wish to offend, and so we hid ourselves away.

Father told me that our kind must not be angry with other men and women merely because of the way that they treated us. They had anxieties we could never understand. He said that we of the hidden had our burdens, but those who lived in the open carried far heavier burdens than ours, which was true.

We also remained hidden to avoid worse than persecution. One night, my father was caught in the open. Two frightened, enraged men shot and clubbed him to death.

I did not harbor any anger toward them. I pitied them, but I loved them as best I could. We have all been brought into the world for some reason, and we must wonder why and hope to learn.

My little windowless residence also served as my school, where I sought to learn, and the most important of those three small rooms was the one lined with mahogany shelves built by my father's father. The shelves were filled with books not wanted by those who lived in the world above.

Each of the deep, comfortable armchairs had a padded footstool. Beside each chair stood a simple wooden cube on which to set a drink, and a bronze floor lamp with a pleated shade of peach-colored shantung silk.

A small table and two straight-backed chairs provided a place to dine. In the days when we were two, we played cards and chess at that table.

These days, I occasionally played solitaire. I didn't much like the game, but sometimes, shuffling the cards or dealing them out, I saw not my hands but instead my father's. His fingers were deformed because they had healed improperly in self-applied splints after a minister had broken them on a Sunday night, when Father was a boy.

I loved those hands, which never harmed a living thing. The pale scars and arthritic knuckles were beautiful because they signified his courage and reminded me that I must never be embittered by the cruelties inflicted on us. He suffered more than I did, and yet he loved life and the world.

The table and most of the other furnishings had been brought here with difficulty or had been built in place by those who came before me.

For six years, I had not needed two armchairs. Most of the time, when reading, I sat in the chair that had been mine since I arrived there. Once in a while, however, I sat in Father's chair, the better to remember him and to feel less alone.

The second room, like the others, was eight feet high. The thick walls, floor, and ceiling were of steel-reinforced concrete through which vibrations sometimes traveled but never any identifiable sounds other than the aforementioned music.

To each side of the doorless doorway, a hammock was suspended wall to wall. The canvas was easy to sponge clean, and my blanket was the only bedding to be laundered.

When Father still lived, on nights when sleep eluded us, we would lie awake, either in the dark or in candlelight, and talk for hours. We conversed about what little of the world we'd seen firsthand, about the marvels of nature that we studied in books of color photography, and about what all of it might mean.

Perhaps those were among my happiest memories, although I had so many that were happy, I wasn't easily able to favor some over others.

Against the back wall, between hammocks, stood a refrigerator. Father's father had once lived without this amenity. My father—an autodidact like me—taught himself to be a fine electrician and an appliance mechanic. He dismantled the refrigerator, brought it down from the world aboveground, and reassembled it.

To the left of the refrigerator stood a table holding a toaster oven, a hot plate, and a Crock-Pot. To the right were open shelves that served as my larder and tableware storage.

I ate well and remained grateful that the city was a place of plenty.

When Father's father discovered this deep redoubt, electricity and a minimum of plumbing were already provided, although the rooms were unfurnished. No evidence existed to suggest that they had ever previously been occupied.

Before Father found me alone and waiting to be killed, he and his father imagined many explanations for these chambers.

One might think this place must be a bomb shelter, so deep beneath the street, under so many thick layers of concrete, that multiple nuclear blasts would not crack it open, reached by such a circuitous route that deadly radiation, which traveled in straight lines, could not find its way here.

But when you removed the receptacles from their mounting screws in any wall outlet, the manufacturer's name stamped in the metal junction box identified a company that, research proved, went out of business in 1933, long before a nuclear threat existed.

Besides, a bomb shelter for only two, in a great city of millions, made no sense.

The third room, a bath, also concrete all around, was not designed with the expectation that the city and its utilities would be atomized. The pedestal sink and the claw-foot tub offered two spigots each, although the hot water was never more than pleasantly warm, suggesting that whatever boiler it tapped must have been far from there. The old toilet featured an overhead tank that flushed the bowl when you pulled on a hanging chain.

During construction, perhaps some official who was also a sexual predator with homicidal desires might have provided for this sanctum under one pretense or another, intending later to erase its existence from all public records, so that he could by force bring women to a private dungeon to torture and murder them, while the teeming city overhead remained unaware of the screaming far below.

But neither a city engineer nor an architect of public-utility pathways seemed likely to be an insatiable serial killer. And when Father's father discovered these cozy quarters back in the day, no gruesome stains or other evidence of murder marred the smooth concrete surfaces.

Anyway, these rooms had no ominous quality about them.

To those who lived in the open, the lack of windows and the bare concrete might call to mind a dungeon. But that perception was based on the assumption that their way of life was not merely superior to ours but also without a viable alternative.

Every time that I left this haven, as I did for many reasons, my life was at risk. Therefore, I had developed a most keen sense of pending threat. No threat existed here. This was home.

I favored a theory involving the unseen world parallel to ours that I mentioned earlier. If such a place existed, separated from us by a membrane we couldn't detect with our five senses, then perhaps at some points along the continuum, the membrane bulged around a small part of that other reality and folded it into the stuff of ours. And if both worlds, in their becoming, arose from the same loving source, I liked to believe that such secret havens as this would be provided especially for those who, like me, were outcasts by no fault of their own, reviled and hunted, and in desperate need of shelter.

That was the only theory I wished to accommodate. I couldn't change what I was, couldn't become more appealing to those who would recoil from me, couldn't lead any life but the one to which my nature condemned me. My theory gave me comfort. If one less reassuring revealed itself, I would refuse to consider it. So much in my life was beautiful that I wouldn't risk pondering any darkening idea that might poison my mind and rob me of my stubborn joy.

I never went into the open in daylight, nor even at dusk. With rare exception, I ascended only after midnight, when most people were asleep and others were awake but dreaming.

Black walking shoes, dark jeans, and a black or navy-blue hoodie were my camouflage. I wore a scarf under the jacket, arranged so that I could pull it up to my eyes if I had to pass along an alleyway—or, rarely, a street—where someone might see me. I acquired my clothes from thrift shops that I could enter, after hours, by the route that rats might enter if they were as born for stealth as I was.

I wore such a costume on the night in December when my life changed forever. If you were a creature like me, you expected that no big change could be positive in the long run. Yet were I given a chance to turn back time and follow a different course, I would do again what I did then, regardless of the consequences.

4

I CALLED HIM FATHER BECAUSE HE HAD BEEN THE closest thing to a father that I had ever known. He was not my true father.

According to my mother, my real father loved freedom more than he loved her. Two weeks before I was born, he walked out and never walked back in, off to the sea, she said, or to some far jungle, a restless man who traveled to find himself but lost himself instead.

On the night that I was born, a violent wind shook the little house, shook the forest, even shook, she said, the mountain that the forest mantled. The windstorm quarreled across the roof, insisted at the windows, rattled the door as if determined to intrude into the place where I was born.

When I entered the world, the twenty-year-old daughter of the midwife fled the bedroom in fright. Weeping, she took refuge in the kitchen.

When the midwife tried to smother me in the birthing blanket, my mother, although weakened by a difficult labor, drew a handgun from a nightstand drawer and, with a threat, saved me from being murdered.

Later, in the calm of morning, all the birds were gone, as though they had been blown out of the trees and swept to the edge of the continent. They didn't return for three days: first the sparrows and the swifts, then the crows and hawks, and last of all the owls.

The midwife and her daughter kept the secret of my existence, either because they feared being accused of attempted homicide or because they could sleep well only if they forgot that I existed. They claimed I was born dead, and my mother confirmed their story.

I lived eight years on the mountain, sleeping as often as not in that cozy little house at the dead end of the narrow dirt track. In all that time, until the afternoon of the day I left, I saw no other human being but my blessed mother.

Eventually the cloistered spaces of the forest were mine to roam at an age when most children would have been denied the wilds. But I had great strength and uncanny intuition and a kind of kinship with Nature, as if the sap of the trees and the blood of the animals were in my DNA, and my mother felt more at peace when I was not in the house. The shadowed woods by day and the moonlit woods by night became as familiar to me as my own face in a mirror.

I knew the deer, the squirrels, the birds in great variety, the wolves that appeared from—and vanished under—the graceful arcing ferns. My community was populated by feathered and furred creatures that traveled by wings or four swift feet.

In the bosky woodlands and in the meadows that they encircled, also occasionally in our yard, I sometimes saw the Clears and the Fogs, as I came to call them. I didn't know what they might be, but I knew intuitively that my dear mother had never seen them, because she'd never spoken of them. I never mentioned them to her, because I knew that hearing of them would distress her and cause her to worry about me even more than she already did.

Later, I would see the Clears and Fogs in the city, too. And I gradually came to understand their nature, as I will explain later.

Anyway, in those years, I was happy, as to one extent or another I have always been happy. The forest was not a wilderness to me, but served instead as my private garden, comforting in spite of its vastness, and endlessly mysterious.

The more familiar that a place becomes, the more mysterious it becomes, as well, if you are alert to the truth of things. I have found this to be the case all of my life.

Shortly after my eighth birthday, my mother would not have me in the house anymore. She could not sleep in my presence. She could not maintain an appetite, and thus lost weight. She didn't want me nearby in the woods, either, in part because the thought of me at home in the forest reminded her that she was not welcome there in the way that I was, but also in part because of the hunter. And so I had to leave.

I couldn't blame her. I loved her.

She tried hard to love me, and to an extent she did. But I was a unique burden. Although I am always happy—or at least not unhappy—I made her terribly sad. The sadness was slowly killing her.

5

MORE THAN EIGHTEEN YEARS LATER, IN THIS FAMILiar yet mysterious city, came the December that changed my life.

When I went out that night, with a backpack slung from my shoulders because I intended to partially restock my larder, I took a pair of compact LED flashlights, the first in hand, the second clipped to my belt in case the other failed. The route from my rooms to the metropolis above was for the most part dark, as are many passages in this world, underground and not, concrete and not.

A five-foot-wide corridor led out of the hammock room for ten feet, where it appeared to terminate in a blank wall. I reached high, to the top right corner, inserted an index finger in the hole that was the only feature on that smooth surface, and pressed the latch-release button in there. The foot-thick slab pivoted silently on a concealed pair of over-under ball-bearing hinges that were set one foot from its left edge.

The resultant opening was four feet wide. After I crossed the threshold, the massive door swung shut and latched behind me.

Even without light, I could navigate the second corridor: eight feet straight ahead, then the curve to the left, and finally ten feet to a cunningly designed louver door. From the farther side, the door appeared to be merely the cover for a large ventilation shaft.

In darkness, I listened, but the only things that passed between the louvers were silence and a draft as faint and cool and pure as the breath of a snowman brought to life by love and magic.

The air carried the scent of damp concrete, the lime that had fluoresced from the walls over the decades. In this section of the city's underworld, I never smelled the decomposing rats or the foul molds that sometimes flourished elsewhere.

Like the pivoting concrete wall, the louver door featured a hidden lock release. It closed automatically behind me.

I switched on the flashlight, and a storm drain formed out of the darkness, as if the blade of light carved it from bedrock. The great cylindrical concrete tunnel appeared sufficiently large to spare the world from a repeat of Noah's flood.

On occasion, maintenance teams in electric vehicles the size of pickup trucks passed through primary drains like this. At the moment, however, I was alone. Over the years, I had seldom glimpsed such crews at a distance, and more seldom still had I needed to flee from them to avoid being seen.

I seemed almost to have had cast upon me a spell of solitude. When I traveled below or above ground, people usually turned away from me and I from them in the moment before they might have seen me.

Otherwise, I would have been murdered long ago.

The most recent major rainstorm had been in late October. The tunnel bored into dryness, the floor littered with the small things—plastic bags, empty beer and soda cans, fast-food containers, cups from Starbucks, a knitted glove, a baby's shoe, a sparkling fragment of costume jewelry—that had settled out of the flow as the last of the runoff withered away.

The amount of debris was not great. I could have walked for miles without stepping on anything. Raised three feet off the floor, however, along both sides of the drain, were maintenance walkways where the surging water rarely deposited trash.

Periodically I passed other louver panels that were nothing more than they appeared to be, and iron-rung ladders that led up to service traps in the ceiling, and the mouths of smaller tributary pipes that, during a storm, fed water to this drain.

In this subterranean maze, earlier drains than this one were built of brick or stone, or concrete blocks. They possessed greater charm than more recent constructions, for they were the work of masons who were also proud craftsmen.

According to metropolitan lore, one crew of masons had been secretly in the employ of a crime boss of that distant era, and they had walled up several of his enemies, some dead but others living. I had never seen one of the small crosses that were supposedly carved into bricks to mark those tombs, nor had I seen any skeletal fingers in the gaps of mortar between stones, like once-questing but long-fossilized pale roots. Perhaps such stories were not true, just urban legends, though I was well aware of how inhumane humanity can be.

When I was halfway to the first intersection of major drains, I spotted a familiar glowing silver-white mist in the distance, one of the Fogs. A coherent and sinuous stream, it swam toward me as if the air through which it moved were water and it were a luminous eel.

I stopped to watch, always curious about this phenomenon and about the other that I called the Clears. In my experience, I had no reason to be afraid, but I admit to feeling uneasy.

Unlike a tendril of genuine fog or an exhalation of steam from a vent, this apparition didn't feather away at the edges or change shape according to the influence of currents in the air. Instead it serpentined toward me, perhaps seven or eight feet in length and a foot in diameter, and as it passed me, it halted and stood on end for a moment, writhing in the center of the tunnel, as if it were a cobra enchanted by the music of a flute. Thereafter it went horizontal once more and shimmered away, a slither of silvery radiance diminishing to a point, and then gone.

I had seen the Fogs and Clears all of my life. I hoped one day to know for certain what they were and what they meant, although I suspected that I might never be enlightened. Or if I discovered the truth of them, there might be a high price to pay for that knowledge.

6

"YOU'RE TOO HIGH A PRICE TO PAY," MY MOTHER declared on the afternoon when she sent me away. "I've lived by my own rules, and I expected a cost, but not this. Not you."

Always as lovely as any woman in any magazine, as any TV star of whom millions were enamored, she had lately looked thin and drawn. Even the evident weariness and the crescents of darkness like fading bruises around her eyes did not detract from her appearance. In fact, they suggested that she was tenderhearted and haunted by some terrible loss, that her pain, like the pain endured by a martyr, was beautiful, which then made her face yet more beautiful than it had been before.

She sat at the kitchen table with the shiny chrome legs and the red Formica top. Near at hand were her medications and her whiskey, which she said was just another medication.

The whiskey seemed to be her *best* medicine, if you asked me, because at worst it made her sad, but sometimes it made her laugh or just lie down and sleep. The pills, on the other hand, and the powder that she sometimes inhaled, could inspire unpredictable moods in which she cried a lot or raged and threw things, or hurt herself a little on purpose.

Her graceful hands transformed everything they touched into elegant objects: the plain glass of Scotch glimmering like cut crystal as she repeatedly traced one fingertip around its whiskey-wet rim, the slim cigarette like a magic wand from which smoke rose as if to signify wishes granted.

I had not been invited to sit down; and so I stood across the table from her. I made no attempt to approach her. Long ago she had some-times cuddled with me. Eventually, the most she could tolerate was an occasional touch, smoothing the hair back from my brow, laying one hand over mine for a moment. During the past few months, even a fleeting touch was more than she could endure.

Because I understood the pain that I caused her, the very sight of me an offense, I was anguished, as well. She could have aborted me, but she didn't. She had given birth to me. And when she saw what she had brought into the world . . . even then she defended me against the midwife who would have smothered me. I could not but love her and wish that she could love a thing like me.

Beyond the window at her back, the October sky lowered gray and bleak. Autumn had stripped most of the foliage from an old syca-more, but in the fitful wind, the remaining leaves shivered like brown bats about to fling themselves into flight. This wasn't a day for leav-ing home, or a world in which to be alone.

She had told me to put on my hooded jacket, and I had done so. She had prepared for me a backpack of food and first-aid items, and I had strapped it on.

Now Mother indicated a wad of cash on the table. "Take that—for what little good it'll do you. It's stolen, but *you* didn't steal it. I do all the stealing in this family. To you, it's just a gift, and clean."

I knew she never lacked for money. I took the gift and stuffed it in a pocket of my jeans.

The tears that had been pent up in her eyes spilled now, but she did not make a single sound of grief. I sensed that she had been rehearsing this scene for a long time, intent on seeing it through without allowing me a chance to improvise a change to the script that she had written.

My vision blurred, and I tried to express my love for her and my regret that I caused her such despair, but the few words that escaped me were distorted, pathetic. I was physically and emotionally strong for a mere boy of eight, and wiser than a child, but still a child if only chronologically.

After crushing her cigarette in an ashtray, she wet the fingers of both hands with the condensation on the glass of iced Scotch. She closed her eyes, pressed her fingertips to her eyelids, and took a few long, deep breaths.

My heart felt swollen, pressing against breastbone and ribs and spine, so it seemed that it would be punctured.

When she looked at me again, she said, "Live by night, if you can stay alive at all. Keep the hood up. Keep your head down. Hide your face. A mask will draw attention, but bandages might work. Above all, never let them see your eyes. Those eyes will betray you in an instant."

"I'll be okay," I assured her.

"You will *not* be okay," she said sharply. "And you shouldn't delude yourself into thinking that you will."

I nodded.

After draining half the glass of whiskey in a long swallow, she said, "I wouldn't send you away if it hadn't been for the hunter."

The hunter had seen me in the woods that morning. I ran, and he pursued. He shot at me more than once and missed by inches.

"He'll be back," Mother said. "He'll be back again and again and again until he finds you. He'll never leave those woods for good until you're dead. And then I'll be dragged into it. They'll want to know about me, every little thing about me, and I damn well can't afford that kind of scrutiny."

"I'm sorry," I said. "I'm so sorry."

She shook her head. Whether she meant that an apology wasn't necessary or that it was inadequate, I can't say. She picked up the pack of cigarettes and extracted one.

I already wore knitted gloves, for my hands might also betray me to others. I pulled up the hood of my jacket.

At the door, as I put my hand on the knob, I heard Mother say, "I lied, Addison."

I turned to look at her.

Her elegant hands were trembling so violently that she could not match the cigarette to the flame of the butane lighter. She dropped the lighter and threw the cigarette aside.

"I lied when I said I wouldn't send you away if it wasn't for the hunter. I'd send you away no matter what, hunter or no hunter. I can't stand this. Not anymore. I'm a selfish bitch."

"You aren't," I said, taking a step toward her. "You're scared, that's all. Scared not just of me but of . . . of so many things."

Then she was beautiful in a different way, like some pagan goddess of storms, highly charged and full of wrath. "You just shut up and believe what you're told, boy. I'm selfish and vain and greedy and worse, and I *like* me that way. I *thrive* the way I am."

"No, you're not those things, you're—"

"*You shut your freakin' mouth, you just SHUT UP!* You don't know me better than I know myself. I am what I am, and there's nothing here for you, never was and never will be. You go and live however you can, in farther woods or wherever, and don't you dare think of coming back here because there's nothing here for you, nothing but death here for you. Now *get out!*"

She threw the Scotch glass at me, but I'm sure she didn't mean to hit me. Her aim was too wide, and the glass shattered against the refrigerator.

Every moment that I lingered was another wound to her. Nothing I could say or do would help her. Life is hard in a world gone wrong.

Weeping as bitterly as I had ever wept—or ever would—I left the house and didn't look back. I grieved, although not because of either my condition or my lean prospects. I grieved for her because I knew that she didn't hate me, that she hated only herself. She despised herself not for bringing me into the world in the first place, more than eight years earlier, but for turning me out into it now.

Behind the low overcast, the day waned. The clouds that had been smooth and gray earlier were everywhere coarse and in places kettle-black.

As I crossed the yard, the wind made dead leaves caper at my feet, in the way that small animals, familiars to a witch, might dance around she whom they served.

I entered the forest, confident that the hunter was gone for the time being. His horror had been greater than his rage; he would not linger with night coming but would return with the bright of day.

As soon as I was sure that shadows hid me, I stopped and turned and leaned back against a tree. I waited until I had no more tears, until my vision cleared.

This would be the last I saw of the house in which I was born and thus far raised. I wanted to watch the twilight begin to harden into darkness around those walls, to see lamplight bloom in the windows.

On those days when the sight of me had most troubled Mother, I had roamed the woods until dusk and had either slept in the yard or, on cold nights, in a most comfortable sleeping bag in the ramshackle detached garage. She always left a small hamper of food for me on the front seat of her Ford, and when banished I ate dinner at twilight, watching the house from a distance, because it pleased me so much to see the windows suddenly blush with warm light and to know that, in my absence, she must be at peace.

Now again, as the black of a starless night mantled the small house, as the wind died with the day and a hush settled over the woods, light came to the windows. Those glowing panes reliably evoked in me a most satisfying sense of home and safety and comfort. When I was welcome inside, however, the quality of the same light, seen from within, was not as golden and as stirring as when seen from without.

I should have left then, should have followed the narrow dirt track out to the distant county blacktop, but I delayed. At first, I hoped to see her pass a window, to get one last glimpse of this woman to whom I owed my existence. When an hour passed, then two, I admitted to myself that in truth I didn't know what to do, where to go, that I was lost here at the edge of the woods as I had never been lost far deeper in the wilderness.

The front door opened, the subtle protest of the hinges carrying clearly to me in the stillness, and my mother stepped onto the porch, backlighted, a mere silhouette. I thought that she might call out to me, hoping I was still nearby, that she might say she loved me more than she feared me and that she'd had second thoughts about sending me away.

But then I saw the shotgun. The pistol-grip pump-action 12-gauge was always loaded in anticipation of unwelcome visitors whom she never named; she called the weapon her insurance policy. She was not holding it casually, but in both hands and at the ready, the muzzle toward the porch ceiling, as she surveyed the night. I assumed she suspected me of lingering and that with this display she intended to convince me that my banishment was final.

I felt ashamed of myself for not honoring her wishes without delay. Yet when she returned to the house and closed the door, I remained in the perimeter of the forest, still unable to make myself set out upon my journey.

Perhaps half an hour passed before the shotgun roared. Even muffled by the walls of the house, the blast was loud in the quiet of the mountain.

At first I thought that someone must have forced his way through the back door or through a window beyond my line of sight, because Mother often spoke of enemies and of her determination to live where they could never find her. I thrashed through the low brush, into the yard, and ran halfway to the house before I realized that no intruder lay wounded or dead in there, no enemy but her worst one, which was herself.

If my death could have brought her back to life, I would have died there in the yard.

I thought that I ought to go inside. She might be only wounded, and in need of help.

But I didn't return to the house. I knew my mother well. When it was important to her that some task be done, she put all her mind and heart into it, and she accomplished what she set out to do. She neither made mistakes nor took half measures.

How long I stood in the yard, in the dark, in the after-shotgun quiet, I do not know.

Later, I discovered that I was on my knees.

I don't recall leaving. I realized that I was walking along the dirt lane only a minute before it led me to the blacktop county road.

Shortly after dawn, I took refuge in a dilapidated barn on an abandoned farm, where the house had burned down and had never been rebuilt. Mice were the rightful tenants of the barn, but they were not too frightened of me, and I assured them that I meant to stay only a few hours.

Mother had included the essentials in the backpack, but also a half dozen chocolate-pecan cookies that she had made herself and that were my favorite.

7

ON FOOT BENEATH THE CITY, I ARRIVED AT AN INtersection where abruptly a rumble rose, the underground thunder of a train, which was the only utility routed deeper than the storm drains. On the rare occasions when a section of the subway flooded, water was pumped up to these tunnels. Before the turn of the millennium, they had pumped it to the sewer lines; but a calamitous backflow once gushed filth through two miles of the subway, requiring weeks of decontamination by hazmat teams, and the existing design was reconsidered.

A city is half beast and half machine, with arteries of fresh water and veins of foul, nerves of telephone and electrical cables, sewer lines for bowels, pipes full of pressurized steam and others carrying gas, valves and fans and filters and meters and motors and transformers and tens of thousands of interlinked computers, and though its people sleep, the city never does.

The city nurtured me and provided me with a secret haven for which I was grateful, but I continued to be a little distrustful of it, and sometimes afraid. Logic insisted that, in spite of its intricacy, the city was only an accumulation of *things*, buildings and machines and systems, that could not develop an awareness or intent. Yet often it seemed that, though I remained unknown to the people of this place, I was known by the city itself, and watched.

If a city had a life separate from its citizens, then it must have a capacity for both kindness and cruelty. As a creation of men and women, it surely shared their evils as well as their virtues.

The rumble of the train passed away beneath my feet, and beyond the intersection of enormous drains, I turned left into a tributary that sloped upward more than the main tunnel. The passageway lacked elevated service walks, and its dimensions required me to proceed a considerable distance with shoulders hunched and head bowed.

I was so familiar with these subterranean avenues and alleys, I might have found my way without the flashlight. But although I ventured out only at night and lived days in the depths, I was born for light and yearned for more of it than my circumstances allowed.

I came to an open cove in the right-hand drain wall, like half of a cylinder, made of curved concrete blocks. It was five feet in diameter, seven feet high, rather like what you'd find if you took the cover off a manhole, except that a manhole was deeper, wasn't open on one side, and remained accessible only through the top.

Overhead, a heavy iron lid featured a recessed nut along the perimeter. From my backpack, I removed the one tool it contained: a foot-long iron rod with a T handle at one end and something like a socket wrench at the other. When this gate key engaged the nut and turned it, a rim latch in the lid retracted from the manhole frame, allowing me to push upward, swinging that cover open on its hinges.

My father's father had appropriated that tool from a street-department truck years before his death. That gate key was the most precious thing I owned. Most of the freedom of movement I enjoyed, such as it was, would be lost if that tool was lost.

After returning the gate key to a zippered compartment of my backpack, I held the flashlight in my teeth, grabbed the frame of the manhole, and drew myself through the open lid and into the basement of the city's central library. All was silent, as should be the case in such a place, the air dry but not arid, cool but not cold.

In this first hour of a Sunday morning, no one would be in the great building. The cleaning crew had gone. The library remained closed on Sundays. I should have the place to myself until Monday morning. I intended to pass only a few hours within those walls, however, before going elsewhere to resupply the larder in my bunker.

The climate-controlled basement was enormous, a single space with rows of massive columns fanning out toward their tops to create graceful limestone vaults. Between the columns, metal cabinets stood on foot-high concrete plinths. Some of the drawers held ordinary files, but others were wide and shallow to accommodate blueprints as well as small stacks of publications that, brittle with age, couldn't bear their own weight and would rapidly deteriorate if piled high.

These were the archives of the city's history, which explained the entrance to the storm drain that was built into the floor. There were other drain caps that, in the unlikely event of a burst water line or other catastrophe, could be opened to ensure that no flood would rise higher than the plinths on which the metal cabinets stood.

I liked that immense space, the colonnades and the curved vaults overhead, which reminded me of photos of the extensive reservoirs constructed by Francois d'Orbay beneath the Water Terrace and gardens of the palace at Versailles. In the moving beam of my flashlight, the shadows of the columns swung aside like great black doors.

A regular elevator and one for freight served the basement, but I never used them. Stairs were silent, safer. Having a choice of enclosed stairwells, I took the one in the southeast corner.

Books, of course, were what drew me to this library. Although Father and his father before him had collected volumes that had been thrown away by those who lived in the open, although I could borrow reading material from thrift stores in which I shopped after hours, many books were not easily found other than in the central library.

The stairs brought me to the walnut-paneled periodical room, where newspapers and magazines could be enjoyed. A short hallway led to the main reading room, a sixteen-thousand-square-foot architectural masterpiece rising from a sea of dark-caramel marble flooring. This immense chamber housed part of the book collection and, beyond that maze of shelves, provided seating for at least five hundred readers at wooden refectory-style tables.

Always before, at this late hour, the reading room had been brightened only by the eerie, ambient light of the city seeping through its high, arched windows. This time, numerous lamps glowed.

I almost retreated, but intuition counseled me to wait, to see, to know.

Decades earlier, night watchmen patrolled the many rooms and corridors of the central library. But in a nation that had nearly spent its way into bankruptcy, sturdy locks and a perimeter alarm were the preferred form of security, because they didn't require salaries, health care, and pensions.

Through the eight-foot-high rows of shelves, which librarians called stacks, aisles led east-west and north-south. As I approached an entrance to the labyrinth, I heard footsteps that were almost inaudible even in this quietude, footsteps so light and quick that they might have been those of a child ghost desperately fleeing from the recognition of his early death.

In the opening before me, crossing an intersection of aisles, a slender teenage girl appeared from the left, which was the north, gazelle-fast, running with balletic grace and landing on her toes. Her shoes were silver, like the winged feet of Mercury, and otherwise she wore black. Her long hair appeared black, too, lustrous in the lamplight, as a pool of moonlit water lies glossy in the night. One moment there, the next moment gone, she seemed to be running for her life.

I heard no pursuer, though her evident alarm suggested that one must be close on her trail. If she was the prey, I didn't know—and couldn't imagine—any predator stealthier than she.

Warily, I entered the stacks. The big chandeliers, hung from the fifty-foot-high ceiling, were not alight. The aisle that the girl had run through lay deserted for its considerable length, illuminated by brushed-steel sconces trimmed with polished brass, like small lamps, fixed high on the six-inch-wide stiles that separated sections of shelving.

These shelves had backs, so that I couldn't look over the tops of the books into the next aisle. Stepping softly, I continued east, into the next north-south passage that paralleled the first, but the girl wasn't there.

The stacks were arranged in a large grid, not as mazelike as the board for that old video game Ms. Pac-Man. Yet it seemed far more baffling than a grid as I cautiously made my way through it, spying around corners, turning this way and that as intuition guided me.

I was heading south, approaching a corner, intending to turn left, when I must have heard something, perhaps the faintest squeak of a rubber-soled shoe. I froze between the last two sconces, not in shadow but not brightly lighted.

A tall, sinewy man hurried through the intersection in front of me, from right to left, apparently so sure of his quarry's location that he didn't glance in either direction as he crossed my aisle and disappeared. I thought that he must have registered my presence peripherally and that he would startle back for a more direct look, but he kept moving.

He'd been dressed in a suit and tie, minus the coat, the sleeves of his white shirt rolled up, which suggested that he belonged here, worked here in a position of authority. But something about him—

perhaps his intensity, his grimly set mouth, his hands clenched in big bony fists—convinced me that his intentions were suspect if not even dishonorable.

I dared to follow him, but by the time I turned the corner, he had vanished. Even as familiar as I had become with the library, this might be his labyrinth more than mine. If his role was the Minotaur of legend and if my role was Theseus, who destroyed such beasts, this might end badly for the good guys, considering that I'd never killed anything, monsters or otherwise.

The girl cried out and the man shouted, *"Bitch, you little bitch, I'll kill you,"* and the girl cried out again. The clump-and-thud of avalanching books suggested that someone must be using the weapon of knowledge in an unconventional fashion.

The acoustics of the enormous room were deceiving. The ornate and gilded ceiling coffers, the limestone walls, the marble floor, the endless partitions of muffling books alternately absorbed and ricocheted sounds until it seemed that the brief battle was being waged in every aisle of the stacks, to all sides of me. Then sudden silence.

I stood in an intersection, head cocked, turning in a circle, my heart racing, fearful that something had happened to her. I recalled that the Minotaur, in the caverns under Crete, ate human flesh.

8 .

HOOD UP, HEAD DOWN AS BEST I COULD KEEP IT AND still find my way, I turned left, right, left, this way, that way, around and back again, through History with all its wars, through Natural

Sciences with all its discoveries and mysteries. Several times I heard sly movement, the light quick breathing of the girl, a muttered curse in a low male voice. I glimpsed him ahead of me twice, turning a corner. I didn't see her, but that was good, excellent, better than finding her corpse.

I discovered the aisle where books were scattered on the floor, perhaps thrown by the girl or pulled off the shelves to foil her pursuer. It pained me to see books treated that way. But she was maybe sixteen, all of a hundred pounds, if that. The man with his sleeves rolled up stood about six two, weighed nearly twice what she did, clearly couldn't control his anger, and threatened to kill her. If she had to destroy the entire library to save herself, she would be in the right. Each book is a mind alive, a life revealed, a world awaiting exploration, but living people are all those things, as well—and more, because their stories haven't yet been completely told.

Then something changed, and for a moment I thought it was just that the small sounds of search and evasion had given way again to utter silence. But the faintest susurration rose, vaguely liquid in character, as though a thousand thin threads of water were gently spilling from bowl to bowl of a tiered fountain that stood almost beyond the limits of hearing.

With that ghost of a sound came a smell that was not native to the library, that was neither the paper of three centuries aging with as many subtly different fragrances as were produced by an array of cheeses, nor the faintest citrus scent of limestone walls, certainly not wood polish or marble wax. This was the half-fresh smell of a half-washed street, and with it came a cool draft not quite strong enough to flutter the pages of the tumbled books on the floor.

Alert to the risk of being discovered, I sought the source of the draft, walking into it, to the south end of the stacks, where I hesitated to move into the open. The book-return station stood to the left, the main desk to the right, and between them a wide swath of glistening dark-caramel marble led to the circular grand foyer with its domed ceiling. At the farther end of the foyer, one of the four main doors, an ornately decorated slab of bronze, stood open to the night.

From out of sight, elsewhere in the stacks, came the sounds of someone running. As I shrank back into my aisle and the threadbare weave of shadows that dressed it, the angry man appeared, angling from the east, past the book-return desk. His attention was so focused on the foyer and the open door that he might not have seen me if I had been spotlighted on a pedestal.

The incident, still unfolding, excited me for reasons that I could not define, and I found myself behaving recklessly, as I had never done before. Certain that the man would exit through the open door and descend the two long flights of exterior stairs to see if he could spot the fugitive girl, I boldly followed him, so that he needed only to glance back to discover me.

Indeed, he rushed through the open door, and I arrived at its threshold in time to see him dashing across the landing and down the lower flight to the public sidewalk, where he looked left and right, searching for his silver-shoed quarry. The broad street had recently been half washed by a street-cleaning truck, which explained why the smell was less fresh than it would have been if rain had done the job, and the susurration arose from the light post-midnight traffic passing over the wet pavement.

As the man stepped off the curb, the better to see farther along the avenue, I realized that the alarm had not gone off when the girl had escaped. And then I noticed that the heavy door, which featured an automatic closer, was held open by the long L-shaped drop bolt that she must have extracted from the hole in the floor where it would have been inserted. She hadn't taken the time to swivel the bolt into its retainer, and now the end of it was caught in a void in the granite of the upper landing of the exterior steps, propping open the door.

The likelihood of the bolt finding that—apparently single—void in the otherwise smooth stone seemed small. I suspected that she had wedged it there to make sure the door remained open wide to admit a draft that would be noticed.

As the frustrated man in the street began to turn back toward the library, I retreated before I might be seen. I raced across the foyer with the intention of returning to the labyrinth of books.

At the sight of the girl in black, I faltered. She hurried through the half-light in the reading area that lay past the stacks, heading toward an interior door at the distant northeast corner of the immense room.

She had faked her escape, which meant she must know a secret haven in the building where she felt safe. And it meant more than that, though I couldn't quite imagine what.

I heard the man cursing loudly even before he reached the top of the exterior steps. I didn't have enough time to reach the stacks across what seemed to be an acre of marble. The moment he arrived at the open door, he'd see me. I darted to the left and vaulted the wraparound counter at the main desk, which was not simply a desk but instead a spacious librarian station appointed with exquisite mahogany moldings, at which patrons could be served from four sides. I crouched below the counter, hopeful that I had not been spotted.

I listened as the bronze door boomed shut, as the primary deadbolts were engaged, and as the drop bolt rang softly as it was seated in the bronze-rimmed hole in the floor. His footsteps seemed to approach my hiding place directly, but then he walked past, so close that I could smell his spicy cologne. In passing, he snarled "bitch" and worse, alternating vicious epithets, as if in fact he hated her enough to kill her. He faded into silence. A door closed in the distance.

After a while, the lights went off.

I got to my feet but didn't leave the shelter of the main desk.

The thirty-foot-tall windows in the south wall began above ten feet of bookshelves and arched to a keystone within ten feet of the deeply coffered ceiling. One of the charms of the city is its night glow, which is never less than romantic, sometimes magical. On this occasion in December, the metropolis shone into the library not with an eerie milkiness, as earlier, but with a convincing imitation of snow light, like a Christmas moon reflecting from a landscape cloaked by a recent blizzard. The EXIT signs above the doors were as red as clusters of holly berries, though I marveled at myself for thinking such a thing and wondered what had possessed me that I should be so light of spirit only minutes after cowering in fear.

Of course, it was the girl. Her gracefulness, her fleetness, her balletic sprint, and the sheer mystery of her presence in the library inspired in me the pleasant expectation that I might be witness to—if not a party to—an exciting adventure.

Although my life was by any standard unconventional, it wasn't full of sparkling encounters and dazzling exploits. I hid by day, reading, listening to music through the earphones of my CD player, thinking, wondering, and from time to time sleeping. By night I skulked through the city, seeking the essentials for survival, as well as a few moments of beauty in places like this, where great culture and fine art came together in sublime architecture. But considering the all-consuming hatred and fury that I inspired on sight, if I sought to participate in an adventure, I would be as unwise as a hemophiliac juggling hatchets.

Books had shown me, however, that all people everywhere wanted their lives to have purpose and meaning. This longing was universal. Even I, in my terrible difference, wanted nothing less than purpose and meaning.

Intuition told me that this girl might be different from other people in her attitude toward me, that she might be at least as tolerant as my mother had been, that she might be a touchstone by which I could test my value as a person without suffering torture and a violent death. I suspected that she might need help and that I, in spite of my limitations, might be of service to her.

I expected no relationship, only a memorable encounter in which I might contribute something that would make a vital difference in her life. Father often said that we are here to learn and give. But how could one give while in hiding, six years alone?

A few minutes after the lights went out, a recorded voice issued from speakers throughout the building: *"Perimeter is armed."*

The angry man must be leaving by the rear entrance, which opened onto an alleyway. An alarm keypad was positioned by that door.

In a building as elaborate as this one, motion detectors tended to report too many false alarms, and therefore they weren't employed. Because of the paper-preserving climate-control system, the windows were fixed, and their bronze stiles and muntins would not be easily penetrated by thieves. Besides, the current criminal class was even dumber than those in centuries gone by, unaware that books had value. And the vandals who might once have enjoyed hiding in here to deface and destroy after hours were, these days, able to get away with such bold in-the-open mayhem that tearing books apart or even urinating in them was boring compared to the assaults on civilization that could be made elsewhere, anywhere. By comparison, the doors were easily alarmed, the perimeter secured; and within the walls, I was free to roam.

I switched on my flashlight and left the librarian station by its gate.

During the eighteen years that I'd been visiting, the grandeur of this building, for hours at a time, had been mine alone, as if I were the king of books and this my palace. In spite of my familiarity with its every nook, I never tired of the place, but now it offered something new. Why was she here? Why hadn't she fled when she had the chance? Who was her enraged pursuer? I hadn't found the library so exciting since the first few times that I had come here with Father.

I hurried across the enormous reading room, toward the door through which the girl had gone. I knew a few hiding places that she might have found, sanctums that even the longest-tenured employees of the library might never have discovered.

If she didn't prove to be as tolerant as my mother, she was at least much smaller than I was and unlikely to be able to harm me before I could flee from her. The memory of her running with great poise, all but gliding through the stacks, still enchanted me, but I reminded myself that people who seemed to be no threat at all had sometimes been those who almost cut me down. Even a rapidly dying man, with nothing left to lose, had been overcome with such loathing that, when I knelt to help him, he used his last breath to curse me.

9

EIGHT YEARS OF AGE, A BOY BUT ALSO SOMETHING far different from other boys, I looked for a place where I might belong.

For five days following my banishment from the little house on the mountain, I traveled overland, mostly by the first two hours of light after dawn and the last hour before nightfall, when those who might venture into woods and meadows for a pleasant hike or a bit of off-season hunting were less likely to be afoot. I slept by night and remained hidden but watchful during the larger part of the day.

Because I soon left the forest that was familiar to me and passed into one I had never seen before, I tried to stay as near to one road or another as possible without moving too often in the open. There were more trees in that part of the world than anything, trees I could name and many kinds that I couldn't, so that I was able more or less to remain within sight of blacktop while trees screened me from those who traveled on it.

I set out that morning before the sun crested the horizon, but already the feathery clouds in the east blazed more pink than blue, the very pink of flamingos that I had once seen in a nature book.

In addition to whiskey, pills, and the white powder that she sniffed, about the only thing my mother liked was nature, and she had maybe a hundred picture books about birds and deer and other animals. She said that people weren't worth spit, none of them. She said that my true father was a shiftless piece of trash, like all the rest of them, and she wasn't ever going to lie with another man or a woman, either, since they were all selfish perverts when you really got to know them. But she loved animals. Even though she loved them, she wouldn't have a cat or dog or anything in the house, because she said she didn't want to own any living thing or to be owned by it.

The flamingo-pink turned darker, almost orange, and I knew that the fiery colors would quickly burn away, as they always did, and the clouds that were so flamboyantly painted now would soon be as colorless as one kind of ashes or another, and the sky behind them all blue. While the orange was still up there, before the sun showed it-self directly and slanted as sharp as glass into the woods, the morn-ing shadows were so black among the trees that I could almost feel them sliding over me, as cool as silk.

In the high orange light of dawn, the car came along that lonely road, which was four or five feet above the woods. A gentle slope of wild grass led down from the blacktop to where I hid. Confident that I could not be seen among the trees and their silken shadows, I did not drop flat to the ground or crouch, not even when the car stopped and the men got out of it. I knew somehow that they were engaged in a piece of business that had their full attention; for them, the whole world had shrunk down to what they had come here to finish.

Three of the men were joking with the fourth. I could hear the laughter in their voices though not the words, but the guy that two of them were holding up didn't seem to be in a mood to be amused. At first he looked weak and sick, maybe drunk, but then I realized he'd been badly beaten. Even from a distance of fifteen feet, his face looked all wrong, distorted. His pale-blue shirt was streaked with blood.

While two men held the one, the fourth man punched him in the stomach. I thought it was a punch, but when he punched the guy again, I saw the knife in his hand. They dropped the stabbed and beaten man off the side of the road, and he slid on his back, headfirst, to the bottom of the little grassy slope, where he lay very still.

The three by the car laughed at the way the dead man slid down through the dew-wet grass, and one of them unzipped his pants as if he might pee on the corpse, though maybe that was only another joke. Just then the one who had done the stabbing hurried around to the driver's door, shouting, "Let's go, you douche bags, *let's go!*"

The car flashed away, the engine noise quickly swallowed by the yawning forest, and the sun came up in the deepest quiet that I had ever heard. I watched the dead man for a while and waited for the car to return, but by the time the colorful clouds had faded to an ashy white, I knew the killers weren't coming back.

When I went to the body, I discovered life in it. The victim's face was horribly battered, bruised. But he still breathed.

A knife with a fancy carved-bone handle protruded from his gut, buried to the hilt. Where not slick with blood, the man's right hand looked as white as the bone around which his fingers folded.

I wanted to help him but didn't know how. Nothing that I could think to say seemed adequately comforting. In my awkward silence, I wondered if I would ever be able to talk to anyone but my mother, for I had never exchanged a word with anyone but her.

Busy with dying, the job almost done, he at first seemed unaware of me. His left eye was nearly swollen shut, the right eye wide and staring as if at something astonishing that winged across the morning sky.

"I'm sorry," I said. "I'm so sorry."

His gaze refocused. He made a low thick sound that seemed to be more an expression of revulsion than an expression of pain.

I wore my knitted gloves, yet when I touched him, he shuddered and clearly would have kicked out and scrambled away from me if he'd not been so weak.

In his raw and desperate voice, words came with bubbles of blood that popped between his lips. "Get away. Get. Get away."

Then I realized not only that had I neglected to pull the scarf over my face, but also that the hood had slipped off my head.

Mother warned me that by my eyes alone I would be known, and the dying man couldn't look away from them. His pallor worsened quickly when he met my stare, as if my eyes did more damage to him than had the bone-handled knife.

With a sudden burst of energy, he snarled a word I didn't know but delivered it with such viciousness that I realized it must be both an insult and a curse. On the repetition of that word, he found within himself a hatred so great that it anesthetized him against the searing pain of disembowelment. He ripped a wider wound as he pulled the knife out of his abdomen, and he slashed at my face, as if to blind the eyes that so offended him.

I pulled back, the blade cut only air, it fell from his hand, his arm dropped to the ground, and he lay dead.

10

BEYOND THE DOOR THROUGH WHICH THE GIRL HAD vanished, a wide hallway with a groin-vaulted ceiling served four rooms that housed specialty collections. One of those was a seven-thousand-volume collection of first editions of important detective fiction, valued at many millions and donated by a famous writer who resided in this city.

Crossing the threshold, I switched off my flashlight. I stood in the dark room, listening.

In any large building designed both for functionality and to please the eye, dead spaces exist here and there behind walls, not needed for plumbing or electrical chases. Some are as large as walk-in closets. If included in the room that they adjoin, these nooks and coves would deform the shape of that chamber. In the interest of eye-pleasing harmony, such cavities are lost behind walls.

A clever architect with a romantic streak and an appreciation for mystery will sometimes find ways to make those spaces accessible through a secret door well concealed in a paneled wall or by some other means. Often, these recovered dead spaces serve as storage, but some architects with a sense of fun and a love of things arcane will make other use of them.

If the fleet-footed girl had taken refuge here among the storied pages full of FBI agents, homicide detectives, private investigators, and amateur crime-solvers of a thousand kinds, she was as quiet as the cadavers that also filled those pages.

The original blueprints for the central library, more than a century old, were archived in the basement. My love of the building's beauty and its books had motivated me to study the plans during numerous visits, years earlier, and I had found two dead spaces of generous proportions.

One was indeed concealed behind a secret door in a paneled wall, elsewhere in the building. It measured eleven feet wide, six deep, and it was beautifully finished with several exotic woods and exquisite millwork. I thought the architect—John Lebow of the firm Lebow and Vaughn—himself had designed and secretly performed the finish work in both hidden rooms, though not in a spirit of fun.

On the back wall, as the focal point of the first space, hung a portrait of a lovely woman with auburn hair and green eyes. She held in her hands a book and was sitting beside a table on which other volumes were piled high. On the bottom rail of the painting's frame, a brass plaque identified her as MARY MARGARET LEBOW / BELOVED WIFE. Her date of death was given as June 15, 1904, more than a year before the construction of the library was completed.

The second secret room, ten feet wide and eight deep, was here with the detective fiction, concealed behind a wall of bookshelves that flanked a nine-foot-by-five-foot painting of the library's main entrance as it had looked when decorated for its first Christmas in 1905. The painting seemed to be fixed in place. But a series of small steel levers, cunningly recessed in the frame's ornate moldings, would release a latch if pressed one at a time in the correct order, thereafter allowing the painting to swing outward on a hidden piano hinge.

The second concealed chamber, likewise beautifully finished with the highest quality woodwork, featured another oil painting, this one of two children: a boy of seven, a girl of nine, each holding a book. The plaque on the frame named them—KATHERINE ANNE LEBOW / JAMES ALLEN LEBOW—and revealed that they died on the same day as their mother.

Through research, I had learned that Mary Margaret Lebow had been a librarian when the architect met and married her. Years later, on a visit to New York City, while her husband remained here to continue overseeing the building of the library, she and the children joined a few of her relatives—and more than thirteen hundred other passengers—for a day trip on the steamboat *General Slocum*. They intended to cruise leisurely from the Lower East Side of Manhattan, along the East River to Long Island Sound. They had not gone far before a fast-moving blaze broke out aboard the vessel. Hundreds of terrified passengers leaped into the water. Few could swim. Those who did not die by fire died by drowning—more than a thousand. June 15, 1904, was the date of the greatest tragedy in the history of New York, until September 11, 2001.

Most of those who perished that day had been members of St. Mark's Evangelical Lutheran Church, at 623 East Sixth Street, to which Mary Margaret's relatives belonged. In their grief, other men might have judged God unspeakably cruel and might have turned away from Him forever, but apparently not John Lebow. In each of those two secret spaces, flanking each oil painting, inlaid in the woodwork were gilded crosses. These painstakingly created shrines to his wife, the librarian, and to their children were also testaments to the architect's enduring hope.

I switched on the flashlight, shone it upon the large painting that also served as a door, and spoke loud enough to be heard by the girl if she sat in the haven behind it. "My name is Addison, although no one in the world knows it—except now you. If you're in there with John Lebow's lost children, I want you to know that in a different sense, I was a lost child, too, and I am still lost, although not a child anymore."

No response was forthcoming.

"I don't mean you any harm. If I intended to hurt you, I would press the three concealed levers in the proper order and pull you out of there right now. I want only to help you if I can. Maybe you think you don't need help. Sometimes, I think I don't need it, either. But we all do. We all need help."

In the painting, evergreen boughs were wound around the columns that flanked the entrance to the library, and wreaths with huge red bows hung on each of the four tall bronze doors. Snow fell into a white-blanketed street, and the world looked more right than perhaps it had ever been since 1905.

"If you don't want to talk with me, I'll never bother you again. I love the library too much to give it up, so I'll visit some nights, but I won't look for you. Take a little time to think about it. If you *do* want to talk, for the next half an hour, I'll be in the main reading room, among the stacks, where the bad man couldn't catch you, where you ran just like a dancer dancing. I'll be in the aisle with Charles Dickens."

I knew her to be bold and quick and not a mouse. But a mouse behind the wainscot, smelling a cat and being smelled by it, just a thin width of cherrywood away, could not have been more quiet than this girl.

11

IN THE MAIN STACKS, EACH AISLE HAD ITS OWN light switch, and I clicked on only the one. The high-mounted sconces with their brushed-steel brass-trimmed shades funneled light down to glimmering pools on the caramel-marble floor.

Having removed the bulb from one sconce, I stood as near to Dickens as I dared, his books in light and I in shadows. If the girl should come, I would not by either intent or accident expose my face to her. Under my hood, reflected light might shimmer in my eyes, but she wouldn't be able to see the color or the details, or whatever quality of them made people want to slash and burn me.

If she came and for a while we conversed like equals, and if then a sudden intuitive understanding of my nature caused her to turn and flee, I wouldn't pursue her but would instead run *away* from her. In time, therefore, after her terror passed, she might realize that I not only meant her no harm but also respected—and did not resent—her antipathy.

To be my friend, maybe you must be like me, one of the hidden. It might not be possible for anyone who lives in the open to tolerate a thing like me. But always I had remained hopeful that, among the millions on this Earth, there might be a few who could summon the courage to know me for what I am and have the self-confidence to still walk part of this life with me. The girl, mysterious in her own right, was the first in a long time who seemed as if she might have that capacity.

Just when I thought she would not come, she appeared at the farther end of the aisle, moving into the light from the last sconce. Standing there in her silvery shoes and black jeans and black sweater and black leather jacket, with her feet wide apart and her hands on her hips, she looked as if she had stepped out of one of those comic books that I don't like very much. I mean those comics in which everyone, good guys and bad guys alike, is very self-assured and tough and determined and proud of himself. They stand with their chests out and their shoulders back and their heads lifted, looking heroic and confident, and their hair is always blowing even in scenes where there is no wind, because they look better with their hair blowing. In the library, of course, there was no wind, and the girl's hair wasn't blowing, but it was long and black and shaggy, so that it kind of looked as if it must be blowing even when it wasn't.

I don't much like the superheroes and supervillains in many of those comic books because, maybe except for Batman, the way they pose dramatically all the time really does reflect how they think of themselves. Very self-righteous, whether saving the world or blowing it up. So in the thrall of power fantasies. This girl looked like she stepped out of a comic book, but somehow I could tell that the way she posed wasn't a reflection of how she really thought of herself.

Or maybe I was deluded. The fallow soil of loneliness is fertile ground for self-deception.

After regarding me from a distance, she took her hands from her hips and approached neither warily nor boldly, but with the same effortless grace that she had shown earlier.

As she stepped into the lamplight that fell across the books by Dickens, I said, "Please stop there." She did. We were no more than twelve feet apart, but my hoodie and the fact that I had disabled the nearest sconce spared her from the shock of my appearance.

As for *her* appearance, I hadn't realized when I glimpsed her in flight that she accessorized and painted herself so grotesquely. In her pierced right nostril, she wore a silver nose ring fashioned as a snake devouring its tail. Pinned to her lower lip, bright against the black lipstick, a polished red bead looked like a drop of blood. Her flawless skin was as pale as powdered sugar, and she emphasized that pallor by applying mascara and creme-stick makeup as thick as greasepaint. With her jet-black and curiously chopped hair, the look was Goth, I suppose, but a personalized version of the standard Goth-girl style. For one thing, the creme formed carefully drawn diamonds, the upper points at midbrow, the lower points two inches down her cheeks, which reminded me of certain harlequins but also recalled to mind a most disturbing tuxedoed marionette that I had once seen in the lighted window of an antique-toy store.

At the center of those black diamonds were eyes identical to those of the marionette. Whites as white and veinless as hard-boiled eggs, anthracite-dark irises with deep-red striations so subtle that they were visible only when the angle of her head allowed the light to find them. Because my life seldom brought me face-to-face with other people, because I was familiar with the variety of human faces and the color range of eyes only from books of photography, I could not say for certain that such eyes were uncommon, but they were so disconcerting that I imagined they must be rare.

"So you want to help me," she said.

"Yes. Whatever I can do to help you."

"No one can help me," she declared with no slightest indication of bitterness or despair. "Only one person could ever help me, and he's dead. You will die, too, if you associate with me, and you'll die cruelly."

12

I STOOD IN THE SHADOWS SHORT OF DICKENS, SHE in the lamplight, and I saw that her fingernails were painted black and that tattooed on the backs of her hands were curled blue lizards with forked red tongues.

"That wasn't a threat, when I said you'll have a cruel death," she clarified. "It's just the truth. You don't want to be around me."

"Who was the one person who could help you?" I asked.

"It doesn't matter. That's another place, another time. I can't bring it back by talking about it. The past is dead."

"If it were dead, it wouldn't smell so sweet."

"It isn't sweet to me," she said.

"I think it is. When you said 'another place, another time,' the words softened you."

"Imagine whatever you want. There's nothing soft here. I'm all bone and carapace and quills."

I smiled, but of course she couldn't see my face. Sometimes it is my smile that most terrifies them. "What's your name?"

"You don't need to know."

"No, I don't. I'd just *like* to know."

The thread-thin red striations brightened in her black-black eyes. "What's *your* name again, lost boy?"

"Addison, like I said."

"Addison what?"

"My mother's last name was Goodheart."

"Did she have one?"

"She was a thief and maybe worse. She wanted to be kind, kinder than she knew how to be. But I loved her."

"What was your father's name?"

"She never told me."

"My mother died in childbirth," she said, and I thought that in a sense my mother had died *from* childbirth, eight years after the fact, but I said nothing.

The girl looked toward the rococo ceiling, where the chandeliers hung dark, gazed up as if the rich moldings around the deep coffers and the sky scene of golden clouds within each coffer were visible to her by some spectrum of light invisible.

When she looked toward me again, she said, "What are you doing in the library after midnight?"

"I came to read. And just to be here in the grandness of it."

She studied me for a long moment, though I presented hardly more than a silhouette. Then she said, "Gwyneth."

"What's your last name, Gwyneth?"

"I don't use one."

"But you have one."

As I waited for her reply, I decided that all the Goth was more than fashion, that it might not be fashion at all, that it might be armor.

When at last she spoke, she didn't give me her surname, but instead said, "You saw me running from him, but I never saw you."

"I'm unusually discreet."

She looked at the set of Dickens novels on the shelves to her right. She slid her fingers along the leather bindings, the titles glowing in lamplight. "Are these valuable?"

"Not really. They're a matched set, published in the 1970s."

"They're wonderfully made."

"The leather's been hand-tooled. The lettering is gilded."

"People make so many beautiful things."

"Some people."

When she turned her attention to me again, she said, "How did you know where to find me, in there with the Lebow children?"

"I saw you leaving the reading room when he was in the street looking for you. I figured you must have studied the blueprints in the basement archives. So did I."

"Why did you study them?" she asked.

"I thought the bones of the structure might be as beautiful as the finished building. And they are. Why did *you* study them?"

For maybe half a minute, she considered her reply, or perhaps she considered whether to answer or not. "I like to know places. All over the city. Better than anyone knows them. People have lost their history, the what and how and why of things. They know so little of the places where they live."

"You don't stay here every night. I would have seen you before."

"I don't stay here at all. I visit now and then."

"Where do you live?"

"Here and there. All over. I like to move around."

Seeing through her bold makeup wasn't easy, but I thought that underneath she might be very lovely. "Who is he, the one who chased you?"

She said, "Ryan Telford. He's the curator of the library's rare-book and art collections."

"Did he think you were stealing stuff or vandalizing?"

"No. He was surprised to discover me."

"They don't know I come here, either."

"I mean he was surprised to discover me in particular. He knows me from . . . another place and time."

"Where, when?" I asked.

"It's not important. He wanted to rape me then, and he almost did. He wanted to rape me tonight. Though he used a cruder word than *rape*."

Sadness overcame me. "I don't know what to say to that."

"Who does?"

"How old are you?" I asked.

"Does it matter?"

"I guess not."

She said, "I'm eighteen."

"I thought no older than sixteen, maybe even thirteen now that I've seen you up close."

"I have a boyish body."

"Well, no."

"Well, yes," she said. "Boyish the way that very young girls can seem boyish. Why do you hide your face?"

I was intrigued that she had taken so long to ask the question. "I don't want to scare you off."

"I don't care about appearances."

"It's not just appearances."

"Then what is it?"

"When they see me, people are repulsed, afraid. Some of them hate me or think they do, and then . . . well, it goes badly."

"Were you burned or something?"

"If it were only that," I said. "A couple of them tried to set me on fire once, but I was already . . . already what I am before they tried."

"It's not cold in here. So are the gloves part of it?"

"Yes."

She shrugged. "They look like hands to me."

"They are. But they . . . suggest the rest of me."

"You're like the Grim Reaper in that hood."

"Look like but am not."

"If you don't want me to see you, I won't try," she said. "You can trust me."

"I think I can."

"You can. But I have a rule, too."

"What rule?"

"You can't touch me. Not even the slightest, most casual touch. Especially not skin to skin. Especially not that. But also not your glove to my jacket. No one can touch me. I won't permit it."

"All right."

"That was quick enough to be a lie."

"But it wasn't. If I touch you, you'll pull the hood off my head. Or if instead you make the first move and pull the hood off my head, then I'll touch you. We hold each other hostage to our eccentricities." I smiled again, an unseen smile. "We're made for each other."

13

AT THE AGE OF EIGHT, WITH NO IDEA WHERE I WAS bound, I came to the city on a Sunday night, aboard an eighteen-wheeler with a flatbed trailer hauling large industrial machinery that I couldn't identify. The machines were secured to the truck with chains and covered with tarps. Between the tarps and the machines were nooks where a boy of my size could conceal himself. I had gotten aboard when the driver had been having dinner, near twilight, in the coffee shop at a truck stop.

Two days earlier, I had run out of things to eat. My mother had sent me away with a backpack full of food, which I supplemented with apples from an untended orchard that I chanced upon. Although I had raised myself more than I'd *been* raised, though I had grown up more in the wilds than in our small house, I possessed no knowledge of what safely edible smorgasbord, if any, forests and fields might offer.

After a day of hunger, early on Sunday morning, I made my way through a sort of pine barrens, where the soil was peaty. The land spread out too flat and the underbrush grew too sparse to allow me to feel safe. For the most part, there was nothing to hide behind but trees, with the boughs far overhead and the trunks not all that thick. When I looked around, I seemed to be in a dream about a vast cloister where thousands of columns stood in no discernible pattern. Through the staggered trees, you couldn't see far in a straight line. But as I passed through, horizontal movement in all that vertical architecture and stillness, I couldn't possibly be missed by anyone who happened to be there.

Voices raised in song should have sent me scurrying toward some distant silent place, but instead I found myself drawn to them. I ran in a crouch and then, nearing the last of the pines, crawled to the tree line. Cars and pickups were parked on a graveled area a hundred yards to my left. Half that distance to the right, a languid river flowed like molten silver in the early light.

About forty people were gathered at the water's edge, singing a hymn, and the preacher stood in the river with a woman of about thirty-five, engaged upon a full-immersion baptism. To one side of the choir stood a man and two children, who seemed to be waiting their turns for salvation.

Directly ahead of me, across an expanse of grass, past all those people, stood a humble clapboard church, white with pale-blue trim. Near the building, in the shade of a great spreading oak, were chairs surrounding picnic tables that appeared to be laden with enough food to provide breakfast, lunch, and dinner during a full day of church and family fun.

The members of the congregation stood with their backs to me, busy with their hymnals and focused on the joyous event in the river. If the minister looked my way, I would be screened by the members of his congregation. I might not have much time, but I thought I would have enough.

I stripped off my backpack, zippered open its main compartments, broke from the trees, and sprinted to the picnic tables. On the grass near them were baseballs, bats, and gloves, also a badminton net not yet erected, rackets, and shuttlecocks. I had never played such games or heard of them, and those items meant nothing to me; I would not be able to identify them, in memory, until years later.

When I tore the foil off a platter, I found thick slices of ham. I wrapped several in the foil and shoved them in the backpack. There were potato salads and pasta salads covered with plastic wrap or lids, pies and cakes, none of them easy enough to pack. But I also found baskets of homemade rolls and biscuits covered by napkins, oranges, bananas, hard-boiled eggs pickled purple in beet juice, and cookies of all kinds.

From a pocket of my jeans, I withdrew part of the wad of cash that my mother had given me, peeled off a few bills, and dropped them on the table. Considered in retrospect, I probably paid far too much for what I had taken. But at the time, shaking with hunger, I felt that no price was too high to satisfy my growling stomach.

Sweating cans of soda and tea and juice were layered in plastic tubs of ice. After I slipped the straps of the backpack over my shoulders, I snatched up a cold Coca-Cola.

Just then someone behind me said, "Child, it's time for the Lord, not breakfast yet."

Startled, I turned, looked up, and saw a man coming out of a side door of the church, carrying a pan piled high with barbecued chicken legs.

Under thinning hair and a high brow, his face was soft and kindly—until he saw *my* face enclosed but not fully hidden by the hood of my jacket. Behind wire-rimmed glasses, his eyes widened as if the darkness of Armageddon had suddenly fallen upon the world and as if he were straining to see what must surely be the devil come to wage a final battle. The pan of chicken legs dropped from his hands, the color drained from his face in an instant, and he staggered two steps backward on abruptly weak legs. When he had taken in the totality of my face, he focused on my eyes, and a strangled sound escaped him.

"I'm sorry," I said, "I'm so sorry, so sorry, so sorry."

My apology meant nothing to him, nor did the cash upon the table, which I pointed out to him. He plucked a Louisville Slugger off the grass, lunged forward, and swung it, cutting the air above my head with enough power to have blasted a ball out of the park if the game had been under way.

I feinted left, he swung, I ducked and dodged right, he swung again and was almost quick enough to slam me. But then he seemed to be shocked by—aghast at—his sudden ferocious assault on a creature as small as a child, and he dropped the bat. Again, he reeled back from me, his face now wrenched with what might have been remorse or even anguish, a flood of tears sorrowing into his eyes, and he put one hand to his mouth as a cry of something like grief came from him.

They were singing louder than ever at the river. No one had yet seen the encounter by the picnic tables.

"I'll go," I said, "I'm sorry, I'll go."

As I broke into a run, I thought that in spite of his tears and his wrenching sobs, he was stooping to grab the baseball bat again. I raced past the back of the church, across mown grass, into a wild meadow, angling away from the river, desperate for the next pine barren, hoping that it would be furnished with more brush and with a topography more friendly to a fugitive.

I never glanced over my shoulder. I don't know whether the churchman pursued me for a quarter mile or a hundred yards, or any distance at all. Perhaps half an hour later, after the land had risen from peaty flats to more solid slopes, when my lungs burned and I began to flag, I paused on a wooded knoll to look back through the trees, whereupon I saw that no vigilantes were at my heels.

Driven by fear that temporarily quelled my hunger, I walked for another two hours, until I found a place that seemed remote enough to be safe. I sat upon a fern-skirted outcropping of rocks to eat some of what I had acquired at the church, my table a broad flat stone, luncheon music provided by birds high in the surrounding pines.

As I ate, I wondered at the farrago of emotions that the very sight of me had stirred up in the churchman with the soft and kindly face. I expected to inspire terror. Likewise repulsion and disgust. But his reaction had been more complicated than that of the stabbed man who tried to stab me in turn, more nuanced than the homicidal loathing of the midwives as it had been recounted to me by Mother. Even in its brevity, the churchman's reaction to me had been almost as complicated as the much longer relationship between me and my mother.

Mother and I had never discussed what I might be, as if it was burden enough to know that I was an abomination from which even she, having carried me within her, most often had to avert her eyes. My body, my hands, my face, my eyes, my impact on everyone who saw me: Any attempt to discuss those things, analyze them, and theorize about my nature only sharpened her aversion to me, sickened her until mere depression became despair.

A bird of some kind, small with a blue chest, dared to perch on the edge of the large flat stone that served as my table. I scattered biscuit crumbs toward it, and the bird hopped closer as it feasted. It had no fear of me, did not expect me to seize it in one fist and crush the life from it, knew that it was safe with me, and it *was* safe.

I thought then that perhaps I should spend my life in the deep woods, where I would be accepted. I could venture into areas of human habitation only at night, to get food wherever I could find it, and only until I might eventually learn to live off the bounty that the wildlands offered.

But even then, young and still unaware of my nature, I wanted more than peace and survival. I felt that I had a purpose that could be fulfilled only elsewhere, among the very people who were repelled by me. I felt I had a destiny, though I didn't know that it would be in the city where soon thereafter I came to live.

Later that very Sunday, in the lengthening purple shadows of twilight, miles from the stone table on which I had lunch, I found the truck stop and the eighteen-wheeler flatbed carrying the tarp-covered machinery. Aboard, I was brought to the city, arriving after midnight.

In the dark early hours of that Monday morning, I first saw the disturbing marionette in the lighted display window of the antique-toy store, as it sat with its back against a hand-carved rocking horse of whimsical design, its tuxedo rumpled, legs bent awkwardly, arms limp, black eyes with red striations seeming to follow me as I walked past.

14

AS I WENT WHERE GWYNETH LED ME BY FLASHLIGHT, along the hallways of the less public areas of the library, I said, "Where are you from? I mean, before the city."

"I was born here."

She named a year and a day in early October, and I halted in surprise. "You're eighteen."

"As I told you before."

"Yes, but you look so much younger that I just didn't think . . ."

She cupped one hand over the lens of the flashlight, letting just enough shine between her fingers to hold back the dark while ensuring that she could face me without a risk of revelation. "You just didn't think . . . what?"

"I'm twenty-six, you're eighteen—and we've both been in the city eighteen years."

"What's so remarkable about that?"

I said, "The day you were born—it's the day I came here as a stowaway on an eighteen-wheeler, in the first hour of that morning."

"You say that as if it must be more than a coincidence."

"I think it must be," I confirmed.

"What is it, then?"

"I don't know. It's something, though."

"Don't tell me it's kismet. There's not going to be anything like that between us."

"Kismet doesn't imply romance," I said a bit defensively.

"Just don't infer it."

"I've no illusions about romance. *Beauty and the Beast* is a nice fairy tale, but fairy tales are for books."

"You're no beast, and I'm no beauty."

"As for me," I said, "my own mother seemed to feel that *beast* was an inadequate word for me. As for you . . . eye of the beholder."

After a thoughtful silence, she said, "If a man is a beast, he's a beast in his heart, and that's not the kind of heart that beats in you."

Her words touched me and left me speechless.

"Come on, Addison Goodheart. We've got some snooping to do."

J. Ryan Telford, curator of the great library's rare-book and art collections, had his name on a wall plaque beside his office door.

By the narrow beam of Gwyneth's flashlight, we passed through the reception lounge where Telford's secretary had a desk. The inner office, with a full bath adjoining for the curator's private use, was immense and elegantly furnished in Art Deco antiques. The girl proved to be knowledgeable about the furnishings and showed me the Makassar-ebony desk by Pierre-Paul Montagnac, the Brazilian-rosewood sideboard with Portoro-marble top by Maurice Rinck, the fine sofa and matching armchairs of ebonized lemon wood by Patout and Pacon, the lamps by Tiffany and Galle, the ivory and cold-patinated bronze sculptures by Chiparus, who was arguably the greatest sculptor of the period, and throughout the tour, she scrupulously kept the light away from me, so that even the back glow did not reveal the slightest hint of my face.

And in respect of Gwyneth, I endeavored to maintain just enough distance between us to be sure that I did not accidentally touch or bump against her.

Until she told me, I had not realized that the art museum across the broad avenue from the library was a subsidiary of it, constructed decades later. Both institutions were among the most richly endowed of their kind in the country.

She said, "Their vast and priceless collections are both in the care of J. Ryan Telford, thief that he is."

"You said rapist."

"Would-be child rapist and successful thief," she said. "I was thirteen when he first cornered me."

I didn't want to dwell on what he had almost done to her, and so I said, "Who does he steal from?"

"The library and the museum, I imagine."

"You imagine."

"Their collections are broad and deep. He might muddy the records of what's in storage, collude with the auditor, sell off a very valuable piece now and then through an unscrupulous dealer."

" 'Imagine' . . . 'might.' You don't seem like a girl who would want to bear false witness."

She sat in the chair at the Makassar-ebony desk, swiveled 180 degrees to the computer that stood on a separate table, and said, "I *know* he's a thief. He stole from my father. Given his position here, he couldn't resist the temptation."

"What did he steal from your father?"

"Millions," she said, as she switched on the computer, and the word echoed off the Deco surfaces as had no other word before it.

15

THE OFFICE FELT SUMPTUOUS EVEN IN NEAR DARK-ness. It reminded me of certain photographs by Edward Steichen: velvet shadows deepening into moody gloom, here and there a form suggested by a reflection of light on a radius of polished wood, the mysterious gleam of Tiffany glass in the pendant shade of a lamp not lit, the room implied rather than revealed, yet known as well as if it had been enraptured by sunshine instead of barely kissed by the ghost light of the haunted city beyond the windows.

The fragrance of the curator's spice cologne lingered in his absence.

Painted by the glow of the computer screen, Gwyneth's face acquired an Asian aspect, largely because her pale skin and dramatic black makeup reminded me of the mask of a Kabuki actor.

She didn't seem to be a rich girl. Of course, I had never before known a rich girl, and had no experience by which to determine if she might be a familiar type among the wealthy. I thought not.

"Your father has millions?"

"Had. My father is dead."

"Is that who you meant, the only one who could ever help you?"

"Yes." She scrolled through the directory on the screen. "My father understood me. And protected me. But I couldn't protect him."

"How did he die?"

"In so many words, the autopsy said, 'Accidental death by honey.'"

"Honey like bees?"

"My grandfather, Daddy's father, had apiaries, hundreds of hives. Rented them out to farmers, then processed and bottled the honey."

"Is that where the family fortune came from?"

A brief soft laugh escaped her. Though she was amused by my ig-norance, the sound was as appealing as any music I had ever heard. I thought that I might like nothing better than sitting with her as she read a comic novel, just sitting and watching her laugh.

"My father married late in life, and I never met my grandfather. But in my family, beekeeping was a passion, not a money machine."

I said, "Well, I don't know a lot about money. I don't need much of it."

From an inner pocket of her leather jacket, she produced a memory stick, inserted it into the computer, and began to download documents.

"My father's the one who hit it big in real estate, but he grew up in the bee business, and he loved artisanal honey. He had a farm out-side the city, and he kept a lot of hives. He also traded honeys with beekeepers in other parts of the country, because they taste different depending on the plants from which the bees harvest the nectar. Daddy loved every kind of honey—orange blossom from Florida and Texas, avocado honey from California, blueberry honey from Michi-gan, buckwheat and tupelo and fireweed honey. . . . He bottled lots of flavors and blends for himself and friends. It was his hobby."

"How can honey accidentally kill someone?"

"My father was murdered."

"You said—"

"The autopsy report said accidental. *I* say murder. He ate some creamed honey, spread it thick on scones. It was contaminated with cardiac glycosides, oldedrin, and nerioside, because the bees had har-vested the nectar from oleander bushes, which are as poisonous as anything on Earth. Considering the dose he received, a few minutes after finishing the scones, he would have broken into a sweat, vom-ited violently, passed out, and died of respiratory paralysis."

As she found another document that she wanted to add to the

memory stick, I said, "But it does sound accidental, doesn't it? To me, it does, anyway."

"My father was an experienced beekeeper and honeymaker. So were the people he exchanged honey with. It can't have happened. Not with all their experience. The deadly honey was the only contaminated jar in his pantry, the only one containing poison. That was wholesome honey once, and later someone added oleander nectar."

"Who would do that?"

"A piece of human debris named J. Ryan Telford."

"How do you know?"

"He told me."

In its silken gloom, the murderer's office retained its air of elegance, of privilege waiting to be enjoyed, of authority waiting to be exercised. But now the sensuous lines of the lacquered furniture, revealed largely by reflections of pale light along the sleek curves of exotic woods, suggested a room as sinister as it was elegant.

More than eighteen years since I'd seen it in the store window, the tuxedoed marionette rose again in memory. The most strange and disquieting conviction overcame me: that if I were to switch on the lights just then, I would discover the loose-jointed puppet sitting on the sofa, watching me as I watched Gwyneth at the murderer's computer.

16

THAT NIGHT IN THE LONESOME OCTOBER, IN THE early weeks of my ninth year, with Mother dead by her own hand, the body perhaps not yet discovered, I arrived in a manufacturing district, cradled in machinery of unknown purpose. The trucker parked his rig in a fenced lot, and after listening and observing for half an hour to be sure the way was safe, I slipped from under the tarp, climbed the chain-link, and set foot in a city for the first time in my life.

The scale of the human accomplishment all around me, seen previously only in magazines and a few books, inspired in me such awe that I would have scurried along those streets with my head down, humbled and heart pounding, even if I had not needed to hide my face to protect myself. I had not known where the truck would take me. I had not prepared myself for the shock of civilization in such an insistent form as this metropolis.

The industrial buildings and warehouses were immense and seemed for the most part old, dirty, worn. Dark windows, others broken and boarded over, suggested that a few of those structures might be abandoned. Occasionally a streetlamp was out, and those that worked were dim because their globes were filthy. Litter collected in the gutters, billows of foul-smelling steam rose from a grate in the pavement, but the scene was no less glamorous for all of that.

I was at the same time fearful and exhilarated, alone in a place as alien as a world at the farther end of the galaxy would have been, yet electrified by a sense of possibilities that might transform in positive ways even a life as hedged with threats as mine. A part of me thought that it would be a miracle if I survived a day here, but another part of me nurtured the hope that in the countless thousands of buildings and byways, there would be forgotten nooks and passages where I might hide and move about, and even thrive.

At that hour, in that year, few of the factories ran graveyard shifts, and the night was quiet. Except for a passing truck now and then, I proceeded all but alone through that rough district. The nearly deserted and dimly lighted streets gave me more cover than I had expected, although I knew that I would eventually come to a more lively—and potentially deadly—neighborhood.

In time I crossed an iron bridge that accommodated both vehicles and pedestrians. On the broad black river far below, the running lights of barges and other boats appeared fantastic to me. Although I knew what they were, they looked less like vessels than like luminous creatures of the water, gliding dreamily past not on the surface but just beneath it, on journeys even more enigmatic than my own.

As I walked, I kept my attention mostly on the river, because ahead of me rose the lighted towers of the city center, a sparkling phantasmagoria at once enchanting and flat-out terrifying, which I could handle only in quick glimpses. On and on they went in serried ranks, stone and steel and glass, of such great mass that it seemed the land beneath them should sink or that the whole world should be tipped by their cumulative weight into a new angle of rotation.

When there was no more river below to distract me, only quay, I could no longer avoid facing the dazzling scene before me. As the humpbacked bridge sloped down, I looked up boldly, directly, and came to a halt, abashed at the splendor and wealth before me. I was an outcast with little knowledge, a child with no accomplishments to justify myself, standing now at what seemed to be the gates of a city of powerful and magical beings, where beauty and talent were required for admittance, where such as me would not be tolerated.

I almost turned back, to live like a rat among the rats in one of the abandoned factories on the farther side of the river. I was compelled, however, to go forward. I have no memory of descending the pedestrian walkway as it sloped down toward the shore, the open railing to my left, a four-foot-high concrete wall to my right, between me and the occasional passing car. Nor do I recall turning north at the foot of the bridge and following the quay for a considerable distance upriver.

As if waking from a trance, I found myself in an outdoor mall paved with herringbone brick, lighted by ornate iron lampposts, furnished with benches, shaded by trees in massive pots. The mall was lined on both sides with shops and restaurants, all closed at a quarter past three in the morning.

Some of the store windows were dark, but others were softly lighted to display their most appealing wares. I had never before seen a retail outlet of any kind, had only read about them or marveled at pictures of them in magazines. An entire shopping area, at the moment deserted but for me, was no less magical than the panorama of the bejeweled city viewed from the bridge, and I moved from business to business, amazed and thrilled by the variety of merchandise.

At the antique-toy shop, the contents of the display window were artfully arranged and lighted, the key items carefully pin-spotted, others illuminated only softly by spillover from the spots. Dolls from various periods, mechanical coin banks, cast-iron cars and trucks, a Popeye ukulele, a fanciful hand-carved rocking horse, and other articles captivated me.

The tuxedoed marionette sat in the softer light, its face white except for its black lips, a single red bead, like blood, upon the lower one, and the big black diamonds that angled around its eyes. From one nostril hung a silver ring fashioned as a serpent eating its tail. The head leaned forward slightly and the lips were not quite together, as though it might impart a secret of great importance.

Initially, I found the puppet to be the least interesting of the items on display. But the window was long, and the contents were so delightful that I moved from the left end to the right and then all the way back again. When I returned to the marionette, it sat where it had been before, but now the pin spot brightened its face instead of the rocking horse behind it.

I doubted that I was mistaken. The light previously had been focused on the horse. The eyes in the center of those diamond shapes, which had been merely black when in shadow, were now, in the brighter light, black with thread-thin scarlet striations that radiated from the center pupil to the outer edges of the irises. They stared straight ahead, so strange and yet with the depth and clarity and something of the sorrow of real eyes.

The longer I met that gaze, the more disquieted I became. Once more I moved from the left toward the right end of the large window, imagining what fun it would be to play with many of those toys. At the midpoint of the display, I glanced back to the marionette and discovered not only that the pin spot still brightened its face but also that its eyes, which had been focused straight ahead, had now turned sideways in their sockets, to follow me.

No strings were attached to the tuxedoed figure; therefore, no puppeteer could be manipulating it.

Instead of continuing to the right, I returned to the marionette. The eyes gazed toward where I'd been a moment earlier.

At the periphery of my vision, I thought the toy's left hand moved. I was pretty sure that it had been palm down, but now it lay palm up. I watched it for a long moment, but it remained motionless, pale and without fingernails, the white fingers hinged in two places instead of three, as if this were an early prototype of humanity, rejected for inadequate detail.

When I looked again, the black eyes with fine red filaments now almost as bright as neon were staring directly at me.

As centipedes seemed to crawl the nape of my neck, I stepped away from the window.

Back then, I didn't know cities or outdoor malls or antique-toy stores, and therefore I couldn't say for sure that such displays as this weren't routinely motorized or otherwise tricked up to keep the browser intrigued. But because, of all things in the window, only the marionette moved, and because the sight of it had troubled me even before it had become animated, I decided that something lower than a sales technique was at work and that continued study of the toy would be dangerous.

As I walked away, I heard what seemed to be a rapping on the inside of the window glass, but I assured myself that I either misinterpreted or imagined the sound.

The cool night seemed to be growing colder. The dirty-yellow moon floated low, slowly sinking down the sky. Out on the river, a boat horn blew three times, so melancholy that it might have been sounded in memoriam of lives lost in those waters.

I began to look for a place to hide before first light—but moments later I found instead two men who wanted to set a living thing on fire and, denied their original victim, settled on me as an acceptable substitute.

17

ON THE DEEP SILL OF THE BIG CORNER WINDOW IN the curator's office lay a folded newspaper. As I waited for the girl to discover whatever she might be searching for on the computer, I picked up the daily and, by the ambient light of the city, scanned the headlines: plague in China, war in the Middle East, revolution in

South America, corruption in the highest levels of the U.S. government. I had no use for such news and put the paper down.

Having taken what she wanted from the computer, Gwyneth pocketed the memory stick and switched off the machine. She remained in the murderer's chair, evidently brooding about something with such intensity that I was reluctant to interrupt her train of thought.

At the corner window, I gazed down at the cross street that bisected the avenue on which the library fronted. I could see for several blocks.

Emergency beacons flashing but without siren, a police sedan glided past on the avenue and arced left onto the cross street. No engine noise or squeal of tires rose to me, as if the panes of leaded glass were a window on a silent dream. When I had come to the city eighteen years earlier, it had been a brighter place. But in these days of electricity shortages and high energy prices, the buildings weren't as brightly lighted as they once had been. As the car receded along the shadowy canyon of high-rises, the murky quality of the night conjured the illusion of an undersea metropolis in which the sedan was a blinking bathysphere descending an oceanic trench toward some deep enigma.

Although the illusion lasted only a moment, it disturbed me to such an extent that a shiver of dread became a shudder, and my palms were suddenly damp enough that I needed to blot them on my jeans. I don't see the future. I don't have the ability to recognize an omen, let alone to interpret one. But that specter of a cold, drowned city resonated with me so profoundly that I could not lightly dismiss it as meaningless, yet I didn't want to dwell on it.

Assuring myself that what had really spooked me was the police sedan, I turned from the window and spoke into the darkness where the girl sat. "We better get out of here. If you've stolen something—"

"I've stolen nothing. Just copied evidence."

"Of what?"

"Of the case I'm building against the murdering thief."

"You've been in here before, at his computer."

"Several times, though he doesn't know it."

"But he was chasing you."

"I came into the library an hour before closing time and hid in the nook behind that painting. Fell asleep and woke after midnight. I was climbing the south stairs with my flash when the door opened above me, the light came on, and there he was, as shocked to see me as I was to see him. First time he'd seen me in five years. He never works so late. Besides, he was supposed to be in Japan another two days on business. I guess he came back early."

"Five years. Since you were thirteen."

"The night he tried to rape me. The worst night of my life, and not only for that reason."

I waited for her to explain that curious comment, but when she didn't, I said, "He's above you on the stairs, you run, and you fake him out so he thinks you left the library."

"Not that easy. He chases me down the stairs. He's fast. In the hallway, he catches me by the arm, swings me around, throws me to the floor. He drops to one knee, arm pulled back, going to punch me in the face."

"But here you are."

"Here I am because I have a Taser."

"You Tasered him."

"A Taser doesn't drop a guy as hard if he's really furious, if he's hot with rage and flooded with adrenaline, totally wild. I should have given him another jolt or two after he went down and I got up, but all I wanted was away from him, so I ran."

"If he recovered that quick, he must really hate you."

"He's had five years for the hate to distill. It's pure now. Pure and potent."

She got up from the chair, a dark shape in a darker room.

Stepping away from the window, I said, "Why does he hate you?"

"It's a long story. We better hide until they open in the morning. He's not as smart as you might think a big-time curator would be. But if it dawns on him that maybe I've been here before at night and that maybe I didn't leave the way it looked like I did, he'll be back soon."

In the first soft flare of her flashlight, the girl's painted face appeared both beautiful and eerie, as if she were a character in an edgy graphic novel in the manga style.

I followed her into the reception lounge, marveling at the ease of our regard for each other, wondering if it might strengthen into friendship. However, if my own mother eventually became unable to endure the sight of me, an amicable relationship between Gwyneth and me was unlikely to last any longer than the moment when, by an accident of light, she glimpsed my face. But I would have liked a friend. I would have loved one.

I said, "We don't have to hide here in the library through the night."

"He set the alarm, and if we trigger it, he'll know I was still here when he left. I don't want him to know that yet."

"But I have a way out that isn't wired into the system."

Phantoms of the library, we descended to the basement, and as we went, I succinctly explained how I traveled through the city unseen and unsuspected.

In that lowest level of the building, at the hinged cap to the storm drain, which remained open as I had left it, Gwyneth said, "You never go by streets and alleys?"

"Sometimes but not often. Only as far as necessary. Don't worry about storm drains. The idea is a lot scarier than the reality."

"I'm not afraid," she said.

"I didn't think you were."

She went down the ladder first. I followed, pulling shut the lid and securing it with the gate key.

The confining dimensions of the tributary drain did not seem to concern her, but nevertheless I explained that it would shortly take us to a much larger tunnel. Shoulders hunched and head lowered, I led her along the gradual downward slope, my mood especially felicitous because I was able to help her. It felt good to be needed, no matter how humble the service I provided.

The smaller pipe entered the main one at the level of the maintenance walkway, three feet above the floor of the bigger drain. With the flashlight, I showed her the drop-off, the sweep of floor below, the high curve of the ceiling.

For a moment we stood there, two dark shapes, finger-filtered flashlight aimed well away from us, so featureless that we might have been mere shadows separated from the people who cast us.

Gwyneth took a deep breath and then said, "It doesn't smell like I expected."

"What did you expect?"

"Bad odors. All kinds."

"Sometimes there are but not often. A big rain washes all the soot and filth down here, and for a while there seems to be as much stink as there is water. Even toward the end of the storm, when the city's been rained clean, you wouldn't want to bathe in the runoff, but it doesn't smell much anymore. When it's dry like now, there's usually just the vague scent of lime or, in the older passages, the faint trace of the silicates in the clay used to make the bricks. If they don't clean out the catch basins frequently enough or if something dead is rotting in one, that can be foul, but it's not a major problem." In my eagerness to share my subterranean world, I was close to babbling. I reined in my urge to be a docent of the drains, and said, "What now?"

"I need to go home."

"Where is home?"

"Tonight I think maybe it should be on the upper east side, where there's a view of the river. It's beautiful how sometimes the morning sun scatters gold coins on the river."

" 'Think maybe'?" I asked.

"I have choices. More places to go than one."

She gave me an address, and after a moment of thought, I said, "I'll show you the way."

We dropped off the service walk to the main floor of the tunnel, so that we could proceed side by side, each with a flashlight. The blackness was not merely darkness but a reduction of darkness, so thick that it seemed to congeal around the twin beams and press those narrow cones of light into even narrower cones.

As we ascended the barely perceptible slope, I glanced at Gwyneth now and then, but she kept her promise and did not look toward me.

"Where do *you* live, Addison?"

I pointed behind us. "Back there. Farther. Deeper. Rooms that everyone has forgotten, where no one can find me. Rather like a troll, I guess."

"You're no troll, and never say you are. Never. But you live by night?"

"I live from dawn to dawn, all day every day, but I go out only at night, if I go out at all."

She said, "There's not just danger in the city by day. There's beauty, too, and magic and mystery."

"The night offers much the same. I've seen things that I don't understand but that nonetheless delight me."

18

THINGS THAT I DON'T UNDERSTAND BUT THAT nonetheless delight me . . .

Two weeks following my arrival in the city, after I had been saved from fire by Father and taken under his protection, we were out on a mission in the hours when most people sleep most deeply, and for the first time I saw a ledge-walker.

Father was educating me in the ways that our kind must operate in a great city, teaching me the subterranean maze, the techniques of stealth that allow us the next thing to invisibility, and how to get into and out of essential places with all the grace of ghosts who can walk through walls.

By means that I'll explain later, he had obtained a key to the food bank operated by St. Sebastian's Catholic Church. Because the church gave away the food to those in need, and because the key had been freely provided to Father, we were not stealing when we entered the food bank after hours, to resupply our larder.

On the night of which I write, we exited the building into the alleyway behind it, where we discovered a power-company truck parked atop the storm-drain manhole that was the nearest entrance to our underground haven. The two workers were apparently in the transformer vault that lay behind the truck, from the open cover of which rose voices and a shaft of light.

Before we could be seen, we hurried toward the continuation of the alley in the next block, where we hoped to find another entrance to the drainage system. This required us to cross a brightly lighted six-lane street, which we were loath to do even though the great majority of our fellow citizens were abed and dreaming.

Father scouted the way, found no traffic, and motioned for me to follow him. As we approached the island separating the six lanes into three westbound and three eastbound, I saw movement four stories above the street, a man walking on a ledge. The sight halted me, for I thought he must intend to jump.

In spite of the cool weather, he wore hospital blues, or so it appeared. The ledge was not wide, but he walked it with a casualness that suggested that he didn't care about his fate. He peered down into the street, whether at us or not I couldn't tell, but also tipped his head back to gaze up at the higher floors of the buildings across the street, as though searching for something.

Realizing that I had halted at the island, Father stopped, looked back, and urged me to hurry.

Instead, I pointed to the walker on the ledge. "Look, look!"

I thought now that the man in blue wasn't reckless, as he had first seemed, but confident, as though he had walked tightropes in circuses the world around. Perhaps the narrow ledge posed no serious challenge by comparison to the death-defying feats that he had performed far above admiring audiences.

A taxi rounded the corner a block away, the driver glorying in the speed that daytime streets did not allow. The flare of headlamps reminded me of our perilous position. If the vehicle had been instead a police patrol car, a man and a boy in hoodies, bent under backpacks, running into an alleyway at that hour, would have invited pursuit.

We were of little interest to the cab driver, who no doubt lived by a hear-no-see-no-evil code. The car sped past without slowing as we dashed into the mouth of the alley.

There I hesitated again, looking up, as the walker turned the corner of the ledge. He stepped nonchalantly from the north wall of the building to the east wall, seemingly unconcerned about a misstep, as if he could walk on air as readily as on stone.

When he moved with such agility from the street to the darker alleyway, I realized that he was no jumper, that he was one of the Clears. His light had not been evident in the brighter street, but here in shadows, he glowed up there on the ledge.

I had seen Clears in unusual places, doing peculiar things, but I had never seen a Clear walking a ledge before. Of course, back then, I hadn't been long in the city.

How to describe a Clear to those who can't see them? The light of which I speak is not a searing beacon but a soft glow, and it has no locus but radiates evenly from them, head to foot. I once referred to it as *inner* light, but the word implies that they're translucent, which they are not, being as solid in appearance as anyone. Besides, their clothes shine as softly as their skin and hair, as if they are refugees from a science-fiction movie in which they were irradiated in a nuclear incident. I call them Clears not because they are transparent, but only because the first inexplicable beings that I saw, as a child, were the Fogs, and when next I saw two of these radiant people together in a moonlit meadow, the name that occurred to me was Clears, for they seemed to be the antithesis of the Fogs.

They were not ghosts. If they were anything as simple as spirits of the dead, Father would have called them that. He could see them, too, but talking about them made him apprehensive, and he routinely discouraged any line of conversation involving either the Clears or the Fogs. The man on the ledge and others like him weren't interested in haunting anyplace or spooking anyone. They didn't rattle chains or turn the air cold by their presence, or toss furniture around the way that poltergeists were supposed to do. They were not anguished or angry as ghosts are reported to be. Sometimes they smiled and often they were solemn, but always they appeared serene. Although they lived invisible to nearly everyone, I believed they were as alive as I was, though their intentions and their meaning were unknown to me and perhaps unknowable.

Father hooked a manhole cover and levered it aside with a tool that he had devised. He called to me that I was risking our lives by dawdling, and reluctantly I turned away from that spectacle above. But as I preceded Father down the ladder, into the tributary drain, I glanced back and up for one last glimpse of the glowing Clear who walked high ledges fearlessly, while I must always worry through backstreets and crooked byways.

19

THE ADDRESS THAT THE GIRL GAVE ME WAS ADJA-cent to Riverside Commons. She lived in a block of handsome detached houses, some of brick and others of limestone, that faced the park. About half were still single-family homes. She occupied the fourth floor of a four-story house that had been converted to apartments.

Under the commons lay Power Station 6, which once stood in plain sight. Decades earlier, to beautify the neighborhood, they buried the utility in a deep and massive vault, and built the park atop it. The workers' entrance, air intakes, and expulsion vents were along the river quay. Station 6, like the basement of the library, could also be entered by a tributary drain in the floor, provided in the event there should be a rupture in the pressurized water lines supplying the natural-gas-powered boilers that fed the steam generators.

Entering through a manhole, we were on the lookout for power-company employees, though fewer staffed the graveyard shift, when the plant produced below maximum potential. The drain lay at the west end of the structure, behind ranks of boilers, turbines, generators, and transformers. Workmen seldom had reason to venture into that shadowy space. Ten feet from the drain, a door opened on a concrete spiral staircase, a secondary exit in the event of an emergency.

I had instructed Gwyneth to go directly to the door, while I eased the manhole back into place. Haste was the key to passing through unseen. We didn't need to be concerned about noise because the spinning vanes of the turbines, the rotors of the generators, and the laboring pumps provided us with cover.

In the stairwell, with the insulated door closed, the clamor fell to a quarter of what it had been. As we ascended turn by turn, it steadily diminished.

With her natural grace, Gwyneth rose in the stair light, not as if climbing but as if she were all but weightless and were drawn up by a draft that I couldn't feel.

The light fell bright enough to reveal me within my hood, and I kept my head down in case she glanced back. I wanted this unexpected adventure to last for a while, wanted to be able as long as possible to share the night with her.

The door at the head of the stairs opened into a dark building that served as storage for the riding lawn mowers and other equipment used to maintain the Commons. With flashlights, we found the exit.

I followed Gwyneth outside but paused, holding the door. As an emergency exit from Power Station 6, it was always unlocked from the inside; but it would be locked from the outside when closed. I didn't have a key. Some homeless people lived in the park, and although most were timid and kept to their hidden nests in warrens of shrubbery, now and then one would be belligerent, stropped to sharp edges by either mental illness or drugs, or both.

This December night, no one approached us. The park lay as quiet as any place in the city could be, and we didn't need to retreat.

We followed a footpath across lawns, past the pond where, in warmer seasons and in a full moon, half-sleeping koi sometimes rose into view. They were thick from eating bread cast to them by daytime visitors, too spoiled to take night insects off the surface.

As if she knew my mind, the girl said, "By now they will have netted the koi and moved them inside for the winter."

At home in my hammock, when I slept, those fish sometimes swam into sight, mottled and pale, fins wimpling in the gentle currents, smoky presences. On the mirrored water of those dreams, I saw my face reflected darkly. The koi shimmering under my reflection had a place where they belonged in this world. Waking from such a dream, I was always filled with longing, yearning for a home in the light, a garden flowering and fruiting as it ought to be.

Now, at the Kellogg Parkway entrance to the Commons, as we stood under a towering pine, Gwyneth pointed to a house across the street. "That's one of the places where I live. Come in for coffee."

Having no friends, I had no experience of such invitations, and I stood speechless for a moment before I could say, "I better not. The night's nearly gone."

She said, "There's almost another hour and a half of darkness."

"I have to go to the food bank, get supplies before they open."

"What food bank?"

"St. Sebastian's."

"Come up, have breakfast. Go to the food bank tomorrow night."

"But I'll be seen going in your place. Too dangerous."

She said, "No doorman. Nobody's coming or going at this hour. Quick up the stairs."

I shook my head. "I shouldn't. I can't."

She pointed to a narrow walkway between her house and the one next door. "Go through there to the alley. At the back, there's a fire escape."

"No. I really can't."

"You will. *Come on.*" She ran into the street in the wake of a passing limousine with tinted windows as black as its paint job.

Before other traffic might appear, I sprinted after her. She raced up the front stairs of the house as I followed the passageway that led to the alley.

The fire escape switchbacked up the building, looking as though it ought to ring loudly beneath my feet like the bars of a xylophone struck exuberantly, but my ascent was quieter than pianissimo. A window framed soft light at the second-floor apartment, and the draperies were only half closed. As far as I could see, the room beyond was deserted. I turned onto the next flight of iron treads.

At the fourth floor, Gwyneth had opened the window for me; but she was not waiting. At the farther end of the dark room, beyond an open door, a cut-crystal ceiling fixture brightened a hallway wall with prismatic patterns.

Switching on my flashlight, I noticed words printed in black letters on the white windowsill, but before I could consider them, Gwyneth appeared beyond the open door and said, "Addison. Come to the kitchen."

By the time I climbed through the window and slid it shut behind me, the girl was gone. I stood in a generously proportioned room as sparsely furnished as a nun's cell: narrow bed, single nightstand, lamp, digital clock. The place smelled fresh, and I could relate to the minimalism.

Across the hallway lay an equally large room, containing only a desk, an office chair, a computer, a scanner, and two printers.

A lamp turned low illuminated a living room that must have been twice as large as my three underground rooms combined, but the place felt like home because of the books. There was, however, only one armchair, as if *her* father, while alive, had never lived here.

Beyond an archway lay a dining area with a table and chairs, open to a large kitchen in which she worked by candlelight. Even those discreet flames in ruby-glass holders were bright enough to risk my revelation.

Although we seemed to have much in common, I suddenly grew wary and felt that I should leave quietly.

Although her back was to me, she said, "There you are. Scrambled eggs and toasted brioche with raisin butter will be quick. Okay?"

"I should go."

"You won't. You're never rude. Pull out a chair. Sit down."

In spite of the one narrow bed, in spite of the single armchair in the living room, I said, "You aren't alone here, are you?"

Breaking an egg into a bowl, attended by her shadow and the shadows of candle flames that quivered on the walls, she said, "There is one who comes and goes infrequently, but I won't speak of that. It's nothing that will put you at risk."

I stood beside the table, unsure what to do.

Her back remained toward me, yet she seemed to know that I had not pulled out a chair. She held another egg, hesitating to break it.

"Everything now depends on mutual trust, Addison Goodheart. Sit down or go. There can be no third choice."

20

EIGHTEEN YEARS EARLIER, DURING MY SECOND WEEK in the city, on the night I saw a Clear in hospital blues walking the high ledge . . .

Later, at home in our deep redoubt, after the groceries were put away, Father brewed a pot of orange-flavored herbal tea, and I sliced a pound cake with coconut icing, and we sat at our small table, It and Son of It, speaking of this and that, until he finished his cake and put down his fork, whereupon he brought up the subject that he felt was more important than our small talk: Fogs and Clears.

He never called them that. He had no names for them, and if he had a theory about what they might be, he wasn't inclined to discuss it. But he had an opinion about what we should do when we encountered them.

His instinct, like mine, told him that the Fogs were nothing but bad news, though of exactly what kind he wasn't prepared to say. Even the word *evil*, he said, was not sufficient to describe them. Best to avoid the Fogs. Certainly never approach one, but on the other hand, maybe it was also wise never to run from them, just as running from an angry dog might invite attack. Feigning indifference to the Fogs had worked for Father and for his father, and he strongly advised me to respond to them always and without fail as he did.

Leaning over the table, lowering his voice, as though even this far beneath the city, all but entombed by a mountain of concrete, he might be overheard, he said, "As to the others, the ones you call the Clears. They aren't evil like the Fogs, but in their own way, they're more terrible. Pretend indifference to them, as well. Try never to meet their eyes, and if you *do* find yourself in close quarters with one of them and eye-to-eye, turn away at once."

Perplexed by his warning, I said, "But they don't seem terrible to me."

"Because you're so young."

"They seem wonderful to me."

"Do you believe I would deceive you?"

"No, Father. I know you never would."

"When you're older, you'll understand."

He would say no more. He cut another slice of cake.

21

BY THE LIGHT OF A SINGLE CANDLE SET NEAR Gwyneth's plate and far from mine, we ate a simple but delicious pre-dawn breakfast of scrambled eggs and brioche with raisin butter. I had never tasted coffee as good as hers.

After six years of solitude, sharing a meal and conversation with someone was a pleasure. More than a pleasure, her hospitality and companionship were also affecting to a surprising extent, so that at times I was overcome by emotion so intense, I couldn't have spoken without revealing how profoundly I was moved.

With my encouragement, she did most of the talking. In but half an hour, the quality of her voice—clear, steady, gentle in spite of her profession of toughness—charmed me no less than the grace with which she moved and the determination that she seemed to bring to every task she undertook.

She was, she said, a recluse from a young age, but she did not suffer from agoraphobia, a fear of open spaces, of the world beyond her rooms. She loved the world and exploring it, though she did so largely under limited circumstances. When the hour grew late and few people were afoot, she ventured out. When the weather turned so bad that no one spent a minute longer outdoors than absolutely necessary, she prowled the streets with enthusiasm. The previous year, a storm of historic power shook the city with such elemental ferocity that its broadest avenues were all but deserted for two days, and in the tempest, she spent hours abroad, as if she were the goddess of lightning, thunder, rain, and wind, undaunted by Nature's fury, in fact thrilled by it, soaked, blown nearly off her feet, fully *alive*.

People were what repelled her. Psychologists called it social phobia. She was able to be around people only briefly and could not tolerate crowds at all. She would touch no one and would not allow herself to be touched. She had a phone but rarely answered it. She shopped almost exclusively on the Internet. Groceries were left on her doorstep, where she could collect them when the delivery boy had gone. She loved people, she said, especially those in books, which was largely how she knew them, but she declined to associate with those who were not fictional.

I interrupted then to say, "Sometimes I think there may be more truth in fiction than in real life. Or at least truth condensed so that it's more easily understood. But what do I know of real people or the world, considering my strange existence?"

She said, "Perhaps you have always known everything important but will need a lifetime to discover what you know."

Although I wanted her to explain what she meant, my greater desire was to hear more about her past before the coming dawn drove me underground. I encouraged her to continue.

Her wealthy, widowed father, sympathetic to her condition and suspicious of psychologists, chose to indulge her rather than force her to seek treatment. As a child, Gwyneth had been a prodigy, self-educated and emotionally mature far beyond her years. She lived alone on the top floor of her father's midtown mansion, behind a locked door to which only he was allowed a key. Food and other items were left outside her door, and when her quarters periodically required housekeeping, she retreated to a room that only she cleaned, to wait until the staff had gone. She did her own laundry, made her own bed. For a long time, except for people on the street, whom she watched from her fourth-floor windows, she saw no one but her father.

Shortly before her thirteenth birthday, she had chanced upon a magazine article about Goth style, and the photographs had fascinated her. She studied them for days. On the Internet, she sought other examples of Goth girls in all their freaky majesty. Eventually she began to think that if she became a Gwyneth different from the one whom she had always been, a Gwyneth who denied the world all power over her and challenged it with her very appearance, she might be able to walk in the open with a degree of freedom. Denied sun, her skin was already as pale as lily petals. Spiked and pomaded hair, heavy black mascara, other makeup, facial jewelry, sunglasses, and faux tattoos on the backs of her hands were more than a costume; they were also a kind of courage. She discovered that too extreme a

Goth look drew attention that she didn't want, but soon she found the happy medium. Thereafter she could live beyond her fourth-floor rooms, although she didn't go out often, wouldn't enter a crowd, preferred quiet streets, and was most comfortable in the night or in the foulest weather.

Her father, as forward-looking as he was indulgent, had prepared for his daughter's future, so that she would be able to thrive after he passed away, a prudent step considering that he died before her fourteenth birthday. Assuming that Gwyneth would be no less a recluse at eighty than she was as an adolescent, assuming that the confidence and freedom she got from her Goth disguise or from any different look she might later adopt would always be limited, he created a web of trusts to ensure her lifetime support. But the trusts were also designed to allow her to draw upon them and benefit from them in numerous ways with the barest minimum of interaction with trustees, in fact with only one man, Teague Hanlon, her father's closest friend and the only confidant that he fully trusted. After her father's murder, Hanlon had been her legal guardian until she turned eighteen; he would be the primary trustee of the interlocking trusts until his death or hers, whichever came first.

Among the things that the trusts provided were eight comfortable though not extravagant apartments located in different but appealing parts of the city, including the one in which we sat now together at breakfast. This choice of residences allowed her a change of scenery, a not inconsiderable boon if her reluctance to go out resulted in day after day during which her experience of the city was restricted to the view from her windows. In addition, her father supposed that because of her natural elegance and her elfin beauty—which she denied possessing—she might attract the unwanted attentions of a dangerous man, whereupon an apartment could be easily abandoned for immediate relocation to another ready haven. Likewise, a fire or other disaster would not leave her homeless for so much as one hour, an important consideration if her social phobia rendered her more terrified of human contact and more reclusive as the years went by. She also kept moving from residence to residence as a means of discouraging well-meaning neighbors from making any attempt to be neighborly.

She rose from the table to fetch the pot from the coffeemaker.

The night was in retreat from the city, first light less than half an hour from possession of its streets.

I declined another cup.

Nevertheless, she poured one for me.

Returning to her chair, she said, "Before you go, we have to settle a few questions."

"Questions?"

"Will we meet again?"

"Do you want to?"

"Very much," she said.

Those two words were not just music, they were an entire song.

"Then we will," I said. "But what about your . . . social phobia?"

"So far you haven't triggered it."

"Why is that?"

She sipped her coffee. The silver-snake ring, as delicate as the nose that it ornamented, glimmered when the candle flame fluttered, and seemed to circle round and round through the pierced nare from which it hung.

"I don't know," she said. "Maybe next time, I'll turn away from you and run, and want to be alone forever."

She stared directly at me, but I was too far from the candle for her to see anything more than a hooded figure with gloved hands, and nothing more visible within the hood than there would have been if I were Death himself.

She said, "Come by this evening at seven o'clock. We'll have dinner. And you'll tell me more about yourself."

"I never go out until after midnight. Too dangerous."

Following a silence, Gwyneth said, "Do you have hope?"

"If I didn't, I would long ago have died by my own hand."

"Belief and trust, twined together, can meet any danger. Do you fear death, Addison?"

"Not my own death. Not the way people fear their death in books. I sometimes worried that my father would die. And when he did, the loss was worse than I imagined. The pain."

She said, "I want to hear all about your father and your life, at dinner."

My heart felt enlarged, not swollen with grief as it had been after Father died, but with complex emotions, swollen but not heavy, buoyant. I reminded myself that the heart is deceitful above all things, though I was sure it did not deceive me now.

I pushed my chair back from the table and got to my feet. "Leave the window open. At that hour, I'll have to be very quick, out of the storm drain and up the fire escape."

Rising from her chair, she said, "The rules don't change."

"The same rules," I agreed. "You don't look, and I don't touch."

She smiled and quoted me: "'We hold each other hostage to our eccentricities.'"

After following me through the apartment to the dark bedroom, she remained in the open doorway to the softly lighted hall as I switched on my flashlight, dimmed it with fingers across the lens, and went to the window.

I turned to look at her and quoted something that she had said earlier. " 'There is one who comes and goes infrequently, but I won't speak of that.' " When she said nothing, I asked, "Will you speak of that at dinner?"

"Perhaps. But as I said before, it's nothing that'll put you at risk. Not in any way."

When I raised the window, the beam of my light reminded me of the words hand-printed on the windowsill with a felt-tip marker, which I had half seen when I first entered. If they were words and not just symbols, they were in a foreign language, and in fact they somewhat resembled letters of the Greek alphabet, with which college sororities and fraternities named themselves.

"What is this?" I asked.

"Remember the sun. Go, Addison. Go, while you still have the night."

Switching off the flashlight, I slipped out of the room, onto the fire escape, where the air was cool, and all around the city seemed to be rising from its dreams, the millions of its cells waking one by one.

As I descended the iron steps, I heard the window sliding shut behind me and the latch being engaged.

Suddenly I was sure that I would never see her again, and the thought was so piercing, so sharp with intuition, that I froze on the iron, there above the alleyway.

22

AFTER A MOMENT, I FOUND MY HOPE AGAIN AND continued down the fire escape. At the second-floor apartment, light still glowed at the window, and the draperies remained partly open. But this time movement in the room caught my attention in passing.

I would not have stopped, would not have moved closer to the glass, if I had glimpsed only the man. But in the room with him was one of the Fogs.

The man appeared to be in his thirties, as ordinary as anyone, with a pleasant face and hair damp from a recent shower. He wore a sapphire-blue silk robe and stood barefoot before an entertainment center, sorting through a small stack of DVDs.

The Fog traveled that living room, swimming through the air from wall to wall, from ceiling to floor and up again, like an eel lazily exploring an aquarium with which it had long ago grown bored. White from end to end, lacking eyes and mouth, in fact without any features whatsoever, it should have seemed no more threatening than a blind worm. But it inspired such repugnance that a sour mash of coffee and brioche rose in the back of my throat, and though I had to swallow hard to force down that acidic mass, I could not look away from the thing, wondering what its intentions might be, for I had never before seen one in such an intimate setting.

On the coffee table in front of the sofa, an ice bucket chilled a carton of orange juice and an open bottle of champagne. A waiting glass, empty at the moment, suggested that the man in the robe would have mimosas for breakfast.

He selected a DVD from the small collection and inserted it into the tray of the player. Oblivious of the circling Fog, he went to the coffee table and poured equal measures of orange juice and champagne into the tall glass, sipped it once, then again, and put it on a coaster on an end table next to the sofa.

As the man sat down, the Fog attacked. I had never witnessed such a thing before, nor had Father or his father, as far as I know. If what transpired next was common, the Fogs took great trouble to conduct their assaults only where there were no witnesses, where their prey was alone and vulnerable. Though only Father, his father, and I could see these creatures, the response of the prey would have alerted anyone present to the fact that something extraordinary was occurring. As the serpentine form abruptly lashed the man and wound around him, he reacted as if he'd taken an electric shock, his entire body stiffening. He tried to move his encircled arms but could not, tried to thrash up from the sofa, without success, and opened his mouth as though to scream, but no thinnest cry escaped him. His face flushed red, features contorting in what appeared to be agony one moment and ecstasy the next, eyes rolling and protuberant with fear, but jaws slackening in surrender, the cords of his neck as taut as cables. Although the predator apparently had no mouth, I thought that it would somehow devour him, but instead *he* devoured *it* against his will. The Fog inserted itself into his silent scream, pressed into his mouth. The beast no longer seemed to be merely coherent mist. Now it looked as muscular, as torsional, as powerful as a python, and it fed itself to him insistently, relentlessly. His cheeks bulged with the mass of it, and his throat swelled grotesquely as the Fog forced itself down his esophagus. As it had wound around him, now it unwound while he swallowed more and more of it, although when his arms were free, he made no meaningful use of his hands, only clenched them into fists to beat on the sofa and upon himself.

I thought that I should smash through the window, go to the aid of the victim, but intuition restrained me. I was not afraid for my life, but somehow I knew that I could not grapple with the Fog any more than I could wrestle into submission a cloud of smoke. This was more than an encounter between predator and prey, more and different. Although I saw no evidence that the man had invited the assault or that he'd even been aware of his peril prior to the attack, every moment of his struggle was characterized not merely by fright and horror but equally by what seemed to be a carnal acquiescence, as if he received the Fog with almost as much pleasure as terror.

The tail of the thing slithered out of sight between the man's lips, his throat swelled obscenely one last time, and he slumped back against the sofa, gray-faced and exhausted. After less than a minute, color began to seep into his skin once more. His breathing returned to normal. He sat up straight and looked around as though bewildered, as if not quite sure what, if anything, had just happened.

Although I had witnessed the event complete, I couldn't say with certitude what it meant. I felt reasonably sure, however, that the Fog still lived, that now it thrived like a parasite within the man, and that the silk-robed host, having been somehow induced to forget the hideous penetration, was unaware of what had taken residence within him.

The man reached for the mimosa on the end table, swallowed a third of it, and returned it to the coaster. He picked up the remote control from the coffee table, switched on the big-screen TV, and put the DVD into play.

Although the window was at an angle to the TV, I had a good enough view to allow me to see what appeared on the screen: a pretty girl of ten or eleven and a grown man. As he began to undress her, I realized that the horror of the recent assault was nothing as compared to the abomination that was about to play out on the big-screen TV.

The man on the sofa leaned forward. The collection of obscene DVDs had belonged to him before the Fog had combined itself with him, and it was he, only he, who smiled now and licked his lips, savoring the atrocity on the video as surely he had enjoyed it often before.

With the stealth that is at all times essential to my survival, I fled down to the alleyway, shaking with disgust, my eyes hot with tears.

I halted and peered up, not at the second-floor window but at the fourth. With such a man living two floors below her, was Gwyneth safe even behind locked doors and latched windows? I considered going back and warning her, but the quiet metropolis began to resonate with the sounds of its earliest-rising citizens. I realized that Gwyneth knew more about the city's residents than I would ever know, and she understood at least as well as I did what corruption and pitiless cruelty might be hidden behind the masks that some people wore.

Faint color had faded the night along the eastern horizon, and soon it would saturate the sky. With gloved hands, I wiped at my eyes, and the blurred surroundings clarified.

I wanted light and cool fresh air and a vast openness into which I could run until I collapsed, but it was my burden to be an object of such loathing that I must shun the light, descend into darkness at dawn, and pass the bright day closed far away from those whom I would offend by my very existence. I hurried along the alleyway, seeking an entrance to the underworld.

23

THE NIGHT THAT I ARRIVED IN THE CITY . . . THE MALL along the river where, through plate glass, the sly marionette watched passersby . . .

The globes atop the ornate iron lampposts glowed like illumined pearls, and flecks of mica in the fired clay of the bricks sparkled underfoot as I walked away from the antique-toy store and north past other shops that offered window displays in which every item remained reliably inanimate.

Before I saw the man, I heard him. A shout, another, a shuddery scream of terror, and then his pounding footsteps.

I will never know who he was, although I suspect that he must have been a vagrant, a homeless person accustomed to bunking in a secret and protected nook somewhere in the open-air mall. He appeared from a break between two buildings, one of them a restaurant, running clumsily in buckled rubber snow boots that made sloppy squelching sounds on the bare bricks. He wore patched khaki pants, a pale-gray sweater over a plaid shirt, a stained corduroy sport coat with badly tattered cuffs, and a broad-brimmed hat the likes of which I'd never seen before and have never seen since.

Flames feathered back from the crown of his hat, but he seemed to be unaware that the danger was more immediate than the two men from whom he was running. As he approached, I pointed to his head and shouted, "Fire, fire!"

He was most likely one of those booze- or drug-worn men who aren't as old as they appear to be, for he looked eighty but moved with alacrity. Rheumy eyes, haggard face, skin sallow and runneled and pocked, tall and thin, with long-fingered hands that seemed as big as garden rakes, he might have been a scarecrow come to life in a cornfield and now footloose in a city that had no use for him.

Whether my warning or a sudden awareness of heat alerted him to the threat, in one smooth motion, with thumb and forefinger, he took off his broad-brimmed hat and flung it away as someone playing in a park might fling a Frisbee. As the fire spread off the crown toward the brim, the bright headwear sailed by mere inches from my face. When the hobo raced past me, I saw a few wisps of smoke rising from his scraggly beard, as if a fire had first been lit—and somehow quickly smothered—in that witches'-broom of facial hair before the hat was set ablaze.

Behind him came two young men, excited and laughing, eyes as bright as those of wolves in moonlight. Each carried a small butane torch of the kind that chefs use to caramelize the surface of crème brûlée and for other culinary tasks. Perhaps they were kitchen hands in the nearby restaurant that had closed an hour or so earlier, but they might have been from somewhere else entirely, nothing more than two delinquents who prowled the night with the intention of burning homeless people alive.

When they saw me, I happened to be in lamplight, still wearing my hoodie, but with my head raised and my face somewhat revealed. Although I was but a boy of eight and they were grown men, the first said, "Oh, shit, burn him, *burn him*," and simultaneously the second said, "What is he, what the *hell* is he?"

With their longer legs, they could outrun me. I saw no option but to dodge this way and that among the benches and tree planters and lampposts that were arranged along the center of the promenade, trying to keep something between me and them, hoping that a night watchman or a couple of policemen might come along, whereupon my attackers would flee in one direction and I in another, lest I ultimately become a victim of my rescuers.

Quick and bold, the two flanked me, herded me, and soon cornered me behind a bench, between two planters. *Click-click, click-click.* The double-action safety switches triggered two hissing jets of blue-tipped yellow flame. The men spat at me, cursed furiously, thrusting like swordsmen with the torches, trying to set me afire at arm's length, as if they feared me nearly as much as they detested me. The flames reflected in their eyes, so that it seemed they must be filled with the very fire that they dispensed through the nozzles of their weapons.

Farther along the promenade, glass shattered and cascaded to the pavement, and a burglar alarm sounded. Startled, my assailants looked toward the noise. Another display window dissolved into glittering fragments that, with an icy ringing, spilled across the bricks, and then a third window, three alarms clanging stridently.

My attackers ran south, and I ran north. They escaped into the night, but I did not escape.

24

FROM GWYNETH'S APARTMENT, I CAME HOME TO MY three windowless rooms in no mood to sleep. I should have slept. This was my time for sleeping. But I couldn't lie down and stay down. It just didn't feel right. Lying in my hammock and closing my eyes, I felt as if sleep would be a kind of incarceration. I was too alive to sleep, more alive than I had felt since I had been a young boy living by day—and some nights—in the wild woods, determined not to bother my troubled mother in the little house on the mountain.

Sitting in Father's armchair, I attempted to escape into fiction, but that didn't work, either. Three different books failed to gather me into their stories. I couldn't focus on the meaning of the sentences, and sometimes the words looked foreign to me, as if they were written with those symbols on the windowsill in Gwyneth's bedroom.

I didn't think it was love that made me restless, although in some way I did already love her. I knew what love felt like, for I had loved Father and, less powerfully, my mother. Love is absorbing, related to affection but stronger, full of appreciation for—and delight in—the other person, marked by a desire always to please and benefit her or him, always to smooth the loved one's way through the roughness of the days and to do everything possible to make her or him feel profoundly valued. All of that I had experienced before, and this was all those things but also a new and poignant yearning of my soul toward some excellence that this girl embodied, not just physical beauty, in fact not physical beauty at all, but something more precious that she epitomized, although I couldn't name it.

I also thought of the man into whom the Fog had forced itself, and I knew that I should do something to bring him to the attention of the authorities. Perhaps he had never committed the crimes that he watched with such twisted pleasure on the TV, but by acquiring those DVDs and viewing them, he encouraged those who had committed those crimes and perhaps worse. What he wished to watch was what he wished to do, and if he watched enough of it, he might one day grant himself his wish and ruin some child's life.

In time, exhaustion overcame me, and though I was loath to lie down, I fell asleep in my armchair, asleep and into dreams. I don't remember what other dreams might have preceded the bad one, but in time I found myself in the open-air mall into which I had wandered on my first night in the city.

In this reimagined confrontation, I appeared twenty-six, not a boy any longer, although the hobo looked exactly as he had been in life, flinging aside his burning hat and fleeing into the night. Pursuing him were not two delinquents but a pair of marionettes as large as men, one of them the puppet from the toy shop and the other a representation of Ryan Telford, the curator from the library and the murderer of Gwyneth's father. Their joints were crudely hinged and, though freed from the puppeteer's strings, they didn't walk but instead approached in a grotesque dance. They were nonetheless quick and not easily escaped, and both carried butane torches. When they cornered me, they spoke, their wooden jaws clacking. Ryan Telford reported what I had glimpsed in the newspaper earlier, "Plague in China," and the nameless marionette with the painted face and the scarlet-striated black eyes said, "War in the Middle East," in a low voice thick with menace. Instead of thrusting their swords of fire at me, they knocked me aside and to the bricks, both screaming wordlessly in rage, clattering past me in pursuit of someone else. When I scrambled to my feet and turned to discover the object of their hatred, it proved to be Gwyneth. She was already gripped in the teeth of fire, and when I rushed toward her, desperate to save her and to take the biting flames unto myself, I woke in a sweat and got up from the armchair.

I had slept away the latter part of the morning, through lunch, into the afternoon. My watch read 2:55.

More than four hours remained before I would see Gwyneth again, but in the first minutes after waking, I felt that the dream must be premonitory, a warning that she was in danger *now*.

I had no phone to call her. I had never before needed a phone. Nor did I have a number at which she could be reached.

Pacing restlessly, trying to quell the shakes with which the nightmare had left me, I knew that going to her right now involved intolerable risk. Sundown didn't come for about another two hours. I had never gone aboveground into the teeming streets in daylight.

During the twelve years that I had been blessed with Father's companionship, he schooled me continuously and well in matters of secrecy and survival. We of the hidden are so hated that we can't afford a single mistake, and most potentially fatal errors are made when you think that some new circumstance requires a relaxation of the rules of conduct that have thus far kept you safe.

As little use as I might be to Gwyneth in a moment of crisis, I would be of no use at all if I were dead.

Gradually Father's training and wisdom trumped the panic induced by the dream.

After pouring peach-flavored tea into a mug and heating it in the microwave, I soaked in the old claw-foot tub in the bathroom and drank the tea. I counseled myself to be patient. I assured myself that, in spite of her social phobia, the girl had more street smarts than I could ever hope to acquire. She knew how to protect herself. Besides, the trusts established by her wealthy father would insulate her from much that was wrong with the world.

By the time I toweled dry and dressed, I regretted missing lunch. I prepared a sandwich and another mug of tea.

When I was nearly finished with the meal, I realized something that seemed peculiar at first blush and that seemed more strange the longer that I thought about it. Gwyneth's large diamonds of black makeup and her highly unusual eyes at the center of those dramatic shapes were uncannily like those of the toy-store marionette, yet I had not mentioned the puppet to her. Neither had I allowed myself to wonder much about those curious similarities.

Minutes later, as I washed my plate and mug in the bathroom, at my one sink, still thinking about the marionette, I was reminded of something that had happened that long-ago October night, after the windows shattered and the two young hoodlums fled with their butane torches.

25

MY FIRST NIGHT IN THE CITY, AND EVERYWHERE glass underfoot . . .

Because my tormentors sprinted south, I ran north but got only a few feet before I collided with the man who moved to intercept me. From concealment, he had witnessed my encounter with the hobo and his pursuers. He had thrown the rocks that shattered the windows and triggered the alarms, for he meant to rescue me, though I didn't at first understand his intent.

He was tall and strong, and I was little, but though resistance might have been futile, I struggled to break free of his grip. He wore a long black raincoat that looked almost like a cape. Holding fast to me with his right hand, he used his left to pull back the hood of his coat, revealing his face. When I saw that he was like me, I ceased struggling and stood gasping for breath, gazing up at him in astonishment.

Until that moment, I had assumed that I must be the only one of my kind, the freak that the midwife and her daughter had called me, a monster to the world, condemned to solitude, until someone killed me. Now I was one of two, and if there were two, there could be more. I had not expected to survive childhood, but here stood one like me, twenty-something and in possession of all his limbs.

"Are you alone?" he asked.

In my shock, I hadn't the wit to answer.

He spoke above the clanging alarms. "Are you alone, son?"

"Yes. Yes, sir."

"Where do you hide?"

"The woods."

"No woods in the city."

"I had to leave there."

"How did you make it here?"

"Under a tarp. On a truck."

"Why come to the city?"

"I didn't know."

"What didn't you know?"

"Where the truck would bring me."

"It brought you to me, so you might live. Let's go. Quickly now."

Hoods up, glass crunching and clinking underfoot, we hurried along the promenade, past the smoking remnants of the burnt hat. When we passed the toy store, where the window was broken, the items in the display were arranged as before, except that the marionette was missing. I almost stopped to confirm its disappearance. But sometimes I knew things with my heart that my mind could not explain, and right then my heart insisted I should keep moving and not look back, and never ask where the marionette had gone because my question might be answered.

By the time we heard the sirens, we were two blocks from the mall, in a cobbled backstreet as dark as a deer path in the woods under a half-moon. A sudden wind broomed away the stillness of the night as the man whom I would eventually call Father hooked the disc of iron, lifted it, and set it aside. Piping across the hole where the iron had been, the wind played an oboe note, and I went down into that sound and into a world that I could never have imagined, where I would make a better life for myself.

Three years would pass before I mentioned the marionette to my father, on the night when he warned me about the music box that was surely more than it appeared to be.

26

WITH SOME EFFORT, I REASONED MYSELF INTO waiting to return to Gwyneth's place until the agreed-upon time. After all, I had known her for less than a day. Although our relationship had developed with almost miraculous ease, if I showed up unannounced at first dark, two hours before expected, regardless of my excuse, I would seem to be disrespecting her wishes. Worse, a girl so afflicted with social phobia that she couldn't bear to be touched would find my eagerness off-putting.

I understood—or thought I did—why she had felt comfortable with me even though she recoiled from most, if not all, of humanity. The extreme repugnance with which people responded to the sight of me, the fact that I was an abomination to them, allowed Gwyneth to think of me as such an outsider to the human race that her phobia hardly applied in my case. At the same time, because I lived in solitude and she in deep seclusion, our emotional lives must have been to some extent similar, and that shared experience in part formed the basis of her affinity for me.

I hoped that she would eventually feel as tenderly toward me as perhaps she had once felt toward her father. I expected no more, and no more was possible between one who could not be seen and one who could not be touched. After six years of solitude, a friend was the most extravagant gift I could be given, the most for which I hoped.

To reduce the risk that the girl would accidentally be exposed to the shock of my face, to allow us a little more light during our time together, and as a precaution against being recognized for what I am in the streets during these busy evening hours, I wore a ski mask in addition to the hood. There were holes only for my eyes and a loose slash at the mouth. I could breathe easily through the knitting, and I was confident that this cold December evening would justify a mask even to the most suspicious observer.

As I passed beneath the city, on my way to her building near Riverside Commons, I decided that because of Gwyneth's condition, I would be unwise to mention those things we of the hidden see that no one else does. She had her mysteries, too, which she acknowledged but kept pocketed. In the interest of not being so exotic that I became entirely alien to her, I would pay out my secrets as slowly as she paid out hers.

This time, I avoided Power Station 6 beneath the park, because more people worked the swing shift than those on the graveyard crew. To facilitate the pumping out of transit-system tunnels in a flood, there are work shafts connecting them to the storm-drain system at key points. From one iron rung to the next, I descended one of these, a thirty-foot-long pipe, five feet in diameter, not far from the Commons. As I neared the bottom, a fast train shuttled past in the darkness below me, which meant that I would have at least three minutes until the next one shrieked through. I needed to go only a hundred yards in the subway tunnel, being careful to avoid the electrified third rail, before coming to an emergency-exit door that opened inward to a switchback of wide stairs leading to the surface.

Some such exits terminated in public places, often stations on the line, and were therefore useless to me. This one, however, had once led to the ground floor of the Fifty-seventh Street Armory, which had been torn down nine years earlier during one of the city's periodic redevelopment frenzies. While the architect's plans were finalized for the ambitious affordable-housing project that was intended for the site, a temporary stairhead shack had been constructed to receive the emergency stairs from the subway. In hard times, the city had yet to find the funding, and the shack still stood, the door always un-locked from the inside.

I needed to cross one secondary street, follow a short block of al-leyway, cross a well-traveled avenue, and navigate a narrow service passage between two grand old houses to arrive behind Gwyneth's place. Only the midblock dash across the avenue gave me pause, for there were streetlamps and the headlights of oncoming traffic. But masked, hooded, jacketed, and gloved as I was, I elicited nothing more than one angry motorist's horn.

At the back of her building, lights glowed warmly in apartments on the first and third floors. Ascending the fire escape, I was much relieved to find the draperies fully closed at the second-floor window through which I had watched the Fog be received into the silk-robed man.

At the top landing, the lower sash of the double-hung window had been left open, the bedroom dark beyond. The door on the farther side of the room stood open to the hallway where prismatic light from the cut-crystal ceiling fixture left spear and arrowhead patterns on the wall, with here and there a bright shard of color broken out of the spectrum—blue, indigo, and red.

When I crossed the windowsill and stepped into the room, I knew at once that something must be wrong.

27

THREE YEARS WITH FATHER, ELEVEN YEARS OLD, learning every day that the city was a kind of forest through which our kind could move as secretly as foxes through ferny woods . . .

At two o'clock one morning, with the key that Father had been given by the man who feared him, yet did not hate him—of whom, more later—he let us into the food bank operated by St. Sebastian's Church. When the facility was closed, its windows were covered by roll-down burglary-proof shutters made of interlocking steel slats, which allowed us to turn on a few lights for easier shopping, with little risk of arousing the suspicion of any police patrol that might pass by.

The building served two functions, food bank and thrift shop, and an interior archway connected the former with the latter. Father had been given permission to clothe himself—and now me—from the secondhand garments in the thrift-shop stock. Before selecting canned and packaged foods, we meant to find new pants and sweaters for me, because I was a fast-growing boy.

The thrift shop offered more than clothing: some used furniture, shelves of well-read books, other shelves of CDs and DVDs, used toys, and costume jewelry. Dishes. Decorative items.

That night I discovered a music box that enchanted me. It was made of wood, intricately painted and lacquered, but what charmed me in particular were four tiny dancers on the top. Three inches tall, beautifully carved and painted, with exquisite details, they included a princess wearing a long gown and tiara, and a prince in formalwear and crown. In spite of its fine craftsmanship, the piece was comical, because the prince and the princess did not embrace each other but instead took two fanciful characters as their dancing partners. The prince had his right arm around a goggle-eyed frog, and with his left hand he held the webbed right hand of that grinning amphibian, as if about to waltz. The pretty princess stood in a similar pose, but she was in the embrace of a creature who had the head, chest, and arms of a man but the legs, hooves, ears, and horns of a goat; he looked especially silly because he wore a cocked wreath of green leaves on his head.

After I wound the box with its key and pushed the switch, the two unlikely couples began to dance to the music, turning around in circles as they also moved along figure-eight tracks. I laughed, but Father watched without even a smile, solemn as he seldom was.

"She dances with the Greek god Pan," he said, "and the prince with something worse."

"They're funny."

"Not to me."

"You don't think they're funny?"

"That's not a waltz," Father said.

"It's not?"

"They changed it into a waltz."

"What was it before?"

The dancers went around, around.

Father said, "They changed it to mock it."

Inside the box, the pegs on the turning cylinder plucked the tuned-steel teeth on the song plate. In spite of being mechanical, the music had at first struck me as sparkling, effervescent. Now it had an undeniably disturbing quality, the steel teeth biting off the notes as if music were a violent and hateful art. As the tempo increased, the royal couple and their partners turned more rapidly, until they seemed not to be dancing anymore but whirling about in a mad frenzy.

Father switched off the music and the four figurines. He plucked out the small steel key that wound the mechanism, and put it in a pocket of his pants.

I said, "Are you taking that? Why?"

"So it can't be played."

"But, sir, then it can't be sold."

"All the better."

"But isn't that like stealing?"

"I'll give the key to our friend."

"What friend?"

"The one who lets us come here."

"Is he our friend?"

"No. But he's not our enemy."

"Why will you give him the key?"

"So he can decide about the music box."

"Decide what?"

"What to do with it."

"The store needs money. Won't he decide to sell it?"

"I hope not," Father said.

"What do you hope he'll do with the box?"

"Smash it. Come on, let's find you those pants and sweaters."

We chose a pair of dark khakis, blue jeans, and a couple of sweaters for me. Father rolled them and stuffed them in a gunnysack that he had brought for that purpose.

In the food bank, following his instructions, after he filled my backpack with light packages of dry pasta and crackers, and after I had filled his with canned goods and blocks of cheese, he said, "You want to know about the music box."

"I just wonder why smash it."

"You know those things we both see that others don't."

"You mean the Fogs and the Clears."

"Call them whatever. I told you don't look at them directly if you feel they're looking at you."

"I remember."

"And I told you it isn't wise to spend a lot of time thinking about them."

"But you didn't say why it isn't wise."

"You've got to figure that out in your own good time. What you need to know right now is that the Fogs, as you call them, sometimes hide in things like that box."

"They hide in music boxes?"

"Not just music boxes," Father said. "In all kinds of man-made things, in anything they want."

"Only man-made?"

"I think only. Maybe it has to do with who made the thing, the character of the person. If the object was made by someone consumed by anger or envy, or lust, or whatever, then the Fog feels drawn to that thing, feels comfortable inside it."

"Why do they hide in things?" I asked.

"Well, I don't know that *hide* is the right word. They go into things like that maybe to dream. To sort of hibernate. I don't know. They're dreaming away for weeks, months, years, decades, but time doesn't mean anything to them, so it doesn't matter."

"One of them is dreaming in the music box?"

"Dreaming and waiting. Yes, I feel it. One day you'll learn to feel it, too."

"What is it waiting for?"

"Someone to see the box and take it home, to take the Fog home."

"What happens when someone takes it home?"

"Ruination," Father said. "Now we've talked too much about this already. If it's dreaming, talking too much about it can wake it up."

We went into the night again, where the man-made city bustled and slept, laughed and wept, danced and dreamed, and waited.

When we were safely below the streets, walking in the path of countless floods long past and floods to come, whispery echoes of our voices spiraling along the curved concrete, I told him about the marionette that, three years earlier, had disappeared from the shop window. He said that this was the very thing he meant when he told me about the music box, and I said but no one took the puppet home, and he said maybe one of the delinquents with butane torches scooped it up as they ran away or maybe, since it had legs, the marionette went somewhere on its own. He said we shouldn't talk any more about it, that if it had been sleeping three years somewhere in the city, we didn't want to talk it awake.

28

ONE THING WRONG WITH THE DARKNESS IN THE bedroom was the smell of it, which had been fresh and clean before. Now a spice cologne faintly seasoned the air. The Goth girl had not used or needed fragrances, and this was the very scent that I had first smelled the previous night at the library.

Another thing wrong was the intensity of the quiet, no clink or clatter of dinner preparations from the kitchen, no footsteps, no word of greeting though I had arrived precisely on the hour. Even the city had gone strangely mute, with no traffic noise or distant music or voices admitted by the open window.

I stood perfectly still, letting the darkness wind its silence around me, as breathless as if mummified in strips of gravecloth, waiting for a sound from her or from the man who had invaded her apartment. I felt alone. As an expert on solitude, I didn't doubt my perception.

Afraid that my flashlight might reveal her body slashed and broken, I hesitated to switch it on, but then of course I did. The mattress had been pulled off the box springs, as if he thought that something might have been hidden between them. The nightstand drawer hung open, as did the door to the walk-in closet. The closet had been searched. The clothes and shoes had been thrown to the floor.

If I had met her only to lose her, this might be the equivalent of the death by fire that I had long expected. Loss can be an incandescent terror equal to any flames.

I hurried to her office across the hall. The drawers of the desk had been turned out, the contents scattered. Her computer was on, and I imagined that he might have tried to search hers as she had searched his.

In the living room, books had been swept from the shelves and tumbled in a pile as if for burning.

Shattered plates and glassware carpeted the kitchen. I startled when the wall phone rang, and then I clattered through the brittle debris to pluck the handset from the cradle.

Because I had never answered a phone before in all my twenty-six years, I didn't think to say hello.

Gwyneth said, "Addison?"

"Yes. Me. It's me. I'm glad it's you, you're okay."

"I knew you'd be there. You wouldn't stand me up."

"He's wrecked the apartment."

"At five o'clock, I was at the window, waiting for the storm. I always like to see the first of it."

"What storm?"

"Snow. It was supposed to be snowing by five, but it still isn't. I saw him park at the curb and get out of his car. He didn't know about that address or any of the other seven. Someone ratted me out."

Remembering the name of the one man whom her father trusted to be her guardian, I said, "Teague Hanlon?"

"If it's him, I'm finished sooner than later. But it isn't him. There's another possibility. Anyway, when I saw Telford get out of that car, I knew if he had the address he also had a key. So I went out the bedroom window, down the fire escape. Addison, will you help me?"

"Yes. Of course. What can I do? Anything you need."

"Let's be careful," she said. "In case someone's listening. I'm gonna ask a couple questions. Just answer yes or no. You understand?"

"Yes."

"Remember the fish?"

"No."

"Last night. The fish that weren't there."

"No. *Yes!* All right," I said, remembering the pond in Riverside Commons, where the koi had been moved inside for the winter.

"Can you meet me there in an hour?"

"Yes. Or sooner."

"An hour. Look for a Land Rover."

"What's a Land Rover?"

"Like a truck. An SUV."

"You drive?"

"I won't be pushing it. Just don't be frightened off by it."

"Don't you be frightened, either. I'm wearing a ski mask now." Belatedly explaining why I hadn't spoken when I'd picked up the receiver, I added, "This is the first time I've ever used a phone."

"It can't be."

"But it is. I don't know anyone to call."

"How do you like it?"

"The phone? It's okay. But I'd rather we were in the same room."

"Fifty-eight minutes now."

"I'll be there," I promised.

She hung up, and after maybe half a minute, so did I.

29

WHEN I WAS FOURTEEN, I GOT MY WATCH FROM A dead man. Father assured me that it wasn't stealing, but I never really thought it was in the first place. Before he finished dying, the man wanted to give the Rolex to Father; and under the circumstances it would have been a great unkindness not to accept it.

On a night in November, we were abroad with little fear of being unmasked and savaged, because pounding cold rain roared down like a judgment. The people of the city were proud of being tough. They said of themselves that they were case-hardened negotiators, brutal competitors, sharp with fools, stripped of illusions by the realities of the streets and therefore not softened by sentimentalism, never looking for a fight but ever ready for one. I can't say whether any significant portion of the population actually possessed all of these qualities or any of them. What I do know is that the city was a comfort machine designed to provide amenities and conveniences, and regardless of how flinty and indurate its people might have been with outsiders and even with one another, they retreated at once from Nature when she turned furious. They took refuge in warm cozy rooms replete with so many forms of entertainment that the wet and windy world beyond their walls could be forgotten for hours at a time.

That night, the sky poured out such torrents that the city was a drum set, every surface a source of rhythms, pavements and windows and canvas awnings, street signs and parked cars, Dumpsters throbbing like tom-toms, garbage-can lids swishing as the wind swirled bursts of rain in imitation of a drummer brush-stroking the batter head of a snare.

Father and I wore rubber boots, gloves, fleece-lined black rain-coats that had hoods secured under the chin with Velcro closures. We hid behind ski masks, too, though pedestrians were rare and, when seen, were bent and hurrying, sheltering under umbrellas that had to be held close over their heads to prevent the wind from turning them inside out.

The storm, which would prove to be the worst of the decade, also sluiced most of the traffic from the streets. In this post-midnight tempest, no taxis were cruising for fares on the deserted avenues. The drivers of the few cabs answering calls were challenged by flooded intersections and blinding sheets of water that overwhelmed their windshield wipers, and they had no time to be curious about us. Even police patrols were at a minimum, perhaps because, as statistics confirm, crime drops sharply during nasty weather because criminals prefer warm and cozy rooms as much as do law-abiding folks.

The outlaws weren't all tucked in their beds or playing video games, however, because we came upon four of them during our explorations.

We had no pressing errand to run, nothing that we needed. We were out and about sightseeing.

In good weather, even at night, we had to avoid well-lighted places and scurry through shadows like two cockroaches anticipating the stamp of a crushing shoe. Most nights, of necessity, our time above-ground was efficiently managed and spent on essential tasks.

When the raw wind shrieked through the canyons of high-rises, when the deluge blurred those monoliths as if intent on erasing in one night a civilization that would otherwise be reduced to dust only by a thousand years of history, *then* Father and I were as free in the city as we would ever be. We could travel where we wished and linger without fear at the lighted display windows of the best stores and galleries on the most elegant streets. As window-shoppers, we could enjoy fine art and the sparkle of luxuries that we would never be able to afford and that, even if a fortune fell on us, we could not purchase without coming face-to-face with a salesclerk who would judge us, by our eyes alone, to be abominations.

On such nights, the freedom to go places we usually had to avoid was no more satisfying than the weather itself, which we relished. Underground, there was no weather, save for the runoff from a storm. We yearned as much for open air and the feel of the sun on our skin and the buffeting wind as we did for daylight. We were delighted by weather so wild that others fled from it, because it was the only weather we could ever experience leisurely and without fear.

We were blocks from the finest stores, in a different kind of neighborhood, when the gunfire started.

The soaring wind and the rush of rain felt and sounded like a flock of a million birds continuously startling into flight around us, wings beating against us, as we walked a street, enchanted by the Beaux Arts architecture of the low-rise commercial buildings dating to the early years of the twentieth century. Some of those structures had been rehabilitated but others were in decline, and lights shone in one of the latter.

As we approached that place, gunshots tunneled through the white noise of the rain, and a pane in one of the ground-floor windows shattered. A door flew open, and a man came through the door into the storm, but his hair didn't even have a chance to get wet before he was shot in the back and folded down onto the sidewalk as if he had no more substance than the suit that he wore.

Inside the building, rapid gunfire from at least two weapons continued for much the lesser part of a minute, and after the last shot, the silence in there sounded as final as the hush in a casket under six feet of freshly spaded earth. The door stood open, but no one stepped outside either to help or to finish off the back-shot man, who was lying on his side and weeping.

The street remained empty of traffic. No light suddenly bloomed in the windows of the surrounding buildings. Nothing moved except the silver skeins of rain and the wind tearing through them.

We were hooded and masked, but we could be known by our eyes alone. Although our genuine concern would surely be met with fear and disgust, we could do nothing but attend the weeping victim.

Father first went to the open door, dared to look inside, stepped out of sight, but returned quickly. When he knelt with me beside the wounded man, he said, "Five men in there, all dead."

We were in the pooled darkness between streetlamps, but if we had been in light, the man still would not have known us by our eyes or perhaps not even if we revealed our faces. In his delirium, he saw not what lay before him but what he wished to see. He allowed my father to lift his left hand from the pavement to check his pulse, but he didn't realize that he was in the company of strangers.

To my father, he said, "Papa Gino, where'd you come from? Ain't seen you a long time." Weariness and bewilderment marked his voice. Death would settle on him soon. Father asked the man for his name, so that he might say a prayer for him. "Don't you recognize me, Papa Gino? It's me, your own Jimmy. All grown up and done real good for myself." Jimmy coughed, and a little blood, black in the poor light, spilled between his lips. Perhaps because my father was holding Jimmy's left wrist, the dying man said, "See my watch, Papa? Bitchin' Rolex, solid gold. You take it. I ain't never given you a damn thing. I wished I could of, now I can. Take it, Papa." When my father did not at once accept the watch, Jimmy began to sob wretchedly and asked to be forgiven, for what we could not know, and his anguish seemed greater than his pain. Twice he spat blood between his words as he said, "Please take it, Papa Gino, it's something I can do, it's a little something." My father took the watch from the wrist and passed it to me, because just the previous week my secondhand thrift-shop Timex had failed. Father thanked Jimmy for the watch and called him son and said it meant a lot to him to have it. He held Jimmy's hand in both his hands and said a prayer for him, and I said one, too, but silently.

In life, Jimmy's face was flat planes and hard edges, but when he didn't live in it anymore, the face changed and became soft and almost kind. His fixed eyes were dark and empty, and the rain washed the tears out of them.

It was a terrible thing when death first entered the world, and even now when it's the way of nature, it's terrible beyond words. Whether it comes for your mother by her own hand or for a stranger who can say nothing in defense of himself except that his watch is solid gold, standing witness to a death leaves you desolate.

We left the dead for others to find and bury, and we went away into the storm, the wind throwing shatters of rain at everything and the sky like a sea above and the whole world drowned in it. We went home from there, to our three windowless rooms, and we didn't speak of dead Jimmy again, as if the gold watch had materialized around my wrist by the working of a magic lamp that I had rubbed.

I didn't sleep at all that night, though Father did or pretended that he did. I worried that *he* might die, and I wondered how I could go on alone without him. I hoped that I might die before him, selfish though that hope might be, but as you know, it didn't work out that way.

30

THE POND IN RIVERSIDE COMMONS WAS ONLY MIN-
utes from Gwyneth's apartment, but apparently she needed an hour
to get there, which left me with time to do something useful. After
turning on the lights and closing the bedroom window that I had
left open, I began work in the living room, picking up the books that
Ryan Telford had thrown on the floor. I smoothed rumpled dust
jackets and returned the volumes to the shelves in alphabetical order
by the authors' names.

When that task was completed, I intended to gather up the broken plates and glasses in the kitchen. Instead I went to the window
at which Gwyneth must have been standing when she saw Telford
get out of his car.

The snow had not yet begun to fall. On the farther side of the
street, Riverside Commons looked darker from here than it had
seemed when I'd been within its boundaries, the low path lights
now mostly screened by trees. It wasn't the biggest park in the city
or even the second biggest, but at that moment the Commons
looked like a place in which you could easily become lost, wandering
into territory that had never before presented itself to park visitors,
where the trees were mutant and the grass as gray as an old man's
hair.

One summer morning two and a half years earlier, they had found
a woman floating dead and naked in the pond, pale and facedown
among the koi, her clothes scattered carelessly on the shore as
though, in the grip of some pagan impulse, she had undressed there
for a swim. She proved to have been a nurse, a wife, a mother of two,

and she lived close enough to the hospital to walk home from work in the early evening. Before long they found the three young men— Orcott, Clerkman, and Sabbateau—who used her like a toy, broke her, and threw her away in a quickly and ineptly staged fake drowning. Orcott had a doting uncle, Benton Orcott, who owned three flower shops and from whom they had borrowed a delivery van. They put an old mattress in the back and called the van their pussy wagon. The crimes were committed on the move, while they took turns driving and riding shotgun, one of them always with the woman. The wife of Benton Orcott, Verbina, despised her nephew, whom she regarded as a useless, depraved doper. Certain that he would damage the van, she inspected it the next morning. Although Verbina was unable to find a dent or scratch, she discovered a nurse's cap under the front passenger seat and in the cap a pair of panties, which one of the rapists had kept for a souvenir but had forgotten to retrieve. She called the police. Two days later, they found the mattress stored for future use in an abandoned building across the street from the nephew's apartment house. The three were high-school graduates who had been unable to find employment in the perpetually bad economy. Their defense attorney lamented that society had failed them. The nurse's name was Claire. The name comes from the Latin *clarus*, which means "clear, bright, shining." In his confession, Sabbateau said that they had chosen her because she "was so pretty that she seemed to shine."

I had not come to the window to wait for the snow or to dwell upon the more depressing moments of the park's history. I disengaged the latch, raised the lower sash, and discovered upon the sill the same Greek-like letters, printed with a felt-tip marker, that were on the sill of the bedroom window. No doubt they were at every window in the apartment. As a cur of cold wind snuffled and licked at my hands, I closed the sash and engaged the latch.

In the small vestibule, I peered through the fish-eye lens to be sure that no one lurked on the fourth-floor landing. When I opened the door, the felt-tip inscription graced the threshold. I closed the door, locked it, and stood there for a moment, wondering.

Those symbols—or most likely words—seemed to be meant to ward off some enemy. They had not stopped Ryan Telford; and they would not have kept out men like the three who had murdered the nurse. Whatever Gwyneth feared most, it had not been born of man and woman.

31

MY FATHER HAD SAID THAT WE SHOULD FEAR equally the Fogs and the Clears, that the latter were, in their own way, as terrible as the former, and that we should regard them with wary indifference. Although I never disobeyed my father, although I never met the eyes of a Clear or sought to attract its attention, I did not fear them. In fact, the sight of them continued to make me happy.

To one degree or another, I have been happy most of my life, in part because the world has infinite charms if you wish to see them. Also, the world's many mysteries fascinate me and inspire in me a hope so profound that I suppose, if I were to express it sincerely and at length in a manuscript more bluntly philosophical than this one, any normal person, those who walk freely in daylight, would find it the work of a Pollyanna and worthy only of ridicule.

Of course I also have periods of sadness, for there is sorrow baked into the clay and stone of which the world is made. Most of those doleful times occurred during the year after Father died, when I found it difficult to be alone after his long companionship.

When I ventured out that night, a little more than five years before I met Gwyneth, I encountered a spectacle so enrapturing that my melancholy melted away. I thought of it as the Convocation. The word felt right to me, though at the time, I didn't know why.

Past one o'clock in the morning, in an August cooler than most, I came aboveground and discovered Clears everywhere I looked. They wore what they always wore: soft-soled white shoes, loose pants with elastic waists, and shirts with three-quarter sleeves, some all in white, others in soft blue, still others in pale green, as if they were dressed to staff the emergency rooms and surgeries at various hospitals. There were men and women of every race, but all of them seemed to be of roughly the same age, early to mid-thirties. They walked ledges, eight or ten or even more to a single building, and they glowed on rooftops, strolled the sidewalks, proceeded boldly down the center of the street, stood in intersections. In the glass towers that lacked ledges, the Clears were at some windows, radiant, gazing out. They traveled the parks, and I saw them descending the steps to a subway station.

Never before had I seen more than three or four Clears in one night. I was delighted by these multitudes.

They neither spoke to one another nor appeared to be engaged in coordinated activities. Each seemed to be going calmly about his own business, whatever that might be, and some were solemn while others smiled. I felt that they were all listening to something I couldn't hear, which might mean that they were telepathic and were attuned to one another, though I had no way of knowing.

The few drivers who were out at that hour were oblivious of the luminous crowd. They drove right through some of them, and it was as if both the Clears and the vehicles were mirages, each unaffected by the others, as though they were from different dimensions, combined in this one scene only by virtue of my gifted eyes.

As I moved in wonder, block after block, a few of the Clears looked at me, and in each instance I turned away at once. But in the split second during which our eyes met, I felt every time as though a cube of dry ice had been swiped the length of my spine, the chill so intense that I wouldn't have been surprised to discover my skin blistered from my topmost vertebra to my coccyx.

They did frighten me then, but only briefly, and I continued to delight in the sight of them. I saw thousands of Clears that night, and never again enjoyed a spectacle like it.

For days afterward, I felt that something new should happen, some event that the city had never played host to before and that no one could have imagined in advance of its occurrence. But time went by, and nothing came to pass that didn't befall the city's people every day. I was mildly disappointed until I thought that perhaps the unimaginable episode that I anticipated had been something that the Convocation had been there not to facilitate but to forestall.

And with that realization, I felt the dry ice sliding down my spine again, though not a single Clear was present.

32

IN THE COMMONS, ON THE FOOTPATH BY THE POND, I waited in a cold that deepened by the minute, thinking I might see the first crystals of ice form on the shallow black water along the shore.

Gwyneth wasn't late. I was a few minutes early. I hadn't quite finished picking up all the broken glass and china on her kitchen floor, but all of a sudden I had felt an urgent need to get out of there. I don't know why. I was overwhelmed by the feeling that when I'd closed the bedroom window, I hadn't latched it, and that someone or maybe something was at that minute climbing the fire escape and soon to enter the apartment with bad intentions.

So affecting was that intuition, I abandoned caution and left by the front door, went down the communal stairs two at a time, at risk of encountering one of the neighbors, and burst into the night as if I had been blown out of the house by an explosion. There was traffic in the street, but I was hooded and masked and gloved, and I dodged across the lanes to a Gershwin-jazz performance of car horns and shrilling brakes.

Just inside the gate to the Commons, I paused under the great pine where Gwyneth and I had stood the previous night, and looked back toward the house, expecting something to be at her living-room window, but it was just a rectangle of unobstructed light. Hopeful that I had not been seen in flight, I continued to the pond, where now I stood in expectation of the first ice.

Because I had earlier remembered the murdered nurse found in the water and now stood near the spot where she had been pulled to shore by the coroner, pity swelled in me, not just for the dead woman and her family but also for the city, though certainly the city did not want my pity. So tender did this feeling become that I knew I was losing the degree of self-control that I needed every minute that I was aboveground.

When I tried to turn my thoughts away from the nurse, they went unaccountably to the marionette, of all things. As irrational as it may sound, I wondered if the puppet had sat on this shore for part of that grim night, watching her pale body float and the koi bump against it under the mistaken impression that it was a great mass of bread thrown to them by admirers. Seemingly irrational, yes, but the thought became an image in my mind's eye, and I felt in my bones that it was true, and I wished that I had not come to the Commons sooner than necessary.

Precisely then the first snow frolicked down the sky, flakes as big as rose petals, wheeling through the bleak dark and flaring in the light of the pathway lamps. They vanished into the black water but gathered on the stiff brown grass and on the pavement. So quickly did smaller snowflakes follow the larger ones in such greater numbers that I knew this would be a storm that the city would long remember, whereupon the night breeze stiffened just enough to be called a wind.

When I looked at the dead man's watch on my wrist, I saw that the moment of our rendezvous had arrived. On time, the Land Rover appeared, following the one-way blacktop service lane, but then she turned off the road and drove across the picnic meadow, to the shore of the pond, switching from headlights to parking lights as she drew near.

The vehicle looked immense, maybe because I knew Gwyneth was petite and I couldn't quite believe that a hundred-pound girl could maintain control of such a formidable machine. I was also a little spooked because I'd never ridden in a motor vehicle before, only under a tarp on a flatbed and only once.

Sometimes your life rolls away with you, like a big stone going downhill fast, as on the day when my mother put me out on my own, and then nothing is ever the same. I could feel my long-stable world in motion again, beginning here, as Gwyneth stopped the Rover beside me, and though the roll can sometimes be a good thing, and you come to rest in a better kind of life, there are no guarantees.

If that night I had listed a thousand ways that my coming life might possibly be different from the one I had lived for the past eighteen years, what I might lose and gain, I would not have proved prescient about anything, and I would have greatly underestimated both the losses and the gains.

PART TWO

The Flame Delights the Moth
Before the Wings Burn

33

I KNEW WHAT A SEAT BELT WAS, AND I KNEW THAT the law required its use. I had never before trusted my life to one, however, and though it sounded simple enough when I read about someone belting up in a novel, I took so long figuring it out that Gwyneth said she wished she could help me. She said it with sweet forbearance, not with impatience or scorn. But if she tried to assist me, we'd almost certainly touch, which she couldn't tolerate.

At last I got it done, though I felt no safer in the belt than out of it. I *did* feel dangerously trammeled. I wondered which was the greater risk: being thrown through the windshield when not wearing a belt or being trapped in a burning car because the belt buckle would not release.

I said, "Does it have air bags, too?"

"Yes, of course."

"What do I need to do about that?"

"Nothing," she said. "Air bags are automatic."

"I guess that's nice."

"Well, it's easy. Anyway, I'm not going to crash into anything."

"Have you ever?"

"No. But I don't drive much, hardly at all."

She switched on the headlights, released the brake, and piloted that monster SUV across the picnic meadow to the service lane as easy as if it were an amusement-park ride gliding on a rail, the steering wheel just for show.

Let me tell you, it was quite a sensation: sitting up in a warm capsule and moving smoothly through the cold night, across the land and then the blacktop, windows all around so you could have a good look at anything you wanted to see. Lots of books have thrilling scenes involving cars or trucks, but none of them prepared me for the sheer delight of that ride, for the magic-carpet quality.

As Gwyneth turned out of the park onto the avenue, I said, "With your social phobia, how did you learn to drive?"

"Daddy taught me. When I turned thirteen, we went way out in the country a few times, just the two of us. He worried that when he was eventually gone, something might happen that I would need to leave the city."

"Something like what?"

"Like just about anything. Anything can happen."

"But if you left the city, where would you go?"

"There's a place. But that doesn't matter right now."

The streets were busy, cars crowding all around us. Delivery trucks. Buses. Well-bundled people on the sidewalks hurried through the wintry night.

I said, "When you got your driver's license, you must have had to be around a lot of people at the DMV or somewhere."

"I don't have a driver's license."

I can't say that I was shocked, but I was a little dismayed. "It's against the law to drive without a license."

"It's illegal," she said, "but it's not immoral."

"What if you're in an accident and hurt someone?"

"With or without a license, an accident can happen. The fault wouldn't be in the lack of a license. The fault would be driving inattentively or recklessly, or drunk."

"You don't drive drunk, do you?"

"No. And not inattentively or recklessly, either."

I considered all of that for a minute, and I guess she wondered what my silence meant.

She said, "Well?"

"Well, I guess it's okay then."

"It's okay," she assured me.

"All right. Good. You see what the snow's doing?"

"Snowing."

"No, I mean the way it floats over the front of the car and up and over the roof and never touches the glass."

"When we're moving, we create a slipstream that floats the snow over us." She pulled to a stop at a red traffic light, and right away the snow stuck and melted on the warm glass. "See?"

"Neat," I said.

A Clear in hospital blues appeared out of the slanting snow and stepped into the street, indifferent to the foul weather. He stopped in the middle of the intersection and turned his head from side to side, the way they do, maybe looking for something but almost seeming to be listening more than looking.

The traffic light changed, and Gwyneth ran down the Clear. I saw him pass through the SUV between our seats, but I didn't turn to watch him recede out the tailgate.

I didn't say anything to her about him. What could I have said? She tolerated my hood and mask and gloves, my inexperience and what must have seemed to her to be my deeply paranoid conviction that most people, if not all, would respond to the sight of me with disgust and violence. If I told her about the Clears and the Fogs, she might decide that I was one kind of crazy too many for her taste, pull the Rover to the curb, and tell me to get out.

Our relationship was delicate, perhaps no less so than the crystal intricacy of those first huge snowflakes that had spiraled around me in the Commons. We had at once accepted each other because we could accept no one else. I admired her brave attempts to cope with her phobia, and perhaps she admired the way that I had coped with what she assumed was my irrational paranoia. We were outcasts, she by election, I by the condition in which I was born, but that did not ensure our friendship. She didn't want the world, and the world didn't want me, and when you thought about that, it became clear that we were less alike than we seemed to be, that strains could easily develop that would lead to an irreconcilable parting.

Already I loved her. I would be content to love her all of my life without touching her, but I saw no indication that she loved me in the same way, or at all. Considering her social phobia, if she were to suspect the depth of my feelings for her, she might recoil, retreat, and banish me. She might not be capable of loving me as I already loved her, let alone in the more profound way that I would surely come to love her over time. I drew hope from the fact that she had clearly loved her father, and I needed that hope because, after living my life with one loss after another, losing this might at last break me.

I hadn't thought to ask, but now I did: "Where are we going?"

"To see someone."

"Who?"

Until this moment, the girl's Goth makeup had seemed exotic and fanciful, but it did not convey upon her an air of danger. Now her face hardened, her mouth became like a crack in stone, her teeth clenched as if she had bitten into something that she wanted to tear apart, and the scarlet bead on her pierced lip glistened and seemed to quiver as if it were a real drop of blood.

In answer to my question, she said, "Nobody knows her name. They say she's dead, but I refuse to believe it. I refuse."

34

THE STREET WAS IN A COMFORTABLE NEIGHBORHOOD, lined with maples, their bare limbs a becoming architecture, a perfect grace when green, and as red as fire in autumn. The yellow-brick house stood behind a shallow front yard and a raised porch trimmed with Christmas lights. A wreath hung on the door.

When Gwyneth parked at the curb, I expected to stay in the car, but she said, "I want you to come in with me. You'll be safe."

"The only house in the city that I've ever been in is yours. The only one. A house is a trap, a place that I don't know and too few ways out."

"Not this house."

"I can't."

"You can, Addison."

I slid lower in my seat.

She said, "They won't harm you."

"Who are they?"

"They take care of her."

"Of the girl with no name?"

"Yes. Come on now. I want you to see her."

"Why?"

She opened her mouth to reply—and had no words. For a moment she stared out at the black limbs of the maples as the wind slowly knitted a white lacework across their bark. She said, "I don't know. I don't know why I want you to see her. But I know you must. It's important that you do. I know it's important."

I took a deep breath and let it out as if with it I would also exhale my doubt.

She said, "I called them earlier. They know we're coming. I told them that you have . . . issues. Serious issues. They understand me, the way I am. They'll be respectful, Addison."

"I guess if you aren't afraid of them, I shouldn't be, either."

In spite of what I said, I dreaded going inside, but I got out and closed the passenger door and waited for her to come around the front of the Land Rover.

Snow at once diamonded her black hair, and the skiff on the sidewalk plumed around her silver shoes.

Just then I realized another similarity between her and the marionette, besides the black diamonds of makeup and the eyes. The puppet wore a black tuxedo with a black shirt and a white tie, and Gwyneth was dressed in black but for her shoes.

I almost turned away from the house, but I loved her, and so I followed her through the gate in a spearpoint iron fence.

"His name is Walter," Gwyneth said. "He's a widower with two young children. He was a medic in the military, and he's a physician assistant now."

She strode more than stepped, and she seemed to skate more than stride, and I thought that this girl would never lose her footing on treacherous ground or slip on ice, so extraordinary was her poise.

Stepping onto the porch, she said, "His sister, Janet, lives here, too. And an older woman, Cora. Janet and Cora are nurses. The patient is never left alone for more than a few minutes."

"Isn't this too many people for you?" I asked.

"They understand my problem. They don't get too close. They make sure there's never more than two in the same room with me. You'll be all right."

"I don't know."

"I do," she said. "You'll be all right."

The bell press sounded chimes, which we could hear through the wreathed door, there on the Christmas-lighted porch.

Almost at once the door opened, and a man said, "Gwyn, we've missed you coming around."

I couldn't see him because I kept my head down, afraid that my ski mask was insufficient disguise, that he would know me by my eyes.

She said, "I'm no less like I've always been, Walter, so there aren't a lot of days I go anywhere. But tonight is . . . special."

With considerable apprehension, I followed her into a foyer with a plank floor and a round, flowered rug. A solemn voice issued from a television in a nearby room.

When Walter said, "This must be Addison," I said, "I'm sorry my shoes are wet," and Walter said, "It's nothing, just a little snow."

I liked his voice. He sounded kind. I wondered about his appearance, but I didn't raise my head to look.

Gwyneth said, "Remember Addison's rules like I told you," and Walter said he remembered, and she said, "Where are the children?"

"In the kitchen. They know to stay there."

"I'd love to see them, I really would, but this is hard on Addison."

I wondered how neurotic Walter thought I was. He probably thought I was past neurotic and all the way to crazy.

He said, "Janet's in the kitchen. She was getting dinner when you called, but she's putting it on hold."

"I'm sorry I gave you such short notice."

"You're like family, Gwyn. We don't need any notice at all. I'll go see if she needs help with the kids or something."

When just the two of us were in the foyer, Gwyneth said, "Are you okay?"

"Yeah. I'm all right. Are you okay?"

She said, "I've been better."

I raised my head and scoped the foyer. An archway on the right led to the living room. Everything was clean and neat and bright and pretty, a place of harmony, absent of conflict. I thought that those who lived here must feel safe, and I was pleased for them, more than pleased, happy that such a life was possible for them and for so many people.

The voice on the television said that the plague in China had actually begun across the border in North Korea.

A woman entered the hallway from the kitchen, and I lowered my head once more. She greeted Gwyneth and introduced herself to me—she was Janet—and I said that I was pleased to meet her, though I looked at nothing but the round, flowered carpet.

Janet led us to the second floor. We waited at the top of the stairs while she went along the hallway to a room at the end, where Cora, the older nurse, tended to the nameless girl.

Because I felt that someone of bad intent had quietly ascended the stairs behind us, blocking the way out, I turned to look, but no one followed us.

Janet and Cora came out of the patient's room, went into another directly across the hall, and closed that door.

"This is important," Gwyneth said.

"I guess it must be."

"I know now why I brought you here."

"Why?"

Instead of answering me, she went down the hallway to the open door, and I went with her. At that threshold, she hesitated. She raised her hands as though to cover her face, but then she closed them into fists, and on the one nearer me, the faux tattoo of a blue lizard flexed as if it might come to life and spring off her skin. Brow furrowed, eyes tight shut, jaws clenched, pulse visible in her temple, she appeared to be in pain or struggling to repress great anger. But then I thought—I don't know why—that perhaps this was the posture in which she prayed, if she prayed at all.

She opened her eyes and lowered her fists. She went into the room. In consideration of me, she switched off the overhead light and used the dimmer on a reading lamp to soften its glow to the point that, within my hood, my eyes could not easily be seen.

I looked at the closed door behind which Janet and Cora had retreated. I looked back toward the head of the stairs.

Crossing the threshold, I saw upon it the cryptic inscription that I had found at the entrances to Gwyneth's apartment.

The large room contained two armchairs, side tables, a dresser, nightstands. There were also two beds, the farther one neatly made and accessorized with decorative pillows, the nearer one a hospital bed.

The upper half of the motorized mattress was elevated, and upon it, reposing in a realm deeper than mere sleep, lay a girl of perhaps six. If she had been an avatar, the incarnation not of a goddess but of a principle, her face would have been befitting for the avatar of peace or charity, or hope, and if she had been capable of expression, her smile might have been miraculous in its effect.

Standing beside the child, looking down at her but speaking to me, Gwyneth said, "If Ryan Telford kills me, if anyone kills me, you have to take care of her. Protect her. At any cost. *Any* cost."

35

THE HOMELESS MAN HAD IN THE NIGHT COME TO the bottom of his current bottle, and subsequently he had awakened repeatedly from dreams of deprivation in which everyone that he had failed during his life returned to thwart his every attempt to acquire even just one more pint of the distiller's art. He was therefore on the move at first light, which was not his habit, to search the commercial alleyways in his territory, seeking redeemable soda cans and other humble treasures in the set-out trash that had long sustained him.

So it was that in a Dumpster he found the badly beaten, naked body of a girl of about three, which he thought was a corpse until from it issued the thinnest mewl of abject misery, like that of a kitten he had once found run down in traffic, with still a minute or two of this world in it. Most of his life, he had chosen to flee from responsibilities. But at the core of him remained the dry kernel of the better man that he had once hoped to become, and the child's muted cry spoke to that remnant. He discovered that he yet had the capacity for pity.

In his worn-thin, patched, and greasy clothes, tangled hair bristling from beneath a stained and half-crushed brown fedora not otherwise seen on the head of a city man in decades, eyes bloodshot blue, nose scrawled over with visible capillaries, he kicked open the door to a popular doughnut shop a block from the Dumpster. With the battered child draped over his long, bony arms, weeping bitterly, shouting "Ambulance, ambulance," he entered among the incredulous customers waiting to place their orders, two of whom were police officers.

Initially but not for long, he was suspected of being the party responsible for the girl's condition. But his discovery of her in the viscous mounds of trash had wrenched something askew in his fragile constitution, and when the girl was taken from his arms, he could no longer stand upright or control his shaking hands, which alternately scrabbled at the floor in useless gestures and plucked at his face and chest as though something offensive clung to him that he was desperate to cast off. He ended the morning not in a jail cell but as a patient in the same hospital to which the girl had been rushed.

The doctors determined that she had been not merely beaten but also tortured, and not once but often, perhaps for half or more of her estimated three years. The authorities were not able to locate her parents. The wide circulation of a pencil portrait of her did not lead to any useful tips from the public, and a photo of her, taken after the bruising on her face faded, likewise brought no leads. They reached the conclusion that she had been imprisoned for most of her short life, hidden away, and in such cases it was with rare exception the mother and father, or one of them, if both were not present in the home, who committed the abuse.

The girl became a ward of the court during her recuperation. In a month, she healed but didn't wake. Sixty days after she was found, the prognosis for her recovery from coma was dismal. An advisory committee of doctors arrived at the unanimous opinion that, although the girl might not be technically brain-dead, she would remain in a permanent vegetative state. The current wisdom of medical ethicists held that a person in such a condition could feel no discomfort from being denied food and fluids. The court ordered the removal of the feeding tube by which sustenance was introduced to her stomach and a cessation of all extraordinary attempts to keep her alive, although the order was stayed for fifteen days to allow any patient-advocacy groups time to file an appeal.

All this Gwyneth told me as we stood on opposite sides of the nameless girl's bed in the yellow-brick house, while outside snow and cold wind slanted through the city, a quiet reminder to its people that the shapen world had the power to erase their mightiest works, though few of them would see it as such. She surprised me when, part of the way through her story, she reached down to take one of the child's hands in hers. Other than her beloved father, when he lived, this was the one person whose touch she did not fear.

Walter worked at the hospital where the girl was given care. He had called Gwyneth to say that the doctors on the advisory panel were certain the judge, who shared their bias against extraordinary care for the comatose, would deny any appeals regardless of their merit and would do so with such timing that the child would be either severely damaged by dehydration or dead before an advocacy group could find a sympathetic judge in a higher court to issue a stay.

"How did you know Walter?" I asked.

"My father once spent a few days in the hospital for a bleeding ulcer. Walter's wife was his day nurse. She was very kind to him. I stayed in touch with her after he was released. When she died so young, two years after Daddy, I convinced my guardian to use some of my inheritance to set up a trust for the education of her and Walter's children."

"And Walter hoped you'd take on the expense of this girl?"

She shook her head. "He didn't really know what he wanted when he called me. He just said he didn't think she was vegetative."

"He's not a doctor."

"No. A physician assistant. But he also said there was something special about this girl, he couldn't define exactly what, but he felt it. He asked me to see her. He sneaked me into her room past midnight when there were few enough people around so I wouldn't go nuts."

"You don't go nuts."

"I have my moments," she assured me.

Indicating the child's limp hand, which Gwyneth held, I said, "Did you touch her that night, too?"

"Yes. I don't know why I had the courage, but I did."

"And you think she's special?"

"Yes."

"Why?"

She bent to kiss the girl's hand. "I'm not sure what I believe about her. But I'm certain I should protect her until she wakes and tells us her name."

"You're so certain she'll revive."

"I am certain, yes. I'm certain even in spite of this . . . ." Gently she pulled the flaxen hair back from the left side of the girl's face, revealing an indentation where temple curved to brow, the mark of some beast whose signature was made not with a pen but with an object stone-hard and blunt.

"How did she get here?"

"I'll tell you over dinner. I don't want to inconvenience Walter and his family any longer. Wait for me on the front porch while I have a word with Janet and Cora."

I went down to the foyer. Someone had turned off the television. Alone, I stood in the warm silence, in the wide archway to the living room, still nervous about being here but nevertheless taking a moment to enjoy the domestic charm.

To the left of the archway, on a console, a candle burned in a clear-glass container with a vented lid designed to keep the candle and its flame contained if it should be accidentally knocked to the floor. The luminary served a shrine, brightening a porcelain of the Holy Mother.

When I stepped into the living room for a closer look at the two framed photographs that flanked the sacred statuette, I saw a woman of whom the camera had captured not only her beauty but also the suggestion of kindness and intelligence. Reflections of the honoring flame unfurled in the chased-silver frames into which the silversmith had worked a pattern of roses.

I stood on the front porch, at the head of the steps, watching the ghost parade of snow shapes sculpted by the wind, ever changing as they capered through lamplight and shadow. The bare black limbs of the maples knocked and rattled an idiot rhythm, and creaked like the stair treads in an ill-carpentered house.

After a minute, Gwyneth came out onto the porch, closed the door, and joined me. "You were okay in there. It wasn't so bad, was it?"

"It was bad, worse than I expected, but not in the way I thought it would be bad."

"Come on. I'm waiting for a couple of calls, but meanwhile we'll grab dinner."

In the Rover, as she started the engine, I said, "Walter's wife, she was kind to your father."

"From what I know of her, she was kind to everyone."

I said, "She didn't just die, she was murdered, wasn't she?"

"Yes."

"Was her name Claire?"

"You know the case, then."

"There were three of them. They dumped her in the pond in the Commons. They threw her away like she was trash."

As heat poured from the vents and the chill relented, we sat together in silence. Not looking. Not touching. But close.

Then she said, "Ryan Telford has a reputation, respectability, much education, a prestigious position, but under all that, he's just like those three. He'll do anything. In the end, for all of their kind, it's about the same thing—power. Having power over others, to tell you what to do, to take what you have, to use you any way they wish, to demean you and break you and make you obey, and finally to rob you of your faith in truth, make you despair that there's no hope and never was. Since last night, he's known I'm a threat to him. That can't be permitted. He's on a tear. He isn't going to stop."

"Can he find out about this house?"

"I don't think he can. Or the place I'm staying tonight. But with his connections, I can't be certain about anything. I shouldn't have asked you to protect the girl. With your limitations, it's too much to ask."

"You did all right for her with *your* limitations. If it were to come to that, I'd manage somehow. But it won't come to that. Do you have proof of Telford's larceny?"

"The proof took time, but I got it. The proof is the easy part. Who to trust with it is a puzzle with half the pieces missing."

"The police," I said.

"The police, the district attorney's office, the courts—you'll find good people in all those places, Addison. But there's also deep corruption there, as well. It's not the city it once was. Everyone talks about justice, but there can be no justice where there is no truth, and these are times when truth is seldom recognized and often despised. It's a hoglot, money is the mud, a lot of it dirty money or tax money wildly misspent, and more people are wallowing in it than you might think. If I put the proof in the wrong hands, it'll be fiddled with until it proves nothing, and suddenly I'll have a lot more enemies than one."

As she drove away from the curb, snow came down like ashes from a burnt-out sky invisible. In spite of its brightness, the city all around us seemed obscure, its millions of rooms offering no certain safe haven.

36

FATHER DIED ON A NIGHT DRAPED WITH HEAVY SNOW. The streets were all but impassable because of a strike of city workers in the Street and Sanitation Department that a cowed mayor would not confront. No plows funneled the powder to the curbs, and no dump trucks stood by to be loaded. Because the storm came rich in snow but without wind, perfectly even layers built up on every horizontal surface, as smooth as buttercream. The tunnel visors on the traffic lights wore white hoods, under which burned cyclops eyes that, when not blind dark, were red or green or yellow. The only vehicles abroad—a couple of four-wheel-drive black-and-white SUVs with police shields on the doors and a winterized ambulance of similar design—ignored those signals and cruised intersections without stopping.

We had read of the predicted storm in the newspaper, during our after-hours visit to the library, and we had prepared for a night of sightseeing enhanced by the magical quality of a city under a spell of snow. Warmly dressed beneath our fleece-lined raincoats, booted and gloved and wearing ski masks, our hoods up and tied beneath our chins, we came aboveground in high spirits.

During the first hour of our tour, we saw many marvelous things, one particularly memorable as we entered the block where stood the great Cathedral of St. Saturnius of Toulouse. The church and its associated buildings occupied an entire block at the broad flat top of Cathedral Hill, with steps plateauing up to its three entrances, each with two bronze-clad doors under a cinquefoil arch. The two Gothic towers soared so high into the night that their spires at moments disappeared into the kaleidoscopic snowfall.

Along the street came a sleigh drawn by a horse nearly as large as a Clydesdale. The snow-muffled clopping of its steel-shod hooves and the ringing of the bells on its harness signified its reality, which otherwise we might have questioned, so fantastic was the animal and the four-passenger cariole that it pulled. A couple occupied the front seat, another couple the back, and they were dressed as if out of Dickens: the women in bonnets and voluminous dresses overlaid with capes, their hands warmed in furry mufflers; the men in greatcoats and top hats, bright scarves around their necks. We thought they must have planned this a long time, as a lark, and it tickled us to think that people would go to such lengths for the sake of frivolity. We waved at them, and they waved at us, and they turned west along the brow of Cathedral Hill.

Inspired by that sight, Father and I broke into a snowball fight in the middle of the street, half a block past the church. We were thus engaged, plumes of laughter feathering away in the icy air, when the police SUV turned the corner and angled toward us.

Perhaps the two patrolmen wanted only to warn us not to continue our game in the middle of the street, although traffic was almost as light as it might be after doomsday. Or perhaps they might have been concerned that we would damage one of the vehicles parked at the curb, inadvertently scooping up a chunk of tarred gravel from a fracture in the blacktop, giving one of our snowballs windshield-cracking impact.

We waved at them to indicate that we understood their concern, and we stepped between two parked cars to the sidewalk, continuing north. But waving and cheerful assent to their authority didn't satisfy them. They swung the SUV around to follow us and, with a spotlight, brought us center stage in the night.

Over a loudspeaker, one of them said, *"Please stop right there."*

When my mother had turned me out, my life had rolled down the long hill of change, but I had enjoyed a better and more stable life during the twelve years after Father saved me from burning. What happened in the next few minutes, however, seemed not like a hill of change but like a cliff from which I was pushed into darkness. I will never be able to recount it without pain.

37

IN THE LAND ROVER, SURROUNDED BY THE CITY, I thought the falling snow began to seem ominous, as though it might be the same storm in which Father had died, the wind having circled the world uncounted times in those six years, returning now for me.

As we headed for the haven to which Gwyneth had fled from her apartment near the Commons, she said, "When Walter lost Claire, it changed him. The brutality of her murder followed by the travesty of the not-guilty verdicts radicalized him."

Of the three rapists—Orcott, Sabbateau, and Clerkman—the last was the son of the longtime president of the union representing the city's police and firemen. The press and all responsible authorities agreed that Clerkman's family connections would in no way affect how the district attorney's office would build a case and prosecute it.

In court, the police chain-of-custody records for evidence in the case showed that the nurse's cap and panties were found with her other garments near the pond. The officer who tagged and bagged those items had since retired and moved out of state; he was too ill to be subpoenaed. For reasons not explained, the prosecution was confident that the evidence records hadn't been altered, that the cap and panties found in the van were not those of the nurse. Therefore, the defense attorney proposed that the aunt of Orcott, Verbina Orcott, who claimed to have found the garments, had foolishly planted them in the flower-shop van to incriminate her nephew, whom she detested and believed to be a heavy drug user. Wasn't it true that she thought her husband was naive and far too financially generous with their nephew? Wasn't it true that they often argued about his generosity? Wasn't it true that subsequent to her giving this trumped-up so-called evidence to the police, her husband filed for divorce? In sworn testimony, Verbina declared that the cap and panties shown to her in court were not the ones she found under the seat in the van, but when subjected to relentless cross-examination, she at times became befuddled.

Although initial statements by the police-department spokesman had mentioned mattress-related DNA evidence matching that of the three defendants and the victim, by the time the trial was under way, the prosecution had no match to the victim or to Orcott, and the DNA evidence regarding Clerkman and Sabbateau was inconclusive. Because the nurse had floated for hours in the pond, water had invaded her every orifice. The deputy coroner testified that he could not obtain perpetrator DNA from the cadaver. For some reason unspecified, the chief coroner was not called to testify.

With such supposedly flimsy evidence, the case might never have been brought to trial, if not for Sabbateau's confession. In court, the defendant claimed he had made a false confession because the two interrogating detectives threatened and psychologically tortured him, so that he feared for his life. And they had not allowed him to call an attorney. Two psychologists testified that Sabbateau had a below-average IQ and suffered from an inferiority complex; as a consequence he was timid and inclined to be fearful even in ordinary situations. They didn't go as far as to claim that Orcott and Clerkman hung out with the pathetic Sabbateau solely because of their kind hearts, but such noble intentions were implied.

The two accused detectives, Hines and Corzo, each other's best friend, didn't acquit themselves well on the witness stand. After the jury returned the not-guilty verdicts, the detectives were eventually suspended for a year without pay. In spite of having no income, Hines and Corzo endured no obvious decline in their living standards, and in fact they rented a bachelor's pad in Las Vegas and spent most of the year enjoying everything that city had to offer, whereafter they returned to their duties, chastened and contrite.

Now, piloting the Land Rover through the steadily thickening snowfall, Gwyneth said, "When the girl found in the Dumpster wasn't protected by the court, when Judge Gallagher started the process of having the feeding tube removed, Walter felt the system was failing her as it failed Claire. Without my name ever being used, Gallagher was persuaded to allow an irrevocable trust to be set up to care for the girl. Custody of her was quietly granted to Walter and to his sister, Janet, so that they could care for her in the house I provided through the trust."

Considering the burden of her social phobia and the restrictions that it placed upon her, I marveled that Gwyneth could accomplish so much. I supposed that she had been taught competence and courage by the father of whom she spoke so highly, as I had been by my father.

"But how could the judge be persuaded to do all that without knowing who funded the trust?"

"Judge Gallagher's mother, Rose, has big influence, because he'll receive a huge inheritance when she dies. The person Rose trusts most in this world isn't her son, who often defies her, but Teague Hanlon."

"Your guardian."

"He told her what could be done for the child if the judge allowed it. Rose was sick that the girl might be starved to death. Never mentioning who had advised her, she told her son that if Walter and Janet weren't given guardianship, a new will would be drawn, granting him a quarter of her estate rather than all of it. The court saw the wisdom of compassion. The wheels of justice turned with express-train speed."

I said, "So much money and effort for a girl you didn't know."

"What else is money for if not for things like this? Besides, you saw her. She's special."

I remembered the face that inspired in me thoughts of peace and charity and hope. "Special, I think. But how?"

"Time will show us. Maybe soon."

The wind brought the fine dry snow fast along the street, and the heavily trafficked street brought us at a more sedate pace to a long block of theaters and restaurants. Through the streaming flakes, I read the titles of the plays and the names of the actors on the marquees.

I wondered what it would be like to sit in such a theater, with the auditorium in quiet shadows and the whole wide world for a while shrunken to a stage evocatively lighted, to sit without fear among hundreds of people and to see a story told, to laugh with them, to share their suspense, and in the most human moment of the play, to cry with them.

Again, I thought of the comatose child, reclining in the bed, like a princess in a play, a princess bewitched, with many years to wait and grow before she would be old enough to be awakened and betrothed by a prince's kiss. And as in a fairy tale, the kiss would also heal the bone of battered temple, so that when the flaxen hair was drawn back, there would no longer be a grievous indentation in her skull.

Perhaps it was inevitable that such a thought would bring to mind Father's battered face and the spray of blood like a nimbus on the snow around his sainted head.

"What's wrong?" she asked.

"Nothing."

"Something's wrong."

"No. I'm all right."

I suspected she still believed that my face was only scarred from burns. I was reluctant to tell her there had been others like me—Father and his father—and that there might be more in the world, we of the hidden. She no doubt thought my father had been like her own, a man of normal appearance who had walked in daylight as well as night, who had gone wherever he wished, whenever he chose. I hoped that she would continue believing just that for a while yet. These tender hours of friendship might come to an end when at last she understood that the thing about us that terrified people wasn't anything as mundane as fire-chewed flesh or any of the ordinary deformities of the human face that have medical definitions, that we were so horrific, even she, with all her tolerance and sympathy, might recoil in fear and disgust.

"I'm all right," I repeated, keeping my head turned away from her. "I'm just hungry."

"We're almost there. We'll have dinner soon."

"Good. That will be nice."

I knew that I had done a fateful thing when I had sought her out in her hiding place in the library. If I were to die in this snow as Father had died in the white night six years earlier, my actions would have summoned this storm and my rebellion against loneliness would have been the death of me.

38

"PLEASE STOP RIGHT THERE."

Spotlighted, Father and I stood on a sidewalk that had become a theater, two actors in a cast of four, the remaining players soon to enter left. The street scene was so minutely detailed, the snow such a masterly effect so exquisitely executed, that I could not deny this stage was in fact the world. Nevertheless, for half a minute, I stood paralyzed by denial, insistent that this must be a theater of dreams from which I would awaken at any moment.

We had contingency plans for various situations that might arise when we were aboveground, and the worst of these was an encounter with the police. Since we never committed crimes, they had no reason to detain us, but on the other hand, they were legitimate authorities to whom everyone should respond properly if approached. In our case, a proper response would be the death of us.

Our tactic in such a confrontation was no different from that of men in ancient times surprised by a pride of lions: *run.* But we had the misfortune to be stopped on Cathedral Hill, in a block that offered few routes of escape. Behind us stood the Museum of Natural History, which occupied an entire block, allowing no alleyway, and which was closed and locked at that hour. Across the street, also a full block on every side, was the Ruthaford Center for the Performing Arts, dark and secured. Our only options were to continue north on Cathedral Avenue or retreat south.

In such a situation, which we had never faced before but which we had discussed, our intention was to wait until the officers were out of their vehicle and approaching, so that when we ran, we might gain a few seconds of advantage while they returned to the patrol car. We dared not let them get too close, however, or they might pursue on foot. The plan was to run in opposite directions, dividing their attention. Because they had no reason to suspect us of a crime, they would react according to the police department's official rules of engagement, which allowed pursuit but did not allow them to shoot us in the back.

"Go south," Father advised me, as the doors of the winterized SUV opened and the officers stepped down to the street.

They were tall and solid men, made to appear even bigger by their dark-blue, insulated winter uniforms. The short quilted jackets ended in elastic hems just above their gun belts, pistols ready in swivel holsters on their right hips.

Father said to them, in the friendliest of voices, "We're too old for snowball fights, but it's such an exhilarating night."

"You live around here?" one of them asked.

"Yes, sir. We do indeed."

In this situation the word *indeed* was code between us, and it meant *run*.

As I turned south, from the corner of my eye, I saw Father slip in the snow on his second step, stagger, slide, and fall.

We of the hidden may be mutants, but whatever we are, we don't have superpowers like mutants have in movies. We are more human than we're perceived to be, subject to the laws of physics, to gravity, to the consequences of our decisions. The frivolity of a snowball fight in the middle of the street invited notice, and inviting notice was, for us, like pulling the pin from a hand grenade.

The shock of Father falling blew out of my mind all of our contingency planning, and I turned toward him in fear for his life, my own peril for a moment forgotten.

As far as the policemen were concerned, the attempt to flee was as damning as flight itself. They drew their guns, one aimed at me, the other covering him, and they said the things that they say in these situations, issued commands. I dared not move, and Father got to his feet as they demanded that he do, arms spread, hands far from any pocket in which he might have a weapon.

He possessed no gun, but that didn't matter. What followed was now ordained, as certain as that all rivers run downhill.

Before he could be told what to do next, before we both might be handcuffed and both surely dead, Father said, "Officer, you need to see who I am. I'm going to take off my hood and ski mask." He was warned not to make any sudden moves, and he said, "Sir, I have no moves to make."

As he untied the drawstrings of his hood, I said, "No." My chest was so tightly banded with horrified anticipation, the breath so heavy in my lungs, that I couldn't speak even that small word twice, but only pray it silently: *No, no, no, no.*

He pulled back the hood, drew off the mask.

After a sharp inhalation of shock, the two men were frozen for a moment at the sight of him. At first but only at first, their wrenched countenances were those of helpless children cornered by a thing that stalked them in their worst dreams, a thing that in the lands of sleep never quite possessed features but that now had a face more terrifying than their worst imaginings.

Father looked at me and said, "Endure."

As if in reaction to the catalyst of that word, the policemen's expressions of childlike terror morphed into disgust, although the terror remained evident in eyes and trembling jaws, and then morphed into hatred, although the terror and disgust could still be seen, so that their faces were grotesque and tormented, galleries of wretched emotions.

The officer to whom Father had spoken shot him twice, and the reports were muffled in the snow-blanketed night, echoing briefly back and forth between the museum and the concert hall, across the deserted top of Cathedral Hill. They were not at all like gunfire but like the thud of fists on a door, sounds like those that wake you and then do not repeat, leaving you uncertain if they were real or of the dream from which you've risen.

Father fell onto his back in soft snow that plumed up and then sparkled down across his black raincoat. He labored for breath, and his twitching hands fanned through the snow at his sides, like birds with broken wings.

In that moment and for a while, I ceased to exist as far as the two policemen were concerned. Their universe was Father's face and Father's dying eyes, and though surely they could see that he was mortally wounded and no threat, they went after him not with guns, but with truncheons, clubbing him furiously where he lay unresisting. Such is the power of our appearance that, once they have killed one of us, their violence escalates, as if they feel that we are yet alive in death and must be killed twice.

I was no longer the small boy whom Father saved from burning. Twenty years old, a grown man, I nevertheless could not help him. I could not help him.

Knowing how the sight of his face and eyes would consume their attention, he offered his life for mine, and when he said "Endure," he meant many things, the first of which was *run*. I could not help him, but neither could I run and leave him there, with no one to stand witness to the last of his ordeal.

I retreated along the sidewalk to the vehicles parked at the curb, slipped between two of them, dropped to the ground, and belly-crawled under an SUV. I moved forward until, from beneath the front bumper but still cloaked in shadow, I could watch them try to break their truncheons on his bones.

I did not weep, because weeping would reveal me, and I owed him my survival, for which he had paid everything. From my low point of view, I couldn't see their faces—and was glad that I couldn't. The viciousness of their assault on a man now dead or dying, the bitter curses and the wordless exclamations of hatred and fear were so savage that the sight of their faces might turn me to stone.

When they were done, they stood for a moment, silent but for their ragged breathing. Then they began to ask each other *What the hell, what was it, what is it, what the shit?* One of them vomited. The other made a sound like sobbing, and although there might have been remorse in it, there were other and worse miseries.

Lying under the SUV, I prayed they wouldn't read my footprints in the snow and drag me into the open.

When they realized that I was gone, their reactions were of two kinds, revealed in rapid-fire conversation. They were afraid that I was another like the one they killed and that if two existed, perhaps there might be others of us even now gathering around one corner or another. And they were overcome by a recognition that they had lost control. Regardless of what we might be, they hadn't proceeded in anything resembling a professional manner, which troubled them with guilt and the fear of punishment.

Because my father had told me of *his* father's death, I wasn't surprised when their first impulse was to climb aboard their patrol SUV and get out of there. As the clink of chain-wrapped tires and the engine noise receded, I crawled into the open. When the officers' fear and confusion abated, when doubt set in and guilt grew greater, they would come back. Before they returned or anyone else came along, I had an awful job to do.

39

GOING ON NINE O'CLOCK OF AN ORDINARY NIGHT, the city would be in its third act of the day, the streets and restaurants and places of entertainment crowded with millions of people living out their stories. This evening, the storm was a counterweight to the allure of things culinary, musical, theatrical, and otherwise enticing, and most people had flown home as if pulled off the stage by fly lines.

Gwyneth pointed out to me that even on those blocks where vehicles were usually lined up, their drivers buying drugs, the NO PARKING signs were being obeyed. Also gone were the usual front-line salesmen, young expendables hoping to avoid jail long enough to be promoted off the streets, some of whom did business in Rollerblades, the better to skate around a corner and away at the first sign of a cop, or at least to get out of sight long enough to dump incriminating merchandise down a street drain before being pursued and arrested.

Gone, too, from their customary corners, were the prostitutes, who could not look sufficiently erotic to attract johns when they were attired in Gore-Tex storm suits and parkas.

Already, in only the second hour of its reign, the blizzard had decreed at least a temporary interdiction against the more public expressions of vice.

I thought of the Fog that entered into the man in the apartment two floors below Gwyneth's, and I wondered how many in this world were hosts to those creatures. Judging by the fact that I saw many more Clears than Fogs, I thought that the latter numbered many fewer than the former. I also didn't think that Clears could enter into anyone. Most people indulged in their vices and clung to their virtues based on their responses to temptation and conflict, not because some Other within them drove their behavior. My guess was that when you descended to a certain depth of depravity, the Fogs could smell you as a hound, catching a murderer's spoor, could track the criminal through forest, field, and moor.

Having seen Ryan Telford in fevered pursuit of Gwyneth in the library and having made an effort to clean up the wreckage that he left behind in her apartment, I suspected that a Fog had climbed aboard him years earlier and was delighted to be traveling in his company.

Through sheeting snow, we cruised a block of a cross street that once had been lined with five- and six-story apartment buildings, a few of which still served that residential purpose. Others had been converted to low-rent offices for a series of fledgling or declining businesses, reminding me of the buildings in which private detectives had their offices in noir novels, and the ground floors were occupied by gin joints, tattoo parlors, and specialty shops dealing in narrow lines of merchandise like vinyl records, psychedelic-era memorabilia, and taxidermy.

At a narrow brown-brick five-story, where the street level had been converted into a garage, Gwyneth said, "Here we are."

With a remote control, she disarmed the alarm system and put up the segmented rolling door. As soon as the back end of the Land Rover cleared the threshold, she lowered the big door again, watching in the rearview and side mirrors until it clunked into place, perhaps concerned that someone might slip in behind us.

When I got out of the vehicle, powdery snow slid off the door onto the concrete. The garage was cold, dimly lighted by an automatic ceiling lamp. The only smell was the faint astringency of lingering exhaust fumes.

Gwyneth indicated stairs behind a locked steel door, though she used the elevator, which could be summoned not by a call button, but only by a key.

On the floor of the elevator car, just past the tracks in which the doors rolled, were the words in an unknown alphabet that she had printed on other thresholds. I had asked about them before, and she had avoided an answer. I didn't ask about them again.

As the car rose from the garage on what I thought must be a hydraulic ram, I faced the floor, to avoid being revealed by the fluorescent lights behind the ceiling grid.

She said, "Not even Teague Hanlon knows about this place. Daddy set up a trust in the Cayman Islands to buy it. The trust pays the taxes and utilities. It's my emergency bolt-hole."

"In case of what?"

"In case of anything. Right now, in case of Ryan Telford. If he found one of my other eight apartments, he'll find them all, because all of those are linked through the domestic trust that owns them."

"Your father set all this up by the time you were thirteen?"

"I think he had a premonition or something, I mean that he wouldn't live long. Though he didn't expect to be murdered—either by honey or otherwise."

We were going to the fifth floor at the top of the building.

I asked, "What's on floors two, three, and four?"

"Nothing. You might not have noticed, but the windows on the first four floors have been bricked shut. This is now designated a warehouse, but nothing's stored on those levels."

The elevator opened, revealing a vestibule. The formidable steel door between that small space and the rest of the apartment could be unlocked only by entering a four-digit code and the star sign into a keypad.

I said, "Such heavy security."

"I'm embarrassed to tell you, but Daddy called me a priceless treasure. This is my vault."

In the living room, she switched on a lamp and then went to set out candles, in the light of which I would be more comfortable. The room was nearly as minimally furnished as the one in the apartment where we had eaten scrambled eggs and brioche, except that this one contained a grand piano.

At the wall of windows, I discovered three Clears on the roofs of the two buildings across the street, a woman and two men, glowing softly. The falling snow, all of it vaguely luminous as it reflected the ambient light of the city, was brighter in their vicinity, but it appeared to pass through them, and it wove no lace mantillas in their hair. One of the men gazed into the sky, and the other two peered down into the street along which we had recently arrived.

The heavens offered nothing but the sea of snow. In the street, on the farther sidewalk, a man bent into the wind, two lengths of his long scarf trailing behind him as if he were a walking weather vane. Also trailing behind him on a leash was a German shepherd, judging by its deep chest, straight back, and sloping hindquarters.

As they passed out of shadow and under a lamppost, the shepherd raised its bowed head and turned its face out of the wind-driven snow to look up as if suddenly aware of me at the window high above, its eyes radiant in the lamplight. I didn't step back from the glass. The Fogs may take tenancy in bad people and sleep dreaming in certain objects, but I have reason to trust dogs.

In the living room behind me, Gwyneth finished strategically placing candles in ruby-glass cups and turned off the lamp.

She said, "I've put a glass of pinot grigio on a coaster on the piano. You do drink wine?"

Turning away from the window, I said, "Father and I would from time to time have a glass or even two."

"I want to hear all about your father."

Not ready to open that door yet, I said, "And I want to hear all about you."

"There's not that much to me."

The most that I could clearly see of her in the lambent ruby glow of isolated votives was her right hand as it gripped a wineglass, in the bowl of which glimmered the reflection of a nearby flame.

"For every small thing I've learned about you," I said, "I'm sure there are a thousand things of greater importance."

"You are a hopeless romantic."

"For instance, do you play the piano?"

"I play and I compose."

"Will you play something for me?"

"After dinner. Music is a better brandy than it is an aperitif."

Her cell phone rang, and she fished it from a jacket pocket.

The ring tone was a bar or two of lovely music, but somehow I knew that the call was bad news.

40

SIX YEARS EARLIER, IN ANOTHER NIGHT OF HEAVY snow . . .

The windows of the performing-arts center and the museum were blind dark, and to the south the towers of St. Saturnius thrust high into a night that had become as Gothic as their finials, crockets, spires, and belfries.

Kneeling beside my father, I looked into his ruined face, that I might always remember how cruel had been his martyrdom and what he had endured to save me. One of his eyes was lost beneath a pool of blood, the socket like a cup and, in that light, the blood as dark as cabernet.

I half expected cathedral bells to ring out across the city in memoriam, a carillon of joyous bells that said *Someone is free at last,* and simultaneously a monody of heavy bells, iron bells, as solemn as those rung for heroes and for statesmen, bells that said *He is gone who was much loved.* But the night was empty of all bells. There were no bells for such as us, no funerals, no crowd of mourners around our graves.

The distraught policemen might return at any moment. Although in part motivated by regret, they were likely to repeat with me the violence visited upon my father.

After rolling up the ski mask that he had taken off and putting it in a pocket of my coat, I slipped the scarf from his neck. I wound that length of wool around his head, covering his face, and secured it with the hood, which I tied beneath his chin, cinching up his sagging, broken jaw.

Snow fell so heavily now through the windless night that, from this midpoint of the block, I couldn't see past either corner. The strike by workers in the Street and Sanitation Department had led to the deserted avenues that enticed us aboveground for a night of play, and now the same strike all but ensured that, here atop the most treacherous slopes in the metropolis, hours past midnight, no one would happen upon me in the next few minutes.

Cathedral Hill was the highest point in the city, which meant the drains were the smallest, because no higher culverts existed to feed them. I could not bring Father's body at once down into our world below the street, for there was no entrance here to a tunnel large enough to accommodate us.

I had only two options, but I didn't like the first. I could drag or carry the body through one of the long, steep streets that led down from this high plateau, block after block, until I reached a largely horizontal neighborhood that would offer entrances to storm drains through which I could travel upright. Even in this feathery down-pour, with visibility diminished, the longer that I stayed above-ground, the more likely that I would be seen either by the returning policemen or others. Besides, I could not carry Father that far, not in snow halfway to my knees, and I was loath to drag him, as a hunter might drag a deer carcass from the woods.

My second option was St. Saturnius. In the full block occupied by the cathedral complex, there were associated buildings, including not just the archbishop's residence and the offices of the diocese, but also a monastery with chapter house, refectory, and a cloister sur-rounding a garden. There was a secret passage off the great hill, but to access it, I had to get Father into St. Saturnius.

Already in those days, and in fact years earlier, churches were locked tight after vespers or any lay activity that might be the last meeting of the day. Previously, they had been open around the clock, and any troubled soul was free to enter and sit or kneel alone. But for a few decades, an unsecured church door in the night had been an invitation to vandalism and to desecration of the altar; such was the modern world.

The various entrances to the cathedral complex were unlocked at daybreak, and I knew of a place where I might remain concealed from anyone on the street until I could gain access. I was twenty and very strong, but my resources were tested as I got the body across my shoulders and carried it toward St. Saturnius.

To take my father to his final resting place, soon after first light, I would have to carry him into the realm of the dead, and then down into deeper places.

41

THE VOTIVE ON THE PIANO HAD A THICK CLEAR-GLASS base and a ruby-red bowl the size of a teacup. In the high-gloss black finish of the Steinway, a halo of reddish light darker than blood surrounded the glass, shimmering in the lacquered ebony, as if it were a faint fire burning underwater.

My sense that the call might be bad news must have been matched by Gwyneth's intuition, because she set her cell phone on speaker mode before she said, "Hello," so that I could be witness to whatever conversation might ensue.

During the chase in the library the previous night, I'd heard Ryan Telford shout only a few words at her. Although I didn't recognize his voice, I knew that he was the caller because of what he said.

"I was led to believe that you were in a sanatorium following your father's untimely passing, some ultra-expensive asylum, hiding under the bed and sucking your thumb, mute and beyond curing."

In the nearly dark room, I stood by the keyboard, and she stood at the heel of the piano, which was a safe though not great distance, but the light of the cell-phone screen was insufficient to reveal her expression.

She said nothing, and after a moment, Telford said, "You're a neurotic little mouse. Afraid of people, geeked up in Goth, scurrying from one little-mouse nest to another, but delicious in your way."

"Murderer," she said calmly.

"What a twisted imagination you have, little mouse. You probably also imagine that more than one of your sad little nests have been visited by a pest-control expert, and that all eight will soon be."

Again, Gwyneth chose silence.

Telford said, "My current business model requires a partner. Did you know? He's as disappointed in the recent turn of events as I am. Too bad you don't have a partner, little mouse. It grieves me that you're alone in this cruel world."

"I'm not alone," she said.

"Ah, yes, your guardian. But he's not reliable anymore."

"He didn't give you this number or those addresses."

"No, he didn't. He wouldn't. But he's on a leash, you know, and more than he realizes. If he ever slips loose, well, then I would have to meet with him and explain the leash laws. Now that I know you're not in a sanatorium and never have been, we should have a date. I'm very attracted to you, mousie."

"I am not alone," she repeated, and in the near dark, I thought but could not be certain that she was looking toward me.

"How brave you are. An orphan, hopelessly neurotic, isolated by your own neurosis, inexperienced. And yet so brave. Brave little mouse, do you ever fantasize about being filled by two men at once? Real men, I mean, not like your precious guardian."

She terminated the call without further comment.

I expected the phone to ring at once, but it did not.

Her wineglass glimmered with candlelight as she raised it to her lips.

I said, "What are we going to do?"

"Have dinner."

"But if he finds this place—"

"He won't. I'll make dinner, we'll eat dinner, and then I'll play the piano for you. I might even have a second glass of pinot grigio."

The kitchen was too small to accommodate two cooks when one of them could not be touched and the other must hide his face.

I returned to the wall of windows and looked down into the street. The snow lay deep enough that tires carving through it no longer exposed the bare black pavement in their wake. The man with the German shepherd was most likely home by now.

Across the street, the three Clears were gone from the roofs on which they had stood. I wondered if they had crossed to this building. I considered sliding open a window, leaning out, and looking up for their telltale glow.

Befitting a tower meant to keep safe a priceless treasure, the windows didn't open. When I rapped my knuckles lightly on a pane, the glass sounded unusually thick. I wondered if it might be bulletproof.

42

FATHER DEAD ONLY MINUTES, THE HAUNTED CITY shrouded in pale cascades, and no safe way to convey a corpse off the hill and through the city other than perhaps by the secret route accessible only through the great church . . .

The imposing Gothic facade of St. Saturnius faced onto Cathedral Avenue, and the north flank lay along East Halberg Street.

As bent as a troll and with an apelike gait, the necessity of urgent action keeping despair at bay, I carried the body of my father across my shoulders, turning left onto East Halberg.

Contiguous with the church, a high stone wall encircled three sides of the square-block property. Entrances at strategic points allowed access to the various buildings that were integrated with the wall along its perimeter. All of those ingresses featured arched openings, and above each a statuary figure stood solemn sentinel, inset in the wall. Surmounting the particular archway to which I carried my father's body stood Saint John the Divine, whose expression of awe was that of a man who saw worlds beyond East Halberg Street.

The wall was so wide that within its uppermost eight feet ran a corridor that connected all the buildings along its perimeter. Here at the base, a seven-foot-deep vestibule lay beyond the archway, illuminated by a single bulb, and at the end of it stood a plain teak-plank door, which would be locked until just before daybreak.

As gently as possible, I lowered Father to the floor of the vestibule and arranged him sitting up with his back to a wall, hands gloved, face wrapped in a scarf. His clothes might have been stuffed with old tattered garments and threadbare towels and socks full of holes, and he a ragman from a children's story in which he had been becharmed and had come alive and had known great adventures, until he stepped out of fiction into this world, whereupon the magic went out of him.

Sewn into the lining of his raincoat were long pockets in which he kept the gate key that allowed us to enter the library and other buildings from below and the combination hook/prybar with which we could manipulate a manhole cover with ease. These things were mine now, and they were precious to me not merely because they made it easier to move around the city but also, and most of all, because they had belonged to him.

In the center of the vestibule ceiling, a wire cage protected a light bulb. Although it was vandalism, though I regretted the damage, in the interest of survival, I worked at the wire with the prybar until I made an opening wide enough to thrust it through and shatter the bulb. Most of the broken glass remained within the cage, but a few tiny fragments sifted through the sudden darkness, thinner than eggshells, crunching underfoot as I returned to the archway and stood just inside it, gazing out at the street.

I had never known such stillness in the city. Stripped of wind, the unseen sky quietly shed insulation, as if trillions of cold dead stars, severely shrunken in their dying, descended now and brought with them the perfect silence of interstellar space. The eerie hush raised a dread in my heart that I couldn't name. East Halberg was a wide, white, timeless sward, and I could almost believe that before me lay a vision of a distant era when the city still stood, but when its streets and plazas and parks were drifted over with the finely powdered bones of its former inhabitants.

If the two cops paid another visit to the block of Cathedral Avenue where Father had sacrificed himself, they did not get there by East Halberg, nor did they use a siren.

I returned to Father and sat beside him. The last dark hours of the night were cold, but the bitter air didn't sting as much as the grief that I could not unwind and pay out, that like a woven vine of thorns cinched my heart. Self-control was essential, and I tried to think of nothing, but into the nothing came the marionette and the music box and the way the little mountain house had looked when the shotgun roared within, which wasn't good, not good at all.

Moments in advance of the earliest blush of light, the monks daily proceeded from their monastery through the large cloister that surrounded a formal garden, unlocking the north and south doors in the

great wall, at the same time that other priests turned on the cathedral lights and opened the street doors for another day.

I stiffened when I heard the clack of the lock bolt disengaged, and
prepared to identify myself as a humble homeless man, head low,
beside my sleeping friend. Fortunately, the door was unlocked, but
the monk with the key did not linger in the cold to see if anyone had
camped out, which I suppose happened from time to time.

Even we of the hidden, who have every reason—but no inclination—to be cynical, tend to believe that we are to a degree safer when
unexpectedly encountering a member of the clergy than when coming face-to-face with anyone else. We are wise, however, not to expect universal mercy from the devout. All these years later, I vividly
remembered the white-clapboard blue-trimmed church by the river,
where one of the faithful, perhaps a deacon, had gone after me with
a baseball bat—and the minister who had broken Father's fingers.

After a minute or so, when I felt that all of the confreres would
have proceeded into the church, I opened the door inward. Beyond
the nearer length of the cloister immediately before me, glimpsed
between the columns that encircled it, lay the garden. In the first pale
light, the evergreen hedges draped in snow looked like sheet-covered
furniture in a house closed for the season.

I leaned through the doorway and confirmed that the cloister was
deserted. Because the vestibule offered insufficient space for me to
maneuver Father onto my shoulders, I dragged him across the threshold into the cloister, closed the door, and lifted him, and went to the
right along the covered walk.

The only entrance to the cathedral I dared use was the north porch,
which offered four doors. I hunched farther forward to keep the un-
gainly weight balanced on my back while I let go of the body with one
hand to open the door to my left.

From inside came chanting as sweet as song. The monks were observing matins, the first of seven hours in the Divine Office.

With the hope that they would be too involved with their prayers to notice me, I entered the north transept. During the night, I had scraped the caked snow off my boots; now I left only wet footprints on the marble floor.

Since first seeing them on a secret visit, I have always admired the fan vaults in the transept ceiling, sixty feet overhead, but burdened as I was and afraid of being noticed, I didn't even try to look up that high.

The cathedral was large, the transept long. When I strained to raise my head a little way, I saw no one in the crossing, where the shorter transepts met the longer nave. Whether they were gathered in the choir or elsewhere, I didn't know.

The body across my back seemed heavier by the moment. My calf muscles began to burn.

Immediately to my left, this side of the baptismal, beyond a columned archway lay a chamber that served a great spiral staircase with limestone treads six or seven feet wide, leading only down. Between two bronze stanchions hung a thick red-velvet rope, blocking entrance to the stairs, and when I managed to push aside one of the stanchions, it scraped loudly against the floor.

The chanting did not cease, and like some medieval body snatcher returning with remorse what he had taken earlier, I carried my dead father down the stairs to the crypt deep under the church, which would provide covert passage off Cathedral Hill and into the lower reaches of the city. At the foot of the stairs, under a carved-limestone tympanum featuring Christ the Redeemer, an ornate bronze gate blocked the way, but it was not locked.

At the moment, the crypt was lighted only by several torchères crowned with gas flames that burned 24/7 to attest to the eternal nature of the souls of those interred here. The space was divided into sections separated from one another only by arcades of columns, and overhead were groin vaults painted with murals. Here the bishops and the cardinals and perhaps some of the most worthy parishioners from the generations of the city were laid to rest.

The floors of the various chambers, all open to one another, had been constructed with subtle integrated slopes, which Father had pointed out to me when long ago we had entered along the route by which I would now leave with him. I passed among columns, accompanied by cowled figures in flaring black cassocks that were really shadows flung about by the leaping gas flames, enhanced by my imagination. I quickly came to the corner toward which the floors would direct the water if the crypt was ever flooded.

After putting Father down, I used the gate key and then hooked the large cover off the drain, leaving a few inches overhanging. Now and then a partial passage of a psalm sung down from the church, but I knew the monks couldn't hear me.

A vertical shaft, four feet in diameter, dropped sixty feet to a drain line large enough for a man to pass through easily in a stoop. These were among the earliest drains in the system, made of brick and mortar but still enduring.

The shaft featured embedded iron rungs for those who needed to service it, but a few of them were loose, and caution was required to avoid losing one's grip or footing. The hole was not wide enough for me to sling the body from my back and go down with it. Anyway, I had no way to sling it.

I had one option, grim as it was, and I hesitated only briefly before sliding Father feet-first into the hole. I turned away but did not cover my ears, because I felt that I should bear witness to every detail of his journey from point of death to his final rest.

The friction whistle of raincoat fabric against brick rose as he fell. He impacted with the larger drain far below and spilled into it, but the slope was too minimal for him to travel farther.

For perhaps a minute, I stood shuddering, forcing back my tears and steeling myself for the descent.

From elsewhere in the crypt, I heard footsteps on stone and then voices echoing along the groin vaults.

43

AS OUR STRANGE COURTSHIP REQUIRED, IF IT WAS A courtship, the dining area was barely lighted: three candles in blue-glass cups on a sideboard, six others at more distance in the open kitchen, none upon the table at which we ate. I had taken off my ski mask but not my jacket, and I ate with my hood still up.

A simple glass chandelier hung by a chain above us, left dark in consideration of me, but its chrome arms were faintly traced by fluttery reflections of the blue candlelight, and the small glass bowls containing its light bulbs took the blue glow and made rings of it around their rims. Our wineglasses and the flatware likewise glimmered, and on the wall behind the sideboard, soft blue light quivered as the flames danced.

She had prepared crab cakes with a slaw of peppers and cabbage, and tiny potatoes sautéed first and then roasted in the oven. All of it was delicious, and I couldn't tell what had been frozen and what was fresh.

I asked, "Who might be the partner that Telford mentioned?"

"I have no way of knowing. He lies as easily as he breathes, so there might not be any partner."

"I think there is one."

After a silence, Gwyneth said, "So do I."

"What did he mean—your guardian is on a leash?"

"We're going to meet him later. Then you'll know."

"You said even he doesn't know about this place."

"He doesn't. We're going out again to meet him."

"Is that safe?"

"Not entirely. But it's necessary."

I liked the pinot grigio. I'd never tasted it before. I liked the shadow of her at the farther end of the table, too, her hands like the graceful hands of a mermaid in a pale-blue dream.

"He sounds entirely wicked," I said.

She laughed softly. "I won't disagree."

"Five years ago, when he . . ."

When I hesitated, she completed my question for me. "When he tried to rape me?"

"You were only thirteen. You said you lived secluded on the top floor of your father's house then."

"Do you have a worst night of your life, Addison?"

I thought of Father shot and bludgeoned on Cathedral Hill. "Yes. I have a worst night."

"Me too. I was living alone on the fourth floor of my father's house when Telford came after me, but Daddy was murdered minutes before, in the kitchen."

I said, "I didn't realize both in the same night."

A sharp knocking came from overhead, three pairs of quick but not heavy raps, like a percussionist in an orchestra striking a hollow wood block with a small wooden hammer.

I've never known the Clears to make a sound, but looking up at the ceiling, I said, "Someone on the roof?"

"There's an attic. But it's nothing. Probably just a water line."

The sound came again: *rap-rap, rap-rap, rap-rap.* She said, "Probably just air in the water pipes."

Rap-rap, rap-rap, rap-rap.

"Always six raps in pairs? How can that be?"

"It's not always the same. Sometimes a rap or two, sometimes a long stutter of them. Nothing to worry about. Just air in the pipes. How are the crab cakes?"

In the gloom, her face was no more revealed to me than mine was visible to her.

"Delicious. You're quite a cook."

"I'm quite a reheater."

I picked up my wineglass, hesitated, waiting for another spate of knocking, which did not come.

After a sip of wine, I said, "Gwyneth?"

"Yes."

"I'm so happy to be here."

"I'm happy, too," she said. "My life has always been so limited. But it doesn't feel limited right now."

44

SIX YEARS EARLIER, IN THE CRYPT OF THE CATHEDRAL, standing by the open drain, in the farthest corner from the entrance, I dared not move because the slightest sound would resonate along the curves of the groin vaults and announce my presence with a choir of echoes.

The four chambers were open to one another, delineated only by the colonnades. Although sound traveled well, getting a clear line of sight to any point would be difficult. I was reminded of the pine barrens through which I'd made my way as a boy, before coming to the church by the river. Those trees, with their lowest limbs high above my head and no underbrush competing with them, were so plentiful that I'd had no long views, and I had none here, especially by the lambent light of the torchères and through the pooling shadows.

I could have gone into the shaft, but when they came to see the cause of the noise, the manhole cover would be lying beside the hole. They would know someone other than a city worker came and went by this route, and I would never be able to return here, where sometimes in the deep of night I found a certain peace.

Whoever they might be, there were two of them. If the tone of their conversation was not conspiratorial, it was at least that of men with opinions that they evidently kept secret between them.

"The announcement won't be for five days, but the word has been received. It's been decided."

"Please tell me it's not Wallache."

"But it is."

"They've all gone mad."

"Say nothing to anyone or I'm toast. This is übersecret."

"But they must know—*he* must know—Wallache's history?"

"They seem to believe Wallache's version of it."

"He's been lucky not to be exposed like the others."

"Perhaps it's more than luck."

"You know my feelings in that regard."

"And yet it's known. It's *known*."

"It's not known widely."

"We have two duties now. One to Wallache, which we should fulfill only to the minimum possible, and one to what is right."

"There are others who feel as we do. Many others."

"Yes, but that's cold comfort when such a decision has been made and you know there's a long darkness coming down."

As suddenly as they had arrived, they departed.

I couldn't make much sense of what they had said, and at the time I didn't have any interest in puzzling through the meaning of it. With Father dead, the seams of my life were split, and I didn't believe that I could sew them up again. My entire life was a secret, and the small secrets of others seemed to be none of my business.

Alone, I went into the hole, from the crypt to what lay far beneath it, as if I were of the dead yet tasked with my own burial. Holding fast to a rung with my left hand, I secured myself to another with the six-inch tether that I had long ago stitched securely to the belt of my raincoat. That short safety line ended in a large snap link that I inspected often enough to entrust my life to it. Feet on a lower rung, tethered at the waist, I had both hands free to use the prybar/hook to snare the overhanging drain lid and muscle it into place, though with considerable noise.

After releasing the tether, I descended in darkness so thick that I breathed it in with the cool air. Although it was nothing but imagination, I felt that the inhaled darkness was not expelled with the exhaled breath.

I knew the number of rungs from top to base of the sixty-foot shaft, and I counted them as I went down to where Father lay tumbled and broken. When I drew near the bottom, I stopped, took a flashlight from a coat pocket, and searched below. At my back, the last four feet on the farther side of the shaft formed an open arch to the larger drain, providing a four-by-four curved opening, through which the momentum of the falling body had carried it feet-first. He had turned on his side, and only the hooded, scarf-wrapped head remained within the vertical shaft.

At the bottom, I knelt, pushed him all the way out into the larger drain, and crawled after him. I struggled to focus on what needed to be done, the physical work, while striving not to dwell too much upon the nature of this package that I needed to convey across a great length of the city.

I had to leave him there for a while in the dark, and hope that no rats found him in my absence. Fewer rats scurried the storm drains than you might think, because those tunnels contained little to feed upon and because, in a Hamelin cleansing, the rushing walls of water from every major rain drowned them, washed them out into the river.

I troll-walked through the tributary drain, where the once-smooth water-struck brick was now pitted and eroded, set in a common bond with headers every sixth course. The next drain, larger in diameter, had been crafted of random-rubble stone with uniform mortar joints; though newer than the brick section, it appeared ancient.

When I came to a modern concrete culvert in which I could stand erect, I ran. A milky trickle of water eased along the center of the floor, glistering like melted fat in the flashlight beam that jostled through the dark. I needed to change tunnels a few times, but in twenty-five minutes, I came to the louvered steel panel that opened to the corridor leading to our windowless rooms.

This warren of passageways beneath the city was not a catacomb in which we of the hidden could be interred in wall niches to work our way to bones. We had to be consigned to water, to the riverbed where we would become significant silt that might nourish all things for which the river served as home.

After my arrival at the age of eight, my father realized the necessity of assembling a burial kit to be used by whoever of us survived the other. Fortunately, I had lived to be strong enough for the task, as daunting now as it was urgent.

The gear was piled in a corner of our book room. A canvas tarp found in a Dumpster had been sprayed on one side with a silicon lubricant supplied on request by the one friend who had given Father a key to St. Sebastian's food bank. Father sewed eyelets into two ends of the tarp and strung draw cords through them. He folded it with the untreated surface and the cords on the inside. There were, as well, two buckets containing nails and bolts and washers and rusted iron fittings of various kinds and the heads of a couple of hammers and all manner of small things, heavy for their size, that we had found on our night rambles and had collected over the years to serve as sufficient weight to sink a body and keep it sunk.

I carried the buckets out of our secret rooms and put them on the elevated service walkway outside the louvered panel. With the folded tarp, I set out at a run to the tributary drain in which I had left the body.

We don't know what those of the aboveground world would do to our cadavers. But considering the violence that most of them visit upon us on sight, we assume they might commit abominations beyond our imagining. We stand and die with courage when cornered, but we do not—must never—let them take our dignity in death.

My gold Rolex marked an hour and ten minutes since I had left Father. He lay as before, unattended by rats, in a stillness that the surface world will never know, not even in this hushed day of windless snow.

I spread the tarp across the drain floor, the lubricant-treated side against the bricks. When I rolled him into the tarp, he jiggled in his clothes, like a mass of odds and ends, shattered and torn not just by bullets and truncheons but also by the long drop through the shaft.

The ends were not difficult to cinch and tie securely, because Father had done good work in the construction of his shroud. The draw cords at one end were longer than those at the other, and fitted with a two-grip wooden handle that he had carved himself.

The silicon-based lubricant, which formed a slick but seemingly dry sheath on the canvas, came with a guarantee that it was durable and would withstand much friction without wear, though surely the manufacturer had never conceived the use to which I put it. Both arms behind me, with a two-hand grip on the handle, I lurched forward in a crouch. The treated canvas slid well enough across the bricks and then over the stone, but more easily on the concrete. I drew him toward his final rest as if I were a father pulling a young son on a sled, but with the roles reversed as I would rather they were not.

I took forty-five minutes to arrive at the two buckets of metal objects. Later, my arms, shoulders, and back would ache as if I had drawn a wagonload of goods; for the moment, duty and grief together were morphine. I untied the knotted draw cords and opened the tarp just enough to fill it with the first bucket and half of the second.

Father and I had calculated the poundage that might sink the package, not at once, but several yards from shore. Anchorage added to the canvas roll, I secured both ends and set out with it once more, this time traveling little more than a quarter of a mile.

The seven biggest tunnels, the terminal drains in the system, ended at different points along the river. Most of them disgorged their torrents into large catch basins, and not until the water in those storage tanks reached a certain height did it pour over the top onto a stepped spillway and into the river. This delay ensured that all trash heavier than papers and feathers would settle to the bottom of the catch basin rather than be washed into the river.

I brought Father to the open end of one of those enormous drains. The concrete catch basin before us might have been fifty to sixty feet on a side and thirty feet deep. Having been cleaned out since the most recent rain, it was dry now and empty but for snow.

To facilitate maintenance, a wide pierced-steel footbridge led from the nearer wall of the basin to the farther. A blanket of snow covered it, pierced in the same pattern as the steel, like a doily. Crossing would be treacherous, but there were safety railings. Besides, I had no choice but to cross it.

Initially I hesitated, wondering if I should wait until night. But darkfall lay long hours away. Besides, the Street and Sanitation Department workers, who dealt with the catch basins, were on strike, with little chance of anyone being in the vicinity, especially in this weather.

The sky shed itself as heavily as it had on Cathedral Hill, such blinding crystalline thickets that I couldn't see the farther shore, as if snow meant for decades were released today because the world did not have decades left until its end. The river remained ice-free this early in winter, and every boat upon it was a working vessel, not a single pleasure craft among the lot, cruising through gauzy white curtains that half obscured them. I doubted that the crewmen would have the time or the curiosity to wonder about me, if they noticed me at all.

Dragging the shroud across the footbridge, I fell twice, once into the railing, once hard to my knees. At the farther end lay the spillway, a series of steep six-inch-wide steps, as broad as the catch basin itself, leading down to the water's edge.

From this closer vantage point, the river traffic appeared no less obscure than it had been from the greater distance, every vessel brightened by running lights as they would be at night or in fog.

I tried to negotiate the spillway steps while controlling the shroud, for I was pained by the thought of Father's remains making an undignified plunge. Only a third of the way down, however, the package got away from me, slid across the corrugated slope, and slipped into the river with the faintest splash.

My legs began to quiver, as if they would fail me, and I sat on the spillway. I said my good-byes and prayers in a voice that trembled not because of the cold.

Even near its engineered banks, the river offered almost a fathom, and the bed rapidly fell off to accommodate deep-drawing vessels. The tied ends of the tarp were not watertight, and I hoped that it floated out far enough to go unnoticed after it sank.

The shroud washed somewhat farther from shore than I anticipated before it disappeared beneath the waves. The added metal was meant less to sink the package than to keep it down when the body began to decompose and, producing gases, sought the surface, as Father had sought it and dreamed of possessing it all of his sequestered life.

In days to come, in the most fierce of storms, the water would swell and race, and his remains would be shifted by the stronger-than-usual currents, moved farther downstream. At some point, too, the ever-shifting silt of the bottom might deposit layer upon layer atop him, until it buried him *under* the river, as in life he lived under the city that enchanted him.

Through the stillness, snow fell not in skeins but in infinitely layered arabesques, filigree in motion, ornamenting the icy air, of an especially intense white in the dove-gray light of the morning, laying boas on the limbs of leafless trees, ermine collars on the tops of walls, a grace of softness in a hard world. You might have thought it would fall forever, endlessly beautifying all it touched, except for the reminder of the river. When the snowflakes met the undulant water, they ceased to exist.

Everything and everyone we treasured in this world comes to an end. I loved the world not for itself but for the marvelous gift that it was, and my only hope against eventual despair was to love something larger than the world, larger even than a near-infinite sparkling universe full of worlds.

I remained on the spillway, recalling many special moments with Father, until the cold finally bit through my ski mask and my layered clothing. When I got to my feet, a cape of snow fell away from me, as if I were a statue that suddenly came to life.

From there I returned to my windowless rooms, now mine and mine alone. For the subsequent six years, I secretly moved through the city, diminished by solitude, until one night in the central library, I saw a running girl dressed all in black but no less graceful than snow in motion.

45

THE TABLE CLEARED, GWYNETH AND I SAT WITH what remained of our second glasses of wine, and although the rapping in the attic arose briefly twice again, she made no further reference to it as she told me about the night that her father died. She knew how the murder had played out, because Ryan Telford had relished telling her in vivid detail.

Her father's long-standing policy regarding Christmas was to give the household staff paid leave from December 22 through the New Year celebration. Almost a decade earlier, he had cashed out of his real-estate investments and had built an unlikely but successful second career working from home. Although his friends, none of whom Gwyneth could endure meeting, thought his new line of work must give him ample time for leisure, he was busier than ever. Come the holiday season, he preferred to be alone, to treat it as a time of peace, just he and Gwyneth, so that she might have not just the fourth floor, but the entire fine residence to roam without fear of encountering a house manager or maid or cook.

The only visitor anticipated throughout the holiday was J. Ryan Telford, who even then oversaw the renowned collections of the city library and the associated art museum across the street from it. For years, the curator had contracted with Gwyneth's father to catalogue and appraise his amassment of rare first-edition books and works of fine art, a small fraction of which were kept in the residence, the majority in a climate-controlled warehouse. Late on the afternoon of December 22, Telford was expected to deliver a year-end report to the house. When he arrived, he also brought with him a bag of fresh scones from the best bakery in the city and a jar of honey.

From time to time, Gwyneth's father had spoken of donating substantial portions of his acquisitions to institutions that he favored, and recently he had decided that the time for doing so had nearly come. Telford had long feared that his theft of key items in the collections might eventually be discovered; and it seemed that fateful moment would soon arrive.

During the previous two years, to ingratiate himself, Telford pretended to embrace the older man's enthusiasm for exotic honeys, and he learned the lingo of beekeepers and honeymakers. In a conversation some days before he arrived on the doorstep with lethal intent, he extravagantly praised an exotic creamed honey that he claimed to have purchased during a trip to Italy, although he would not reveal the plants from which the bees collected nectar. Arriving that December afternoon, he presented Gwyneth's father with a bottle of the acclaimed ambrosia, from which he'd stripped the label. In a spirit of fun, he challenged his host to identify the unique flavor.

They went at once to the kitchen, where Gwyneth's dad uncapped the honey, breathed deeply of it, put out plates and knives and cups, and set about brewing a pot of tea. While his host was distracted, Telford tore open the bag of scones and placed it in the center of the table, the biscuits spilling from it as if from a cornucopia. Earlier, one scone had been cut in half, spread with another, benign creamed honey, and pressed together again. Telford put that one on his own plate, as if he'd just then split it. He stirred the knife in the honey but didn't use any, and by the time that his host returned with the teapot, the curator sat at the table, ready to eat.

All parts of the oleander plant are supertoxic, including the nectar, and symptoms of poisoning appear as soon as a minute or two after even a minimal dose of the toxin has been swallowed.

Gwyneth's father lavished the creamed honey on his scone, ate half of it with enthusiasm, trying to determine the exotic flavor, and started on the second half when suddenly he broke into a heavy sweat. His face paled, his lips went gray, and he dropped the scone to put one hand to his chest. With a sound that Telford likened to a baby gagging on pureed vegetables, the victim thrust up from his chair. Because oleander is a cardiac stimulator, his heart would have been hammering perhaps as much as two hundred beats per minute. Already finding it difficult to breathe, he collapsed to his knees, and then onto the floor, on his side, where he spasmed helplessly.

Telford finished his own scone and then took his plate to the sink, washed it, dried it, and put it away. He poured his tea down the drain, rinsed and dried the cup, and put that away as well.

On the floor, the victim vomited and died. If he had vomited sooner and emptied himself more completely, he might have survived. But honey's fabled palliative powers and its sweetness helped keep the mass of poisonous quickbread in his gut.

Telford wiped his prints from the handle of the honey knife and, holding it with a paper towel, put it on his dead host's plate. Two scones remained. He wrapped them in the torn bag to take them with him, for they were delicious and would make an excellent late-night snack, but with lemon marmalade instead of honey, which he detested.

From Gwyneth's father, and from a few of the servants, Telford had learned of the daughter with social phobia who lived in seclusion on the fourth floor. And then one day he had seen her when he had been leaving her father's second-floor study after a meeting. She was eleven then, and Goth was not yet her personal style. Head down, holding something to her breast that he couldn't identify, she raced along a hallway and disappeared up a staircase, evidently heading for her high rooms.

She was lithe and quick. *A sprite,* he thought, *a sylph who lives wingless in the air.* She seemed the fairest and most tender girl that he had ever seen, and he wanted her so passionately, so vehemently, that if her father and the household staff had not been present, instead just the two of them, he would have pursued her, dragged her down, and torn the clothes from her. He would have taken her without regard for the consequences.

Although Telford had certain bondage games and minor physical cruelties that he enjoyed administering, he indulged in them only with discreet partners who took pleasure from receiving attentions of that kind. He had never forced himself on a woman, though he had often wanted to do so and had fantasized about rape. He had never been attracted to children before, either; but now he wanted urgently to break both taboos and take the young girl by force.

Alarmed by the intensity of his desire, he restrained himself and managed to let the girl's father escort him from the second floor, downstairs to the front door, without revealing his turbulent state of mind and fierce lust. In the nearly two years that followed, he thought of her often, and in his dreams, she served as his slave.

Telford had already decided to murder Gwyneth's father to ensure against the discovery of rampant larceny when, just a month before the poisoned honey, he saw Gwyneth again. He was waiting for the master of the house in the front drawing room when the girl, now thirteen, passed the open archway, hesitated, glanced at him with the expression of a startled doe, but said nothing and hurried away.

In spite of her Goth style or perhaps because of it, he wanted her more intensely than before. Thereupon he knew that when he fed her father poisoned honey, he would time it to the Christmas season when just she and the old man were in the house, and when the latter lay dead in the kitchen, he would spend a most satisfying night on the fourth floor.

He would have to kill her, of course. But he had always known that he could kill if the reward was great enough. He was a man of considerable sophistication.

Because of the recent ability of the authorities to identify perpetrators by their DNA, he would dispose of her body by taking it to some remote location, drenching it with gasoline, and setting it afire. First, however, he would have to break all of the teeth out of her corpse and keep them to avoid identification through dental records.

The house was in fact a mansion, and it included a garage in which four vehicles were stored. He would load her body in the trunk of her father's Mercedes S600 and drive it away for burning.

After she had been reduced to blackened bones and greasy ashes in the abandoned rock quarry that he'd found well outside the city, he would return the car to the garage. He would go into the house to open the front door and leave it that way, with some object belonging to the girl left on the threshold to prevent the door from closing. He would depart by a side entrance. After an investigation, the police would believe that the highly neurotic and fearful daughter, having found her father dead, fled the house. And when they never found her . . . Well, it was a big and sometimes dangerous city where thirteen-year-old girls, possessing more street smarts than Gwyneth, disappeared with regularity.

The curator was surprised not by his depraved desire or by his capacity for extreme violence, but he was amazed at how quickly and elegantly—and with what cunning detail—he planned the disposal of her corpse. He almost felt as if there might be a second self within him, another and even more confident J. Ryan Telford who had been waiting, perhaps impatiently, for him to recognize their combined potential.

Now, on the night of the murder, Telford went from the kitchen into the house manager's office. He found a desk drawer divided into compartments and devoted to keys: those for the four vehicles, for the front door, and for numerous other locks, all tagged and clearly labeled.

He did not use the elevator, lest he alert Gwyneth, but climbed the stairs to the fourth floor. The landing offered a single door that granted access to her apartment. As quietly as possible, he disengaged the lock, entered a foyer, and closed the door behind him.

Leaving the foyer, Telford found himself in a large drawing room furnished with antiques and emblazoned with at least a score of huge red poinsettias to provide it with the spirit of the season. The girl admired poinsettias, and her father gave her everything he could to compensate for her cloistered existence.

The curator found her on a window seat in her bedroom, back against the niche wall, legs drawn up on the upholstered seat, in full Goth, the cityscape as her backdrop. She was reading a book.

The instant Gwyneth saw him, she knew that something monstrous had happened to her father and that something no less horrific might soon happen to her. She realized that a mere scream would not save her, and that her only chance would be to encourage him to believe that she was even weaker, more shy, and more timid than he thought.

As he approached her, she looked down at the book, as if she were so detached from the world that she didn't understand what his appearance meant, and she pretended to read, although in such a way that he would know it was mere pretense and that she was afraid. He pushed a button on a wall plate and put down the automatic pleated shades that covered the windows beside her. He sat on the window seat near her feet and watched her pretend to read, enjoying her attempt to hide her fear.

After a minute or two, he told her that her father was dead, and he described in detail what he had done and the consequence of a good dose of oleander toxin. Because he wanted so much to see her grief, she grew determined to deny him tears. She failed to have that degree of self-control, and the tears came, although she didn't sob or make any sound. By the thirst in Telford's voice, Gwyneth knew that her tears excited him. She made no effort to blink them away, for they had become a tool with which to manipulate and deceive him.

He didn't touch her yet. From what her father had told him, he knew the anguish that the slightest touch would cause her; therefore, he savored the dread with which she anticipated his hand on her skin.

In fact, when he finished telling her about her father's fate, he began to explain what he was going to do to her, where he would caress her and all of the ways by which he would enter her. "When I'm finished with you, cutie, you'll wonder why a simple touch once offended you, and you'll feel soiled so deeply that there will be no hope of ever being clean again. It'll feel like not just one man violated you, but as if the whole world rubbed up against you and used you."

She didn't need to fake her tremors. The pages of the book rattled in her hands, and she put it down beside her, though she still did not look at him. She crossed her arms over her breasts.

He spoke of a certain pleasure that a girl could give to a man, and he asked her if she had ever dreamed of doing that. He had a list of obscene questions, and he kept pressing them upon her so that it almost felt as if he were touching her.

At first she said nothing, but then a strategy occurred to her. She didn't think her father would have told him more about her than that she suffered from social phobia; and perhaps a member or two of the household staff had given him another few details. She had not yet spoken, and perhaps he knew so little about her that he could be led to assume that an inability to speak was part of her condition. The more neurotic and emotionally disabled he believed her to be, the more convinced he would become of his absolute power over her, and the more likely it would be that he might grow careless.

As Telford continued his salacious monologue, he watched Gwyneth with the sharp stare and hunger of a wolf circling a lamb. Now she responded not merely by cringing and drawing into a huddled posture on the window seat, but also with wordless sounds of misery and tortured apprehension. When he demanded answers to his lewd questions, she strung together half-words and short clusters of syllables that meant nothing, grunts and sputters and thin mewls of distress that might have inspired pity in another man, though Telford had no pity. After a few such exchanges, he arrived at the conclusion that, although she could read, she was incapable of speech, that she was either limited by some physical impediment or by a developmental disability.

Words are the wellspring of the world, and language is the most powerful weapon in the ancient and still unfolding war between truth and lies. Telford stood a foot taller than Gwyneth, weighed twice her hundred pounds; he was bold where she was timid, cruel where she was gentle. When he realized she couldn't speak to plead or to accuse, or to shame him, he was further inflamed by her helplessness. Into his eyes and across his flushed face came an expression so brutish and so carnal, Gwyneth feared that in addition to all the ways that he promised to abuse her, he would at the end of the ordeal tear into her with his teeth.

He no longer called her Gwyneth. He didn't call her "girl" anymore, and he didn't even deign to address her as "you." He had several names for her, all of them coarse, many of them obscene.

At last he ordered her off the window seat and to the bathroom adjoining her bedroom. He said, "I want the nose ring for a souvenir and that red bead on the lip. We'll scrub away all the stupid Goth stuff, so I can see the little girl beneath, the fragile bird that so desperately wants to be a hawk."

With coltish unsteadiness, making thin sounds of distress, Gwyneth preceded him into the bathroom. Step by step, she frantically considered ways to distract him or to tumble him off his feet so that she might have a chance to run, but he was strong and made stronger by his lust, by his profound desire to commit those cruelties and ultimate transgressions about which he had previously fantasized.

In the spacious bathroom, he ordered her to undress. She feared that if she hesitated he would slap her, that the slap would open in him a door to an even darker place than the one his mind currently inhabited, that it would lead to a sudden acceleration of the planned rape and murder. Tears still slid down her face, smearing her Goth makeup, tears for her father, not for herself, and her tremors were uncontrolled. As she began to unbutton her blouse, she turned away from him, facing the vanity, eyes downcast, as if desperately modest.

She heard him pull the drain-control lever that engaged the stopper. She raised her head to look into the mirror above the vanity, not at herself but at what lay behind her, and she saw him in reflection as he leaned over the tub to crank the hot-water faucet. In that posture, he was at last vulnerable. She spun around and shoved him hard. He toppled into the bathtub, crying out in pain as the gushing water scalded him.

The elevator would be far too slow, and if she stumbled and fell as she raced down the stairs, Telford would catch her. He might snare her easily anyway. Darting through the open bathroom door, she heard him floundering out of the tub, and instead of sprinting through the apartment to the front door, she went directly to the nightstand on the right side of her bed, yanked open a drawer, and snatched up the small aerosol can of Mace.

She knew that he was almost upon her. She turned, saw him three steps away, and thumbed a stream of the chemical into his eyes, as her father had instructed. Telford cried out. As if he had collided with a wall, his forward motion became a backward stagger. She seized the advantage, squirting him in the nose and mouth.

Mace causes no permanent injury but is highly effective. Tears burst forth, vision blurs completely, and a kind of blindness-with-light ensues for a few minutes. Inhaled even slightly, it forces the target to struggle for breath, and although he is in no peril, he feels as if he might suffocate.

Even disabled, breathless, unable to see anything but smears of color that melted together without form, Telford swung both arms wildly, frantic to strike a blow or catch a fistful of her hair, or snare her by an article of clothing. She dodged, crouched, scurried away from him, out of the bedroom, through the rest of the apartment, where the delicate poinsettias, against which she brushed, scattered broken scarlet bracts in her wake, just as the promise of the season now lay broken beyond repair.

She descended the stairs two at a time, crashing to each landing with both feet, and came off the sixth flight into the foyer without once daring to look back. She hurried out into the early night, where the air was as cold and moist as that in an icehouse, although the settled soot and the hard edges of the city were not yet masked by the first snow.

Four doors to the east stood the Billingham mansion, equal to—though more pretentious than—her father's house. The front steps were flanked by broad stone walls on which rested two massive carved-stone lions in the position of the Sphinx, heads raised and faces solemn, blank eyes gazing toward the street not as if alert for prey, but as if watching for the first rough beasts of Armageddon.

The Billinghams, known to her by their family name but never glimpsed, were on an extended stay in Europe and the street swarmed with traffic; therefore, Gwyneth made no attempt to cross the four busy lanes, but instead ran to the watchful lions. The flanking lime-stone walls diminished as the stairs ascended, and she scrambled onto the farther of the two, lying atop the polished-granite cap, be-side the lion, which was at least twice her size. She eased her head forward to look past the big cat's chest, west toward her father's house.

Never did she consider screaming for help, because whoever might respond to her would want to protect her or console her, and their natural inclination would be to reach out, to take her hand or pat her shoulder or put an arm around her, and she could not tolerate being touched. They would ask questions that she must answer. She didn't wish to hear their voices, because then her required response would allow them to hear hers. She was loath to share with strangers any part of her true self, not even her voice, which she had never shared with her father's household staff.

As she lay belly-down, the cold granite leached away her body heat. She was not dressed for the out-of-doors, and her tremors of fear quickly became violent shudders.

After a few minutes, peering past the lion that sheltered her, Gwyneth saw Telford exit her father's house and descend the front stairs. He wore his overcoat and carried a white bundle that must have been the scones in the bag that might have incriminated him in some way if he left it behind. To her dismay, he turned toward her.

She could tell that his vision, while improved, was not normal, because he proceeded like a man in no hurry, his face thrust forward as if in doubt of the way before him. When he passed a lamppost, he turned his head from it, the light too bright for his stinging, dilated eyes.

As Telford approached, his breath steamed from him as if he were a dragon bespelled into the form of a man. Gwyneth *knew*, in passing, he would instinctively look to his left and up, and in spite of his compromised vision and the night shadows in which she was lying, he would see her. What she *knew* proved to be only what she feared, and the curator went past, oblivious of her, cursing softly in a voice strained by fear.

Two houses farther east, he got into a car parked at the curb. Over the rush of traffic in the street, Gwyneth couldn't hear the engine start, but a graveyard's worth of ghosts plumed up from the tailpipe, feathering away among the skeletal branches of an overhanging tree.

Telford's Cadillac faced toward the girl, but from her higher position, the intervening limbs of another tree obscured most of his windshield, and she could not see him behind the steering wheel. She felt certain that she had escaped him for the night, but she remained prostrate and motionless in the dark of the lion.

Although surely he had splashed cold water in his eyes to dilute the Mace and though he must have been anxious to be gone, he waited another five minutes before gaining enough confidence in his vision to pull out from the curb into the street. He drove to the end of the block and turned south on the avenue.

The girl hurried home and locked the front door behind her. She ventured to the kitchen doorway to confirm her father's death, and at the first glimpse of his lifeless face, she turned from him, unable to endure the sight. She could have drowned in a black sea of grief, but such surrender would have dishonored her father, who believed in perseverance in the face of any loss or misfortune. She fled to the fourth floor.

Telford would expect her to dial 911 to report a murder, but she would never make that call. Uniformed officers, detectives, personnel from the coroner's office, reporters, and unknowable others would descend upon her, besiege her, a plague of locusts stripping her of privacy and hope. Their stares relentlessly upon her, their questions requiring a thousand answers, all those hands reaching to reassure her, to take her arm when her knees grew weak, technicians gathering evidence in her rooms, perhaps a trip to a hospital to be examined for injury and to assess her emotional condition: That prospect was intolerable. She would be destroyed by it.

Furthermore, if Telford had been as careful eliminating evidence of his presence as he'd claimed, nothing could link him to the death of her father. In her rooms, he might have left fingerprints only on the entry door and the bathtub fixtures. Even bleary-eyed and frantic to leave before authorities arrived, he would have taken time to wipe those surfaces. If he proved to be as methodical as she expected, he had established an alibi for the hours he had meant to spend in their house. In the end, wouldn't it be her word against his? And were the police likely to believe a respectable curator or a Goth-obsessed, neurotic thirteen-year-old girl with acute social phobia?

Gwyneth packed a few essentials in a satchel belonging to her father. Leaving the front door standing open, she left the house and made her way to the nearest of the eight apartments that, with considerable foresight, her father had prepared for her if he should die.

Safe for the moment, she called Teague Hanlon and told him all that had happened. He wanted to call the police, but when he listened to her reasons for not doing so, he understood that relying on the usual authorities would lead to her destruction, not to Telford's imprisonment.

"If Telford is ever brought to justice," she told Hanlon, "I'm the one who will have to gather the evidence against him, in my own way and in my own good time. I have lost so much. The kindest father in the world. I will never relent. Never."

46

ALTHOUGH OUR WINE WAS FINISHED BEFORE HER story, the candles were a long way from guttering, and they blued the darkness of the dining area.

I said, "So it was declared an accidental death."

"Death by contaminated honey, yes."

"But weren't the police looking for you?"

"Not actively. An appeal was made to the public, through local TV and newspapers, asking anyone who saw this lost and afflicted girl to report her whereabouts to the police. But it was a picture of me with my father, taken a year earlier, before my Goth look, the only photograph of me since I was an infant, and of course I no longer much resembled that girl."

"The only photograph of you in all that time?"

"If you allow your picture to be taken, you don't know who might see it a month from now, a year. Strangers looking at your photo, staring at you, *studying* you . . . It's not as awful as being in the presence of strangers, with them touching and talking to you and expecting you to reply. But it's bad enough. I can barely tolerate the thought of it."

We shared a minute of silence.

Considering her psychological problems and the limitations they imposed on her, considering that I could venture from my underground haven only in the quietest hours of the night, cloaked and hooded and at risk of being murdered on sight, our encounter and the way that our friendship continued to unfold seemed miraculous. I yearned for more than friendship, but I understood that love, given and received, was impossible. Even an imperfect princess could be awakened to the fullness of life only by a kiss from a genuine prince, not by such as I. In spite of my yearnings, I remained satisfied not to pursue the impossible and to settle for the miraculous. Now my greatest fear was that we might lose what we had together and go our separate ways, or be separated by death.

At last I said, "But in time, the court might declare you dead, and then what will happen to the trusts that support you?"

"I remained in seclusion for three months, never once going out, grieving Daddy, in touch with no one but Teague Hanlon. At the end of that period, he told the authorities that I had found my way to him, that as my guardian, with my approval, he'd placed me in a sanatorium in a quiet country setting, so that I could rest, get psychological counseling, and learn either to overcome my social phobia or to live better with it."

"On the phone, Telford said you were in a sanatorium."

"And so he thought all these years. Until last night."

"And the authorities believed Mr. Hanlon?"

"Of course. Not just because he was my guardian, but because of who he is."

"And who is he?"

Although I could not see her face in the blue-tinted dark, I suspected that she was smiling when she said, "My guardian," and thereby made it clear that, regardless of all that she had shared with me, some of her secrets were still hers alone.

She said, "I had no close relatives, only one friend, who was also my guardian, so there was little risk of an advocate stepping forth to ask that, in my interest, the court investigate my current condition and treatment. Besides, the bureaucracy in this city is so indifferent that Child Protective Services as often as not assigns kids to temporary homes where they're beaten or sexually abused, or overdrugged for ADHD until the clean sharp edges are worn off their souls, and everyone knows it. No one would think a foster home in this town is automatically superior to an expensive asylum."

After a brief silence, I said, "I'm sorry you had to see your father dead, in the condition that he was."

"I thought I turned away too quickly for the image to stay in my memory. But it remains. Vivid and terrible. There will never be any forgetting it."

Into my mind's eye came an image of my father's broken face, one eye obscured by blood pooling in the socket.

She pushed her chair back from the table and got to her feet. "I promised to play the piano for you."

I followed her into the living room, where the candles flickered in red-glass cups, though the ambience was no less melancholy than it had been under the influence of blue glass.

When I stood beside the bench on which she sat to play, Gwyneth said, "Don't crowd me, Addison. Since Daddy died, in order to play well, I have to feel that I'm playing just for me and him. Go sit and leave me to it."

Another candle glowed on the small table beside an armchair, and I settled there to listen.

With her back to me, she said, " 'Sonata quasi una fantasia,' in C-sharp minor."

The moment that Gwyneth began to play, I recognized Beethoven's "Moonlight Sonata," and I came to my feet, shaken, because of all the music that Father and I had listened to on our CD player, this was the one piece that moved us equally, that we could never hear too often. It is music that speaks to the deepest reaches of your soul, and you are lifted higher, ever higher, by the adagio, in my opinion more so even than in any of the masses that Beethoven composed.

I went to the wall of windows and stood gazing out at the snow, which fell no less heavily than before. The wind had abated somewhat and had become capricious, though lazily so. The flakes were no longer driven at an angle through the street. Instead, they gathered into half-formed figures that dissolved a moment after they took shape, an eternal procession of spirits, settling softly to the Earth like crystalized notes of music, bringing the melodies of a higher sphere.

The title "Moonlight Sonata" had not been Beethoven's, but had been appended to the piece by a friend to whom the music brought to mind the beauties of Lake Lucerne as one glided across the water in a boat, by moonlight.

In the night, through the snow, came three Clears, the same that earlier I had seen on the roofs of buildings across the street, two men and a woman, she dressed in hospital whites and they in hospital blues. As Clears sometimes do, these three didn't merely walk into view, but glided through the air, standing upright, as if being flown by wires in a stage production.

Two of them touched down in the street and stood looking this way and that, but the woman floated to the windows, as if drawn by the music. When she passed through those panes, a few feet to the right of me, no glass shattered. She walked now as if gravity limited her, when obviously it did not, and as she crossed the room, she was a lamp from which darkness shrank before creeping back in her wake. She stepped out of the living room, through the dining area, through the open archway to the kitchen, where she moved out of sight. She must have gone into other rooms, because shortly she returned, not by a door, but manifested out of lath and plaster, passing through a wall as easily as I could stroll through curtains of fog.

The Clear went to the piano and stood gazing down at Gwyneth, neither smiling nor frowning, watching with calm interest. The girl wasn't aware of being observed, nor could she see the soft glow of the Clear, which fell upon her and across part of the keyboard. She played as if only I and the memory of her father were with her.

After a moment, the visitor turned from the piano and walked toward me. Obeying Father's admonition, I looked out of the window, avoiding her eyes. I imagined that meeting her stare might transform me as, in classic mythology, meeting the stare of Medusa could turn flesh to stone. Father had never explained what would happen to me if I insisted on being eye-to-eye with a Clear, but he had been wise in all things, and I had no reason to doubt his advice.

The radiance of the Clear settled upon me and silvered the windowpane. I was aware of her face mirrored in the glass as she looked over my right shoulder, but I dared not meet the eyes even in reflection. After a hesitation, she passed through me, through the window, into the night, and I thought that perhaps she lived in a different dimension from mine and was capable of exploring this world, though I could not cross into hers.

She drifted down through the falling snow and joined her two companions. They walked along the street in the direction that the man and dog had gone earlier.

The sonata came to an end, but Gwyneth must not have wanted praise for her playing. After the briefest silence, in the thrall that follows the final note of any soul-felt piece of music, she brought forth another melody from the keyboard. As quickly as I had recognized "Moonlight Sonata," I knew this piece as well, but not its title. These were the beautiful but sad strains that, on certain nights, found their way into my windowless rooms and haunted me, the music for which I'd never been able to identify a source, as though it issued from another world invisible.

I crossed the room and stood behind and to one side of her, still at a respectful distance, so that she could continue to imagine she was playing only for herself and her lost father, but near enough that I could *feel* the music as well as hear it. Music is sound, sound consists of vibrations in the air, and these particular vibrations resonated with the marrow in my bones, with the tissues of my heart.

When Gwyneth finished, she sat with her head bowed, her hands resting on the keyslip, her face blushed by trembling candlelight.

She said nothing. I knew that I should give her silence as long as she wanted it, but I asked in a whisper, "What was that music?"

"The first was Beethoven."

"Yes, I know. 'Moonlight Sonata.' But the second?"

"It's my own composition. I wrote it in the week after my father died. It's an expression of the pain . . . the pain of losing him."

"It's beautiful. I didn't know you had such great talent."

"Don't be so awed. It's just a thing I can do. A gift. It's not work to me. I didn't earn it."

"You must have recorded the piece you just played."

She shook her head. "No. It's music only for him and me. And, this time at least, for you."

"But I've heard it before."

"You can't have."

As she began to play it again, this time pianissimo, I said, "But I have heard it many times. In my rooms under the city. And I can never trace it to a source."

I stood in silence as she played the piece through to the end. The last note traveled away from us like a slow bird floating higher on a warm current of air.

After a silence, I said, "I really do hear it some nights."

"I believe you."

"But if you've never recorded it and no one else ever has . . ."

"Nevertheless, you've heard it. I don't know how. But I think I might know why."

I didn't quite follow the logic of not-how-but-why, and yet I asked, "Why?"

At first she replied with silence, but then: "I don't want to say—and be wrong. I don't want to hope for the wrong thing."

Her cell phone rang. She put it on SPEAKER. "Hello?"

All silken tones had been washed from the voice by bad whiskey, and the words came rough and low, as if spoken through a stone-filled craw. "Miss Gwyneth, it's me."

"Is something wrong, Simon?"

"Some guys they're lookin' for you."

"What guys?"

"Neighbors at two of your apartments called me, said these guys came around askin' about you. Your neighbors they didn't much like the look of these guys, thought I should know."

"My neighbors hardly ever see me come and go. I don't know them, Simon, so how do *you* know them?"

"Well, Miss Gwyneth, they're friendly, and I gave 'em my number in case, you know, there was ever a plumbin' leak or somethin' when you weren't in residence."

"The neighbors have the number of the property-management company, and that's all they need. Simon, I told you never to talk about me to anyone."

Her tone of disappointment seemed to distress him. "No, no, I never did. I never talked about you. I told 'em the other name, not your real one, and all we talked about was stuff, you know, just this and that, the way people do."

She got to her feet. "But you gave them your phone number. Simon, you've got to get out of there right away."

"Out of here? Out of my nice little place? Where would I go?"

"Anywhere. Those men will be coming for you."

"But, Miss Gwyneth, those neighbors, they have just my phone number, not my address or even my last name."

"The men who'll be coming for you have connections, friends in high places, resources. They'll find you eventually."

"But where would I go? I don't have anyplace else to go."

"Go to my guardian. I'll call him and tell him to expect you."

"Even in good weather that's too far, Miss Gwyneth. In this blizzard, it's impossible far, I mean for a man my age."

"You still don't drive?"

"My history, they'll never give me a license, Miss Gwyneth. Who needs to drive in the city anyway? I got my bicycle and taxis, I do all right, but you can't bike in deep snow, and no taxi is comin' out in this storm."

She hesitated, and then said, "I'll come for you, Simon. I'll drive you."

"If those guys come around here, I won't tell them the littlest thing. Not even the littlest. You know I won't, Miss Gwyneth. I'd die first."

"I know, Simon. But I don't want you to die, and it might come to that. I'll be there in half an hour."

"Bless you, Miss Gwyneth, I'm sorry to be trouble to you. You're an angel, and I didn't mean for anythin' like this."

"I know you didn't, Simon. Half an hour. Okay?"

"Okay."

She terminated the call. "Telford and his kind pass for human but they're animals."

"They're not animals," I said. "Animals kill only what they need to feed themselves. Animals suffer but they cast no blame for their suffering, and they never envy. Who is Simon?"

"A man who almost lost his soul but found it again. Come on."

47

THE FIRST TIME I SAW REAL DOGS, NOT JUST PICTURES of them, I was eight years old and recently banished by my mother from our house.

Between the church where I was almost beaten and the truck stop where I stowed away aboard a flatbed, I passed through woods alive with whip-poor-wills and tree frogs, crossed wild meadows where flocks of yellow butterflies swarmed up like fallen petals of the sun to which they sought return, before I came upon kept land encircled by a half-collapsed split-rail fence, a pasture where no live-stock grazed.

Towering masses of clouds hung low and irregularly across the sky, the electric-blue of late afternoon visible between them. The westering sun flamed across the upper slopes of the cloud moun-tains, which were kettle-gray underneath, but golden at their sum-mits. The waning day lay between storm and serenity, in an hour of indecision when any scenario might play out.

I vaulted the rail fence and began to hike the field. I had covered perhaps a quarter of it when two dogs came bounding through the grass from my left. One was a German shepherd, the other a mix of shepherd and perhaps a hound of some kind.

Because dogs were the most domesticated species on the planet, I assumed that they wouldn't be as peaceable as the wild animals of the woods in which I had grown up. Bonded as dogs were to people, surely they shared the prejudices of them. I expected to be attacked and left to bleed to death as they circled and snarled their hatred.

I raced through the grass, though not at a pace that defeated dogs. When they caught up with me, they didn't lunge, but instead paralleled me, one on each side, grinning foolishly, tails wagging.

I stopped running, concerned that my fear might be conveyed to them, but I kept moving at a walk. They loped ahead of me, gamboling together, play-biting, tumbling, springing to their feet once more. I feared them still, but it was a delight to watch them frolic.

When I was halfway across the field, they returned, panting, and sniffing. They smelled the church-picnic ham in my backpack. I had eaten two slices for breakfast, but one remained in a side compartment of the pack, wrapped in aluminum foil.

I thought perhaps dogs might after all be as amenable as the animals of the woods. Those creatures had been more of a family than my troubled mother. Without taking off the backpack, I reached the zipper of the side compartment in which I'd stowed the ham. I unwrapped it, tore it into pieces, and fed it to the dogs.

They had perfect manners, each waiting patiently as I gave the other a chunk of ham, back and forth, until the meat was gone. They didn't snap the morsels from my fingers, but took them with soft mouths. When I said, "No more," they didn't insist on further treats.

Just then a voice called out, "They won't bite. They're good old boys."

Fifty or sixty yards away, a man wearing a shooter's jacket with satchel pockets ambled toward me, carrying a shotgun across the crook of his left arm. In spite of the weapon, he seemed unthreatening, but that would change when he drew closer and saw my face under the hood.

I pulled my scarf up to my eyes and sprinted, expecting a warning shot or a command to the dogs that would set them upon me. Neither came. I leaped the collapsed fence and fled into more woods.

The dogs accompanied me in a spirit of adventure. I shooed them away, but they would not go. They weren't seeking more food, and by their demeanor I thought I understood. I dropped to one knee and with my gloved hands rubbed behind their ears and scratched beneath their chins. I told them that they must go at once, before their master thought I might steal them. Just then, he called out, much closer than before. Upon my further insistence, the dogs turned away and re-treated to the pasture, though they went with their tails between their legs, looking back repeatedly, as if chastened by my dismissal.

Years later, after other experiences with dogs, I wondered if their species were shaped and charmed to serve as four-legged guides able to assist in leading humanity back to our first—and lost—home. By the example of their joy and humility, by wanting nothing more than food and play and love, by the deep satisfaction that they take from those humble things, they belie all creeds of power and fame. Al-though they have the teeth to tear, it is by swish of tail and yearning eyes that they most easily get what they want.

And as it happened, in a critical hour, dogs did prove to be all that I imagined and more.

48

THE CITY STEADILY SUCCUMBED TO THE BLIZZARD, but Gwyneth did not. The chain-wrapped winter tires churned through soft powder and spat it out in compacted wads. Snow fell at nearly two inches an hour, and already more than half a foot mantled the ground, but she still thought this was a perfect night for speed, pressing the Land Rover faster, faster, making it slalom around a few stalled vehicles that busy tow trucks had not yet snared, taking corners as if the danger of tipping and rolling were obviated by some ruling she had won in court against the laws of physics.

Even as young as I was, I remembered a time when the plows were quick into the streets and the cleanup began even as the storm was still rising toward its peak. These days, judging by the delay in response, you might have thought the city relied, as in an earlier century, on brigades of shovelers who needed time to bundle against the cold and fortify themselves with spirits before reporting, and on wagon sleds and dray horses to haul away the accumulation.

Simon, to whose rescue we were riding, turned out to be the homeless man who, in search of redeemable soda cans to cash in for whiskey money, found the badly beaten, naked little girl in the Dumpster. Decades before that discovery, he had been a young artist whose career was taking off. But something about success scared him so much that, with alcohol as his copilot and a tendency to burn business relationships as if they were slips of a magician's flash paper, he managed to stall out and crash so spectacularly that in one year he went from sleeping in a penthouse to passing his nights in a bedroll under bridges.

After his breakdown in the doughnut shop, where he brought the battered child, and after he was released from the hospital, he gave up alcohol overnight, without the help of drugs or counseling, or a twelve-step program. Lifting a glass or a bottle of the old poison to his lips, he recoiled from the stench of it, and when he tried to sip it, invariably he vomited. The smell and taste were as foul to him as the malodor in the Dumpster. Each time that he tried to drink, he was forced to confront the realization, which he'd made in the hospital, that it was not merely weak but also evil to throw away your life when so many had their lives or the promise of their future taken from them by cruel people or by the brutal forces of nature.

He lived, sober and industrious, in an eccentric neighborhood, an enclave of picturesque 1920s-era bungalows on a loop of two-lane called John Ogilvie Way, in the southeast borough, near the river.

During the first half of the nineteenth century, the city rang with more harmonies than discords, and everywhere there were things to please the eye. But during decades when the government turned to expert planners, much of the past was considered déclassé, if not abhorrent. Architecture that raised in the mind an appreciation of history was deemed embarrassing because much of that history was considered unfortunate, if not shameful. No place could be made for what was quaint or charming or noble. Anything that might be seen as the work of sentimental primitives was torn down and replaced by massive buildings seemingly inspired by Soviet apartment blocks and by forests of steel-and-glass office towers that blazed in daylight as if they were more glorious than the sun that shed it.

The bungalows of John Ogilvie Way became popular with painters, sculptors, and ceramics artists who lived in them and used them also as their personal galleries. The neighborhood survived long enough to become a tourist attraction, a cultural asset about which the city boasted. Because contemporary art is said to be about the future and progress, about abstraction and the impossibility of knowing truth, it is embraced not just by genuine aficionados but also by those who despise the past. So Ogilvie Way remained, encircled by structures that, in their bold expressions of brute power and command, looked as if they were from a parallel world in which Hitler triumphed.

In appreciation of Simon having saved the nameless girl, Gwyneth had bought a house in this enclave so that he could live there rent-free and seek again to explore his talent. It was a spacious dwelling in spite of being a bungalow, with a deep front porch and elements of

Craftsman style. Lights were on in all its windows. She drove a block past Simon's house and parked on the farther side of the street.

We got out of the Rover.

"We can't go directly to the front door," she said.

"Why not?"

"Have to scout the place in case they found him. If something's happened to Simon, I'll never forgive myself. I said I'd be here in half an hour, and I wasn't."

Consulting my Rolex, I said, "Thirty-five minutes is pretty close. Five minutes can't have made a difference."

"Something tells me that it did."

Even past eleven o'clock at night, lights shone in the windows of nearly all the bungalows. I supposed that artists, who didn't have to live by the hours of a standard business day, might be most creative when the rest of the world began to grow quiet, that with their talent might come circadian rhythms different from those of us who lacked their particular gifts.

The street reminded me of one of those winter paintings by Thomas Kinkade, charming houses and cobbled walkways and evergreens draped with snow as glamorous as bejeweled ermine, the whole infused with warm light expressed in unexpected but convincing ways. The scene was steeped in magic, but magic has two forms—light and dark.

From a pocket of her coat, Gwyneth withdrew a small can of Mace and handed it to me. From another pocket, she took her close-contact Taser.

We crossed the street and passed through the narrow side yard of the dark bungalow next door to Simon's, into that backyard. A stately monastic evergreen of some kind rose to sixty feet, providing us with a shadowed and sheltered observation point under the hood and habit of its snow-laden boughs.

Simon's house lay quiet in the white downpour, plucked by this weaker and fitful wind but unmoved, so snug that it seemed to welcome drifts that might bury it and insulate it further from the world. No shadows moved beyond the lighted windows.

The only strangeness was a pale fan of light that repeatedly arced wide and then contracted across the back porch, irregular in its timing, not accompanied by any sound. When we moved out from the tree, toward the low garden wall that separated the properties, we saw that the light came from the house and that it was measured out by an open door, which again and again eased almost shut only to be blown open each time by the changeable wind.

"Not good," Gwyneth said.

We crossed the garden wall, the yard, and ascended the steps with a wary urgency. On the porch, we heard a voice inside, but it was that of an announcer backed by music and must have come from a television.

With her usual daring, Gwyneth crossed the threshold. Although the only two residences I had ever entered in the city were both hers, and although this bungalow felt like a trap, I followed her without hesitation.

"Close the door," she whispered.

I wondered if that would prove wise, but I closed it quietly.

We were in an open space, with a small kitchen to the left and to the right a larger area that might have been intended as a family room. Simon evidently lived largely in this back section of the bungalow, for it was furnished with a bed, two armchairs with small tables, an old chifforobe, and a wall-mounted TV currently tuned to a news program. These quarters were nearly as modest as my three rooms, but I supposed that to a man who had lived on the streets and who had slept under bridges for thirty years, the accommodations seemed palatial.

On the TV, an enormous cruise ship lay at anchor near the mouth of a harbor, and the newsreader said something about the authorities denying the captain the right to dock.

Far beneath the city, under countless tons of concrete and steel, radio waves or microwaves could not be received. During my adventures aboveground, every time I had a glimpse of television, it intrigued me. I always reminded myself, however, that Father said we were better off without TV, that it was an instrument of change that could make us into people we would not like to be.

My mother had no television in her remote house, and yet she had become less than she wanted to be. Perhaps she watched a lot of TV as a child in her parents' home and everywhere else that she lived before she had gone to the mountain house. There was so much that I didn't know, that I might never know, and many things that I didn't understand about the psychology of those people who lived their lives openly aboveground.

Anyway, Simon's quarters were essentially a studio apartment, which he kept spotless. No grime. No dust. As a consequence, the broken vase and the smear of blood on the blond-wood floor were the visual equivalent of a shout.

49

SHE WAS A GIRL WHO OPENED DOORS, NOT BECAUSE she wanted to open them, but because she knew that she needed to open them.

The chocolate-brown paneled door between Simon's living quarters and the other rooms of the bungalow seemed like a monolith to me, a formidable slab beyond which lay something to be feared, either past or future violence. If the choice had been mine, I might have left right then; but the decision was Gwyneth's.

The door opened to a short hallway. To the left were a bath and a room used for storage, both doors open and lights softly aglow. To the right lay the studio in which Simon created his works. No one, dead or alive, waited for us in those spaces.

At the end of the hall, we entered a gallery that had once been two rooms. Fixed to the rafters of the open-beam ceiling, pin spots brightened walls that were enriched by oil paintings that astonished and amazed, appealing equally to emotion and intellect. He excelled at figurative painting, both portraits of single individuals shown from head to foot and groups of people engaged in communal activities in a variety of exquisitely detailed and rendered locations.

Gwyneth said, "They've taken him."

"Where?"

"Not to Telford's apartment, not anywhere they would be seen with him. They think they can carve out of him the address of my ninth apartment."

"You said he doesn't know where it is."

"He doesn't. In fact, he doesn't even know it exists."

"What can he tell them?"

"Nothing. And even if he knew, he wouldn't tell them. Clearly, he didn't tell them I was coming here to take him someplace safe, or they would just have waited for us."

"What will happen to him?" I asked.

For a moment forgetting the terms of our relationship, she looked at me, and an instant before our eyes met, I bowed my head, not willing to trust that my ski mask would be sufficient to ensure against her sudden and vehement rejection.

She switched off the pin spots, leaving the gallery faintly illuminated by the inspill of hallway light, and she went to a window to stare out at the snowy night.

Although I didn't know Simon except through Gwyneth and through his stunning paintings on the surrounding walls, I felt we must do something. I repeated my question: "What will happen to him?"

"They'll torture him, Addison. And when he gives them nothing, they'll have to kill him."

"All just to get to you?"

"I told you, Telford has stolen millions. And there are many millions more to steal from the warehoused collections of the museum and the library, items that won't be missed for years, especially considering that Telford controls the inventory logs. And he alone decides what paintings, sculptures, rare books, and illuminated manuscripts will be taken out of storage to be featured in special shows. So he won't be caught easily, as he might be if someone else had that power."

I didn't know what to say or do. I was a creature from the deep dark, an outsider who had known but one friend, Father, in the past eighteen years, and no friend at all since he died. I had thought that, with Gwyneth, in spite of her social phobia, I was learning how people were with one another, how they acted and reacted and interacted, what they said and how they said it, what they wanted, what they hoped for—more than I could learn from books alone. I thought that I might eventually discover, through her, how people arrived, if they ever did, at an understanding of the *why* of their lives, because the why of mine weighed heavily on me and seemed unanswerable.

But if I had learned anything in the past twenty-four hours, it wasn't knowledge that I yet understood how to use. I didn't know what to say or do. I didn't know. I just didn't.

I couldn't hear her crying. She stood there as quiet as the snow falling in the light of the streetlamps, yet I was certain that she wept. Tears had no scent, as far as I knew, but my five senses were not the instruments by which I became aware of her grief, nor was it merely intuition, but instead a perception more profound, one that I couldn't name.

If I had been allowed to touch this sweet girl, I would have put my arms around her. In her current mood, however, with her emotions raw, she might not just recoil from a touch, but might instead fling herself away from it as if she'd taken an electric shock. And then my violation of the rules surely would have opened a gulf between us that could not be bridged.

She turned from the windows, crossed the gallery. "Come on."

"What are we going to do?"

"I don't know."

I hurried after her along the hallway. "Where are we going?"

"I don't know."

We left the rest of the lights on, the television as well, and we stepped out of the kitchen onto the back porch as the network newsreader said, "—to our reporter Jeffrey Stockwell in Mumbai, India."

If possible, the snow fell heavier than before, as if the sky were emptying itself, so that when the last clouds shed all their substance, there would be nothing above us but blackness, no moon or stars, no sun in the morning. Right now, all was erratic wind and whirling snow, a beautiful chaos.

As we approached the Land Rover, Gwyneth said, "Death is here tonight. Not just with Simon. Death is with us. Do you feel him?"

I didn't answer, because the answer wouldn't have heartened her.

Once again, after six years, I had something to lose, and my fear was great.

50

THE NIGHT OF LIGHTNING, THE SKY ON FIRE, WHEN we stood exposed and survived . . .

During our time together, Father and I explored the city in many fierce storms, not just the one in which a dying man gave me a gold watch. On a night in July, in my sixteenth year, the heavens opened to release a sea, and we went abroad in our high boots, black hooded raincoats, and ski masks. We splashed through torrents and across flooded streets, as if we were mariners washed overboard but, by some sorcery, able to walk on water in search of our ship.

We stood in the great park, which the city surrounded, and all that would be warm and green under the sun was cold and black. The lamplight along the winding walkways silvered the rain and the faint low mist created when the droplets dashed themselves apart on the pavement. Those serpentine paths withered away past shrubs and trees, milky and vaporous before they turned out of sight. On that night, the pathways seemed mysterious and promised to lead to a revelation, but we knew them to their fullest lengths, and they did not lead anywhere except elsewhere in the park.

So near that the crash of thunder came simultaneously, a great blazing bolt of lightning sheared the sky above the mown meadow in which we stood, angled eastward, and struck the spire—which was a lightning rod—on the roof of a high-rise across the street from the park. The thousand lights of the building fluttered but did not go out, and I was certain that for a moment the spire had glowed red.

I was very afraid and wanted to take shelter, but Father assured me that we wouldn't be taken by lightning, that no storm would finish us. If we were to die short of old age, the killing blows would come from weapons wielded by the hands of our fellow citizens. Although I did not believe that we enjoyed any dispensation from Nature's rage, I reined in my fear as best I could and stood beside him, trusting in his wisdom.

The black shell of the sky cracked again and again, and some of the fissures zigzagged toward farther targets that we couldn't see, while others seemed to leap from point to point in the heavens, as if there were gods who warred with one another.

Between cannonades of thunder, Father spoke of the power of nature: each storm bolt as hot as the molten sun, earthquakes that brought down buildings as if they were as fragile as termite mounds, tornadoes, hurricanes, tsunamis. "Nature is an exquisite machine that is never violent except when contending forces within it need to be rebalanced. And then the violence is nearly always short-lived, a day or two of storm, ten minutes of tsunami, a minute for tectonic plates to shift and accommodate each other. Nature doesn't make war for years on end, and she has no malice."

Humankind, on the other hand . . . Well, that was a darker story. Adam and Eve, he said, hadn't sought forbidden knowledge so much as they sought power, the power to be as gods. Great power could be a beautiful thing when men and women who had it were inclined to use it wisely and with kindness. But few were so inclined. When a leader used his power over the ruled for the purpose of settling scores and inflating his self-esteem, for remaking society according to his own grand designs, class warfare and genocide ensued.

I didn't know his purpose in telling me this, and as I started to ask his meaning, one of the last bolts of the fierce display split a giant oak a hundred feet from us. Flames spurted out of the cleaved trunk, as if the core of the tree had always been molten but contained. Half the oak pulled up steaming roots and toppled, but the other half stood defiant, and the deluge quickly put out the fire.

When the pyrotechnics concluded and the sky brought forth only rain, Father said, "When men in power decide that things need to be rebalanced at any cost, the violence is never brief and never really directed solely at the imbalance that supposedly inspired it. The rule of law becomes the rule of violence. Revenge becomes a synonym for justice. No city is safe from such horror, no nation, no time in all of history. Be ready to recognize the moment. Be always ready."

I had many questions for him, but he would not answer them. He was finished with the subject, which clearly distressed him. He never spoke of it again in the remaining four years that we were together.

Whenever I looked back on that night and considered what Father had said, I sometimes thought he knew or suspected something that he was loath to share even with me. Perhaps in a dream or in a moment of clarity close to clairvoyance, he had discerned the shape of things to come, and had been in awe of the supreme grandness or the terrible power of those events, to the extent that he could not speak of them, but only hope that he had not in fact seen clearly.

51

GWYNETH PILOTED THE LAND ROVER AS IF SHE WERE a Valkyrie, from Viking lore, whose wings had been clipped, as if she needed urgently to find the fallen warrior assigned to her before he died and, in the moment when his soul emerged from his body, *drive* his spirit to Valhalla. Earlier she had seemed reckless behind the wheel. But now, though she drove faster and took corners more sharply than before, she seemed not heedless and not even imprudent, but shrewd, as if she knew where she was going and why, though her route seemed random as she sometimes doubled back upon it.

In our pell-mell plunge through the city to Ogilvie Way, she had been motivated by fear for Simon, but now the flame in her was anger, not focused on Telford and his associates, but on herself, for having been too late to the artist's bungalow. She was angry, not with Simon, but again with herself for having failed to see that when he rebuilt his life, he'd be proud of his recovery and of her faith in him, that he would be pleased to be regarded by her neighbors as someone who had been entrusted with her keys, and would thus endanger himself. Such a thing as righteous anger exists, especially but not always when it is directed at oneself.

I was distressed, however, by the *extent* to which Gwyneth blamed herself. To me and for all time, in all matters that might arise, she would always be blameless, for I knew the purity of her heart.

Nothing that I could say would induce her to accuse herself less bitterly, so that for the moment I was merely along for the ride—and quite a ride it was. We slalomed around more stalled vehicles than before, tested drifts sloping out from parked vehicles, drove on the sidewalk along a cross street where two SUVs had collided and were blocking the way. When the drivers of city plows sounded their horns, admonishing her to cut her speed, she only blew the Rover's horn in return and eased down farther on the accelerator, churning through the all-but-deserted snow-choked avenues.

Although her route seemed impromptu, I knew that it was taken with purpose, because a few times she slowed, stopped, and considered a residence or a business, as if this might be a place where Simon had been taken. Then she either shook her head or muttered something under her breath, and we were away again, the tire chains softly burring through compacted snow, louder on the ever-fewer occasions when they bit down to pavement.

"Why would he have a partner?" Gwyneth asked. "He doesn't need anyone to help him steal these things. He has easy access. And all kinds of ways to conceal the theft. Why share with a partner?"

I didn't think the question had been addressed to me; she was clearly thinking out loud. Besides, although she led a severely circumscribed life, limited by her social phobia, she had vastly more experience than I. Perhaps she knew enough about the ways of the world to puzzle out the reasons for a criminal's behavior, but I was a naïf and knew it.

Before I could regret my uselessness, she answered her own question. "Of course! He needs a fence! If he sold these things himself, the buyers would know he isn't rich enough to have such pieces in a collection. They would suspect that he was looting the museum and library. He needs an art dealer with at least an okay reputation—and a heart for larceny." She let up on the accelerator and repeated, "Yes, of course." She hung a U-turn on the avenue, thumping across the raised median rather than taking the time to drive to the next inter-section. "Goddard. Edmund Goddard."

"Who's Edmund Goddard?"

"He deals in high-end fine art and antiquities, gallery sales and auctions. He has a sterling reputation, but not with me."

"Why not with you?"

"Daddy worked with many of the better dealers to build his collec-tion, but after a few experiences with Goddard, he never did business with him again. He said Goddard was a man of such sharp practices that one day he would cut himself instead of others, and cut himself mortally."

On a street of luxury shops, she pulled to the curb in front of a large gallery, where the sign announced only GODDARD. Laminated to the interior of each of the four big windows was a three-inch border of beveled mirror, meant to create a jewel-box effect that, with the assistance of cunningly designed lighting and black-velvet backdrops, presented just four paintings as if they were diamonds of priceless character.

They were postmodern abstracts that I found not merely ugly but also depressing. I admit that I don't understand art that isn't in the least representational. But I feel no need to understand it.

"I know where Goddard lives," Gwyneth said. "But I'm drawn to this place."

She pulled away from the curb, turned left at the corner, and turned left again into an alleyway that led behind the stores that faced the avenue. The back door of the gallery stood wide, and a man in a long overcoat shoved a large carton through the open tailgate of a Mercedes SUV.

Free of his burden, he turned toward us. He was tall, stout, and totally bald. From a distance, I couldn't determine his age, only that he might be somewhere between forty and sixty. A lot of men, even the young, had embraced baldness for many years; and it wasn't easy to tell who earned the look and who faked it.

Gwyneth braked twenty feet short of him, put the Rover in park, doused the headlights, switched off the engine. "That's him. That's Goddard."

"What now?" I asked.

"I have no idea."

We got out of the Rover and approached Goddard, and he said to Gwyneth, "There's nothing here for you, girl."

"I'm looking for Simon."

As we closed the distance between us and him, he drew a pistol from a coat pocket and aimed it at her. "That's far enough."

I had no illusion that we could win a duel with Mace and Taser against a pistol, and neither did Gwyneth. She said, "You wouldn't shoot me and put your swanky life at risk."

"If you give me the slightest reason," he said, "I'll shoot you *and* your mysterious friend, and I'll piss on your corpse."

52

THE ALLEYWAY WAS LIT ONLY BY A FEW WIRE-CAGED security lamps above the back entrances to some of the businesses, and the one above the door to the gallery had been extinguished. The blanket of snow didn't brighten the way, for the flanking walls of the six- and eight-story buildings crowded close and blocked the ambient light of the city. Along the length of the alley were strange and tortured shadows, though I thought they must be only the shapes of things and not the things themselves.

Far enough from Goddard to feel certain that he was not able to see my eyes within my hood, I stared directly at him, but I still couldn't guess his age. Fat smoothed out whatever lines time might have carved in his face. His voice had sounded as though he lived entirely on mayonnaise and butter but never quite cleared his throat of them; and even in this poverty of light, he had about him an air of dissolution.

"I'm looking for Simon," Gwyneth repeated. "Will you pretend you don't know who I mean?"

Goddard waved the gun in a dismissive gesture but at once brought it back on target. "I'm past all pretense. What would be the point now? He's not here."

"Where are they holding him?" she asked.

"Why should I bother to tell you? It's over now, all of it, even if Telford refuses to see."

"Simon has no idea how to find me. There's no point in hurting him."

"There's no point in any of it, anymore," Goddard said, "but I don't care enough about your Simon to tell you anything. Unless . . ."

"Unless what?" she asked.

"I'm leaving the city. You should, too, if you want to live."

"I think I'll stay awhile."

"I've got a private island, everything I need."

"Except integrity."

His laugh was wet and low. "Integrity isn't a survival trait, little girl."

"You said 'unless.' Unless what?"

"You might not think so, but I can be sweet," Goddard said. "I'm a man of culture, of highly refined taste and much experience. Out of this rat race, with nothing more to win or lose, you'll find that I'm quite compatible. You might even find, after all, that you don't mind being touched."

I had begun to wonder if he and Gwyneth were not talking about precisely the same thing. There seemed to be implications in his words that didn't quite relate to Simon and Telford. Now his proposition was so outrageous that I thought he must be to some degree unhinged.

He said, "Leave the city with me, and on the way, I'll call Ryan Telford and tell him we're both out of it, you and me, there's no reason for him trying to squeeze information out of your artist friend Simon. It's all over now. It's wasted effort."

For a moment, the quality of her silence suggested that she might be considering his proposal, but then she said, "You'd only take me to Telford."

"Little girl, tender as you are, if you came with me, I'd betray a hundred Ryan Telfords. I'd shoot a hundred of them dead for you, and my own mother if she were still living."

In this gloom, the falling snow was not as bright white as it was elsewhere, and in the shelter of the buildings, the wind proved not as fickle as before, so that the night seemed less chaotic. And yet, listening to their conversation, I felt as if everything was cockeyed, and I wouldn't have been much surprised if the buildings suddenly tilted at precarious angles or if the pavement rolled like a ship's deck under my feet.

Gwyneth chose silence again, and the longer it lasted, the more I wondered why she didn't take offense. Then she said, "There are a few things I would need to know first. Not that they matter anymore. But just for my satisfaction."

"This island of mine is eleven acres with—"

"Not that. I'm sure your island is lovely and your preparations complete."

"Then what? Ask me, dear. Anything."

"You sold pieces for Telford."

"Quite a few. Some belonging to your father."

"Among them were many famous works. Stolen works."

"Yes, famous to one degree or another."

"If the buyers ever sell or display them, they'll incriminate themselves."

"I have only a single buyer for everything Ryan brings to me. A consortium. And the consortium never intends to sell anything that it buys."

"Then how could they hope to profit?"

"Profit is not their motive," Goddard said. "The consortium is comprised of some of the world's richest men. They wish to acquire certain meaningful works of art from the heritage of the West, so that they can destroy them."

I couldn't keep silent. "Destroy them? Destroy great works of art? But why?"

"They're fools," Goddard said. "Less than most men, but fools nonetheless. Like voodooists, they believe that each iconic thing they burn or shatter or melt down will strengthen their cause and weaken their enemy. From their kingdom in the Middle East, they intend soon to destroy the West entire, but first they want the personal satisfaction of eradicating some of its most precious and inspiring creations, piece by piece."

Sickened, I said, "But that's insane."

"Insane and evil," Gwyneth said.

"Quite insane," Goddard agreed. "But insanity is everywhere these days, and celebrated. Insanity is rapidly becoming the new normal.

Don't you think? And as for evil . . . Well, we all know that evil is relative. Has your curiosity been satisfied, little girl?"

"One more thing. The Paladine marionettes."

Clearly surprised, he said, "What about them?"

"Through surrogates, I've tracked down, purchased, and destroyed four of them."

Another wet laugh escaped him, a sound hardly more mirthful than the sodden wheeze of a consumptive. "You're no different from the gentlemen of that consortium."

"More different than you could conceive," she disagreed. "They destroy what is precious and inspiring. I don't. I need to know if there were only six. Only six were ever announced, but maybe you've held back a couple, waiting for the price to rise."

"Why are you concerned about imaginary marionettes if you still have two of the originals to find?"

"I need to know. That's all. I need to know."

"There were only six. They're kitsch, not art. I don't expect them to appreciate in price. If there had been seven or eight, I'd have sold them when the selling was good. Come with me tonight, and I'll reacquire the remaining two for you. We'll burn them together. Oh, little girl, I have a thousand stories to fascinate you, the truth of the world, what happens behind the scenes. You'd find me witty and charming company."

Without hesitation, she said, "I'd rather slit my throat."

Goddard pushed a button on the raised tailgate of the Mercedes, and stepped out of the way as it closed automatically. "I'd shoot you for your insolence, but you'll suffer worse if I just leave you to a less swift fate. You'll wish that I'd shot you, that nothing worse had happened to you than being tortured as even now the fools are torturing your Simon. Tell me, little girl, why does it disgust you to be touched?

Is it perhaps because when you were much littler, your daddy diddled you?"

"Ah, there it is," she said, "the fabled wit and charm."

He gripped the pistol in both hands, and for a moment, I thought he would kill us. But after a silence full of menace, he said, "Both of you stay together and move back past the Land Rover, along the driver's side, and then twenty feet behind it."

"We aren't going to rush you," she assured him. "I believe what you've told me. Poor Simon's beyond saving now. You have nothing we want."

"Move back anyway."

We did as he ordered, and watched him drive away into the storm. The tires of the Mercedes cast up pale clouds of powder, exhaust fumes smoked the night, and the brake lights briefly made of the clouds and fumes a blood mist before the SUV turned right into the cross street and out of sight.

Gwyneth started toward the Land Rover, but I said, "Wait," and when she turned to me, I stepped back to make absolutely sure that she could not see anything of my face. "Father told me never to forget the moth."

"What moth and what about it?"

"He said, 'The flame delights the moth before the wings burn.'"

She was as shadowed to me as I to her, a girl shape, dark in the night. "Is there more?"

"Eighteen years ago, my first night in the city, the night you were born, I saw a marionette in the window of an antique-toy store in this open-air shopping mall along the river. There was something strange about it."

"Odds are that's one I've found and destroyed."

"You've made yourself up to resemble it."

"To somewhat resemble it," she acknowledged.

"The Paladine marionettes? *Six* of them?"

"It's cold out here. I'll explain in the Rover."

"Tell me now. Why would you make yourself up to resemble that . . . that thing?"

I could see that she tilted her head to look up into the sky, and when she lowered it, she repeated what she had said to me once before. "Everything now depends on mutual trust, Addison Goodheart."

"I just need to know," I said. "I don't distrust you."

"Then get in the Rover with me or go. There can be no third choice."

The night, the snow, the girl, the hope for a future, the fear of unending loneliness . . .

Into my silence, she said, "I'm not a flame, you're not a moth."

"I am not a moth," I said, "but you shine brighter than any light I've ever known."

"This is a night of change, Addison. I see that now. And we have little time to do what needs to be done. There is no third choice for you."

She returned to the Land Rover, got behind the wheel, and closed the driver's door. I followed her.

PART THREE

What Might Have Been and
What Has Been

53

IN ORDER THAT YOU MAY UNDERSTAND TIMES PAST
and how they were, you need to know that my mother admitted that
she often considered infanticide. During my first three years of life,
on five occasions, she came within a moment of murdering me.

I remember a summer night, weeks before my mother banished
me, when whiskey in a squat glass with a yellow rim, white powder
inhaled through a silver straw, and two pills of some kind mellowed
her into a maternal mood. She insisted that she, with more Scotch
over ice, and I, with a glass of orange juice, should sit together in the

pair of bentwood rockers on the front porch, for what she called "a little quality time."

Seldom did she want to talk at any length, and more seldom still did we sit together for the purpose of companionship. I knew that her tenderness was genuine, the truest of her qualities, and although she had flushed it to the surface of her heart with powder, pills, and whiskey, I was no less happy to sit with her than I would have been if this expression of affection had come to her naturally, as now and then it did.

Even before we settled down, we moved the rockers from the porch to the front yard, because we both marveled at the vast twinkling arc above us. A greater quantity of stars pierced the black sky than I had ever seen before, as though the lamplighter of the galaxy had walked the spaceways overnight and rekindled all the suns that had burnt out during the last thousand millennia. As we sat leaning back, faces tipped toward the heavens, I saw many things figured in the stars, all kinds of wonders in addition to the named constellations, and I could recall no happier time on the mountain than that hour bathed in starshine.

For the first and last time, Mother spoke of her childhood. Her parents had been university professors, one of literature, the other of psychology, and I supposed that was where she had gotten her love of books. She said that she had grown up wanting nothing material, but she had grown up nonetheless in desperate need. I asked her what she needed, if maybe it was love, and she said she could have used some love, for sure, but the desperate need was for something else. I asked what that might be, but she didn't answer me. When my mother chose not to answer, the only safe course was to honor her reticence.

She recalled a few of the happier experiences of her youth, and her little stories were fun to hear, though they would have been more enjoyable if the tone in which she told them had not been melancholy. In spite of the felicitous moments that she remembered, Mother seemed to wish that she'd never had a childhood, perhaps because all delight was fleeting and because the promise of one day was not fulfilled even just until the next.

As we sat there on the mountain, the plenitude of pure-white stars seemed fixed in their positions, although of course all of them—and Earth, as well—were moving ever outward toward a void at terrifying velocities. I realize in hindsight that Mother and I, in the bentwood rockers, likewise seemed to be going nowhere at the moment, though in reality we, too, were speeding forward aboard the train of time, on different journeys, as would become clear within weeks.

When she proceeded from stories of her childhood to recounting the five times when she had nearly murdered me during my first three years, incidents of which I had no memory, a faint note of anguish underlaid her melancholy. Otherwise nothing changed in our posture, demeanor, or attitudes toward each other. The episode was not fraught with strongly expressed feelings, and there were neither apologies nor accusations. In her former life of robbery and other crimes, she had succeeded only at the cost of discarding all morals and also the better emotions that came coupled with them, and she couldn't be expected easily to regain sentiments that she had discarded with such finality. And I could not justify anger, because I knew I was a burden to her, because she tolerated and even nurtured me as best she could even though I disgusted and frightened her, and because she had saved me from the midwife.

In retrospect I understand that, there under the sea of stars, when she revealed the five times that she had nearly murdered me, she wanted not merely to relieve her guilt by acknowledgment of it. More than that, she wanted me to be her confessor, to bear witness to her contrition, and to give her absolution. I was six months old when she determined to drown me in my bathwater, but though she could push me under and watch the bubbles streaming from my nose, she couldn't bear to hold me down long enough to kill me. On the ten-month anniversary of my birth, she felt certain she could smother me with the birthing blanket that the midwife would have used, but she threw it in the fireplace and burned it instead. When I was fourteen months, she spent two hours obsessively sharpening a kitchen knife and then put it to my throat—though she couldn't make the fatal cut. Six months thereafter, an overdose of the drugs that she called her medicines seemed sufficiently merciful so that she might follow through with the plan, and though she mixed the lethal cocktail with apple juice and gave it to me in a nippled bottle, she snatched it away from me when I began to suck. She said that I was nearly three when she led me into the woods, going far enough from our little house to be sure that I would not find my way home, and there she intended to leave me to the mercy of the various predators that prowled those forested mountains and valleys. She told me to sit down in a small clearing and wait for her, though she had no intention of returning, but just then two wolves, lantern-eyed in the green shadows, appeared from among the surrounding ferns. In terror and regret, she snatched me up and ran with me to the house, and after much whiskey and some powder, she reconciled herself to the fact that she was not capable of infanticide.

She didn't say that she was sorry, but sorrow like a river ran beneath her words. Although she wanted me to grant her absolution, I was not then—nor am I now—ordained with such a power. I could only say to her, "I love you, Momma, and I always will."

We sat there in the yard, in the rocking chairs, for a while longer.

I couldn't say with certainty if it was ten minutes or an hour. We sat in silence, and the stars that crowned the night seemed to descend around us, until the house and the woods and the lane that connected us to the outer world all disappeared as if behind a veil, and a great host of diamond-white stars sparkled above and to every side of us, an encapsulating dome of stars under which we were safe.

54

PREVIOUSLY, GWYNETH HAD SEEMED TO TURN aimlessly from street to street when in fact she had been guided by a purpose; but now she was indeed making her way by whim and notion.

The city appeared less real than before, fading into falling snow not as though shrouds were being cast upon it, but as if it were retreating. The high-rises immediately around us stood their ground as always, but those that I knew to be a block away looked as though they had moved an additional block. Those buildings at any greater distance were pale shapes, their glowing windows like befogged running lights, as if they were enormous ships long docked but now cast off and setting sail swiftly away.

She said, "Charles Paladine was a much-hailed artist. He painted what he sometimes called abstracted abstracts, and though he said such things and even sillier stuff, no one in the arts community laughed at him. In fact, he was exceedingly well reviewed and, by the age of twenty-eight, he sold out every show, whether here, in New York, or London, and Goddard Galleries represented him exclusively.

He went from triumph to triumph. He was said to be the next Jackson Pollock, the next Robert Rauschenberg, the next Andy Warhol, all rolled into one modern master. Then Paladine did something peculiar that endangered his reputation. He stopped painting abstracts and became obsessed with realistic scenes featuring marionettes."

I said, "Black tuxedo, black shirt, white tie, top hat."

"Yes, that one, but also others—men, women, and children. The scenes were exotic, moody and disturbing, sometimes featuring several marionettes and sometimes only two. The marionette you mean, the one in the antique-toy store, was often the most prominently featured, but in paintings where other marionettes were the focus, the one in the tuxedo always at least lurked in the background, half shrouded by one thing or another, or in shadow, but always there. The critics who praised Paladine's abstracts were puzzled by his new direction. They had proclaimed him a genius for so long that they couldn't at first be harshly critical. But their positive reviews weren't quite as adoring as before, and some of them openly lamented that he had abandoned abstracts."

"I've never understood abstract art," I admitted.

"Sometimes I think no one does, but they have to pretend or be considered uncool and unsophisticated. My father liked to quote the critic Paul Johnson, who once referred to Jackson Pollock's work as 'inspired linoleum.' Daddy deeply disliked the marionette period of Paladine's career, but he said that at least the artist had been putting something recognizable on the canvas instead of the blobs of nothing and nihilistic scratching that had made him rich."

She drove around a city plow that moved too slow to please her, and coming the opposite direction was a second plow. She maneuvered fast between them in a center lane that was as yet uncleared, and both drivers gave her a blast of their horns in disapproval.

"What happens if a policeman pulls you over?" I asked.

"Won't happen. Anyway, Paladine sold his marionette paintings, but at a lower price—until he killed his wife and two children, a boy of ten and a girl of twelve. In some of the paintings, he'd used their faces as the faces of the marionettes. When they were dead, he beheaded them—"

"I don't like these kinds of stories."

"It doesn't exactly bring a smile to my face, either. Paladine beheaded *and* dismembered his wife and children. Then he sewed their heads and limbs back on, though loosely, with coarse black thread. He painted their faces white, added black details, and drew bright spots of rouge on their cheeks."

With cloaks and robes and cerements of white whirling and billowing and swooning in every quarter, the city looked as if it must be populated by more ghosts than living people, and all those spirits were agitated in their haunting.

I said, "Did he ever explain himself? In court, I mean?"

"No need for either a trial or an asylum. After he finished with his family, Paladine painted his own face like that of the marionette you saw in the shop window. Then he went to the roof of his four-story house, right here in the finest neighborhood in the city, and threw himself into the street."

I shuddered. "Why?"

"We'll never know why."

"Where do the *real* marionettes come into this?"

"Police found the six of them in Paladine's studio, which was there in his home. They were identical, like the one you described. He had carved them from cubes of yew wood and crafted their joints and painted them himself. Do you know the yew tree, Addison?"

"No. I've not had much experience of trees since I was eight."

"The yew is the graveyard tree, symbol of sorrow and death."

"What happened to the six?"

"Oh, they were sold to collectors. His paintings of marionettes soared in price—I won't say 'value'—following the murders and the suicide. Many Paladine collectors no longer wanted his work from that period, but certain . . . *enthusiasts* purchased multiple paintings. And each of the six hand-carved marionettes brought a serious price when Edmund Goddard put them up at auction."

I said, "All this happened before you were born."

"Yes. Before you came to the city."

"And then, when you turned thirteen, you used the marionette as the inspiration for your Goth look. Why?"

"I happened to see photographs of it in a magazine article."

"Yes, but why make yourself like it?"

Instead of answering the question, she said, "As you heard me tell Goddard, through surrogates I've tracked down and purchased four of the six. I personally oversaw the burning of them."

"Are you going to buy and destroy the other two?"

"I haven't known where they are. Which greatly worried me."

"Worried you—why?"

We arrived at the traffic roundabout in Washington Square, where atop a plinth, the first president and legendary warrior sat on his horse, his stone face solemn, as though he issued a challenge to the city, if not to the world, a call to rise to his vision of truth and liberty and honor. Three Clears in hospital whites stood around the statue, looking for whatever it is they seek, waiting for whatever it is they anticipate.

Gwyneth drove three-quarters of the way around the circle before taking one of the avenues that radiated from it. A first-pass plow had cast the snow from the street onto parked cars, which by morning would be so buried that they would look like a series of igloos along the curb.

Throughout these two nights together, I had feared that if I pressured her too much to reveal her secrets, I would trigger her social phobia, that she would retreat from me or even terminate our friendship. But now I knew that her life and mine shared points of intersection long before we met, beginning in fact on the night she was born. In light of that puzzling discovery, I resolved to press her a bit more insistently.

"Why are you worried about the last two marionettes?"

"I'm not as worried as I was. We have an appointment at one o'clock. We can't be late."

"Appointment with whom?"

"You'll see."

I returned to the more essential matter: "Why are you worried about the marionettes?"

She hesitated but did not resort again to silence. "Over time, after to some extent I adopted their image, I gradually came to realize . . . I'd made them aware of me."

"Aware of you?"

"Yes."

"The six?"

"I know what I feel, and I know it's true. But you don't have to think it makes sense, that's okay."

Perhaps right then was the moment to tell her about the Fogs, the Clears, the music box with mismatched dancers, and my conviction that the marionette in the shop window had been aware of me, too. I almost followed that impulse, but then I said instead, "What is there to fear from toys?"

"They were never toys."

"All right. But what is there to fear from puppets?"

"I don't know what, and I don't want to find out."

The wind found its strength again and hurled the snow at us so furiously that the flakes, smaller now, ticked faintly against the windshield, as if by virtue of their numbers and persistence, they would pit the glass and eventually dissolve it, so that the storm could claim the interior of the Rover and us, as it had claimed the city's streets.

A thought occurred to me, and I shared it with her. "Earlier, when we were having dinner. The rapping. In the attic."

"Air in the water pipes."

"Are there water pipes in an attic?"

"There must be."

"Have you gone up there to look?"

"No."

"Is there a way from your apartment into the attic?"

"A trapdoor in a closet. But it's held shut with two thick bolt latches, and it's going to stay that way."

"If you want, I'll go up there and look."

She said calmly but firmly, "No. I'm not going up there, you're not going up there, no one's going up there tonight, tomorrow night, or ever."

55

FOR A BLOCK OR MORE, I LISTENED TO THE METRO-nomic thump-thump of the windshield wipers, which nearly matched the resting pace of my heart, and I listened to the wind, which at times shook the Rover as if to get our attention and compel us to understand what it was striving to communicate with its keening, huffing, and quarrelsome blustering.

Although I counseled myself to let her answer it in her own time, I could not help but ask again the question that she had sidestepped. "When you turned thirteen, why did you use the marionette as inspiration for your Goth transformation?"

"I was timid, and I wanted to look tough. I wanted to look edgy. I was afraid of people, and I thought the best way to keep them at a distance might be to act a little scary."

Although what she said seemed to be explanation enough, I sensed that she had given me only a partial answer.

She must have known what I was thinking, because she elaborated, though the added words were a continuing evasion. "After I realized that I'd made them aware of me, I could have changed my appearance, gone to some other Goth look. But I knew by then, it wouldn't matter. They were already aware of me, and they wouldn't forget me merely because I no longer resembled them. I had opened a door that could never be closed again. I guess now you're convinced I'm kind of crazy."

"Not as much as you might think."

Her cell phone rang. She fished it from a pocket, glanced at the screen, put it on SPEAKER, but said nothing.

For a moment, the line spat out static, but then Telford said, "I know you're there, little mouse."

"Let me talk to Simon."

Telford pretended to be confused. "Simon? Simon who?"

"Put him on the phone."

"You want me to put someone named Simon on the phone?"

"He doesn't know anything."

"You may be right about that."

"I saw Goddard tonight," she said.

"What a loser."

"Goddard knows it's over. There's no point to what you're doing. It's over."

"His associates don't think it's over. They've been a great help to me tonight, and still are."

"Let me talk to Simon."

"There's a man here, maybe his name is Simon, maybe it's not, I can't say. You want to talk to him?"

"Put him on."

The line hissed faintly, sputtered, and Gwyneth waited.

At last Telford said, "He doesn't seem to want to talk. He just lies there on the floor, staring at nothing, his mouth hanging open, a disgusting beard of vomit on his chin, and he doesn't even try to clean himself up. If this was your Simon, let me tell you, he had no manners, no common sense, no survival instinct. You should hang out with a better class of people."

She took a moment to blink back tears, biting her lip so hard that I expected real blood to flow around the bright bead of faux blood. In spite of her emotional turmoil, she handled the Land Rover as well as ever. Finally she said, "It's over, and you better make your peace with that."

"Oh, are you going to the police?"

She didn't reply.

"Three things, little mouse. One, I don't think you can really tolerate being put in a room for questioning, to have all those big burly policemen around you, touching you. Two, the way you look and the way you are won't give you a lot of credibility. You're a tasty little bitch, but you're also a freak."

"You said three things. That's two."

"Three, those associates that Goddard lent to me? Now that he's turned coward, they work for me. And you know what, little mouse, both of them are former policemen. Isn't that interesting? They have friends in the department. Lots of friends, little mouse."

I admired her aplomb as she said, "You can still save yourself. There's always time to save yourself until there's no time left."

"Brilliant, little mouse. In addition to all your other fine qualities, you're a philosopher. There's always time until there's no time left. I will write that down and study it. When I see you, maybe you can elucidate."

"You won't be seeing me."

"I've got considerable resources, little mouse. I'm certain that I'll find you."

She terminated the call and returned the phone to a pocket of her coat.

She'd lost a friend in Simon. I couldn't think of anything to say that might be consoling. Perhaps there had been a time when death was not in the world, but it was here now, with a vengeance, and it would come for us as it had come to Simon, if not this very day, then the day following, or a year from now, or in ten years. When we say "I'm sorry for your loss," we may mean it, but we are also sorrowing for ourselves.

I said, "This one-o'clock meeting that you mentioned—it's ten minutes to one."

"We're almost there."

Initially the snow had been beautiful, but not so much now. The softness and sparkle still charmed, but the storm occluded the sky, denying us the stars. At the moment, I needed to see a firmament of stars, needed to gaze past the moon and through the constellations, needed to see what can't be seen—infinity.

56

THE 1930S ART DECO MOVIE THEATER—THE Egyptian—had been an architectural wonder in its heyday. All these years later, abandoned and in a state of decay, the building still possessed a little magic. A suggestion of glamour remained in spite of its deteriorated facade, even in spite of the defacing graffiti, a Joseph's coat of luminous paints. The vandalism glowed in neon shades of green and orange and yellow and blue: the initials of the perpetrators; acronyms that meant nothing to me; crudely drawn snakes and fish and zombie faces; symbols that I could not interpret but also a swastika and a crescent moon embracing a five-point star. According to Gwyneth, in the final phase of its commercial life, the Egyptian had run X-rated movies. Its marquee, which once enticed with the titles of films that later became American classics, instead boldly trumpeted titles that were crude double entendres or as blunt as SEX CRAZY. That business model had a short life, viable only until porno films became an in-home entertainment option, and these days the Egyptian was nothing more than a message board for barbarians. Now the only word on the marquee was CLOSED. Those large black letters were ominous to me. I thought a day might come when that one-word declaration would be hung across every entrance to this once-shining city fallen into ruin.

As Gwyneth parked at the curb in front of the theater, she said, "They were going to tear it down and build a hospice. But new health-care regulations—they're a swamp, and every bureaucrat a gator."

"Seems a strange place for a meeting."

"They might be watching his house, so I didn't dare go there."

"If he's being watched, maybe they followed him here."

"When he was young, he had a career in the Marine Corps. He was an intelligence officer. If they tried to tail him, he'd know. He'd have called me to switch the meeting somewhere else."

We hurried through the snow to the center pair of eight doors, which she knew would have been unlocked for this rendezvous. The lobby smelled of mold and stale urine and rancid popcorn oil so ancient that cockroaches would decline to feed upon it.

In the beam of Gwyneth's flashlight, the golden-marble floor, inlaid with patterns of Egyptian hieroglyphics in black granite, was cracked and filthy. We might have been archaeologists who'd dug into a tomb long buried under desert sand, where the body of a pharaoh, well-cured in tannin and wrapped in linen, waited for Anubis to send its spirit back from the House of the Dead.

Debris crunched under our feet as we crossed that enormous dark chamber toward an open door in one corner, where milky light spilled across the threshold. Back in the days of newsreels, comedy shorts, and double features, this might have been the manager's office; but now it lay barren and deserted except for Teague Hanlon.

I entered that chamber with the protection of my gloves, hood, and ski mask. I bowed my head, and I intended to keep it that way, but the girl's guardian had another idea.

Mr. Hanlon's voice—gentle yet firm, clear and almost musical but not unserious—reminded me in some ways of Father's voice, which disposed me to like him. "Addison, I know you have issues, I am not to look at you under any circumstances, and I respect that. I've long been accustomed to Gwynie's rules, and I'm sure she's told you that I honor them. I won't look at you, not even sideways. All right?"

"Yes. All right."

"Gwynie has told me what I may say to you and what she prefers that I not say, and I will abide by her request. But I feel that you should know what I look like, know at least that much of who I am. It's going to be essential that you trust me in the hours to come. Trust will be easier for you if you look at me and see no deception. From this moment on, I'll focus my attention only on dear Gwynie."

Warily, I raised my stare from his zippered boots to his black slacks, to his long overcoat, which was buttoned at his throat, a white scarf partly revealed beneath it. In one gloved hand, he held a navy-blue knitted sailor's cap.

Gwyneth said, "Telford won't say it directly on the phone, only imply it, but Simon . . . they killed him."

"God be with him," Mr. Hanlon said. "He didn't have an easy life, and now a hard death."

His head was somewhat large at the brow, his chin and jaw a bit small, like a pear standing on its stem. In spite of the slightly odd proportions, his pleasant face served as a recommendation. White thinning hair, disarranged when he pulled off his cap, was tangled and standing up in wispy twists like a fledgling's feathers. For a man his age, his brow remained remarkably smooth, and a spray of creases at the corner of each eye seemed not to signify a life of much squinting in disapproval, but one of much laughter.

To Gwyneth, her guardian said, "It's harder every day to hold him off. He wants the larger part of the principal in the primary trust, for his pet projects, and he thinks there has to be a way around the trust provisions. I tell him it's all yours until you've died, but his mind is a riot of schemes, which he keeps pressing on me. He comprehends your legal protections, but he doesn't respect them. He keeps saying that your father provided for you too lavishly, and even suggests that the fortune wasn't fairly earned, which is a slander at the very least, as anyone who knew your dad can attest."

"It doesn't matter," Gwyneth said. "I'd give it all to him tomorrow if by giving it I could . . . change things. You know it doesn't matter anymore."

Mr. Hanlon's sweet face hadn't been made for anger. But his pleasant features conformed to a solemn sadness that frightened me. Based on what the girl had just said and on her guardian's grave expression, I thought she must be afflicted not just with social phobia, but also with something worse, an incurable illness without visible symptoms.

He said, "Gwynie, are you still sure that now is the time?"

"Aren't you?" she asked.

After a hesitation, he nodded. "Yes. I'm afraid that I think you're right."

"The fact that you called me today with this information, that it has at last come into my hands—it's confirmation."

From a coat pocket, Mr. Hanlon withdrew a key on a stretchy green plastic coil. He gave it to Gwyneth. "There are two in his retinue who know precisely what he is. His secretary is one of them. He has a room at the back of the first floor, but he won't participate."

"He doesn't need to. He's done enough."

I wondered whom they were talking about, but I didn't feel that it was my place to ask. If I needed to know, she would tell me.

Mr. Hanlon said, "The security system is armed. The audio function has been disabled, so the alarm won't sound in the house, and the keypad won't emit tones when you enter the disarming code."

Gwyneth accepted from him a piece of paper on which were printed four numbers and a symbol.

"Although no siren will sound in the house, a signal will be sent to the security company's monitoring station. You have just one minute to enter the numbers and the star key in order to prevent an armed response from them."

Although I was accustomed to going into locked places where I wasn't supposed to venture, I never did so with the intention of committing a crime. Listening to Mr. Hanlon, I grew uneasy, though I had to assume that Gwyneth likewise harbored no criminal intent. I loved her with such devotion that I could not do otherwise than trust her. In mere hours, trust had ceased to be a choice and had become, with love, the foundation of all my hopes for the future.

Mr. Hanlon said, "His private apartment occupies the entire third floor. You'll find what you need in the living room. He usually takes a tablet of Lunesta before bed. He should be sound asleep, down a long hallway, in his bedroom. If you're reasonably quiet, he won't know you're there."

Sensing that the meeting had reached an end, I looked down at the floor, worried that Mr. Hanlon would forget his promise to me and would turn to say good-bye, quite naturally looking straight into my eyes.

Perhaps I needn't have been concerned. He said, "Addison, you take care of this girl."

"I'll do my best, sir. But I suspect she'll end up taking care of me."

I could hear his smile in his words. "You're probably right. Our Gwynie is a force of nature." He said to her, "I'll see you in a little while?"

"That's the plan."

"You're really sure you must do this?"

"Very sure."

"May God be with you, child."

"And with you."

Mr. Hanlon accompanied us across the lobby, where we trod upon the hieroglyphics, which included silhouettes and symbols of some Egyptian gods: Osiris, Horus, Isis, Neph, Amen-Ra, Anubis. He let us out, and as we hurried to the Land Rover, he locked the theater doors.

By the time Gwyneth started the engine and switched on the headlights, her guardian was nearing the end of the block, shoulders hunched and head lowered into the wind.

I said, "Shouldn't we give him a lift?"

"He doesn't have far to go. If they're watching his place, we don't want to get anywhere near it."

She drove away from the curb, into the iced city as white as a wedding cake. That image sparked another, and into my mind came the figure of a groom standing on the top layer of such a cake. He was the tuxedoed marionette. Imagination is a wonderful but occasionally disturbing gift. In my mind's eye, no bride stood with the groom, but he smiled as if he anticipated her arrival at any moment.

I said, "Why did you tell him there were things you preferred he not say to me? What things were they?"

"You'll know soon enough."

"Do you have some . . . illness?"

"Illness? Why would you think so?"

"You said you'd give all your money away if it would change things. You said it doesn't matter anymore."

"You worry too much, Addison. I have no illness. Truly. And you know I never lie."

"I never lie, either. But sometimes I evade. And so do you."

After a silence, she said, "You're an interesting guy."

"I am?"

"Yes, and you better be."

"Better be what?"

"Interesting."

"I don't understand."

"Doesn't matter. I understand. Now, hush. I need to think."

The streets were at last deserted except for us and the plows. The bright yellow beacons swiveling on the roofs of those vehicles alchemized snow to gold, and on the walls of nearby buildings, waves of sulfurous beacon-cast light chased wolfish beacon-cast shadows.

57

ON A WARM JUNE NIGHT WHEN I WAS FOURTEEN, there were fireflies in the great park, hundreds of them gliding silently through the dark, familiar to me from my time on the mountain but mysterious in the metropolis. I fancied that they were tiny airships aboard which minute passengers were bound from their world to another peopled by their Lilliputian kind, passing through ours and wondering at the strangeness of this place. That was the first and last night we saw fireflies in the city, as if they had not been borne here by Nature's intention, but instead had materialized at the will of some other power that meant their throbbing lanterns to warn us away from—or guide us toward—something of importance.

Later on the same night, traversing an alleyway, we heard a man calling out to us, his voice weak and tremulous. "Help me. I'm blind. They blinded me."

We found him lying beside a Dumpster, and trusting in his claim of blindness, we dared to go to him and examine him by flashlight. He was perhaps fifty, dressed in an expensive but rumpled suit ruined now by bloodstains. He had taken blows to the head. His bruised and swollen face made me afraid for him. Blood oozed from his split lip and from the gums around two broken teeth. His eyes followed not either light or movement, but instead tracked our voices, as he tried to see what he heard. He was strong enough to stand with help, but he was too broken to walk on his own. We were wearing gloves, as usual, and we assisted him, Father to his right and I to his left. A block and a half away, there was a hospital, and in that warm night, our sweat was cold as we risked exposure to get him to those doors.

As he shuffled between us, he said with some bewilderment that this was a safe neighborhood, that he'd had no qualms about walking two blocks even at that late hour. The three men had been waiting in this unlighted alleyway. They stepped out in front of him, thrust a pistol into his abdomen, seized him, and dragged him into the dark. He had twelve hundred in his wallet, credit cards, a watch worth fifteen thousand, a diamond ring worth five thousand, and he thought that if he surrendered all of that without protest, his assailants would not harm him. He knew a man who had, some years earlier, been unfortunate enough to be mugged while carrying little of value, and in frustration, the robbers had beaten him severely. In this case, they were incensed that he had so much, more than they deemed was fair, and they accused him of stealing it from others, one way or another, him in his fancy suit and Gucci shoes, and they beat him in disapproval of his affluence. He lay unconscious, for how long he didn't know, and when he woke, his skull felt as if it were in pieces, held together by skin and hair, and he was blind.

We assured him that the blindness would be temporary. Although we couldn't know if that was true, his eyes were without wounds, and clear. We got him within a few feet of the entrance to the hospital and told him that we couldn't go inside with him, though we didn't explain why. "The doors are in front of you," Father said. "They're automatic. Just two steps, they'll open, you're inside where someone can help you." En route, the victim had asked our names, and we'd avoided giving them. Now he surprised me by reaching out and touching my face, insisting that he must know what his two Samaritans looked like. A ski mask on a June night would have drawn attention to us; we relied on light jackets with deep hoods and, until called to this task, on discretion. No sooner had his fingers begun to trace my features than he snatched his hand away. Because his face was bruised, bloodied, badly distorted by swelling, I couldn't easily interpret the nuances of his expression, though it was one kind of horror or another. Without a word, he stumbled away, the pneumatic doors hissed open, he staggered inside, and we sprinted into the night as if we were his assailants, not his rescuers.

Several weeks later, reading the newspaper after midnight in the central library, we came upon a story about a mugging victim who was searching for two men who had assisted him. We recognized him only because the story included two pictures—one taken post-recovery that meant nothing to us, the other taken in the hospital by a police officer. He had regained his sight. His name was Robert Pattica, and he hoped to find us and reward us for our kindness. We neither wanted nor needed a reward. Considering that Mr. Pattica had touched my face and therefore knew something of my difference, we couldn't help but doubt that his motives were as he claimed.

The most interesting thing in the article was what Mr. Pattica said about fireflies. When he touched my face, though blind, he saw fireflies as he remembered them from his youth in farm country, and though they were familiar, they were also strange, because he thought of them in a way he never had before; they seemed to him like tiny airships sailing silently through the dark. The vision had been so entrancing that he couldn't get it out of his mind, and he was in the process of selling his home in the city, changing careers, and moving back to the town where he had been raised, where there were fireflies and wildlife aplenty, which he hadn't known he missed until now.

Father and I didn't know what to make of that.

We were certain that, if Mr. Pattica had seen my face, he would have either fled in terror or, in spite of his injuries, attacked me. We endured too much over the years to believe that, upon revealing ourselves, we would be embraced. The only abovegrounder who had been kind to Father was the friend who'd given him a key to the food bank, and even that individual found it difficult to meet with him more than once every year—and briefly—to confirm that he remained well.

But what about the fireflies? How could Mr. Pattica have seen the fireflies to which I had stood witness earlier that night, and how could he have arrived at the same simile that had occurred to me— tiny airships in the dark? We could conclude only that the blows he had taken to the head had not only temporarily blinded him but had also conferred upon him an equally temporary clairvoyance.

We were fortunate because his brief psychic vision distracted him from what his fingertips could have told him about my face.

Of course we were aware that temporary clairvoyance was a lame and unlikely explanation. The ordering of this world, however, is so abstruse, so deep and complex, most explanations that people embrace to make sense of moments of strange experience are inadequate. Our very existence as thinking creatures is an astonishment that can't be solved. Every human cell, with its thousands of protein chains, is more complex than a 747 or the largest cruise ship, in fact more complex than the two combined. All life on Earth, in its extravagant variety, offers itself for study, but though we probe to ever deeper layers of its structure, the meaning eludes us.

There is no end of wonders and mysteries: fireflies and music boxes, the stars that outnumber all the grains of sand on all the beaches of the world, pinhead eggs that become caterpillars that dissolve into genetic soup from which arise butterflies, that some hearts are dark and others full of light.

58

AT 1:40 IN THE MORNING, GWYNETH PARKED AT THE curb on the south side of the cathedral complex, steps from the break in the compound wall that served the residence of the archbishop.

"Here?"

"Yes."

"What are we doing here?" I asked.

"Visiting."

She turned, reached over the console, groped for something on the floor behind her seat, and snared a laundry bag with a drawstring closure.

"What's that for?" I asked.

"Convenience."

The frozen and crumbling sky, the countless shoals of crystals swimming down the night, the street a quiet sea of white . . .

We climbed a snowbank compacted by a city plow, forged across a buried sidewalk, and disturbed the pristine white coverlets on the steps leading up to a much broader doorstep under a columned portico.

When she took from a pocket the key on the stretchy coil of green plastic, I said, "Not really?"

"What?"

"This isn't the place I was expecting."

"What place were you expecting?"

"I don't know. Just not this."

"Well, this is the place," she said.

"Wow. We should take off our boots."

"We didn't take them off when we went into Simon's place."

"It was just a bungalow, there was an urgency to the moment."

"There's an urgency to this moment," she said, "and who's to say this place is more sacred than poor Simon's bungalow?"

Nevertheless, I unzipped my snow-caked boots and shucked them off, and so did she. We were both still wearing athletic shoes, and hers were the silver ones on which she had flown like Mercury through the library stacks.

The key worked, the deadbolt retracted, and we went into the spacious foyer, which was round and paved with marble. Next to the door, the numbers on the keypad of the security panel glowed a soft green. The audio function had been disabled, as promised, and the indicator light above the words PERIMETER ARMED blinked silently to announce a violation of the premises. Having stripped off her gloves and shoved them in a jacket pocket, Gwyneth held in her left hand the paper that her guardian had given her. I shone my flashlight on the code, and with her right hand she entered the four numbers and the star symbol. The indicator light stopped blinking and went dark.

Trust. Our relationship hinged on trust. And I *did* trust her. But I was nevertheless nervous. My mouth went dry with apprehension.

The stairs were not an architectural feature and did not open into the foyer. We ventured into the large drawing room, probing left and right with our flashlights. This was one of the chambers in which the archbishop entertained, for among his responsibilities was the work of establishing bonds with the leaders of the city's political, business, arts, and faith communities. Several elegantly furnished seating areas, Persian carpets, and exquisite antiques were balanced by marvelous paintings of scenes from Scripture, marble statuary of Biblical figures, including one of the Holy Mother, and small icons on various tables and consoles. There was also a large portrait of Christ by an artist unusually observant of detail and superbly skilled at creating an illusion of depth, so that the image appeared three-dimensional, and for a moment I could not breathe.

The stairs were behind a corner door in the drawing room, and we climbed to the third floor. At the head of the stairs, another door opened onto an antechamber that offered two chairs. It was lighted only by a flickering electric candle in a glass chimney that stood before a shrine to Mary.

I whispered, "We shouldn't be here."

"But we are."

"Why?"

"We have two things to do before we can go back to my guardian."

I remembered then that he had asked her if he would see her in a little while, and she said that was the plan.

"What two things?" I asked.

"Trust me," she said, and turned to the apartment door.

I thought the door would be locked, that we would be foiled by the lack of a second key. But it was not locked.

When we crossed the threshold, I expected darkness, but a couple of lamps glowed. The light made Gwyneth hesitate, but then we stepped into a different world from the ground-floor rooms, which had clearly been part of the residence of a prince of the church.

Here, the living room reminded me of pictures of homes furnished by interior designers who specialized in soft contemporary style. The upholstered furniture, covered in rich golden silk except for two red chairs, featured waterfall edges and round plump arms, and the legs were tucked back out of sight, so that each piece seemed to float an inch off the floor. Tables laminated in exotic lacquered woods in shades varying from silver to gold, scarlet accent pillows, and large canvases of bold abstract art finished a space very like those that, in magazines, belonged to au courant novelists, avant-garde artists, and movie stars who described their taste as "simple glamour."

I was surprised that the living room contained no smallest representation of things sacred. But the most striking thing about it was the pair of marionettes on the fireplace mantel. They sat with the support of decorative metal stands, facing each other from opposite ends of a painting in which several black arcs made with a wide brush were stark against a white backdrop, spattered across with blue like the blood of some extraterrestrial species.

59

AT THE END OF THE LIVING ROOM, ON THE RIGHT, A hallway led to the rest of the apartment. Although the hall was mostly dark, a rectangle of light issued from an open door, catching the tight nap of the pale-gray wool carpet at such an angle as to make it appear pebbled. From that room came two solemn male voices.

Sensing my trepidation, Gwyneth whispered, "Talking heads."

Baffled, I whispered, "What?"

Because she was more familiar with TV than I would ever be, she said with quiet certainty, "Just TV. News or late-night talk."

Obviously, the archbishop remained awake, and I thought we should leave at once.

She thought differently, returned to the cold fireplace, and whispered, "Come on. Hurry. Help me."

As I went to her, she opened the cloth laundry bag and put it on the hearth.

I said, "But this is stealing."

"No. This is a cleansing."

Although I believed that she didn't lie, I assumed that she could be misguided.

"They know I'm here," she whispered. "They know."

The marionettes still faced each other from opposite ends of the mantel. Their striated eyes had not turned toward us.

"I don't think I should touch them, Addison. Will you take them down and put them in the bag?"

"But why is it not stealing?"

"I'll send him a generous check for them if you insist. But put them in the bag. *Please.*"

In a state of quasi-bewilderment, not quite able to believe that I was in this place and engaged upon such a task, I tried to lift one of the puppets, but it was secured to the metal brace that disappeared under its tuxedo jacket. When I tried to lift the brace, I discovered that it was screwed to the mantel.

"Hurry," Gwyneth urged.

I worked the tuxedo jacket up the brace until I found the cord that tied the marionette in place. As I fumbled with the knot, the arch-bishop entered from the hallway.

He carried two suitcases and, upon seeing us, dropped them so abruptly that one of them fell over. He said, "Who're you, what're you—" Then Gwyneth turned toward him, and he recognized her. "You."

He wasn't wearing a cassock, rochet, stole, pectoral cross, or Roman collar, nor was he wearing the simple black suit of a priest, nor robe and pajamas. In comfortable suede shoes, khaki slacks, and a dark-brown wool sweater over a beige shirt, he might have been anyone, a schoolteacher or accountant, preparing to catch an early flight and wing away on holiday.

Tall, fit, he had the handsome but pale and sharp-featured face of one of the tort lawyers who ran ads in certain magazines, seeking clients for class-action lawsuits. His hair was thick for his age, quite curly, still more blond than gray.

He didn't at once approach us. If he began to step closer, I would back away. At this remove, he couldn't clearly see the eyes in the holes of my ski mask. I remembered well the church by the river and the man with the kindly face, who had come at me with a baseball bat. Among other implements hanging from the rack of fireplace tools on the hearth was a long-handled poker, which would perhaps do more damage than a Louisville Slugger.

"There must be an agent of the devil among my confreres, and perhaps more than one," he said.

"Your Eminence, Archbishop Wallache," Gwyneth said and nod-ded to him, as if we had come calling by invitation.

Father and I never read the entire newspaper, and I did not keep up with ecclesiastical news, but the name resonated with me. I had heard it six years earlier, as I stood by the open drain in the crypt beneath the cathedral. Two men, never seen, met in the farther reaches of that place to share a secret that meant nothing to me at the time but that, I now realized, involved news of whom the Vatican had selected to be the next archbishop.

Please tell me it's not Wallache.

But it is.

They've all gone mad.

Say nothing to anyone or I'm toast. This is übersecret.

But they must know—he must know—Wallache's history.

They seem to believe Wallache's version of it.

Now, Archbishop Wallache said, "I assume you haven't come to me at this hour for a blessing." His courtroom face produced a smile that I would not have thought it could, one warm enough to charm any jury. "Are you admirers of the marionettes?"

"Why would you have such a foul thing here?" Gwyneth asked.

"I grant you that the subject is macabre and their history is dark, but the workmanship is lovely. For another thing, they were a gift, and it is rude to turn down a sincerely offered gift."

"A gift from Edmund Goddard," she said, coloring the name with contempt.

"May I say also that, when one spends every day among people of faith, always bringing the hope of Christ to those who need it, there is a tendency to become too sunny in temperament, to lose track of the truth that Evil walks the Earth and that the battle against it remains always urgent and desperate. Having such a reminder of great wickedness keeps one alert to the possibility of error in one's own life."

Gwyneth said, "So you keep them on your mantel to remind you that evil is real and that anyone can be tempted."

"Yes, exactly."

"So have they been effective, have you avoided error since you've had them?"

He could hold a smile with the apparent effortlessness of a world-class high-wire walker maintaining balance far above a tense crowd of upturned faces. "If I may be allowed a question of my own, I should ask what you want with them."

"I want to burn them. I've bought and burned the other four."

"You wish to destroy icons of evil, and yet you make yourself up to resemble them."

She did not respond.

Indicating me with a gesture, the archbishop said, "Who is your masked companion? Is he what would be called your muscle?"

Instead of answering him, Gwyneth said, "I'm taking these last two marionettes to burn them. If you want to call the police and tell them how you kept these things on your mantel as reminders to be on guard against evil and to avoid wickedness yourself, by all means do so. They might believe you. Most of them. So many years have passed, almost twenty-five, since those murders that a lot of people might have forgotten the most gruesome details of what Paladine did to his family. However, that's the kind of thing cops don't forget. I'm sure they'll want to know why Goddard would think to give them to you."

If he was a man who could take offense, he was too diplomatic to show it. If he had feathers, they would never ruffle. He consulted his wristwatch and said, "I've no use for the things anymore. You may burn them—but you may not take them. That's a gas-log fireplace. The flue is open, and it draws well. You see the remote control lying by the rack of tools? You can switch on the flames with that."

Gwyneth picked up the remote, clicked it, and blue-orange flames at once licked up around the realistic-looking ceramic logs.

"The wood of the yew tree," the archbishop said, "is pliable because it retains its natural oils decades after it has been cut and shaped. They should burn well and quickly."

I returned to the marionette that I had been trying to loosen from its brace.

"Not you," Archbishop Wallache said.

"Sir?"

"Not you. *She* must take them down and consign them to the flames. Or I really will pick up the phone."

"I'll stop you," I said.

"Will you really? I suspect not. I'm a good judge of people, masked or not, and you seem to me to be a lamb, not a lion."

"I'll do it," Gwyneth said. "I'm not afraid to do it."

I said, "He won't stop me."

"I don't know what he might do. I'll burn them myself."

I thought I saw the marionette's eyes turn sideways to regard me. But when I looked directly, it still stared across the mantel at its twin.

60

GWYNETH'S HANDS TREMBLED, SO THAT SHE HAD some difficulty slipping the knot in the cord securing the marionette to the metal stand that braced it upright. When she freed the thing, she held it by its arms and lifted it off the mantel with an obvious dread that infected me.

The archbishop said, "It won't bite."

As Gwyneth took a step backward and began to stoop to throw the puppet into the flames, she cried out as if stung, threw it down on the hearth, and backed up another step.

I said, "What's wrong?"

"It moved."

"I didn't see."

She rubbed the palm of her left hand over the back of her right, the palm of her right over the back of her left, as though she felt the blue lizards of her faux tattoos wriggling on her skin and meant to smooth them into stillness.

"I was holding it by its upper arms. I felt . . . its muscles tensed."

"But it's made of wood," the archbishop said with a note of amusement. "It doesn't have muscles."

The marionette was lying on its back, one arm at its side and the other across its chest, one leg bent. The top hat had fallen off, revealing carved and painted hair. Its hinged mouth sagged open, the square chisel-blade teeth like the jaws of an unsprung trap.

Gwyneth cautiously extended her right leg to kick the hateful thing up and into the firebox.

"No, no. That isn't permissible," said the archbishop.

"There aren't any rules."

"My rules," he said, and held up a cell phone, which he had evidently taken from a pocket of his slacks. "I've already entered 911. I need only press SEND. Use your hands, girl."

With no intention other than persuasion, I took a step toward Wallache, but Gwyneth said, "Addison, no. Your eyes."

As I lowered my head and eased back, the archbishop said, "What about your eyes?"

Gwyneth withdrew her gloves from a jacket pocket.

"Bare hands," the archbishop instructed.

In response to the look of contempt that she turned upon him, he only brandished the cell phone.

Gwyneth put the gloves away, hesitated, hesitated, hesitated, suddenly bent down and snatched the hateful icon off the hearth. For a moment, she seemed to be struggling to shake it loose of her, and I couldn't tell if one of the thing's hands had in fact closed tightly around her thumb or if that was a detail conjured by my imagination, but then she flung it into the firebox, and the gas flames at once ignited the puppet's costume.

Perhaps the effect was a consequence of the pliancy of the oil-rich yew wood, but the marionette appeared to writhe in agony, flexed and twisted and seemed to seek handholds on the ceramic logs, as if it might clamber out of the fireplace and carry the consuming flames to us, setting the entire room ablaze.

A sound like the wooden heels of wooden shoes drumming hard against marble broke the spell that the sight of the twitching puppet cast over me. I looked at its twin, which still sat upon the mantel. Although I was certain of the source of the sound, the abomination sat motionless, its legs stretched out in front of it, hands upon its knees, as it had been posed previously. Because the mantel was somewhat high, if I hadn't been tall enough, I wouldn't have noticed, scattered on the stone, a few chips of the high-gloss black paint with which the puppet's shoes were made to look like patent leather.

In the firebox, the marionette lay still across the logs, and tendrils of foul-smelling black smoke seethed like spirits from its shrinking form and were either drawn up the chimney by a draft or escaped through it into the night and storm.

When I looked at Gwyneth, she was squeezing her right thumb with her left hand, and when she opened the hand, blood glistened, oozing from a cut on the pad of the thumb.

"She needs a bandage," I told the archbishop.

"No, Addison. I'm okay. It's not much of a cut."

In spite of Wallache and his cell phone, I went to the remaining marionette, snapped the cord that bound it to the metal brace, and lifted it off the mantel.

An ink spot appeared in the center of my vision and spread to the perimeter, but I hadn't gone blind, because in that darkness floated the music box from which Father had plucked and pocketed the winding key years earlier. As bright as a stage, illuminated by a light that had no source, the lid offered four dancers, as before. The prince and princess were dethroned, and in their place were Gwyneth and I, but dressed as they had been. She danced with the man-goat Pan, I held in my arms the goggle-eyed frog, and the four tiny figures waltzed along the inlaid tracks to cold and brittle music. The goatish god halted in the dance to bury his face in his partner's cleavage, she threw back her head as if in ecstasy, the frog grinned to reveal teeth as pointed as needles, which no real frog had ever possessed, and flickering from the grin came a snaky black tongue, which the figurine of me bent forward to capture in its mouth.

I don't believe that I was released from the vision, but instead *thrust* myself out of it; and if I hadn't done so, I suspect that next I would not have been merely observing my image on the music box but would have found myself there in its place, the scaly demonic form in my arms, in a hellish kiss with twining tongues.

Although I thought that I had been gone from the archbishop's private apartment for a minute or longer, the unnerving vision must have occurred and ended in an instant, because neither Gwyneth nor Wallache reacted as if I had seized up. I threw the marionette atop the burning remnants of its twin, and the ribbons of foul black smoke didn't merely seethe from it but *leaped* to the flue as if they were raveling up the chimney and onto some cosmic spool that turned at high speed.

The archbishop said, "What do you think you've achieved by this pointless ritual?"

We didn't answer or look at him, but watched until the black smoke faded to gray and the charred marionettes shrank in a tangle of withering limbs, until the fire split their torsos and, through the curtain of blue flames, red coals glowed deep in those cracks.

"Are you done here?" asked Wallache. "Or would you like to burn a sofa cushion, perhaps an entire armchair?"

"We're done," Gwyneth said.

"Good. I'm in a hurry, if you don't mind."

"Last-minute trip?" she asked, indicating the two suitcases.

"As if it's any of your business."

"There's nowhere for you to go, Your Eminence."

"I grew up in worse snow country. I can drive through this."

"Not what I meant. Would you like all the funds in my trust, for your good works? You may have the money now, if you want."

No longer able to summon a smile, he said, "You are demonic."

"Outside the storm zone," she said, "airports will be open. But what about your flock, all left behind?"

A note of defensiveness at last blurred the sharp edges of his self-confidence. "There are many good priests in this diocese to see after them in my absence."

"Yes," she agreed, "many *good* priests," by her tone implying that she did not include him in that category.

As when she and Goddard had sparred verbally with each other in the alley behind his gallery, this conversation had a subtext that I couldn't quite grasp. Although I didn't know where Wallache was going or why, Gwyneth seemed to have—or intuit—that information.

Recovering his poise, the archbishop said, "If you would like to confess your vandalism, Gwyneth, and I assume much else as well, I will prescribe a proper penance."

"I've made other arrangements," she said, dropped the key to the residence on the floor, and walked out of the apartment with me close behind.

In the antechamber, I said, "We have to bandage your thumb."

"This will be good enough," she said, and she pulled a knitted glove onto her right hand.

Following her down the stairs as she worked her left hand into the other glove, I said, "You seem to think he's not fit to be what he is, where he is."

"It's not just what I think. It's the truth."

Crossing the drawing room, where in paint and bronze and stone, the many sainted founders of the faith looked sadly down, I said, "But why is he unfit?"

"Others under his authority broke their vows in a most terrible way. He didn't do what they did, but he engineered a cover-up of what they did, less for the sake of the church than for the sake of his career, with no justice for the victims. And he engineered it in such a way that he left few if any fingerprints in his wake."

I thought I knew to what she alluded, and if I was right, I did not want any further details.

Outside, the street receded left and right like the white bed of a river, and turbulent currents of snow flooded through the air.

61

LEAVING THE ARCHBISHOP'S RESIDENCE BEHIND, Gwyneth at first pressed the accelerator too hard, so that even with four-wheel drive and tire chains, the Rover fishtailed along the street, whereupon she gave it more gas, which didn't help matters, before she eased back on the pedal. When the vehicle became stable and we were proceeding at a somewhat safer speed than a bank robber's getaway car, I relaxed my grip on the seat and lowered my bracing feet from the dashboard to the floor.

I said, "Anger doesn't solve anything."

"I wish it did. If it did, I'd anger away all the troubles of the world."

She hadn't mentioned a destination. Again, she seemed to be driving a route chosen at random, but by now I knew that whatever map guided her this night, it had not been drawn by a whimsical cartographer.

"Where is he going?" I asked.

"Wallache? I don't know."

"Back there, you did seem to know."

"All I know is that he's going in a circle, and wherever he goes, he'll only find the same thing that he's running from."

"What is he running from?" When she did not reply, I said, "Sometimes it seems you know something I don't know but should."

I could hear the smile in her voice. "Addison Goodheart, you are so well named. I love your innocence."

For a minute or so, I reran her words several times in my mind, and at last I said, "I don't think that was a put-down."

"A put-down? How can it ever be a put-down when a girl says she loves you?"

Let me tell you, I parsed and pondered those words, diagrammed the second sentence in my mind, and worried about what subtext was eluding me this time. Finally, I replied, "You didn't say that you loved me. You said you loved my innocence."

"And you *are* your innocence. It's as fundamental to you as water is to the sea."

Although words are the world and were the birthing of the world, there are no words to express what I felt at that moment, no words for the dimensions of my joy, for the great buoyancy that overcame my spirit, for the depth of my gratitude, for the brightness of my hope.

When I could speak, I said, "I love you, too."

"I know."

"I'm not just saying it."

"I know."

"I mean because you said it."

"I know. You love me. I know."

"You really know?"

"I really do."

"How long have you known?"

"Since we met in the library. You were standing there in shadow by Charles Dickens and you said, 'We hold each other hostage to our eccentricities.'"

"I think I also said we were made for each other."

"Yes, you did. But it was when you said the other thing that my heart seemed almost to fall out of me. When we love someone, we're held hostage by fate, because if we lose that person, then we, too, are lost. When you said we hold each other hostage, you declared your love as clearly as it could be said."

How strange it is that one can be rendered unable to speak as much by ecstasy as by terror. Fear never silenced me more effectively than this.

At last I said, "Can there be such a thing as love at first sight?"

"The great poets have always said there is. But do we really need poets to convince us?"

"No. Not me."

"Not me, either."

Staring through the windshield, I didn't see the snow or the veiled city. There was nothing to see, nothing worth seeing except her face.

I wanted to touch her, just my hand to her face, but she could not bear being touched, and I wanted to stare into her eyes, but I dared not let her look into mine. Our eccentricities were more than merely peculiarities of our character; they were cruel conditions of our very existence. Our situation should have seemed hopeless, should have reduced me to despair. But regardless of what we couldn't have together, we could still have our feelings for each other, and at that moment, knowing my feelings were reciprocated was such a grace that my bliss could not be deflated by any arrow.

She said, "We've got to return to Walter's and get the girl."

"The girl without a name? Why?"

"Everything's happening so fast. But before we go to Walter's, I want to see your rooms, where you live."

"What, you mean now?"

"Yes, now. I want to see where you've hidden from the world for eighteen years."

62

ON AN APRIL NIGHT WHEN I WAS TWELVE, SHORTLY after I finished reading a novel about a lucky coin, Father and I went out into the post-midnight city, where in spite of the faint but lingering odor of automobile exhaust, the sweet smell of spring was in the air, as was the expectation of change, with the trees in the parks leafing out anew.

In the great park, in the pavilion, on the elevated floor of the bandstand, a slant of moonlight polished a penny and brought it to my attention. I snatched it up, neither because we were profoundly poor, which we were, nor because we had much need of money, which we didn't, but because of the book that I had recently read. I showed it to Father, declared that I had found my own lucky coin, and began to imagine aloud what miraculous benefits it might bestow upon us.

He could always hold his own with me in games of fantasy, but that one did not charm him. In the spring warmth, as we slowly walked the perimeter of the pavilion, gazing out at the meadows pale with lunar frost, at the woodlet guarding its darkness, at the black lake floating the full moon like a raft upon its waters, he told me that there was no such thing as luck. To believe in luck, you must believe that the universe is a roulette wheel and that instead of paying out to us what we have earned, it pays out only what it wishes. But it is not a spinning wheel of chance, it is a work of art, complete and framed by eternity.

He said that because we live in time, we think that the past is baked and served and eaten, that the present is coming out of the oven in continuous courses, and that the future is not yet even in the mixing bowl. Any thoughtful physicist, he said, well schooled in quantum mechanics, would agree that all time exists simultaneously, which I subsequently learned was the case. In truth, Father said, at the first instant of the universe, all of time was present, all our yesterdays and today and all our tomorrows, everyone and everything that was and ever would be existed at that moment. But more amazing still, in the first instant that the universe came into existence, the fabric of it also included all the infinite ways that things might have been, countless of them terrible in the extreme and countless others glorious. Nothing is predetermined for us, and yet all our possible choices are threads in the vast weave of things, so that we have free will even though the consequences of our will are predictable. Father said we were given a sense of time's progression because our minds are not able to cope with the reality that past, present, and future all exist simultaneously and that all of history existed in the first instant of the universe's being.

To help me understand, Father said that I should think of the universe as a giant painting rendered in more than three dimensions; some scientists say eleven, some say fewer, some say more, but no one knows—or will ever know—for sure. In an art gallery, when you stand too close to a large canvas executed in only *two* dimensions, you can see the artist's brushstrokes and certain details clearly, but you can't understand either the full effect of the piece or the artist's intentions. You have to step back and step back again, and some- times yet again, in order to grasp the totality of the work. To understand the universe, our world, and all life in the world, you have to step *out of time*, which for living humanity is not an option, because we are a part of this painting, characters within it, able to perceive it only as a continuing series of events, episodes. However, because we are conscious creatures with the gift of reason, we can seek and learn and extrapolate from what we learn, and conceive the truth.

In a universe in which past, present, and future came into existence all at once, complete from beginning to end, with all possible outcomes of every life woven through the tapestry, there is no chance, only choice, no luck, but only consequences. A penny polished by moonlight is only a penny, though its existence—minted by thinking creatures for the purpose of commerce in the present and investment in the future—might be a kind of miracle, if you're imaginative enough to credit miracles. He said that the penny would not bring us luck, that even if it had been a million dollars, it would not of itself bring us luck and change our lives, that what happened to us was of our election—and therefore allowed us more hope than luck could ever provide.

I was only twelve that April night, but already worn to wisdom by the friction between me and the world aboveground. When Father took luck away from me, I was not downcast but exhilarated. The penny didn't mean anything, but what I did with the penny mattered. I put the coin down on the bandstand floor, where I had found it, in the hope that whoever discovered it next might, by the loving guidance of someone like my father or by his own heart, be led to the revelation to which I had been led.

And so, more than fourteen years later on a snowy night, I knew with conviction that Gwyneth had not been dropped into my lap by Lady Luck. She and her love for me were one of the infinite number of ways that things might have been, but now they were what *was*, by virtue of countless decisions that she and I had made, moment by moment throughout our lives, which we could never hope to track in retrospect.

I could only lose her if, from this moment forward, I made wrong choices, or if she made them. But I would take those odds rather than the odds that luck offered.

63

IN THE MAIN ROOM OF MY SUBTERRANEAN HOME, Gwyneth moved along the shelves, reading the titles on the spines. "I knew there would be books, and I knew what the character of them would be."

Her presence here was the most magical turn of events in this night of myriad wonders. Gladness expressed itself in my covered countenance, in my voice, manner, action. The girl was fully aware of my happiness, and she delighted in my delight. I could not take my eyes off her, and in respect of that, she did not turn her eyes toward me.

"Your courage humbles me," she said.

"Courage? Not really. I'm a coward by necessity. We always had to run from any threat."

"To live in these cramped spaces, without sun, for eighteen years, the last six without company, and always with the expectation that there would never be more than this, to endure that and not be driven mad . . . Sanity in such circumstances takes more courage than I possess."

With that, she gave me a somewhat different perspective on my life, and I didn't know what to say.

She said then, "What do you want to take with you, Addison?"

"Take with me?"

"What's most precious to you? Don't leave it here. After we go, you won't ever be coming back."

I couldn't fully comprehend her meaning, and it seemed that I must have misheard what she said. "Not coming back? But where would I live?"

"With me."

"You mean in the apartment with the piano?"

"No. We're not going back there, either. That's over. All of it is over. We're moving on to something new."

Until then, I would not have thought that great happiness could coexist with fear, but the latter came upon me without fading the former. I found myself trembling, not in either dread or rapture, but in a kind of neutral expectation.

"We have a lot to do in the next few hours," she said. "So hurry and decide what you don't want to leave behind, and let's be going."

Trust, I told myself, and I did trust.

Pressed between two books on one of the shelves, an envelope contained a photograph, a simple snapshot, that I never wanted to be without. From between the front cover and the endpaper of a special book on another shelf, I withdrew an index card on which Father had printed words of special meaning to me. I slipped the card into the envelope and tucked the envelope into an inside pocket of my jacket.

I followed Gwyneth to the passageway that led from the hammock room—which was also my kitchen—and there I paused to look back. I had lived more than two-thirds of my life in those windowless rooms, and for the most part they had been years of contentment and hope. I felt as though ten thousand conversations between Father and me were recorded on those concrete walls and that if I could only sit quietly and attentively enough, with adequate patience, they would replay for me. Nothing in this world, not even the most mundane moments of our lives, is without meaning, nor is any of it lost forever.

In leaving, I had neglected to turn off the lamps. I considered going back through the rooms to extinguish them, but I didn't. I left them aglow, as the lights in a shrine are never put out. Following Gwyneth, I allowed myself to imagine that the bulbs in those lamps would prove to be blessed with uncanny life and that if, a thousand years from now, some adventurous explorer of storm drains were to come across that haven, he would be welcomed by lamplight, by books perfectly preserved, and would know that in this humblest of places, in ancient times, many treasured hours had been passed in happiness.

64

SNOW SHEETING THROUGH THE HEADLIGHTS, THE streets vacant except for the laboring plows, the people of the city sequestered in their warm and civilized rooms, the wind keening across the windshield and along the passenger door beside me . . .

Gwyneth drove a route familiar to me, and only minutes after we set out, her cell rang. She glanced at the screen, put the phone on SPEAKER, and said, "I would pray that Simon haunts you forever, but he deserves his rest."

"How touching that you should care so much for a useless burnt-out boozer who couldn't even keep from pissing his pants at the end."

Ryan Telford's voice was throatier than before, and in spite of his cocky words, he sounded shaken.

When she said nothing, Telford pressed into her silence: "You were right that he didn't know where you have a ninth apartment. The only useful thing we got from funky Simon was how he came to know you in the first place."

Gwyneth stiffened but still did not speak.

"He saved a little girl from death in a Dumpster, probably so drunk at the time, he didn't know what he was doing. And because he saved her, you saved him. Your weakness, Miss Mouse, is that you're a sentimental little bitch."

"Where are you?" she asked.

Instead of answering, he said, "With the Internet, it's easy to find an old news story."

He paused. The sound he made suggested that he was straining at something, a weight that was difficult to lift or the lid of a jar too tight to unscrew. He muttered a curse.

Gwyneth waited.

The curator said, "The newspaper story and follow-ups tell me the hospital where the girl was treated, how she became a ward of the court, how she was in a coma, a vegetative state. Then the stories end. There's like a press blackout or something, nothing about her fate. Did she die? Is she still alive, with the brain of a carrot?"

When Telford paused again, Gwyneth handed me the phone to hold, so that she could drive with both hands, and she accelerated.

The curator grunted, made that straining-to-lift sound again, and then took a couple of deep, shuddery breaths. "Remember I told you two of Goddard's guys, they now work for me, they're ex-cops?"

"I remember."

"One of them knows these people who are tight with the judge in the news story. In fact, they have a hammerlock on the good judge. They can call him day or night, ask for anything, and he'll pretend to be delighted to help no matter how much shit they throw at him."

Gwyneth took a corner so suddenly and so fast that I was thrown against the passenger door and almost dropped the phone.

Telford said, "This time, Judge Gallagher didn't have to jump through flaming hoops to please them. He just had to tell them what happened to the girl, the one the court records call Jane Doe 329."

"Don't touch her," Gwyneth said. "Don't."

The curator seemed to strain at something again, and I imagined that he must be tied to a chair and struggling to be free of his bonds, though that made no sense.

He said, "If you don't come here, I'll do to Jane Doe 329 what I promised I'd do to you five years ago. She doesn't raise my flag as high as you do, little mouse. She's pale and she won't even be aware of how good I am when I jam it to her."

"She's a child."

"But she's pretty enough, and they've fed her right, exercised her every day, so she does have nice enough muscle tone."

"I'm on my way," Gwyneth said.

"For her sake, I hope so."

"Twenty minutes."

"You sure that's enough time?"

"Twenty minutes," she insisted.

"Twenty-one will be too late."

He terminated the call. I pressed END on Gwyneth's phone.

"You have the Mace," she said. "I have the Taser."

"They'll have guns."

"We have momentum."

"I saw my father shot down."

"Hope for a little luck."

"There's no such thing as luck."

"No," she said. "There's not."

65

THAT WE SHOULD MEET IN THE WHIRL OF LIFE THAT spins more people apart than together, that we should find in each other so much that was compatible, that we should lift each other out of doubt and out of weakness into conviction and strength, that we should fall in love in spite of being unable to consummate it physically, a love that was of mind for mind, heart for heart, soul for soul: This rare gift was priceless. And the elaborate chain of cause and effect from which it arose exceeded in intricacy and in beauty the most exquisitely decorated Fabergé egg, or a hundred of them.

To preserve that love and to have years in which to explore a fraction of its passageways and sanctums, we must now make not one wrong decision, either of us, but do from moment to moment the right thing in the most effective manner.

We passed a plow that must have broken down. Its rooftop beacon shone bright, but the waves of yellow light were pent up and stilled in one glowing ball. Headlights doused, driver's cab deserted, door hanging open, engine quiet, flakes melting on its still-warm housing, the big vehicle canted on a curbside ridge of compacted snow.

Minutes later, in a residential neighborhood, I wondered at the number of houses with windows aglow. In a few instances, people might have forgotten to switch off their exterior Christmas lighting before going to bed, although of the fraction of houses decorated for the season, light issued from the windows of fully half, their occupants evidently still awake, as were the residents of many other homes. The novelist F. Scott Fitzgerald said that the real dark night of the soul was always three o'clock in the morning, and those sixty minutes between three o'clock and four were reliably and literally the darkest in the city. Not this night.

On the street lined with bare-limbed maples, cars at curbside and mounds of plowed snow allowed no place to park. Gwyneth killed the engine, set the brake, and we got out of the Rover in the street directly in front of the yellow-brick house, leaving one lane open for traffic.

The gate in the wrought-iron fence, the porch steps, the door, each salient point on the final approach seemed full of threat, as the cold wind and the snow at our backs pressed us to cross the threshold and enter whatever hell lay beyond. Telford knew we were coming. There could be no hope of stealth.

Before Gwyneth rang the bell, I said, "Maybe this is the time, this once, in spite of who we are, maybe this is the time to call the police."

"Telford has nothing to lose now. If he sees police, he'll pull the pin and blow it all up. And what kind of police might come? Can we hope they'll be the kind who take an oath seriously? And will they come at all? On this night of all nights, will they still answer a call? From here on, Addison, we're alone, we're all alone, everyone alone. We'll be late in two minutes."

She rang the bell.

When no one responded, she opened the door, and we went inside, where Walter lay dead in the archway between the foyer and the living room. He had been shot more than once.

Lamps lit the living room, the candle at the shrine to the Holy Mother flickered, the voices on TV spoke in soothing tones—Walter and his sister had been watching it at this hour—and Janet lay in a lake of blood, having died a slower death than had her brother.

Her brutal murder long behind her, the lost wife, Claire, smiled eternally in the two photographs framed in chased silver.

Gwyneth's Goth makeup couldn't fully conceal her anguish. The thick mascara colored her tears as black as her grief.

The newsreader on the TV said something about a moratorium on all international air traffic in and out of the United States, but we couldn't consider his breaking news because the stairs commanded our ascent, as the steps to the gallows call forth those condemned.

In the upper hallway, we passed the open door to the children's bedroom, where the nurse named Cora had been brought to be murdered with them. There were no children there now, no nurse. They had gone and left their bodies behind them.

In the room where the nameless girl received care, Ryan Telford sat on the edge of the bed in which Cora should have been sleeping. He bent forward with his forearms on his thighs, hands between his knees, a pistol gripped in them. He looked up as we entered the room and smiled, but there was no humor in his smile, only the feverish glee of a rabid jackal.

66

TELFORD'S HAIR HUNG AS WET AND LANK AS IF HE had just stepped from the shower, but this was the greasy wetness of sour sweat. In his pale glistening face, the centers of his bloodshot eyes appeared less like black irises than like portals to the lightless realm of his mind. His ham-pink lips were overlaid with gray, as if he had gone for a touch of Goth himself.

"Little mouse, you're a masturbation fantasy."

"You're not," she said.

"Who's the masked man, Kemosabe?"

"Don't you recognize him, the hood and all? He's Death."

"I don't think Death goes skiing."

His voice was as throaty as on the phone, and perhaps weaker.

"You don't look well," Gwyneth said.

"I would agree."

Soaked with sweat, his shirt clung to him, and his pants were spattered with blood, but the blood wasn't his.

Moving to the nameless girl's bed, looking across it at Telford, Gwyneth said, "You were in Japan."

"The Far East isn't good for business anymore."

"So you came back ahead of schedule."

"Not soon enough."

Concerned that we were now surrounded, I asked, "Where are your two . . . associates?"

"Bastards spooked and ran."

"*After* slaughtering a family," I said.

"That doesn't faze them. But I have one of my moments, and they run away like little girls."

"Moments?"

That mirthless smile again. "You'll see." Gwyneth put her contact Taser on the nightstand.

"I'm not up for it, either," Telford said, and put his pistol aside on the bed where he sat.

She said, "When did your symptoms start?"

"A little light-headed late morning. Slight queasiness midafternoon. Fever by dinnertime. Then wham."

"It goes fast."

"Express train."

In my recent trips to the library, I had not read newspapers. Fragments of things heard on TV in the past two nights suddenly coalesced in my mind, and I understood why I had seemed to be missing some subtext in Gwyneth's conversations with Edmund Goddard and the archbishop.

I have always been of the world but little in it. In this case, the price of isolation was ignorance.

Gwyneth began to put down the safety railing on her side of the girl's hospital bed.

"Better not touch her," Telford advised.

"I'm taking her out of here."

"I've touched her. Pretty much all over. Sweet thing. Succulent. She'll die of it now."

Gwyneth pulled back the sheet and blanket. The sleeping girl's pajamas had been disarranged.

I looked away.

"Couldn't manage more than touching," the curator said. "But it was lovely—the sharing."

Abruptly he wrapped his arms around himself and doubled over, almost toppling from Cora's bed. He made that keening noise, as if he were straining to lift a heavy weight, but it was a more tortured sound and went on longer than when he'd been on the phone. He looked as if he were coming apart inside and was trying desperately to hold himself together. Something that didn't look like vomit and that smelled worse drooled from his mouth.

Having one of his moments.

Gwyneth leaned over the bed, adjusting the girl's pajamas. "Addison, in the nightstand drawer, you'll find a bottle of alcohol, a package of cotton pads, and adhesive tape. Please set them out for me."

I did as she asked, glad to be useful. I worked with my left hand, keeping the little pressurized can of Mace in my right.

When Telford recovered, he sat up straighter and wiped his mouth on his sleeve. The tears on his eyelashes and those sliding down his face were tinted with blood. He looked around as if trying to recall the nature of this place and how he had gotten here.

Gwyneth withdrew the plastic cannula from the vein in the girl's left forearm and let the drip line dangle from the bag of fluid that hung on the IV rack. She said, "I don't think this is necessary, but just in case," and with alcohol, she swabbed the point of insertion from which she'd withdrawn the cannula.

Having oriented himself, Telford said, "What're those stitches in her side?"

"We had the feeding tube taken out two days ago," Gwyneth said.

"I didn't like the look of them. Turned me off. Otherwise, she's a tender little thing. A bit sloppy from lying around all this time, but all in all, prime enough."

"She's a child."

"How prime does it get?"

Gwyneth placed a cotton pad over the puncture in the forearm and taped it down.

Turning quarrelsome, Telford said, "Hell's bells, the bitch is brain-dead and contaminated. What're you doing? What's the use? Why do you care anyway?"

"She's special," Gwyneth said.

Picking up the pistol that he had claimed to be too weary to use, he said, "How's she special?"

Instead of answering him, she pulled the blanket off the bed and threw the top sheet back, so that it draped over the footrail, exposing the girl in her pajamas, head to foot.

"How's she special?" Telford repeated.

Gwyneth rolled the girl onto her right side, facing away from us, and said, "Addison, help me with this blanket."

Telford raised the gun, pointing it at the ceiling, as if to get our attention. "I'm talking here." He must have been even weaker than he appeared, and the weapon must have been too heavy for him, because his wrist kept going limp, the gun wobbling this way and that. "Why is this little slut so special?"

"Because everyone is," Gwyneth said.

"She's just a little slut."

"If that's so, then I must be wrong."

"You're wrong as shit, that's what you are."

Together, Gwyneth and I placed the blanket on the bed, so that half of it was draped over the side.

"You're special, too," she told Telford.

"What kind of crack is that?"

"It's not a crack. I'm just hoping."

She rolled Jane Doe 329 toward us, onto the blanket, and then onto her left side, almost to the edge of the bed.

"Hoping what?" Telford asked.

"Hoping you use what time you have left to save yourself."

We draped the dangling length of blanket over the girl and sort of tucked it against her back.

"You know I'm dying, bitch. Screw hope." He struggled up from the second bed, as loose-limbed as a drunk. "I gotta tell you something."

Gwyneth grabbed the farther hem of the blanket, and pulled it across the insensate child, thereby wrapping her completely.

Telford stumbled two steps forward and grabbed the other bed railing with his left hand to steady himself.

I raised the Mace, and Gwyneth said, "No. That'll just make him crazy. And then what?"

"Little titmouse, you want crazy, go to North Korea. Maniacs. Lunatic bastards. TV says this thing the lunatics engineered, it's a twofer."

Gwyneth said, "Addison, get your arms under her, lift her off the bed. Do it now."

I didn't want to pocket the Mace. Maybe it would drive him crazy, the burning in his eyes, but maybe that would be good, even if he had a loaded pistol.

"Do it now, Addison."

"Hey, Lone Ranger, you hear it's a twofer?"

"I heard," I assured him as Gwyneth took the Mace from me.

"Ebola virus, Lone Ranger, *and* flesh-eating bacteria, and *way* pumped up, the shit's totally *enhanced*, airborne, they say worse than atom bombs. It eats you up from the inside out. How's that for bad?"

I got my arms under the girl and lifted her from the bed. Strong with terror, I was amazed that she felt so light.

The pistol tumbled from Telford's hand onto the bed. Dripping sweat, weeping bloodier tears than before, he leaned hard across the railing, not to retrieve the weapon, but instead to spit in Gwyneth's face. The thick, disgusting wad of spittle contained more than mere saliva.

67

IN THIS FALLEN WORLD, THERE ARE THINGS YOU hope for but never expect to receive because there is no luck and never was, but also because they are things of such great value that not all the good you could do in an entire lifetime would be enough to make you worthy of them. If one of your hopes is fulfilled, if that precious thing ever comes to you, it comes to you as a grace, and every day of your life thereafter, you need to give thanks for the gift. The girl I met in lamplight near Charles Dickens—she was my grace, all I wanted or would ever want.

I stood there helpless, with Jane Doe in my arms, and Telford spat in Gwyneth's face, a foul phlegm that he worked up for a final outrage. He laughed shakily, and there was amusement in it, a giddy delight, almost rapture. "A gun's too easy, titmouse. You die like me, just like me."

She snatched a corner of the top sheet and blotted her face, but I knew that couldn't be good enough to spare her.

"Die like me, like me." The curator drew out each *me* like squeezed air escaping from the pinched neck of a balloon. He was a man and a monster, too, a monster and a clown amusing himself, and if he had possessed the strength, he would have capered in his delight.

God help me, I almost dropped the comatose girl to seize the gun and kill him. A rushing noise swelled in my head, like cataracts of water falling from a hundred feet, flecks of static in my vision, ice in my marrow, for I was overtaken by wrath and almost consumed by it, but I didn't drop the girl.

Gwyneth said, "Let's get her out of here," and I said, "The bathroom, hot water, soap, *wash yourself*," and she said, "Move, move, now, let's go."

A seizure took Telford. His entire body spasmed. He bent over the bed and poured out from his mouth a steaming mass that was not anything he had eaten, that was part of the essential substance of himself. With the sound of bowels liquifying and the knocking of bones, he collapsed onto the floor and out of sight.

"Come on," she said, *"Come on,"* and led the way out of the room, past the bathroom where there would be hot water and soap, along the hallway, to the stairs, and I could do nothing, nothing but follow her, my legs weak with the weight of the girl in my arms and with the burden of my terror.

As I descended the stairs, the malodor from the archbishop's fireplace rose around me, the foul stink of Paladine's marionettes in flames.

I halted, and Gwyneth must have known, for as she continued down the stairs in front of me, she said, "It's nothing, they're not here, it's arrant deception. Like the rapping in the attic. Come on."

Across the foyer, past dead Walter. The door, the porch, the gate in the spearpoint fence, every salient point along the way was no less ominous than it had been when we'd passed it earlier.

Gwyneth raised the tailgate, and I gently slid the blanket-wrapped girl into the cargo space of the Rover.

Along the street, two or three people were digging their parked vehicles out of the snow. Their labor had a frantic quality, and not one of them looked up from the job to see what we were about.

Closing the tailgate, I said, "Do you have sanitizing gel in the glove box, anything, do you have anything? I'll drive."

"You don't know *how* to drive. I'll be all right, Addison."

She settled behind the steering wheel, and I had no choice but the passenger seat, and then we were rolling. Rolling, but where and to what?

68

WHO WE OF THE HIDDEN WERE, WHAT WE WERE, why we ever existed, explained the mystery of music issuing out of the ether.

Days after that grim night in the city, when I had quiet time to reflect, I realized that Father had never heard the beautiful but sad melody that sometimes found its way into my deep three-room safehold. He had been laid to rest in the river a year or more before the first piano notes came from the air around me as I sat reading.

Sometimes the nocturne played only once, those clear notes flowing in crystalline passages, and my mind was engaged by the brilliance of the melodic structure, my heart roused by the purity of emotion embodied in the music. I recognized the acute grief that had been the composer's motivation, and knew it must have been the consequence of losing someone, but I also admired the talent and the wise intention that had subdued the bitter emotion and had drawn from it the strains of sorrow that were a better testament to the beauty of whoever was lost. On other occasions, the piece repeated two and three times, as often as five, and repetition carried me past all wondering about the identity and motivation of the composer, until the music spoke for me alone and expressed my feelings about *my* losses.

If Father had been alive when the phenomenon began, if he had heard that nocturne and, in seeking its source, had been as mystified as I was, he would have raised a question for exploration: By what agency could a piece of piano music be conveyed halfway across a city and deep beneath its streets, making use of neither wire nor wireless technology, playing sweetly without benefit of receiver, amplifier, or speakers? Fascinating conversations would have led to all manner of speculations, from speculation to conjecture, from conjecture to supposition, and finally to a working hypothesis, which might in time be discarded and the process begun again.

Father could never have gone from a hypothesis to the conviction of a theory, because while he lived, he never knew the true nature of the hidden. What we are and why we exist explains the agency by which Gwyneth's music was conveyed to me by extraordinary means, there at the end of an age. If I had not met Gwyneth, if her biological father had not been the man of insight and true grace that he was, if her father's closest friend hadn't been Teague Hanlon, perhaps I never would have learned what we are, and would have died in an ultimate riot of nihilistic violence.

On that night of Telford's death, I discovered what I was and who I am. What might have been but never was . . . Well, it all became possible again.

69

THIS SNOW FALLING, SNOW ON SNOW, SEEMED LIKE none before it, not because it fell as dense as tropical rain, but because of what I now knew of the implacable plague. That knowledge served as a corrective to my vision, so that I saw in this descending whiteness not merely the suggestion of peace inherent in all snow, but peace eternal.

A great city is the hope of mankind. This isn't to say that the future lies in cities. A whistle-stop is also the hope of mankind. A humble village, a county seat, a state capitol, a great metropolis: Each is the hope of mankind on Earth. As is any neighborhood. A life in isolation might be a life in preparation, as mine seemed now to be, but it is not a life complete until it is lived with others who complete it. Although I had been an outsider, welcome nowhere in its boroughs, the city was home to me, its people my people even if they did not wish to be, and this fast-falling snow might as well have been ashes from a crematorium in a death camp, its descent a piercing sadness.

The nameless girl lay blanketed and comatose in the back of the Land Rover. Gwyneth drove. I worried. Worried and accused myself for not using Telford's gun on him, and prayed to hold off despair.

Gwyneth said, "How often do you get a cold?"

In our current circumstances, the question seemed curious. "What do you mean?"

"Only one of those words had more than a single syllable."

"How often do I get a cold?"

"Is there any word in that you need defined?"

"I don't get colds," I said.

"How often have you had the flu?"

"Never. How would I possibly catch a cold or the flu? I've had virtually no contact with people, sick people or otherwise. I've lived almost in isolation."

"What about the man you called Father? Colds, the flu?"

"Not in the time I knew him. He had no more contact with people than I did."

"Toothache?"

"No. We floss and brush. We're very diligent about it."

"That must be miracle floss, a magic brush. Not one cavity?"

"What is this about?"

"Ever cut yourself?"

"Of course."

"Ever had an infected cut?"

The Clears distracted me from answering her. We were still in a residential neighborhood, where they could be seen from time to time, as they could be seen anywhere, but suddenly they appeared in numbers. One in hospital blues crossed a lawn where, in the early hours of the storm, children had rolled together a snowman, using discs of reflective orange plastic for its eyes, a tennis ball for its nose, and what appeared to be the keys from a toy piano for its teeth. Another in whites passed through the wall of a house and came toward the street, leaving no rubble and bearing no wounds from his passage, and two in greens glided down from a roof to drift across a yard, all of them moving atop the mantle of snow rather than through it. On a branch high in a bare-limbed tree, a glowing woman in blues stood as if sentinel, and as the Land Rover approached, she turned her head to stare down at us, and in spite of the distance, though being in no danger of coming eye-to-eye, I looked away, as Father had told me always to do.

Gwyneth said, "How long do you need to ponder it?"

"Ponder what?"

"Ever had an infected cut?" she repeated.

"Not with Bactine and iodine and bandages."

"You're very careful about your health."

"I have to be. I can never go to a doctor."

"What do you fear, Addison?"

"Losing you," I said at once.

"What did you fear most before you ever met me?"

"Losing Father."

"And what else?"

"Father being beaten and badly hurt. Being beaten myself."

"There must be more you feared."

"Seeing other people hurt. A man shot in the back gave me this Rolex. It was the worst thing to watch him die. Sometimes I'm afraid to read the newspapers in the library because they contain so many stories of suffering."

"Do you fear the policemen who killed your father?"

"No. I don't fear anyone until I see murder in his face."

We still hadn't talked much about Father. I hadn't told her that the men who killed him were police officers.

Accustomed to the prevalence of mysteries in the world and still reluctant to ask questions that, though she had professed her love, might cause her to withdraw, I didn't inquire how she had come upon that information.

"What do you hate?" she asked.

I thought a moment. "Only what I fear."

"*What* you fear. That's a most unusual answer in this world of hatred."

Before I could consider what she said, we turned a corner onto a major avenue, drove through three Clears, and came upon a gathering of their kind that reminded me of that night five years earlier, a year after Father died, when I encountered the grand spectacle that I called the Convocation. Now, the city lay dimmed by the seething veils of winter, and the high-rises tiered away into the obscuring weather until those beyond a block might have been only shapes in a murky mirror, mere reflections of nearer buildings. Through the white gloom, standing in air and descending slowly like glowing ornaments being hung upon the night by invisible hands, came Clears of both sexes and all races, in their white shoes and white or blue or green uniforms, from whatever other dimension and into ours. Upon touching down, each of them at once walked away, with the brisk purpose that perhaps hospital personnel displayed on a busy night in the emergency room.

Until the past few minutes, the sight of Clears always lifted my spirits. Although I believed that in their eyes could be glimpsed some power or knowledge that, though it might not turn me to stone, would shake me to my core, I felt happier in their presence than I was when they weren't around. But they did not gladden my heart now. Ordinarily, if anything can be said to be ordinary in this world, some of them were solemn while others smiled. This time, not one smile could be seen, and their demeanor seemed to be one of deep, inconsolable sorrow. The great beauty of their incandescent descent chilled my heart, and finally I understood something of what Father had meant when he said that the Clears, although not evil like the Fogs, were in their own way terrible, for their power was supremely grand and formidable.

I closed my eyes, unable to bear that beauty anymore, and after a moment, Gwyneth said, "Have you ever had a sore throat, headache, indigestion, ulcers in the mouth, hay fever?"

"What does any of that matter?"

She said, "You will not die of the plague."

"I'm in the world more now. I'm at risk of contagion, just like you. I wish you had washed your face."

"Trust," she insisted.

70

BEFORE I EVER CAME TO THE CITY, FATHER'S BENE-
factor had given him the key to the food bank. I was never told the
man's position, and the only name that I had for him was Our
Friend. Although this stranger cared about us and our welfare, although he could once or twice a year meet with my father for a few
minutes and not strike out at him, Our Friend did not trust himself
to restrain a violent impulse through a longer encounter. And because Our Friend suffered a bout of depression bordering on despair
after each meeting, Father felt that he should impose upon the man
as seldom as possible and that I should impose upon him not at all
until Father had died.

When that day of misery arrived, and after Father lay at rest on
the river bottom, I composed a note as he had instructed me and,
that night, I took it to the food bank. The note said: *Father has died. I
have done with his body what he instructed. He wished me to tell you how very
much he loved you for your tolerance and how much he appreciated your generosity. I know that you told him the key would be mine when he passed away,
but he wanted me to ask you just the same if I might keep it. I will never take
more than I need from either the food bank or the thrift shop, and I will try
never to be found on the premises, never frighten anyone there by revealing
what I am, for I would be most aggrieved to ever bring pain or dishonor to the
food bank or anyone who staffs it. I miss Father terribly, and I don't think that
will ever change, but I will be all right. He wanted me to assure you that I will
be all right.*

Because Father had told me that Our Friend had a sense of humor and because I knew he would understand the meaning of my last three words, I signed the note *Son of It.*

Father had instructed me to seal the message in an envelope and to leave it in the center drawer of the desk in the smaller of the food bank's two offices. The arrangement with our benefactor was that any missive would be answered overnight if possible. When I returned, I found a different sealed envelope from the one that I had left, and in it a reply. *Dear boy, I was profoundly saddened to receive your news. I have always kept your father in my prayers, and I will keep him—and you—in them as long as I live. You may of course have the key. I wish that I could do more for you and be more of a comfort, but I am weak and so afraid. I accuse myself daily of cowardice and insufficient charity. As your father might have told you, for much longer than I knew him, I have suffered periodic depression, though I do always bounce back. Each encounter with your father precipitated a bout of the most severe despair, blackest depression, in spite of his great heart and gentle nature, and his face appears in dreams from which I wake as terrified as a child. This is my shortcoming and of course no fault of his. Do not hesitate to ask me for whatever you may need. Each time that I can be of help, I have a chance to mend my soul. God bless.*

Because I knew that Father would be most proud of me if I were to respect Our Friend's unfortunate vulnerability to depression and if I were as self-sufficient as possible, I asked for nothing more during the following six years. Every few months, I left him a note so that he would know I was alive and well.

On the night when Gwyneth faced down Ryan Telford to save the nameless girl, I met Our Friend, who was not, after all, a stranger to me. These years later, I still think of him with great affection, and I wish that I could send him a note to let him know that I am well, but he has been dead for a long time.

71

AGAINST THE SIGHT OF SOLEMN CLEARS DESCENDING, I kept my eyes closed until Gwyneth pulled to a stop and switched off the engine. When I looked, I found that we were in an alleyway, parked on a garage apron, athwart its two roll-up doors.

"Where's this, what now?" I asked.

"You'll see. We won't be here that long, but we can't leave the girl. Anyway, she's coming around."

"She is?"

"She will."

We got out of the Rover, and she put up the tailgate, and I took the bundled child into my arms again.

Following Gwyneth along the side of the garage, snow almost to the tops of my boots, I kept my head down, because the cold sharp wind stung tears from my eyes. I had been humbled, too, and filled with dread by the presence of so many Clears in the avenue, and I was afraid to look into the sky.

We came into a snow-choked area between the garage and the back of a two-story brick house, where all the windows were as black as if they had been painted over. Walls marked the property line, and the space felt like a miniature prison yard. The back porch didn't extend the width of the residence, and to the left of it, a pair of narrow rain doors sloped away from the house, covering a short flight of exterior stairs that led to a basement. Evidently in anticipation of us, someone had swept the snow off the doors. Gwyneth opened them.

I followed her down, through the door at the bottom, into a warm basement that smelled of hot coffee, where bare bulbs in old ceramic sockets were recessed between exposed beams, striping the room with soft-edged bands of light and shadow. The space was used for storage, but it wasn't packed full or cluttered. There were neatly labeled cartons, several pieces of old furniture, including a tattered armchair, and along one wall a folding table on which a coffeemaker warmed a Pyrex pot.

Gwyneth directed me to put the nameless girl in the armchair, and after I had done so, she gently extracted the child from the blanket, which she folded and put aside on a stack of cardboard boxes.

In slippers, flannel pants, a pale-blue cardigan, and a blue-and-white-checkered shirt, Teague Hanlon shuffled out of shadows and put two mugs of coffee on one of three metal barrels of different sizes that stood like an array of primitive kettle drums. "Gwynie takes hers black and said you would as well."

"I do," I assured him.

"How's the child?" he asked.

"She's coming around," Gwyneth said.

Just then a series of small kittenish sounds issued from the girl, as if she were waking from ordinary sleep and regretted leaving a sweet dream not quite finished.

"This is hard for me," Mr. Hanlon said. "I hope you understand, Gwynie."

"Of course I understand."

Mr. Hanlon crossed the room to the door through which we had entered the basement, where he engaged two deadbolts.

Gwyneth picked up her mug of coffee and sipped it, watching the girl intently. "You can take off your mask to drink the coffee, Addison. Neither of us will look at you."

To remove the ski mask, I would have to untie my hood and slide it back, thereupon being entirely exposed, which I never was outside of my rooms deep beneath the city. The thought of such vulnerability distressed me so much that I almost declined the coffee.

But I was cold, not from the short time that I had spent in the open, but from thoughts of plague and death. I needed the fragrant brew. If she said there was no risk, I could only believe her.

As soon as I stripped off the mask, I pulled the hood over my head again and tied it loosely under my chin.

The coffee tasted strong and good, and even through my gloves, the mug warmed my hands.

With his head bowed severely like a penitent monk sans habit, Mr. Hanlon returned to the coffeemaker to fill a mug for himself.

The child raised one hand to her face and traced her features with her fingertips, as if she were not merely confused but also blind and trying to identify herself by touch. She shifted in the armchair, lowered her hand from her face, opened her mouth, and let out a long sigh. Nearly three years of coma seemed to fall away from her as easily as a single night of sleep. Her eyes opened, huge and gray and limpid, and focused at once on Gwyneth. Her voice was hoarse when she said, "Mama?"

Gwyneth put down her mug, went to the girl, and knelt before her. "No, honey. Your mother's gone. She's never coming back. You're safe now. No one will hurt you anymore. You're safe with me."

Head still lowered, Mr. Hanlon returned with another mug. "Her mouth will be dry. I made sweet tea for her. It's cooled enough." As soon as Gwyneth took the tea from him, he returned to the coffeemaker and stood with his back to us.

I sensed that his discretion might be no less for his benefit than for ours, and I wondered why he was so different now from the way he had been in the Egyptian Theater.

As I sipped coffee and, from the shadow of my hood, watched Gwyneth and the girl, I realized that whatever might be happening in this basement was as beyond ordinary human experience as were the Fogs and Clears. The child returned to full consciousness not as any doctor might have expected, not as any other victim of coma would have returned, not gradually and with weakness, but rapidly and with her physical strength intact. She had sufficient coordination to hold the mug of tea and drink from it. Gwyneth spoke so softly that often I couldn't hear what she said, and though the girl did not respond, she listened intently and focused her luminous gray eyes on Gwyneth, who smoothed her hair and touched her face, her arms, so tenderly, reassuringly.

Sooner than seemed possible, the girl put aside her tea and got to her feet. She leaned against Gwyneth, though perhaps she did not need that support.

To Mr. Hanlon, Gwyneth said, "Did you get the clothes for her that I requested?"

He turned toward us but didn't approach. "They're on a chair at the kitchen table. I left it dark upstairs in case something . . . someone comes around looking for you. The only light in the kitchen is the range hood, but it's enough. There aren't any windows in the half bath, so you can turn the lights on in there."

Holding Gwyneth's hand, the child walked on coltish legs that she had not used in nearly three years and that shouldn't have easily supported her. I watched the pair until they moved out of sight on the stairs, and then I watched their shadows accordion after them across treads and risers.

In a world rich with wonders and mysteries, there are also miracles.

To keep his distance from me, Mr. Hanlon began to travel the room, stopping at each piece of furniture or stack of cardboard boxes, pondering it as if he were browsing in a shop where he had never been before, evaluating the merchandise.

"Addison, I assume you know what has come into the world."

"A plague, you mean."

"*The* plague, I think, after which the long war between mankind and microbes will have ended."

Remembering Telford, I said, "It's going to be bad."

"It'll be worse than bad. Latest word is that they engineered the weapon, the bug, for a 98-percent mortality rate. It exceeded their expectations. Then they lost control of it."

"I'm scared for Gwyneth. Telford was dying and he spit on her."

Mr. Hanlon looked up, surprised, but then turned away at once. "Where did Telford find her?"

"He got to the child before we did. She's contaminated, too."

He was silent, not because he had nothing to say but because he had too much. Then: "Though I always hoped for better circumstances, I'm honored to have you in my home at last. Addison Goodheart is a more appropriate name for you than Son of It."

· 72

TEAGUE HANLON, BOTH GUARDIAN TO GWYNETH and the benefactor who had given Father a key to the food bank and the associated thrift shop, was not the high-priced attorney that I might initially have imagined. Once a fighting marine who'd gone to war, he was now a priest and the rector of St. Sebastian's, the man to whom Gwyneth's father and mine had turned when in need, the man who worked through Judge Gallagher's mother, his parishioner, to ensure the transfer of the nameless girl into Gwyneth's custody. He was the nexus of our intersecting lives.

We were in the basement of the rectory behind St. Sebastian's on this terrible night, and Father Hanlon didn't wear the Roman collar here that identified his office when he was in public.

Prior to his revelation, the chalice of my heart had been filled to the brim with emotion, and now it overflowed. I sat on the edge of the armchair, searching for an adequate response and at first finding none. The intense tide of feelings did not wash me away. I had taken a master's degree in stoicism before I learned to walk. I needed only to sit quietly for a moment, seining those deep waters for the right words.

I said, "You fed us all these years."

"The food wasn't mine. It was all donated."

"You clothed us."

"With secondhand garments also donated."

"You kept our secret."

"The least expected of a priest who hears confessions."

"You never raised a hand against Father."

"I saw his face only a few times."

"But never harmed him."

"I was able to meet his eyes only once."

"And didn't harm him."

"I should have made myself meet them again and again."

"But after each encounter with him, you fell into despair."

"I suffered periodic depression before I ever knew about you and the man you called Father."

"Yes, but the very thought of us made those depressions blacker.

You said so yourself in your note to me, and we gave you nightmares, yet still you sustained us."

Standing with his face in his hands, he spoke in Latin, not to me, but perhaps in prayer. I listened, and though I didn't understand the words, his great distress was evident.

I rose from the armchair, took a couple of steps toward Father Hanlon, but halted, for it was not given to me, in my difference, to be able to comfort people. In fact, quite the opposite. As on the night when Father had been brutally murdered while I lay watching from under an SUV, I felt inadequate, useless, and I was ashamed of my helplessness.

The Latin words crumbled in his mouth, falling from his lips in broken syllables, and he faltered in the prayer, taking deep shuddery breaths and expelling them with tortured sounds that might have been half sobs of grief and half expressions of disgust.

Given my twenty-six years of experience, I could only imagine that my presence was the cause of such powerful, unchecked emotions. I said, "I'll go. I never should have come here. Foolish. I've been foolish. And reckless."

"No. Wait. Let me pull myself together. Give me a chance."

He had given us so much that I owed him anything he asked.

When he regained control of himself, he went to the door through which we had arrived and seemed to check the locks to be certain that he had secured them. He stood listening to the storm, his back to me, and at last he said, "It's an east wind, like the one that parted the sea." That thought led him to another, and he quoted: "'They have sown the wind, and they shall reap the whirlwind.'"

Although there was much I wanted to say, I knew that I should not. His mind and heart were out of alignment, and only he could bring them into harmony.

He said, "The North Koreans, what's left of them, announced a short while ago that birds don't contract the disease, but they do carry it. There's no quarantine that can prevent birds from flying."

They made movies and wrote books about planet-killing asteroids, stories that evoked a frisson of horror in audiences and readers. But in the end, no million-ton mass from outer space was necessary to put an end to civilization. The murder of one man could be committed with something as small as a few drops of nectar from the oleander plant instilled in honey, and all of humankind could be murdered most efficiently by something even smaller, a mere microbe of malevolent invention.

Still turned to the door, the priest said, "Your father didn't know what he was, but there was no reason that he should. Do you know what you are, Addison?"

"A monstrosity," I said. "A miscreation, freak, abomination."

73

THE WIND RATTLED THE BASEMENT DOOR THAT Father Hanlon faced, and as if he knew my thoughts, he said, "It may seem to be the wind that tests the door, but on this night of all nights, it's more likely to be something far worse than wind. These aren't the times of which Saint John the Evangelist wrote in Revelations. Armageddon would be an hour of horror *and* of glory, but there is no glory in what's coming, no final judgment, no new Earth, only bitter tragedy on an unthinkable scale. This is the work of men and women in all their perversity and transgression, the love of power in the service of mass death. On such a night, the darkest spirits are likely to be drawn from their usual pursuits, taking to the streets in gleeful celebration."

The delicious aroma of coffee gave way to the stench of burning marionettes. Remembering Gwyneth's words to me as we left the yellow-brick house with the girl, I said, "That's how the marionettes smelled in the archbishop's fireplace. But the stink is deception. Nothing's out there."

"Don't be so sure," he cautioned, and pointed to the doorknob, which worked violently back and forth, not as the wind could ever have moved it. "Whatever wants in, it will bring with it doubt. Did you know that the artist Paladine's last will and testament required that a marionette be included in his casket?"

"There were only six, and Gwyneth found them all."

"This one wasn't like the six. Paladine carved and painted this one in his own image, and they say it looked uncannily like him. His mother was his sole living relative and heir. A woman with unhealthy interests and strange beliefs that perhaps she had inculcated in her son. She had him buried precisely as his will directed, in a little-known cemetery that attracts people who wish to be laid to rest in ground that isn't hallowed, that has never been blessed by anyone of any faith."

The foul odor had grown stronger, and although the door stopped rattling and the knob stopped turning, I said, "Deception."

"You must learn what you are, Addison, so that you won't doubt anymore and won't any longer be vulnerable." He turned his back to the door but still didn't look at me. He stared down at his hands, which he turned palms up. "Doubt is poison. It leads to a loss of faith in yourself, and in all that's good and true."

The storm wind struck great blows at the house, and although the rectory was a sturdy structure of long-standing brick, it creaked overhead.

Father Hanlon lowered his hands and took two steps toward me, but he didn't attempt to make eye contact. "You're not a monster, miscreation, freak, or abomination. You've seen yourself in mirrors, I assume."

"Yes."

"Often?"

"Yes."

"And what did you see?"

"I don't know. Nothing. I'm blind to it, I guess."

He pressed me: "What is the deformity that makes you an object of such instant hatred and rage?"

"Father and I spent many hours in speculation and conjecture, but in the end there's no way for us to know. It's something in our faces, especially in our eyes, even in our hands, that others see in the first instant they look at us, but it's something we can't ever see. Lots of people recoil from spiders, don't they? But if spiders had the capacity for complex thought, they wouldn't have a clue why they were so often loathed, because to one another, spiders look appealing."

"You've come close to the truth," the priest said. "But you are not to be compared to spiders." He came to me, stood before me, but didn't look up. He took one of my gloved hands in both of his hands. "The man you called Father told me about your arrival in the world. Your biological father was shiftless, irresponsible, perhaps even a criminal, and he was never known to you. Your mother was a damaged woman but not entirely lost. You were born of man and woman, as are we all, but with one crucial difference. You were born with that difference perhaps because the world was moving toward a time when such as you would be needed."

"What difference?" I asked, breathless in expectation of the answer. I knew that a difference shaped my life and made of me an outcast, though I didn't know the nature of it. In this mysterious world, I was the central mystery of my life.

"Though born of man and woman, you aren't an heir to Adam or to Eve, and neither was your second and better father. By some grace beyond my understanding, beyond anyone's, you don't carry the stain of original sin. You have a purity, an innocence that the rest of us can sense in an instant, as surely as a wolf can smell the spoor of a rabbit."

I began to deny that I possessed such innocence, but he silenced me with a squeeze of my hand and a shake of his head.

"Addison, I dread looking at you worse than I have dreaded anything else in life, because I see not only you, but also what you are and what I am not. When I look at you, I see into myself as I never do otherwise, every sin of my life in a vivid kaleidoscopic collection of past toxic moments, more than I could recall in a lifetime of examining my conscience. When I look at you, I see what should be, and I know that I am not as I should be, and I recognize in totality every time in my life that I have gone wrong, every small unkindness, every meanness, every lie and unworthy thought relived simultaneously and in an instant."

"No," I protested. "You're a good man."

"Better than some, perhaps, but far from perfect. In my youth, in that unconventional war, when the enemy was never easily identified, sometimes I shot in fear, when I couldn't be sure that shooting was entirely justified—"

"But, sir, self-defense—"

"Is never a sin, but sometimes I *knew* shooting wasn't justified, a delay was necessary, further consideration, further inquiry, but I didn't inquire or delay. Surrender to fear is an invitation to doubt. There is lust and greed in every heart, son, and bitter envy. Perhaps there's envy more than anything, and it's worse than most passions. Even as a young priest, I had unworthy ambitions, a desire for praise and position that outweighed the desire to counsel, save, and serve."

I didn't want to hear his confession. I asked him please to stop at once, be quiet, and he fell silent. He still held my hand. He was trembling. So was I. Quaking.

If my difference was as he identified it, I would rather have been an abomination, a freak so hideous that my twisted face drove men to sudden insane violence. How much worse to be a mirror to their souls, to know that when they looked at me, they experienced in an instant all the errors of their lives, both petty and profound, that they felt the pain they had caused others and knew themselves to an extent that they were not meant to know themselves while still in the flesh, to a degree that no one could bear to know himself until he was but a spirit, in the docket, and free from the possibility of further error.

The priest raised his head, and though I still wore the hood, there was sufficient light for him to see my shadowed features and to stare into my eyes. Across his face came such a look of mental agony and profound sorrow that, even though no rage accompanied it, no antipathy, I was distressed for him, anguished that I should have such an effect on anyone, and afraid for both of us.

Shaken, I looked away from him. "You're the first I've ever known who isn't driven to violence by me, by Father, by just the sight of us."

"It's despair and hatred of their own errors that makes them want to kill you, to put an end to that painful self-awareness. I feel the same urge and resist it, though I doubt that I could ever resist it with the courage of your mother. Eight *years*."

With that statement he put my childhood and my mother in a new light, and I stood astonished to think of her as a woman who remained moral enough—who *loved* me enough—to endure the intense mental and emotional anguish that Father Hanlon had just described.

"And if your mother had something of a saint in her character, well then a case might be made that Gwyneth's father ought to be canonized. He not only endured *thirteen* years, but he loved her with all his heart and would have endured much longer if he hadn't been murdered."

The house creaked in the buffeting wind, the basement door shook in its frame as though it might break loose of its hinges, the knob rattled back and forth, back and forth, but at that revelatory moment I didn't care what might be loose in the night or what might burst in upon us.

74

MINE IS THE KIND OF STORY IN WHICH NAMES should not much matter, certainly not full names, first and middle and last, not for every person stepping onto the stage. Had a story of this kind been told in the third person instead of the first, by some writer just two centuries earlier than my time, he or she would have used even fewer names than I have employed, and some characters would have been identified only by their occupation, such as Archbishop or Priest. Back in that time, had the story involved royalty, the king would have been known as nothing more than the King, and the queen's name would have been the Queen, and the valiant little tailor would have been known as only the Little Tailor. Even in that long-past age but certainly centuries prior, the story might have been told with animals in all the roles, and their names would have been only what they were, such as Tortoise and Hare, Cat and Mouse, Lambkin and Little Fish, Hen and Mr. Fox. That would have been the way because, in those times, life was simpler, and people had a clearer sense of right and wrong than they possessed later. I will call that long-ago period the Age of Clarity. No writer or reader would have imagined that an analysis of a villain's childhood traumas was needed to explain his wickedness, for it was well understood that a life of wickedness was a choice that *anyone* could make if he loved wickedness more than truth. For twenty-six years, I lived in the Modern Age, when it was said that human psychology was so complex, the chain of motivations so recondite and abstruse, that only experts could tell us why anyone did anything, and in the end even the experts were loath to render a definitive judgment of any particular person's specific actions. But although this story is *of* the Modern Age, I have not written it *for* that age. Nevertheless, though we know Gwyneth's father by his deeds and by his selfless love for her, and though I have gotten this far without saddling him with a name, it seems to me that because he was *not* representative of his times, not emblematic, that I should use his name, if for no other reason, to signify that he was a light in a darkening world. Surnames do not matter much anymore, so I will use only his first, which was Bailey. The name derives from the Middle English word *baile,* which means "the outer wall of a castle."

Bailey was present in the delivery room when his daughter came into the world and when his wife died in childbirth. The reactions of the attending physician and the nurses were not as radical as those of the midwife and her daughter who delivered me, but Bailey was aware of a curious tension and some antipathy toward the baby, not anything as strong as detestation but an uncongeniality, a want of tender touch and sympathy, almost a quiet shunning.

His beloved wife had died. A confusing mix of emotions stirred through him, grief and rejoicing, neither entirely suitable to the moment; but having always been an excellent judge of people and their states of mind, he felt that even in his current condition, he could trust his intuition. What he read in the faces and the actions of the medical team first puzzled him and then concerned him. He suspected that if the death of his wife and the failed effort to resuscitate her had not distracted the doctor and the nurses, if their attention had been entirely on the baby, their reactions to tiny Gwyneth might have been even less tender. He counseled himself that they had no reason to bear an animus against the infant, who was beautiful and helpless and unusually serene, that his fear for the safety of the child was nothing more than a reaction to the unexpected, devastating loss of his wife. But he could not persuade himself.

The swaddled baby had been set aside in a bassinet that was in fact a lozenge-shaped white-enameled basin, pending the official weighing and transfer to the neonatal-care unit. No sooner had the effort to resuscitate his wife failed than Bailey let go of her hand and went directly to his daughter. When he picked her up and looked into her as-yet-unfocused eyes, he knew himself to a degree that he had never known himself before, and a flood of remorse for certain past actions nearly brought him to his knees.

He withstood the wave of emotion, and his mind, always quick, had never been quicker as he tried to make sense of the effect that Gwyneth had on him. According to Father Hanlon, Bailey had been not merely a good man, but also scrupulously honest and honorable; successful, but humble in his success. If he had been corrupt, or if he had been ruthlessly ambitious in his rise from poverty to wealth, perhaps his reasons for remorse would have been so numerous and serious that he would have dropped the infant on her head, right there, right then, and blamed his weak grip on the grief that racked him. Instead, he held fast to her, overcome by a conviction that she was precious not only in all the ways that a daughter was precious to her father, but also for reasons he could not explain.

He thought the effect she had on him might be proof of some psychic ability that she was too young to be able to control. She might be a telepath or an empath, if that was a word, a clairvoyant or a mind reader. He didn't know which of those she might be or if she was any of them, but he knew that she was something. He suspected that the explosive examination of conscience she had triggered in him could not have been what the physician and the nurses experienced. If they had endured anything that invasive and intense, their reactions would have been more dramatic; their quiet shunning would no doubt have been more hostile. Perhaps when still linked to her mother by an umbilical cord and in the few minutes after it was cut, Gwyneth had a lesser effect than after she'd been breathing on her own for a few minutes, her heart no longer in sync with her mother's heart, the electrical activity in her brain more vital by the minute.

Some on the hospital staff thought Bailey eccentric and others judged him imperious when he insisted that his daughter not be taken to the neonatal-care unit but that instead she be given a private room where he could stay with her and tend to her himself, according to the instructions of a nurse. Eccentric or imperious, or even if mentally unbalanced by grief, he was treated respectfully and his demands were granted because he was a well-liked man but, in truth, because his foundation had given the hospital millions in grants. No one on its staff or in its administration wanted to put at risk any future millions that might come to the institution.

As soon as he could, Bailey phoned Father Hanlon, his parish priest. Without explanation, he inquired as to the availability of a particularly devout nun, someone who had taken her vows young and whose experience of the world was largely limited to her convent and to prayer. Preferably she would be in the contemplative rather than the active life, if such a one could be given a dispensation to leave her cloistered circumstances for this assignment. Bailey needed such a relative innocent to come to the hospital that night, to assist him with the care of his newborn and motherless daughter, for he didn't trust a nurse, any nurse, in the room alone with her.

Even in those days, the city was home to fewer religious orders than in the past. The number of *moniales* residing in convents was lower than in yesteryear, when the church was stronger. Nevertheless, as a consequence of Bailey's former generosity and Father Hanlon's persuasiveness, Sister Gabriel, of the Sisters of Charity of St. Augustine, though in the active life rather than the contemplative, proved to be an ideal choice, for she was an untroubled soul, yet wise to the ways of the world and effective in dealing with the most secular of individuals in a manner that made them pleased to do as she felt best.

In addition, as a result of her meditation and contemplation, Sister Gabriel was a mystic with an awareness beyond the five senses. The very sight of Gwyneth troubled her but also filled her heart with gladness, so that she could endure the searing introspection caused by the very sight of the child and be uplifted by it. On only the third day of the infant's journey in the world, the nun told Bailey that his daughter had been born in a condition of absolute purity, that somehow she was not burdened with the sad inheritance of the first-made in Eden. How this could be, Sister Gabriel could not say, given that Gwyneth was born of man and woman, but her certainty was such that, were she to be told by a superior that her perception was in error and that to insist upon it might be an occasion of mortal pride, she would have insisted just the same, because this was a truth that pierced her. Bailey knew it to be true, as well, the moment that he heard it.

Gwyneth was taken home from the hospital, and for the next four years, Sister Gabriel visited daily, to assist with the child's care. At the end of this period, she believed that Bailey could manage the situation himself, because Gwyneth was by then intellectually and emotionally mature beyond her years, aware of the great gift of her innocence, of the necessity and difficulty of preserving it, and of the danger of a world hostile to one such as she. Sister Gabriel elected thereafter a contemplative and cloistered life and never ventured again beyond the walls of her convent.

During those same four years, Bailey had so often experienced the involuntary examination of his conscience, which occurred when he but looked at the girl, that he came to fully understand himself and his past errors. He arrived at a state of perfect contrition, so that he could enjoy her company and she his, in as normal a fashion as any father and daughter.

He had by then divested himself of his real-estate empire and re-ordered his investments so that management of them could be left largely to others. He devoted himself to Gwyneth and embarked upon a most unlikely second career as a novelist, under a pen name, which proved amazingly successful in spite of the fact that he never toured or engaged in much publicity.

To explain Gwyneth's reclusive, almost monastic, existence, Bailey told the household staff and others in his life that his daughter was afflicted with fragile health, a compromised immune system, though in fact she never had as much as a cold or a headache. Later it was said that she suffered from social phobia, which in fact she did not. The girl's nature was such that she thrived on seclusion and devoted herself to literature and music and study. She and her father believed that hers was to be a life in waiting, that the day would come when her purpose would be clear and that in the meantime she needed only to be patient.

When she hit upon the scheme to disguise her nature and thereby be able to go out into the world, her father was at first reluctant to grant permission. But Gwyneth was nothing if not persistent, and she proved that her plan was workable. In the magazine photographs of the Paladine marionettes, she recognized a portrait of evil that would be the perfect mask to hide her true nature and to dissuade people from looking closely at her, so that if she could avoid being touched, and thereby known, she could dare to venture tentatively and cautiously out of the house in which she had, until then, passed her entire life.

When I had asked why she imitated the look of the marionettes, she had said that it was to overcome her social phobia, that she felt she needed to look edgy. She was afraid of people, and she thought the best way to keep them at a distance might be to act a little scary. I had known at the time that her answer was incomplete, that she was keeping something from me. The full truth was that she and I were two of a kind, that whereas I lived by day underground and aboveground only by night, she moved safely in the city by spackling over her true nature with Goth makeup. Her strange, disturbing eyes, black with red striations like those of the vile marionettes, were contact lenses, nonprescription because she had perfect vision, custom-made for her by a company that produced all manner of prosthetics for actors of stage and screen, as well as for the growing number of people who chose to escape unsatisfying, mundane lives by donning costumes not just for fantasy and gaming conventions but also for more and more of their lives outside of their office jobs.

Much of that I learned from Father Hanlon as we sat together in the rectory basement, with the house creaking around us and the storm rattling the door, if indeed it was the storm and not a bestial hand, though Gwyneth shared some of her story with me later.

I still had questions, not the least of which was, *What next?*

This might not be the last winter of the world, but by all the evidence, it was likely to be the last winter to which the people of this city or any other would stand witness. The contagion out of Asia, spread by man and bird, might have a hundred-percent mortality rate among the infected. However, if we were what we now believed ourselves to be, we were not heir to the ills of this fallen world.

I said, "If Gwyneth and I—and the child—aren't destined to die from what those madmen have unleashed, what's our future and how do we ensure it?"

If Father Hanlon knew the answer, he had no time to tell me, for just then Gwyneth returned with the girl.

75

DRESSED NOW IN SWEATER AND JEANS AND SNEAKers, with a coat draped over one arm, the nameless six-year-old girl came down the basement stairs, fully alert and smiling. No evidence remained that she had been comatose for years. Her sweet smile seemed to shame the storm, or whatever wanted to be let into the house, because the door stopped rattling and the rectory ceased its creaking.

Following the child, Gwyneth appeared, dressed as before but with all the Goth makeup washed off. She did not glow as the Clears glowed, but I will tell you that she glowed anyway, for no other word quite conveys the wattage of her beauty, skin as clear as rainwater, eyes reflecting summer heavens here in the winter of the world, not luminous, no, this girl of flesh and blood, but radiant nonetheless. The serpent ring was gone from her nose, the red bead missing from the corner of her mouth, and her lips were no longer black, but the red-pink of certain roses.

Of the child, Gwyneth said, "Her name is Moriah," and I asked, "How do you know?" and the child said, "I told her." Of Moriah, I inquired, "Do you remember what happened to you?" and she responded, "No, I don't remember anything of the past," and I said, "Then I wonder how you remember your name." She said, "I didn't remember. It was spoken to me just when I woke, a whisper in my mind, *Moriah.*"

Father Hanlon closed his eyes, as if the sight of three such as us would undo him, although his voice didn't tremble when he said, "Addison, Gwyneth, and Moriah."

Gwyneth came to me, stood before me, and considered my shadowed face within my hood.

"Social phobia," I said.

"Not a lie. People did terrify me, their potential. My social phobia wasn't a mental affliction, but a choice."

Throughout much of her eighteen years and much of my twenty-six, we had known the world more through our books than through direct contact. We should not have been surprised that of those many hundreds of volumes, we had for the most part read the same books, which we began to discover there in the rectory basement.

When she untied the drawstrings under my chin, she touched my face, and a new light entered my heart. Her voice soft and loving, she began to recite a poem by Poe, one of the last he had written. " 'Gaily bedight, A gallant knight, In sunshine and in shadow—'"

I continued: " 'Had journeyed long, Singing a song, In search of Eldorado.'"

When the drawstrings were untied, I put a hand to the hood, to keep it in place, suddenly fearful of letting her see me in full light. I found it difficult to believe that I was what Father Hanlon said that I was, easier by far to believe that I was a hideous thing that a stabbed man, dying by the roadside, hated and feared more than he hated and feared dying.

She skipped from the first stanza of "Eldorado" to the fourth and last. " ' "Over the Mountains Of the Moon, Down the Valley of the Shadow, Ride, boldly ride," The shade replied,—"If you seek for Eldorado!" ' "

I lowered my hand from the hood, and she pushed it back from my head. "In every way," she said, "you are so beautiful, and you will be beautiful forever."

Overcome by wonder, I kissed the corner of her mouth, where the bead had been, and the nose from which the serpent ring had hung, and her eyes that no longer needed to be concealed from a hostile world, and her brow, behind which she lived and hoped and dreamed and knew God, and loved me.

76

AS ALWAYS SEEMED TO BE THE CASE, BY THE TIME I began to imagine the shape of the immediate future, Gwyneth already knew what came next, what came after what came next, and what came after *that*, as well. Regarding foresight and wise planning, she was her father's daughter. Before picking me up in the Land Rover, by the pond in Riverside Commons, more than eight hours earlier, she had by phone set the appointment in the Egyptian Theater, had arranged for her guardian to expect us, with the child, in the darkest hour of the night, and had suggested that he might be required, perhaps with unseemly haste, to perform a duty of his office before daybreak.

I was honored that she should want my proposal, joyous when it was accepted, and somewhat dizzied when Gwyneth took from around her neck a delicate gold chain on which hung a ring fashioned from a nail. Either the nail must have been very old and worn or the point had been rounded with a file. The shank was bent into a smooth and perfect circle, and the head, which resembled in shape the setting for a diamond, was engraved with a tiny lazy eight, the symbol for infinity. The artist, Simon, made it for her because he believed she had freed him from the self-crucifixion of his addiction. In an accompanying note, he wrote that one day she would meet a man who would so love her that, if his sacrifice would spare her from death, he would straighten the nail and drive it through his own heart.

"Simon was as melodramatic as he was talented," she said, "but he was also right."

Father Hanlon had only begun to explain the necessary simplicity with which we must proceed when from the house above us came the hard crash and then the brittle ringing fall of shattered glass, as if not one window but three or four had exploded simultaneously.

Not even Gwyneth, with all her foresight, had anticipated such a frontal assault in the penultimate moment.

Regarding the basement ceiling with apprehension, Father Hanlon said, "The stairhead door locks from the kitchen, but not from this side."

I snatched up a chrome-and-red-vinyl chair, which might once have been part of a dinette set, and hurried to the stairs. On the landing at the top, I was relieved to discover that the door opened toward me rather than into the kitchen. I tipped the chair onto its back legs and jammed the header under the knob, bracing the door shut.

By the time I returned to the basement, heavy footsteps sounded in the rooms above. They blundered first in one direction and then in another, as though the intruder must be drunk or confused.

"Who is it?" Moriah asked. "What does he want?"

I didn't know, couldn't guess, but judging by Gwyneth's grim expression, she had at least a firm suspicion.

Among the old furniture stored in the basement was a prie-dieu that had previously been in the sacristy of St. Sebastian's but had been moved when it was replaced with a new one. The padded kneeling bench was wide enough for two. Father Hanlon stood on the other side of it, his face averted but his voice steady and full.

In the house overhead, something crashed over with thunderous impact, perhaps a breakfront or a tall chest of drawers, and dust sifted down upon us from the basement ceiling.

I didn't want to delay our vows for even a minute. But if these were the last hours of the world as we had known it, nothing was less important than it had been, and in fact everything was more important than it had ever been before. And so I said to the priest, "Are you sure this is right? I'm not of your church."

"By your nature," he said, evading my eyes, "you are of all churches and in need of none. Never have I conducted a marriage service with fewer doubts than I have now."

If a house could be eviscerated, the sound that now came from the ground floor must be guts of wire torn through cartilage that was lath and through flesh that was plaster. I imagined that someone leaped to a chandelier, his full weight depended from it, swinging like a crazed ape, the dangling crystals clinking against one another and plummeting to the floor like glass grenades amidst the cracking-knuckle sounds of chain links torquing and the hard stutter of mounting screws stripping out of the junction box in the ceiling. Again the building shook as something heavy fell from a height. The lights dimmed, fluttered, and chased flurries of moth-wing shadows across the basement, but we were not cast into darkness.

"Addison, wilt thou take Gwyneth, here present, for thy lawful wife, according to the rite of our Holy Mother the Church?"

"I will."

As the marriage service continued, the tumult overhead seemed surely to be the work of an entire wrecking crew of psychopaths, of many eager hands wielding sledgehammers and prybars, smashing glass, splitting wood, ripping up flooring, tossing furniture in a frenzy of destructive glee. A series of explosions sounded not like bomb blasts but like the *whumps* of aircraft breaking the sound barrier, as if numerous visitors were being imported from a distant kingdom, coming into the house at tremendous speed, great hands of air clapping to announce each arrival. But though they raised a racket, they didn't call out to one another or curse, or rage, as if they were creatures who never spoke except to deceive and who, in this late hour of the world, no longer had any reason to lie, no purpose for their tongues.

Yet our voices were clear through the roar, and before long Gwyneth said, ". . . to have and to hold, from this day forward, for better or worse, for richer or poorer, in sickness and in health, until death do us part."

At last, whatever beast or horde of beasts might be laying waste to the rectory, a destroyer arrived at the braced door at the top of the basement stairs and shook it more violently than the exterior door had been shaken earlier. The chrome header of the chair shrieked against the twisting doorknob. With the bone-in-socket sound of an animated skeleton, the pivot pins rattled in the knuckles of the hinge barrels, the latch bolt squealed in the plate fixed to the door frame.

Speaking sacred names that sealed our vows, the priest joined Gwyneth and me in matrimony, that we should face together whatever might lie ahead of us, the two of us now one, always one throughout our days on Earth and ever after.

We sprang to our feet. Pulling on her coat, small and quick and perhaps afraid, Moriah headed toward the exterior door, and Father Hanlon shepherded us after her, through bands of light and shadow, with dust descending from the cracked ceiling as if in reminder of our origins. There we paused, and Gwyneth put her arms around him and said that she loved him. If the contact tortured the priest, it exalted him as well, and if his face was wrenched with anguish and sorrow, it was also informed by hope. I said that he should come with us, and he said that he couldn't, that he needed to remain behind to comfort the dying.

He gave me a sealed envelope and said that it held a treasure, and

I tucked it into an inner jacket pocket with the envelope that contained the only things I had taken from my three windowless rooms.

The basement door opened onto nothing worse than icy wind and hurled snow. Climbing the stairs and sprinting across the yard, we didn't dare look back to see by what bleak light the previously dark windows of the rectory might now be brightened and what grotesque forms and ghastly shadows might loom behind them.

When the three of us were safely in the Land Rover, Gwyneth reversed into the alley, and for a moment I could see past the side of the garage, into the lamplit passage between that building and the property wall, along which we had made our way moments earlier. Snow falling in thick torrents, shuddered by capricious wind into strange writhing forms, playing tricks with light and shadow, might conjure legions of demons in the imagination, but I believe that what I saw in pursuit of us was as real as the snow through which it forged.

If it was a man, it was a dead man with moon-pale eyes, clothed in rags and here and there strigose with splintered bones like sticks and straw bristling from rips in a scarecrow's costume. If it was a dead man, it was the artist Paladine, for it carried in the cradle of its right arm what, seen through the veils of churning snow, might have been a marionette. If it was a marionette, and not an illusion, there were no strings for its wooden hands to pull, yet the man-sized puppet conveyed it through the storm.

Gwyneth shifted into drive. The tires spun out wet ravelings of clotted snow, but then found traction, and we were away into a city enchanted and haunted, its towers shining high into the night, but under it a black abyss.

77

GWYNETH TURNED THE CORNER ONTO A BROAD avenue where skyscrapers sought a sky beyond their reach and blurred into the upper depths of a sea of snow. Before us lay a display of pageantry beyond all of our experience, a *tableau vivant* with a shining cast of thousands, tens of thousands, wondrous and exhilarating but also a scene of drama so dire that I was chilled.

She had always been able to see them, of course; and she could see them now, which is why she let our speed fall. On the older towers crafted by masons, the Clears stood side by side on every ledge, aglow in their hospital greens and blues and whites, like candles in endless tiers of votive cups, and in the buildings of steel and glass, they stood at every window, in the snow on every setback. Where the roofs of the lower buildings were visible through the white veils, the Clears stood there, too, and atop the marquees of theaters, on hotel porticoes, and upon the stone pediments that surmounted grand entryways. They gazed down into the street, solemn multitudes, standing witness now and until there was nothing left to which they might attest. I knew without needing confirmation that they were arrayed like this on other avenues and cross streets, on the roofs and in the trees of residential neighborhoods, in other towns and cities and nations, wherever there were people who would fall sick and into death.

From the rear seat, Moriah said, "I'm scared."

Nothing I could say to her would gentle away her fright. During whatever hours might remain for this world, fear was unavoidable, fear and remorse and grief and fierce, desperate love. In the thrall of such emotions, Gwyneth let the Rover drift to a stop in the middle of the street, and I opened the door and got out and stood in awe and terror, turning, looking up at the thousands who stared down.

Disobedience brought time into the world, so that lives could thereafter be measured to an end. Then Cain murdered Abel, and there was yet another new thing in the world, the power to control others by threat and menace, the power to cut short their stories and rule by fear, whereupon death that was a grace and a welcoming into a life without tears became no longer sacred in itself, but became the blunt weapon of crude men. And though the blood of Abel had once cried out from the Earth, we had come now to a time when so much blood had been spilled over the millennia that the throat of the Earth was clotted and choked, and fresh blood could not raise a voice from it.

Gazing up at the shining multitudes, turning, turning, I spoke to them from my heart, because I knew they could hear that even more clearly than they could hear my voice. I reminded them of the many millions of children, of the fathers who loved and the mothers who cherished, of the simple-minded who in their simplicity were without blame, of the humble and the would-be chaste and the would-be honest and those who loved truth even if they didn't always speak it, who struggled daily toward an ideal that they might never reach, but for which they yearned. There was hatred among people, but there was also love, bitter envy but also gladness for the fortune of others, greed but also charity, rage but also compassion. No matter how ardently or eloquently I might plead the case of humanity, however, I knew that this radiant audience would not, could not, prevent what was coming, that after we had brought ourselves to this pass, they could not be guardians but only witnesses. The world was run by our free will, and if they were to step down from their ledges and rooftops to undo what had been done, they would take from humanity our free will, after which we would be nothing more than robots, golems with hearts of mud and regimented minds. If some people chose to seek the power to strip the Earth of human life and if others of good intention did not take all necessary steps to defend against such madness, the consequences were as certain as that thunder will follow lightning. These shining multitudes did not stare down with cruel indifference, but with love and pity and grief that perhaps exceeded all of the grief that would wash through the dying nations in the days to come.

My face was stiff with frozen tears when, from the corner of my eye, I saw movement in the street. One Clear had come down among us for the purpose of leading three children to me. They were all under the age of five. I knew them by their bruises and their scars, by the emaciation of forced starvation that hollowed the faces of the twin boys, by the bleeding abrasion that encircled the girl's neck, which was evidence of the coarse ligature with which she had nearly been strangled. They were like me and Gwyneth and Moriah, outcasts once hated and reviled, now heirs to all the world.

The Clear was the same woman who had visited the ninth apartment while Gwyneth played the piano piece that she had composed in memory of her father. I remembered what she had told me the first night that we met, when she had prepared for us scrambled eggs and brioche with raisin butter. I had asked if she lived alone, and she'd said, *There is one who comes and goes infrequently, but I won't speak of that.* This Clear was the one who came and went.

The great host of Clears gathered above me were too far away for me to look into their eyes. In spite of Father's warning, I met the eyes of this woman, and he was right when he'd told me that I would find them terrible. They were terrible in the sense that they were august and imposing and exalted, blue and yet as clear as glass, containing depths that no eyes I'd ever seen before could contain, as if I were looking through them to the end of time. By her stare, this woman settled a solemn awe upon my heart, and I was frightened by the degree to which I felt humbled and by the intensity with which I felt loved, and I had to look away.

The three children were small, and there was room for them in the backseat with Moriah.

We drove a block in silence, and we knew that however far we might go, we would find the multitudes shining and observant and sorrowing, sentinels to the end.

Suddenly more traffic appeared on the streets, far less than you would expect on a night of good weather, more than I had ever seen in a snowstorm. The drivers were heedless of risk, as if all of them were being pursued.

In Ford Square, the Jumbotron loomed like a giant window that offered a somber view of our future as it was already playing out in Asia, where the dead were lying in the streets and desperate mobs struggled to board ships already overcrowded. The news crawl listed American cities where deaths from the swift-moving plague were being reported, and the geographic spread was so wide that already it should have been clear even to the most confirmed optimists that there would be no refuge.

When three snow plows crossed an intersection in front of us, one after the other in a train, moving fast with emergency beacons flashing, Gwyneth said, "They aren't serving the city now. They're fleeing it."

We fell in behind them, and they cleared the way for us, though that was not their intention.

Soon we reached the outskirts of the last borough, where we first saw looters. Bent-backed and frenzied, like figures from a nightmare of lupine predators, they poured out of shattered store windows, pushed grocery-store carts, pulled laden slat-sided wagons as if they were dray animals, loaded SUVs and cars with the latest electronic gear and all manner of luxury goods, some of them as wild-eyed as spooked horses and others as giddy as little children on a birthday-party treasure hunt.

The Clears stood witness to this, as well.

By the time that we were passing through the suburbs, the city plows no longer leading us, many of the sacked businesses were on fire, and the looters were stealing from one another now, defending their swag with guns and tire irons and pickaxes. A man in burning clothes ran across the street in front of us, still clutching a box bearing the Apple logo as the flames leaped from his coat to his hair and broiled him, screaming, to the pavement.

78

BY DAWN, THE SNOW STOPPED, AND WE WERE DRIVing through territory that had been less heavily blanketed, the roads clear except for some vehicles driven by desperate or panicked people, most of whom didn't seem certain of where they were going, recklessly bound nowhere in particular.

We were at first puzzled that the roads were not choked with traffic, that thousands weren't fleeing to remote places, even though they knew escape was impossible. Then we heard on the radio that the president had ordered Homeland Security to close off major arteries out of cities that offered international air traffic and shipping, because the first wave of plague reports were coming from those metropolitan areas. The hope was to contain the disease. We had gotten out just in time.

The pointlessness of the government's action was made clear when a squall of cedar waxwings burst into flight from a berried hedge, fluttering across the road, up and away, reminding us that birds were a vector. For its spread, the plague didn't depend on travelers from Asia debarking from planes and cruise ships.

Although tired, we were loath to stop short of our destination. The previous night, when Gwyneth had driven to the pond in Riverside Commons and given me my first ride in a motor vehicle, she mentioned a place in the country that her father had prepared for her, in the event that, for whatever reason, she ever needed to leave the city. We hoped to make it to that haven before nightfall.

In the backseat, Moriah slept. The three exhausted young ones were bunked down in the cargo space behind her.

At a Mobil station and convenience store in a quaint country town, a man dressed in khaki pants and shirt lay dead and befouled outside the raised doors of the repair garage. The establishment was otherwise deserted, but the pumps were working. We didn't have a credit card. Steeling myself for the horror, I chased the pecking crows from the corpse, found the right plastic in his wallet, and filled the tank of the Land Rover.

In the convenience store, I loaded a handbasket with snack crackers, granola bars, and bottles of apple juice, provisions for the last leg of our journey.

Gwyneth's father, Bailey, had given her both detailed directions and a map, but once she'd entered the destination in the Land Rover's navigation system, we no longer needed to consult them.

Whether Bailey had intuited why the likes of his daughter were being born into the world or whether he simply thought that in a crisis she would be safe only far from the nearest people, we will never know. The cabin was remote, on considerable acreage owned by her trust; and within a year of its completion, Bailey ordered trees to be felled across the one-lane dirt track and weeds to be seeded along its route to encourage Nature to take back the trail as quickly as possible.

A caretaker named Waylon, something of a modern mountain man, hiked into the property once a month and stayed for three days at a time, ensuring that it was maintained. He wasn't likely to be staying there now, and when Gwyneth could not raise him by phone, we thought he must be already ill with the plague or dead.

By noon, the wintry landscapes were behind us. We had removed the tire chains. Among the golden meadows, backdropped by green pine forests, here and there a lone house stood, or a house and a barn, behind pasture encompassed by split-rail or ranch-style fencing. Although they might once have appeared picturesque and welcoming, they were now held in a stillness like miniatures inside snow-globe paperweights but without the snow, the sunlight falling so plumb that no building cast a shadow, all of them standing silent, stark, and lonely.

Shortly before three o'clock in the afternoon, the navigator warned us that the paved county road would lead to a dead end within a mile. From there we would have to proceed on foot.

We had traveled two-thirds of that mile when the dogs began to appear. Labradors, German shepherds, golden retrievers, and various mixed breeds came from the fields and woods, angling ahead of us, bounding onto the shoulder of the road and then running alongside the car, grinning up at us, tails lashing the air. We counted twenty of them, and we couldn't imagine whose dogs they were or where they had come from, but their joyful behavior assured us that they were no threat.

The pavement ended at a line of metal posts spaced close enough to one another to prevent the Rover from passing between them. Beyond lay a dirt road rutted, rocky, and unpromising.

When we got out among the dogs, they were without exception eager and affectionate, panting but neither growling nor barking. They milled around us, pleading with their soulful eyes for a touch, a scratch. The four children were enchanted by the animals, and for the first time I saw the three younger ones smiling.

We had nothing to carry other than granola bars and cellophane-wrapped packets of peanut-butter-and-cracker sandwiches, with which we stuffed our pockets.

The map promised to guide us through the wilds by a series of nature's landmarks. The dogs seemed to think they had been hired as scouts, for they gathered in a pack and set out ahead of us, glancing back to be sure we were following.

The dirt road began in a curve, and when we rounded it, we came upon the gunmen.

79

FORTY FEET AHEAD, A JEEP WAGON HAD BEEN PARKED crosswise to the dirt road. Four men outfitted in hunter's camouflage and carrying fully automatic rifles were gathered near the tailgate, but when they saw us, they separated and took up defensive positions, three of them using the vehicle for cover.

The one still exposed shouted at us to halt. He said we could come no farther, that there was no disease in their land and that they meant to keep it that way. But though they might have been too distant to be turned violent by our difference, I thought that the speaker was pale and gray-lipped as Telford had been, and in this cool air there seemed to be a thin sheen of sweat on his face, so that I could only conclude that they were in denial of their peril.

I told them that the six of us were not infected, that we only wanted to pass through to a place of our own a couple of miles to the west, but they were not disposed to believe me or even to care whether I told the truth. The leader squeezed off a burst of four or five rounds, over the heads of the dogs and wide of us, and demanded that we retreat.

As if the gunfire must have been a summons, more dogs began to appear out of the tall grass in the meadow to both sides of the road, startling the four men. They seemed not to emerge from hiding, but instead almost to effervesce out of common wild grass. Twenty or thirty of them came forth to join those already leading us, until there were perhaps fifty in the pack.

The mysteries and wonders of the city were the mysteries and wonders of the world, as prevalent here as anywhere, as we would learn in the days to come. The dogs gathered around us, to all sides, as if they were our praetorian guard, the extraordinary nature of the pack evident in the animals' perfect silence and in the way in which every one of them turned its gaze on the Jeep and the gunmen gathered around it, not in threat but as if challenging them to set aside their fear and behave humanely.

I wasn't sure what we should do, but when the dogs began to move, Gwyneth said that we must move with them. They led us into the meadow, where rabbits bounded away but did not distract our guardians, and in a wide arc around the Jeep wagon before returning to the track.

The gunmen watched in silence, and if one of them thought the safest course was to cut us down with a spray of bullets, he didn't act upon that opinion. Whatever happened to those men, we never saw them again.

Into primal woods where afternoon sunlight laddered down through branches, the dogs led us along winding deer trails. Feathery ferns, like an aviary of immense green wings that might catch a draft and soar, arced away into the piney gloom. Ahead of me, the children followed Gwyneth, all of them repeatedly melting into shadows and reconstituted in sunlight, as if the forest wished to remind me that what had been given could be lost.

The cabin wasn't as simple as it sounds, a sprawling structure of tightly fitted logs caulked with what might have been elasticized stucco, under a slate roof hung with copper gutters that had acquired a green patina. A veranda encircled four sides of it.

While we stood in the large clearing that the house occupied, before going inside, Gwyneth said that of the many provisions stored therein, included were three years' worth of food. But she wondered how we could possibly feed fifty dogs as well.

As if in answer to her question, the dogs retreated to all arms of the surrounding woods and, within a minute, were gone as if they had never existed. In the days to come, they would keep us company, but they would never eat anything that we offered, sniffing what we had to give them but rejecting it as though it offended their keen sense of smell. From time to time, the dogs wandered away among the trees, not all at once but each to its own schedule, and when they returned, they seemed to be well fed and content. Eventually, we would learn their secret.

80

THE TWINS' NAMES WERE JOSHUA AND JUSTIN, AND the girl who had come with them, Consuela, was not related to them. The boys, starved thin in punishment for the distress they caused their mother, soon fleshed out, and the bleeding evidence of near strangulation in time faded from the girl's neck without leaving a scar. The depression in Moriah's skull did not fill out, but her hair concealed it, and she did not suffer any ill effects from it, for she was smart and quick and full of laughter.

They wanted Christmas that year. We cut down a suitable tree and decorated it with holly gathered from the woods and with shiny metal ornaments made from tin cans and painted by hand.

In the main room stood a Steinway, on which Gwyneth played for us songs of the season. She sometimes said she didn't know a tune that we mentioned, but whenever she tried to play it, she found the right keys and the music flowed without a wrong note through the cabin.

Because his daughter was musically talented, Bailey had stocked this forest home with other instruments: two clarinets, a saxophone, two violins, a cello, and more. We agreed that, by next Christmas, at least I and perhaps Moriah would have learned to play an instrument with which we could accompany Gwyneth's piano.

81

ON THE MORNING OF JANUARY 6, WHEN I CAME INTO the kitchen to help make breakfast, the back door was open, and Gwyneth stood at the porch railing, staring across the clearing to the woods, where the trees were skirted with lingering shadows and crowned with early sunlight.

Outside, the day was mild for that time of year, and Gwyneth was in the grip of sadness, which from time to time troubled both of us, though none of the children.

When I stepped beside her and put an arm around her, she said, "Do you feel it?"

"What?"

She didn't reply, and after a minute or two, I knew the cause of her melancholy. Neither silence nor sound, neither scent nor the absence of it, neither the quality of the sunlight nor the color of the sky offered any evidence that an age had fully ended and a new era had begun. Yet I had no doubt that they were gone to the last, all their vast wealth without an owner, all their amusement parks and taverns and dance halls without celebrants, every city and hamlet without a single voice, every ship upon the sea a ghost ship, and the sky traveled now only by birds.

"So soon," she said.

It didn't bear thinking about, but it was our gift, as it was the gift of those who had come before us, to be able to think, to reason and reflect, and with the gift came the compulsion to use it.

If there were other thinkers out there in the quiet vastness of the Earth, they were like Gwyneth and me, small groups in far-flung locations, alert to the wonder and mystery that were woven through-out the fabric of the day.

The following morning, the animals came out of the woods into the clearing and some even ascended the steps onto our veranda. There were several deer and a family of brown bears, raccoons and squirrels and wolves and rabbits. And dogs sat observant or frolicked among the other species. Former predators basked in the early sun beside former prey, watched the lingering veils of mist wither up into the morning light, wrestled playfully or chased one another without fear or menace, and so it has been ever since.

During my first eight years, when I had spent much time in the woods, no animals had feared me or stalked me. If my mother had abandoned me deep in the forest, as she once meant to do, she would have been surprised to discover that even wolves would have been my good companions. At the time, that community of the winged and the four-footed had seemed natural to me, which it had been at the start of time, which it now is again.

82

THE FOREST DEEP AND PRIMAL HARBORS NOTHING that kills, and in it now grow trees of which there are no photographs or descriptions in the books in our extensive library. The new trees and new vines produce scores of fruits never known before or at least not in the age recently passed. Some of the fruits are sweet, some savory, and it is with these that we are nourished and on these that the dogs and all other creatures, from bears to mice, now feed. If ever we grow a little tired of the flavors and textures of what the trees and vines produce, we at once think of new ways to prepare and serve them or else new fruits appear, different but no less delicious.

Sometimes, when I glance out of a window and see a laughing child riding bareback on a brown bear, an old fear twists through me, but it does not last.

83

ON A DAY LATE THAT JANUARY, I READ AGAIN "EAST Coker" by the poet T. S. Eliot, and saw something that I had forgotten: the stark but beautiful metaphor by which he described God as a wounded surgeon whose bleeding hands apply a scalpel to his patients so that "Beneath the bleeding hands we feel / The sharp compassion of the healer's art." I wondered then if it was that forgotten metaphor that worked on my subconscious to see the Clears in hospital garb or if instead Eliot was a greater visionary even than his admirers claimed.

84

IN OUR NEW HOME, THE WINDOWSILLS AND THE thresholds of doors do not bear any of the words that Gwyneth printed on the entry points of her other residences, as there is no need for them anymore. The alphabet she had used was early Roman derived from the Greek through Etruscan. Expressed in Latin, it would have read *Exi, impie, exi, scelerate, exi cum omnia fallacia tua,* which translates into English as "Depart, impious one, depart, accursed one, depart with all your deceits." If she was protected from Fogs and whatever else might take up tenancy in marionettes and music boxes and people, Ryan Telford was not stopped by words composed with Magic Markers, perhaps because nothing curled within him except his own evil.

85

IN ALL THE MANY BOOKS THAT I HAVE READ, THERE exists much truth and wisdom, but in not a single volume has the truth of lovemaking been revealed. When I lie in the arms of Gwyneth, in ecstasy, it is essentially not about sensation but about passion, and passion is not of the flesh but of the mind and heart. No writer ever told me that there is no self in the act, that the desire to give drives out all thought of receiving, that lovers become one, transported, that I am her and she is me, that we find ourselves not engaged in seduction and surrender but in the throes of creation, not consumed by desire but by astonishment, given for a moment the very power that brought into existence the universe, so that we, too, can create life. She carries now a child.

86

ON THE STEINWAY ARE PHOTOGRAPHS IN HANDMADE frames. Among them is the one I retrieved from my windowless rooms on the night when Gwyneth told me that I would never be returning there. It is a snapshot of my mother on a day when she didn't drink too much and smiled more readily than usual. She is lovely, and you can see in her eyes and in her graceful pose the promise that was never fulfilled. I found it in a zippered compartment of the backpack that she gave to me when she turned me out.

There is, too, a photo of Gwyneth's father, who is the very picture of kindness, whose eyes are deep with intelligence. Now and then I find myself staring at him for long periods, and sometimes when I sit alone on the porch or am hiking in the woods, I talk to him and tell him what we have been doing and reading and thinking lately, and I thank him not just then but every day, for I would have no life if he had not lived his.

Father and I never took photographs of each other. We had no camera and we felt no need to preserve memories when we were always together and were certain to keep them fresh by recalling them in conversation. But the envelope given to me by Father Hanlon in the basement of his rectory contained a photograph of Father. The priest had taken it as Father sat in an armchair, lamplit and shadowed like those artful portraits of famous individuals taken by the great photographer Steichen. He greatly resembled an actor who was once very famous, Denzel Washington: milk-chocolate skin, a crisp tight cap of hair, a broad and pleasant face, a smile that angels might envy, and dark eyes that seem to be the still points around which the universe turns eternally.

I have also framed the index card on both sides of which Father had written for me what he said was the one thing I must never forget after he was no longer there to remind me. He willed me these words: *But with one exception, all things pass from this world and time erases not just memories but entire civilizations, reducing everyone and every monument to dust. The only thing that survives is love, for it is an energy as enduring as light, which travels outward from its source toward the ever-expanding boundaries of the universe, the very energy of which all things were conceived and with which all things will be sustained in a world beyond this world of time and dust and forgetting.*

I have written this account for the benefit of my children and their children and their children's children, so that they might know how the world once was and how it came to be as it is. Not only is there no killing now of man by man or even beast by beast, but there seems to be no death except of grasses and flowers and other plants with the changing of the seasons, until spring revitalizes. If death should be forgotten, that might not be as good a thing as it at first seems to be. We must remember death and the temptation of power that it represents. We must remember that by claiming the power of death and using it to control others, we lost a world and in fact more than a world.

Since the day that we arrived here, we have not seen either Fogs or Clears. We believe the former no longer have visitation privileges to the Earth, and perhaps the latter are not needed here anymore. If ever I should glimpse a serpentine form of congealed smoke weaving through the forest or see a shining form wearing hospital scrubs, in snow descending, I will know that somewhere the compact has been broken and onto the stage of the world has come again the tragedy. Until then, there is joy, which by the way does not, as was once thought, require contrast with fear and pain to keep its zing.

About the Author

DEAN KOONTZ, the author of many #1 *New York Times* bestsellers, lives in Southern California with his wife, Gerda, their golden retriever, Anna, and the enduring spirit of their golden, Trixie.

www.deankoontz.com

Correspondence for the author should be addressed to:

Dean Koontz
P.O. Box 9529
Newport Beach, California 92658